I0654322

Guardians of Allon
Book Three

Overthrow

Shawn Lamb

GUARDIANS OF ALLON – BOOK THREE
OVERTHROW by Shawn Lamb

Published by Allon Books
209 Hickory Way Court
Antioch, Tennessee 37013
www.allonbooks.com

Cover illustration by Robert Lamb

International Standard Book Number: 978-0-9964381-1-7

Other Books by Shawn Lamb

Young Adult Fantasy Fiction
ALLON ~ BOOK 1
Published by Creation House, a division of Charisma Media

Published by Allon Books

ALLON ~ BOOK 2 ~ INSURRECTION
ALLON ~ BOOK 3 ~ HEIR APPARENT
ALLON ~ BOOK 4 ~ A QUESTION OF SOVEREIGNTY
ALLON ~ BOOK 5 ~ GAUNTLET
ALLON ~ BOOK 6 ~ DILEMMA
ALLON ~ BOOK 7 ~ DANGEROUS DECEPTION
ALLON ~ BOOK 8 ~ DIVIDED
ALLON ~ BOOK 9 ~ IN PLAIN SIGHT

THE GREAT BATTLE – GUARDIANS OF ALLON – BOOK ONE
REPRIEVE – GUARDIANS OF ALLON – BOOK TWO

PARENT STUDY GUIDE FOR ALLON ~ BOOKS 1-9
THE ACTIVITY BOOK OF ALLON

For Young Readers – ages 8-10
Allon ~ The King's Children series
NECIE AND THE APPLES
TRISTINE'S DORGIRITH ADVENTURE
NIGEL'S BROKEN PROMISE

Historical Fiction
GLENCOE
THE HUGUENOT SWORD

MORTALS

Sir Niles of Pollux – age 60, King's Champion
King Berk – age 42
Queen Myla – age 35
Prince Akilles – age 12, son of Berk and Myla
Prince Blaine – age 10, son of Berk and Myla
Prince Calder – age 8, son of Berk and Myla
Prince Delwin – age 5, son of Berk and Myla
Archimedes – age 63, First Jor'ellian priest
Wilbur, Vicar of Jor'el
Colin – age 22, son of Sir Niles
Lieutenant Markes
Danior

Council of Twelve

Sir Abner of Garwood – age 30	Southern Forest
Sir Gordon – age 24	Meadowlands
Baron Zared – age 35	Delta
Slater – age 55	Northern Forest
Lord Patrin	South Plains
Baron Fenton	North Plains
Mather	Highlands
Jarret	East Coast
Rafe	West Coast
Orson	Midessex
Count Hagan, Royal Treasurer – age 40	Lowlands

IMMORTALS

Captain Kell, Commander of the Guardians of Jor'el
Armus, 1st Lieutenant
Gresham, vassal
Zinna, archer
Jedrek, warrior
Mona, shape-shifter
Eldric, physician
Wren, huntress
Priscilla, Wind Guardian
Barnum, warrior
Valmar, warrior
Chase, Sea Guardian

SHADOW WARRIORS

Dagar
Tor
Carvel, Shadow Archer Commander
Griswold
Ashby, Shadow Archer
Commander Altari
Commander Witter
Nari
Fitch
Pathas
Martel

Chapter 1

SURROUNDED BY ROLLING HILLS AND FOREST, WALDRON CASTLE sat nestled in a plain of Midessex. The site was selected for being the most central in Allon. This made the travel almost equal in distance from the far most provinces.

The plain made Waldron visible for miles, and gave the occupants a clear line of sight to any approaching enemy. The walls rose fifteen feet high with square turrets at the intersections. The entire compound enclosed the thirty acres needed to house the royal family, soldiers' barracks, armory, castle chapel, quarters for the priests and Jor'ellian Knights and other sundry buildings necessary to the functioning of daily life.

Built during the first ten years of King Tristan's reign, the splendor of Waldron rivaled that of the Temple of Jor'el. Now, after more than two centuries, the castle showed its age. Portions crumbled due to neglect.

A crisp autumn wind stripped the branches of the remaining leaves. The colder temperatures warned of winter's approach. Servants busily went about preparing for the upcoming season. With twilight fading, torches and small braziers lit the battlements and corner turrets for the nightwatch.

From the armory courtyard came the sound of swordplay. A boy of twelve years exchanged parries with a man of sixty. The boy stood tall for his age, lanky with shoulder-length blond hair. His baby blue eyes shone with determination against his older more experienced opponent. The lad wore only a jerkin over his linen shirt, no overcoat or cloak. Despite the chill, swordplay required exertion and made him perspire.

Sir Niles barely moved in deftly handling the boy's determination. Keen dark blue eyes took in every detail of the lad's movement. Niles wore the overcoat of his leather uniform trimmed with azure blue, complete with insignia and medallion of his position. The breeze ruffled a full head of dark hair. The neatly trimmed beard moved when the corners of his mouth formed a smile.

"Patience, Highness. Moving too fast on the attack will trouble your balance."

The Prince broke off with a huff of annoyance. "How can I test my balance if you continue to stand there? Move! Do something. Attack me." He assumed the first position.

"Given your present mood, you will not be able to parry any attack."

"Arrogant, knave! You are the King's Champion. If I can't defend against you, I might as well fight my little brothers!"

Niles drew to his full height for a scolding. "Akilles! What is the first rule of a Jor'ellian cadet?"

Prince Akilles lowered his sword and came to attention. With a proud tilt of his head, he replied. "To respect Jor'el, the King and one's teacher."

"Very good. Shall we start again?" It was more a statement than a question.

When Akilles attacked, Niles moved to defend. The Prince stumbled yet quickly regained his balance. Niles' laughter at the miscue enraged Akilles. The emotion translated to his fighting, which became a bit too spirited. Niles responded to the aggression by using more sophisticated moves. Soon Akilles did all he could to defend against the master.

In a desperate move, Akilles ducked and thrust out. Niles shifted right to avoid being impaled. However, the tip of Akilles' sword became entangled in the chain around Niles' neck. Akilles jerked to free the blade. The violent action made Niles' head and shoulder stooped down, throwing him off balance. The force broke the chain. The medallion fell to the ground.

Frightened, Akilles dropped his sword. "Niles?"

Niles straightened and reached for his throat.

"Did I wound you?"

"No."

"Here now!" A man rushed over. By his mature features and scattered grey strands in brown hair, he appeared a few years older than Niles. He wore clothes that appeared a cross between priestly robes of blue and silver and a uniform similar to Niles. He wore the same insignia. A sheathed sword hung from the belt around his waist.

"Master Archimedes, I didn't mean it!" Akilles spoke a hurried apology.

"I know. You reacted to being attacked." Archimedes sent a scolding glare to Niles.

"We did get a little too spirited," admitted Niles. He picked up the medallion. The engraved image featured an eagle clenching a crown with a sword through the crown. Niles examined the broken chain.

Seeing the damage upset Akilles further. "I didn't mean to break it."

"Of course not. You defended yourself," said Archimedes.

Niles examined it again. "Nicked the medallion also."

"Will you need a new one?" asked Akilles.

"A new chain most certainly, but the medallion is not so scarred as to need replacing," Niles replied in a reassuring tone.

"That is your responsibility, knight," said Archimedes firmly. "I think the Prince has had enough for one day. It will be dark soon."

Niles let Archimedes know his displeasure at the interference. "This was *my* pupil's last practice bout of the day."

Cautiously, Akilles watched the terse exchange. "I do need to get cleaned up for dinner."

Niles smiled at the Prince. "Run along. We'll try something less stressful tomorrow."

Akilles flashed a timid, apologetic smile before leaving.

"Be glad it was me who witnessed this *spirited bout* and not the King. He warned you about going too hard on the Prince," said Archimedes.

Niles pocketed the medallion and accosted Archimedes. "If you were the King's Champion, would you go easy with him? Would you jeopardize the life of the future *king* with casual lessons? Enemies give no quarter."

Archimedes didn't immediately reply, the frustration clearly seen in his expression. "You would have made a poor priest."

Niles burst out laughing. He clapped Archimedes on the shoulder. "Then I guess Jor'el knew where we both belonged. You as a priest and me a knight."

Archimedes spoke with sarcasm. "I was this close to beating you." He made an indication with his thumb and forefinger. He chuckled. "You're right, of course."

"Oh, now that was worth having the chain broken to hear you admit."

"In reference to Jor'el! Not how you handle Akilles."

Niles heaved a casual shrug, smiled and left. After moving a short distance from Archimedes, a younger man of thirty years joined Niles on trek to the armory. The young man's hazel eyes twinkled when he smiled.

"You and Archimedes still going at it?"

Niles grinned. "I don't think he'll ever get over me being victorious."

"I don't think you would have been content as a priest."

He glanced along his shoulders at the younger man. "Archimedes said something similar. I do prefer being the King's Champion compared to the First Jor'ellian."

They reached the armory just as a soldier emerged. "Pardon me, Champion. Sir Abner." He moved aside and made a brisk salute.

Niles gave a quick acknowledgement, as he and Abner went inside. He took hold of Abner's elbow to draw him into a nearby office. After locking the door, he asked, "Any news?"

Abner shook his head. "Nothing. At least that makes a connection to Zared."

Niles tugged at his lower lip. "Something uneasy is stirring, and I'm certain it deals with Zared." He withdrew the medallion from his pocket. His brows deeply furrowed as he stared at the image.

Abner came alongside Niles' shoulder. "How did the chain break?"

Niles made a curt wave of impatience. "Not important." His thumb rubbed along the etching. "If I didn't know better I would swear ..." he moved close to Abner, his voice lowered to a dreaded whisper, "it's the Dark Way."

Abner didn't flinch or refute, rather gave a sober nod.

"The problem is how to tell Berk. Zared has practically taken up residence here."

"Would Berk believe you?"

"*That* question gnaws at me." Niles' expression turned worried. "Zared so pollutes his mind with circular reasoning that he's grown apathetic to his faith." He laid hold of Abner's arm. "What about the Council? Can you, Gordon or Slater speak to the issue of Zared's influence?"

"We've tried. He rebuffs us by citing Zared's superior intellect," replied Abner with frustration.

Niles' concern grew deeper then turned hopeful with a suggestion. "Enlist Patrin's aid. Surely Berk will listen to his dear friend. A man who named his infant son after the King."

With dreaded emphasis, Abner said, "Patrin now sides with Zared."

The news startled Niles. "What caused his shift?"

Abner shrugged. "I don't know. Slater, Gordon and I noticed the change in attitude after he returned from the harvest. We can only surmise something happened during the summer, for he stood with us in the spring session."

Niles once more stared intensely at the medallion. "What about the rest of the Council? Has anyone else changed his stance?"

"No. Fenton remains indifferent to anything while Mather's quiet attitude makes it hard to determine his thoughts. Jarret and Rafe are too preoccupied with pirate raids on the coasts. Orson is weak of mind, agreeing with whoever makes the strongest argument. Hagan is stubborn and obstinate." Abner sighed with resignation. "With Berk barring Wilbur from our meetings, I fear we have lost our collective voice to one man."

Niles moved to the window. Now dark outside, torches illuminated the armory courtyard. He hoped for a more favorable report. Alas, the situation had grown worse. His attention shifted between looking out the window to the main building and his medallion.

After a moment of heavy silence, Abner asked, "What about the Queen?"

Niles answered over his shoulder. "Still firm in her faith, but her influence is also being overshadowed by Zared."

"Well, that isn't hard to manage since she and Berk never had a good relationship."

"Ay," groused Niles. "When they first married, Wilbur believed she could bolster him. Alas, that hasn't happened."

"Have you spoken to the Vicar about your concerns? In his position, he may provide answers we can't uncover."

Niles left the window to return to his desk. "He advises caution."

Abner flashed a wry smile. "You haven't taken his advice."

The humor was met with Niles slamming a fist on the desk in rebuke. "Nor will I until I uncover what darkness is threatening the stability of the royal family!"

"Easy, my friend. I jest, perhaps poorly, but you know I fully support you."

Niles attempted to calm his temper and cocked a small grin. "I *do* know. And I can't thank you enough."

"No thanks are needed. Being Jor'ellians, we have taken the same oath. As friends, well … that goes without saying." Abner smiled.

"I'm afraid dangerous days ahead will test our friendship."

Abner scowled in refute. "You know the history of Garwood. Like my ancestor, Dunham, I will not waver in support of the House of Tristan."

Niles noticed the truth of the younger man's word reflected in his eyes. "Then let us make a pledge. No matter what happens, we will fulfill our sworn oath to Jor'el and the king." He held out his hand to take Abner's arm.

Abner grabbed Niles arm at the elbow. He looked straight at his friend. "I so swear! Jor'el take my life if I forfeit my oath."

"May he do the same to me."

The watch called the time of six in the evening.

"Go. Berk doesn't like anyone being late for a banquet," said Niles.

"Aren't you coming?"

Niles made a weary shake of his head. "Council members only."

Abner appeared puzzled. "As the King's Champion, you're present at all meetings and banquets."

"So I argued, but to no avail. The King will be without my protection this night." Niles escorted Abner to the exterior door of the armory. "Keep your wits sharp and your ears open."

"You can depend upon me."

Niles patted Abner's shoulder in sending the younger man on his way. He watched until Abner entered the main building. Sounds of activity resonated from the Great Hall.

In the shadows of the trees to the west of Waldron, he watched the castle. Even in the darkness, he stood unusually tall. Fingers nervously tapped the hilt of a sheathed dagger. He wore no sword. The violet hue of his narrow eyes glowed with the effort of concentration. He muttered under his breath in a different language. Suddenly, he drew his dagger, ready to confront danger.

"Relax, Gresham," said a voice a moment before he appeared from the deeper shadows of the forest.

"Kell! You could have given me warning." Gresham slammed the dagger back in the sheath for emphasis.

"No, something uneasy is causing a disturbance. Any communication could be hazardous." Kell stood six inches taller than Gresham, making him seven and half feet by standard measure. He wore both sword and dagger, looking every inch a warrior. Golden eyes shone with authority.

"Good to know you feel it too. What about the others?"

"Ay. They complain of it interfering with any attempts to discern the source."

"Indeed! No matter how hard I try, I can't discern anything from Berk or Myla." Gresham put up a staying hand to still any reply. "I know Berk is weak in faith, *if* he has any at all. But Myla is devout. I should be able to get some sense of her. Some feeling regarding her state of mind."

Kell's black brows knitted with concern at the report. "What about Archimedes or Niles?"

Gresham shook his head then hastily added at noticing Kell's displeasure, "A fleeting sense of angst on their part. Yet, when I try to push further, the repelling happens." He drew close to Kell to continue in a hushed whisper. "I swear it's the Dark Way."

Kell didn't answer; he didn't have to. Agreement showed in his expression.

Gresham groused, "Surprised it took Dagar this long. I never considered him the patient type."

"Nothing is done outside of Jor'el's timing."

"You hope—"

"I know!" snapped Kell.

Gresham didn't back down at the outburst. "Kell, you've been affected by the punishment like the rest of us—if not more so being captain. So don't try to fool me. Remember, I'm an Original also."

Kell exhaled to regain his temper, yet slow to respond. Gresham's continuing direct gaze made him admit, "Ay, it has been frustrating at times."

"Kell—"

This time the captain raised a silencing hand, his expression stern. "I do not waiver in my conviction that Jor'el's timing is perfect! Nor should you."

Gresham recanted. "I don't. However, being a legend is tiresome. I long for our restoration."

"Time for our return is sooner than it was."

The response made Gresham's ire flare again. "Oh, stop being cagey! You're our captain. Jor'el doesn't keep you ignorant."

"In this case, he has! I don't know when, just that it will happen."

At the rebuke Gresham softened his attitude to ask, "Why not tell you?"

Kell hesitated, not for annoyance rather how to answer. "Perhaps my ignorance is part of the punishment for the Great Battle. Yet I'm *certain* Jor'el will keep his promise to us—and the mortals." With a hand on Gresham's shoulder, Kell directed his attention back to Waldron. "Despite the failing of Tristan's descendants, the kingdom has experienced two hundred and sixty years of relative peace. Now the Dark Way threatens it. The form of threat is what we need to discover."

"Agreed, but I'm not sure whether I should push past the block or not; especially if Dagar is behind the hindrance."

Kell focused his attention on Waldron. Like Gresham, Kell's golden eyes began to glow with effort. Suddenly, he winced in pain.

Gresham grabbed the captain in support. "Kell?"

He blinked several times to recover. "The blocking is unusually strong. Yet I sense what you do in regards to Archimedes and Niles. Going further could be hazardous, more for discovery than actual effort."

"So what do we do?"

Kell thought before replying. "Keep watch. I have someone to meet."

Disturbed in spirit, Niles made his way to the castle chapel located along the western wall. Very few people frequented the chapel these days. The priest in charge wallowed in discouragement bordering on disinterest. Oh, he saw to duty when required, but barely kept the chapel clean. Each day, Niles discovered more signs of neglect. It pained his heart to witness the deterioration. However, he needed renewal in his spirit to fight depression.

Two lit candles illuminated the altar. The rest of the chapel remained in darkness. Being familiar with the layout, the dimness didn't trouble Niles. He easily moved from the entrance to the altar. He knelt and bowed his head. Usually, he prayed for strength and wisdom on how to serve an increasingly apathetic king. Tonight was different. His soul felt burdened like never before.

"Jor'el, there is a troubling darkness I cannot discern. Is this a threat to Berk or to you? Help me understand so I can act on your behalf and that of your appointed king."

Niles took a seat on the front pew to meditate. His mind was drawn back to the history of how Tristan became king. He knew it well for having studied history and Verse most of his life. However, what Tristan accomplished during his one-hundred-year reign became undermined by the weakness of his descendants.

The deterioration began with Tristan's grandson Lewin. Whereas his grandsire and father remained devout, Lewin acted out of duty. Being sixty years old when crowned king, Lewin was already set in his ways thus accomplished little during his twenty-year reign.

Having no son, Lewin's eldest daughter, Reena, became queen. She married Gowin. This proved a bad match from the beginning, which grew worse over a forty-year reign. Scandal plagued the royal family due to Gowin's desire for other women. The crown passed to their only legitimate son Segar, who exceeded his father's lechery.

With each succeeding monarch, the generations drifted further from Jor'el. They kept the institutions Tristan established, and the kingdom remained unified in commerce and purpose. However, by the time Berk succeeded his father, the secular trumped the sacred.

Niles blinked back tears during his meditation. Only three hundred and fifty-two Jor'ellian Knights remained faithful to their oath to defend the Almighty's honor and protect the kingdom. "How much longer can we continue?" he asked with distress.

"You already know the answer."

Niles bolted up at hearing the voice. Darkness hid the speaker. "Who's there? Show yourself."

Footsteps came from the direction of the nave. Niles held the hilt of his sword ready. An unusually tall man stepped into the rim of light coming from the altar candles. He had black hair and light colored eyes that reflected the golden glow of candlelight.

"You're not a priest, so who are you?"

He smiled, friendly and reassuring. "You have nothing to fear from me, Sir Niles of Pollux, King's Champion."

"You know who I am, but I don't know you."

"Well, let's just say the one who knows all, knows us both." He nodded toward the altar.

Niles' curiosity turned to realization. "A Guard—"

"Friend. Let's leave it at that." He again smiled.

The momentary reassurance passed, as Niles studiously regarded him. "Dark times are ahead. That's what you came to tell me."

"Dark times are here. You must be ready."

Niles assumed a braced posture. "I will keep my oath."

The glow of golden light in the eyes grew intense. "You and your oath will be sorely tested."

"Jor'el knows my heart is loyal, why else send you?"

"As divine favor to bolster your courage. More than that," he briefly glanced from Niles to the altar, "I cannot say."

Niles heard pain behind the words and tried to offer encouragement. "Can you at least tell me if a legend has a name?"

A bittersweet grin appeared. "Kell."

Shock registered on Niles's face. "Captain!" He began to kneel, when a hand caught him.

"No. Give homage to him who is worthy." When Niles straightened, Kell continued. "Once I leave, you will not remember our conversation, only that Jor'el has strengthened you to face what is to come." The Guardian captain stared earnestly at Niles. "Defend and preserve the House of Tristan, King's Champion."

18

Niles made the Jor'ellian salute. "As Jor'el commands, Captain." He watched Kell retreat into the shadow. Suddenly, Niles flinched as if struck with a headache. He staggered and sat on the front pew. After a brief moment, he looked up at the altar. "By your strength, I will fulfill my duty." He bowed to the altar and left.

Chapter 2

INSIDE THE GREAT HALL, MERRY VOICES ROSE IN LAUGHTER and conversation. King Berk and Queen Myla sat upon their thrones at the high table. With heavy lines of age and a full head of gray hair, one would hardly believe Berk's age of forty-two. Many men of similar age appeared in better health than the King.

Queen Myla starkly contrasted her husband in appearance. Seven years younger, her fair beauty inspired much admiration at court, and much jealousy. She smiled at the entertainment, and applauded when finished. While the tumblers cleared the floor, she leaned close to Berk.

"Everyone is present save Sir Niles. Is he ill-disposed that he cannot attend us this evening?" she inquired.

Berk's amusement turned to immediate annoyance. "Why interrupt my enjoyment with tedious questions?"

"Hardly tedious. He is the King's Champion, your protector, and always present—" She stopped when he slammed his fists on the table.

"I grow tired of his oppressive presence!" Berk's bellowing drew attention.

Myla fought displaying irritation. "There is no need to shout and disturb our guests"

"I'll shout if I want! This is my banquet."

To contain her exasperation, Myla gripped the arms of her chair. Berk's temper grew worse of late. Reasoning was of little help.

Those present watched the royal couple, some with concern, others quietly snickering. Bravely, a thirty-five-year-old man approached the high table. He bore his tall sturdy frame with a graceful command of movement. He smiled, a pair of bright blue eyes fixed upon the King.

20

"Sire, your banquet is the envy of all. I don't know how you continue to outdo the last one, but each time you succeed." He crossed his hands over his chest in a gesture of humility yet clutched at the collar of his doublet. He bowed his head.

Berk guffawed a merry laugh. "Ah, Baron Zared, you always find the words to soothe me."

"I speak only truth, Sire."

A loud clearing of the throat caught attention. Zared and Berk turned to the person responsible, a twenty-four-year-old golden brown-haired nobleman.

"You have something to say, Sir Gordon?" demanded Berk.

"No, Sire. A piece of food became stuck." Gordon took a lengthy drink in pretended recovery.

Unconvinced, Berk stared at Gordon. Abner sat beside Gordon. Berk's interest prompted him to slap Gordon between the shoulder blades.

"Is that better?" asked Abner.

"Ay. Thank you." Gordon then spoke to Berk. "My apology, Sire."

Berk's intense gaze shifted between Abner and Gordon.

"Musicians, play the King's favorite!" said Lord Patrin. He sat nearest the high table. He nodded to Zared, who assumed a more pleasant disposition.

"Perhaps, we shall start the dancing a little early," Zared suggested then appeared embarrassed by his own idea. "Unless the Queen is too fatigued from her recent misfortune?"

Myla flashed a thin smile at the obvious jab. "My lord, I would not deny the King if *he* chooses to dance."

"What if I *choose* to defer the honor to the Baron, how would you respond, Madam?" Berk's challenge once more raised the level of concern among the guests.

Myla and Berk locked eyes in an obvious battle of wills. The knuckles on her hands turned white from clenching the arms of the throne. Abruptly, she faced forward and said, "I would comply, Sire."

"I'm sure of it." Berk smirked in triumph. He signaled the musicians to begin.

At the strike of the first note, Zared held out his hand to the Queen. With elegant dignity, Myla rose to join Zared on the dance floor.

Gordon shifted uneasily in his seat. He used his hand to cover his mouth in a gesture of swallowing when reality he muttered to Abner. "His goading of her is insufferable."

"She can hold her own."

Gordon squarely looked at Abner. "Do you really believe that?" When he didn't answer, Gordon pressed him. "Abner."

"No," he replied under his breath before shoving a piece of bread into his mouth.

At the proper point in the music, other couples joined in the dance. Being bachelors, Abner and Gordon remained seated.

Niles made his way from the chapel to the main hallway running the length of the Great Hall. Being cooler weather, the doors were closed to maintain the heat in the room. During the warmer months, the doors stood open to allow for cooling breezes. Niles didn't enter the Hall. Defying the King would cause Berk's anger to explode. In fact, he heard Berk bellow about something. Although he couldn't hear clearly, he became concerned for the Queen. The increasing hostility of Berk toward Myla created uneasiness on her behalf. Duty compelled Niles to stay close in case of need, but, oh, how he wished the doors stood opened for ease of listening!

Niles turned the corner of the rear corridor that ran behind the Great Hall to the kitchen. Servants used this hallway for transport of food or anything needed by the royals and their guests. Buffets with food, cups, pitchers and other necessities lined the wall. Several servants walked toward the kitchen, thus didn't spy the ten-year-old boy sneak toward one buffet. Recognizing the lad, Niles chose to watch. He tried not to smile.

The boy glanced to where the servants headed, snatched a meat tart off the buffet and began to run off with his prize. Niles stepped forward to block the boy's path. Looking over his shoulder for danger, the boy didn't see Niles and ran into him. Niles caught the lad to keep him from falling.

"Going somewhere, Cedric?"

The boy gaped in fear. "Si—Sir Niles!" He looked at the tart in his hand and quickly hid it behind his back to pretend innocence.

"Cook makes delicious meat tarts."

Cedric lowered his head in shame. He brought his hands forward to hold the tart up to Niles. "I'm sorry. With my father so busy, I didn't get dinner."

"I know Alvin tends to get overwhelmed in his duty sometimes, but are you certain he didn't leave you anything to eat?"

Cedric lifted his head, his large eyes filled with hurt. "I swear he didn't. For some reason this banquet troubles him more than usual. I went to meet him for dinner like usual, only he wasn't there, and no food on the table."

The hurried, upset answer made Niles ask, "What of your mother and sister?"

"Earlier, Father told Mama to take Janna into town for the night. He doesn't like Mama to be here when there is a banquet." Cedric shrugged, obviously disturbed by the situation. "I don't know why."

Niles knew. Some of the noblemen became rowdy when drunk, and no woman was safe. As royal head chamberlain, Alvin made certain female servants were never alone or totally absent during a banquet if possible. When a worried Cedric glanced up at him, Niles flashed a reassuring smile.

"Go. Enjoy the tart."

Cedric's eyes grew wide with surprise. "Really?"

Niles chuckled. "Ay. Go quickly, someone is coming."

Cedric briefly glanced over his shoulder at hearing footsteps then bolted in the opposite direction.

Alvin arrived, and appeared very curious. "Why is Cedric running off?"

Niles made a lopsided grin. "Just being a boy."

Alvin grew suspicious. "What did you let him get away with this time?"

"Dinner."

The answer deflated Alvin. "I came to find him for that reason."

Niles drew Alvin into an alcove to speak confidentially. "He's concerned for you and uncertain why you sent Candice and Janna to town."

"You know my reason, so don't play coy."

"Then why not send Cedric also?"

"Because the boy needs to learn his duty."

Niles scowled with disapproval. "How? By being forgotten?"

Offended, Alvin began to leave when Niles prevented him.

"What about this particular night troubles you more than usual?"

Alvin hesitated due to obvious anxiety. Niles' jerk on his arm prompted a response. "Everything," he replied in a harsh whisper then changed to discrete. "The *baron*'s influence is interfering with my duties. I can barely get near the King, save to be given orders; which mostly come from *him* even with the King standing there." He sighed with painful regret. "I should have sent Cedric also."

"Doubtful he would have gone. He's as stubborn as his father."

Alvin huffed a chuckle. "So what did he take?"

"A meat tart. Pretend you don't know," Niles said with a wry smile.

Commotion from the main hallway caught their attention. Both men made their way to the corner. A door to the Great Hall stood open with a lady-in-waiting at the threshold.

"Your Majesty!" she called.

Myla hastened from the Hall down the corridor, away from Niles and Alvin.

"Leave her be and shut the door!" they heard Berk shout.

The lady complied.

"I wonder what happened now?" groused Alvin.

"I intend to find out." Niles followed Myla. He avoided rushing in an effort not to draw attention, yet diligent enough to overtake her at an intersection to another hallway. He simply smiled when she noticed him fall in step beside her.

They continued to the family quarters on the opposite side of the castle. Two Jor'ellian Knights guarded the entrance to the royal wing. They came to attention to salute the Queen and King's Champion.

Upon passing the stairs leading up to the bedchambers, Niles asked, "Are you not retiring to your quarters?"

"No," her answer came short and sharp.

Further down the hallway was the family salon and dining room. Noise of conflict came from the dining room.

"The boys!" Myla exclaimed. She lifted her skirt to start running.

Niles stopped her just short of the door. His protective warning made her comply about not entering. He drew his sword and rushed into the room. His blustery entrance startled the young princes. To Niles' relieved annoyance, Akilles and his brothers engaged in roughhousing. Ten-year-old Blaine and eight-year-old Calder joined together in attacking Akilles. The eldest managed to keep them at bay by using chairs for defense along with a long wooden spoon for a sword.

Myla appeared from behind Niles. Her fear turned to irritation. "What is going on here?"

At her scolding, the boys dropped their weapons of spoons.

"It was all Akilles' idea!" said Blaine.

"You two attacked me," refuted Akilles.

"You boasted about defeating Sir Niles and dared us to fight you."

Niles roughly cleared his throat and sent an admonishing glare to Akilles.

The Prince flushed red. "I didn't say *defeat* exactly."

"You did. Calder heard you, didn't you?" Blaine nudged his brother.

Calder shyly shrugged, obviously still embarrassed at being caught.

Myla gave a motherly scowl. "It's growing late. Time for bed."

"Is the banquet over?" asked Akilles.

"The banquet is none of your concern. Setting a good example for your brothers *is* your responsibility!" she rebuffed.

Akilles went to object when Niles again cleared his throat along with a shake of his head. The Prince took the warning and spoke with formality. "Ay, Ma'am." He turned to his brothers. "You heard Marmi, off to bed."

Blaine frowned, yet made the obligatory formal goodnight to his mother. Calder acted more willing in bidding her goodnight. He took hold of Akilles' hand. "Can we play this again tomorrow?"

Akilles flashed an indulgent smile. "Ay."

"Not in the dining room. I suggest the armory. It is better suited with fewer items to break," said Niles.

"Ay," Akilles agreed. He left with Calder.

Myla sighed with great relief as she sat in the chair.

Seeing her emotional turmoil, Niles shut the door. "What happened to make you leave the banquet so early?" She hesitated to speak, so he sat on the footstool. "You know you can trust me."

Her small shaky smile showed confidence while her voice disturbed. "Oh, Niles! He grows worse! He made me dance with that ... *baron!*" She fought against speaking anything worse by tugging on her fingers.

Her unusual disturbance brought forth his concern in the form of a question. "Did Zared act inappropriate?"

"His whole manner is inappropriate! The way he manipulates Berk with smooth words and idle flattery. I asked about your absence, which immediately angered Berk. *He* approached and proceeded to work his wiles. But his manner—" her voice grew low and hushed. "There is something odd that I have noticed of late. Whenever Zared speaks to Berk, he reaches for his collar, almost grasping it." She demonstrated. Niles mimicked her action, which made her say, "Ay, like you reaching for your ... Wait, where is your medallion?"

He slightly colored with embarrassment. "A bout with Akilles became rather spirited and broke the chain." He pulled them out of his pocket to show her.

With renewed vigor, she held his arm. "Don't let Zared turn his attention to my son! If you can't serve Berk in your appointed capacity, protect Akilles."

Niles' brows leveled. Her fear ran deep enough to cause worry for her son like Alvin for his family. Indeed, Zared's growing influence proved unsettling.

She mistook his brief silence. "Niles, please!"

He softly smiled. "I will. Now tell me what was said, for you are not a woman easily intimidated."

She waved him off. "It doesn't matter. What matters is the safety of my sons, especially Akilles."

Niles' faced grew harsh. "You feared the commotion in here because he threatened them! At a public banquet? The cad."

"Not exactly."

"Then what *exactly* did he say?"

The battle to speak or remain silent played across her face. "I can't tell you."

"Before Jor'el, you know I will keep your confidence."

She flashed a thin smile. "I know, but I can't."

Everything within Niles wanted to force the issue, for anything threatening the royal family he took personally. True, as the King's Champion he swore to protect them, but Myla and the princes held a special place in his heart.

"I see my reluctance to speak has wounded you," she said.

He didn't reply; he couldn't due to frustration.

She took his hands. "Cousin," she began with sympathy.

"*Shhh!!!*" he warned, and cast a glance at the door. He leaned down close to speak. "We agreed to keep it secret when you came to court, remember?"

"I need an ally in the place," she replied in a private plea.

"You have one." He squeezed her hand. "Our agreement was so I can act freely. More than ever, it is paramount to be discrete."

She swallowed back her emotions. "Please, promise to protect my sons."

"I promise. I'll escort you to your chamber to rest."

"No, I'll be fine. Go to Akilles."

Niles stood then thought to ask, "Where was Delwin?"

She lightly chuckled. "The day's activity so wore him out that he fell asleep before dinner."

He smiled. "I didn't think so active a five-year could ever grow tired. He'll certainly be hungry come morning. And," he stressed, "I *will* escort you to your chamber, since it is on the way to Akilles' room."

Akilles finished changing for the night when his valet answered a knock.

"Sir Niles, Highness," announced the valet. He moved aside for Niles to enter.

"Leave us, Gilby," Niles instructed the servant.

"Who will see to the prince?"

"Me." Niles nudged Gilby out the door.

After Gilby's departure, Niles noticed the way Akilles stood, braced and warily cying him. For a moment, neither spoke then Akilles broke the silence.

"Why are you not with Father? It's your place to be with him at state functions."

"He did not require my presence."

"You mean he threw you out," groused the Prince.

Niles raised an arched brow at the surly comment. "I never entered the hall to be *thrown* out."

Akilles confronted Niles "Something happened at the banquet that upset Marmi, didn't it?"

"Ay," Niles replied in a level voice.

Akilles' frustration came spilling forth. "How could he be mean to her?"

Niles shrugged. "That is something only he can answer."

Akilles sat on the bed with a hard *plop*. "He's grown so angry lately."

"A king has much on his mind. It sometimes effects his emotions—"

"No! It's not like him! It's …" Akilles turned from Niles. Even in profile, the angst was obvious when he bit his lower lip.

Niles approached the bed to inquire. "It's *what?*"

Akilles vigorously shook his head. "Not what."

Niles sat on the bed to continue the probing. "A person, then?"

The Prince gave a reluctant nod.

Niles took hold of Akilles to get his full attention. "Akilles. By my vow to Jor'el, you know you can trust me."

The Prince leaned closer. His voice barely above a whisper, "Zared! I can't see my father without him being there. It didn't used to be that way. Why is he even around?"

"I'm afraid I don't have the answer to that question."

"But you're the King's Champion and always with Father!"

Niles tried to temper his words. Akilles was already upset. No need to agitate him further. "I'm only around when the King summons me. Being a knight, I'm not privy to Council meetings or private discussions. My duty is the safety of the royal family. To that end, I concentrate my energies."

Sudden understanding shone upon Akilles' face. "Marmi sent you here for my safety."

Niles held Akilles' shoulder for reassurance. This was not a statement he could, or would, deny.

Discomposure made Akilles look to his feet. His spoke with dreadful resignation. "I must fear my own father—"

"No! Others seek to reason with him, so we act out of caution. That is all." Niles' attempt at reassurance did little to ease Akilles' mood, as told by the welling tears in the lad's eyes. "Let us recite the Jor'ellian

Creed to ease your mind so you can sleep." He began and Akilles repeated.

> "There is one Lord.
> He is the Infinite, the Almighty.
> By His will, I live.
> By His power, I serve,
> And His honor, I defend.
> My mind, heart and strength belong to Him."

During the reciting, Akilles relaxed, which made Niles hopeful. "Now, rest with ease, my prince."

Chapter 3

KELL MADE HIS WAY NORTH FROM WALDRON CASTLE. HE MULLED over conversations from earlier in the evening. Being at half-strength while dealing with trouble the last four hundred and ten years proved frustrating. Gresham wasn't the only one wondering when they would be fully restored. Kell heard the same complaint from the others. Unfortunately, the answer proved elusive, for no matter how many times he inquired of the Almighty, Jor'el gave him the same answer: *when the time is right.* True, Jor'el provided clues in the Book of Prophecy about the return of the Guardians. This would happen in connection with the Daughter of Allon and a male descendant of Razi through Tristan, but gave no timetable.

Over the centuries, the Guardians passed from legends into oblivion. The idea that such powerful immortal beings existed and interacted with mortals became viewed as nonsense or childish whimsy. The dismissive attitude increased the Guardians' angst and desire for the time of restoration.

Although Tristan reinstated the worship of Jor'el and established a mortal government dedicated to the old traditions, the Guardians remained covert, waiting for the fulfillment of prophecy.

Interaction with the faithful remnant became infrequent. The most activity for the Guardians since Tristan happened during Segar's reign. Gowin's illegitimate sons posed continual threats. Despite Segar's dissolute character, he was the direct descendant of Tristan thus needed protection. In clandestine roles, the Guardians interceded to prevent the royal family from completely falling apart.

When the threats grew too deadly, Jor'el sent two others to aid the twelve: Egan, a warrior, and Ridge, a ranger. Although bolder in their intervention, Egan and Ridge maintained the secrecy of being Guardians. After the danger passed, Egan and Ridge returned to the heavenlies. This once more left the twelve to fend off any threats.

The past year, a new unsettling sensation renewed apprehension regarding the fate of the kingdom. Subtle attempts to gain covert intelligence were met by a repelling force. This increased anxiety. Direct contact maybe the only way to gain intelligence. Yet, as the disinterest grew among the mortals, granting of divine insight or perception became severely limited. Niles was among the few select mortals given such privilege.

Kell smiled in recalling Niles' inquiry. *Can you at least tell me if a legend has a name?* For a brief moment, it felt good to speak to a trusted mortal, yet also grievous. He came to warn the faithful Jor'ellian of impending trouble. Now, he traveled to the Region of Sanctuary to bring the same ominous message to the Vicar.

Before the Great Battle, transcending the physical realm to journey from place to place did not drain a Guardian's lifeforce. Now, dimension travel had to be used sparingly to conserve energy, thus reserved for times of dangerous urgency. They could still outrun any living creature to cover vast amounts of miles on foot. Kell made the normal mortal four-day horseback journey in one night.

For a moment, Kell paused at the tree line to observe the Temple of Providence. Each of Allon's twelve provinces contributed to the Temple. The pillars of marble were quarried in the far range of the Northern Forest where it bordered the foothills of the Highlands. Images of Verse and Allon's history were carved onto the pillars. These guarded massive wooden doors hewn and gilded with gold by the craftsmen of the Southern Forest. Twin bell spires of gleaming white marble topped with golden steeples rose to the heavens. The bells came from the sister provinces of the North and South Plains. White marble with gold accents composed the entire facade of the Temple. Arch shaped windows of colored glass were blown and assembled in Midessex. At certain times of day, the Temple reflected the sun's rays in a brilliance of white with a dazzling kaleidoscope of gold and rainbow colors.

Kell winced with distress, as so many memories filled his mind. It used to be that on any given day, a hive of activity came and went from the Temple. No more. Despite its majestic reason for existence, the gates remained close when before they stood open for all to enter. The magnificent bells once tolled every hour. Now they rang three times a day, morning, noon and sunset.

Tristan also rebuilt the Fortress of Jor'el for training Jor'ellian Knights. At present, it too suffered from lack of numbers. Two thousand once inhabited the compound. Now, the most dedicated Jor'ellians served at Waldron, with scarcely two hundred living at the Fortress. Just over three hundred Jor'ellian Knights remained loyal to their oath.

Kell bowed his head and cupped his hands together. He spoke a low prayer in the Ancient language of the Guardians. A glow between his hands shone through the gaps of his fingers. When the light faded, he glanced up to the sky. "Your will be done, Almighty One."

Kell boldly proceeded to the Temple. Without being seen, he passed the Jor'ellians at the front entrance. Inside the magnificent Temple, he paused halfway down the aisle. A man knelt almost prostrate in front of the altar. With compassion, Kell watched. Although he couldn't hear any spoken words, his spirit sensed the mortal's great burden. This is why he came, in response to another heartfelt prayer.

No sound of footsteps echoed in the chamber when Kell walked the aisle to stand beside the man. "Wilbur," he spoke with tenderness.

Startled, Wilbur struggled to sit back on his knees. The aged white head lifted to see who spoke. His eyes widened. "Kell!" he spoke with awe. When Wilbur struggled to rise, Kell helped the old Vicar to his feet. Wilbur cast a cautious glanced toward the front door. "Were you seen?"

"No. This time I came as myself and not as Captain Seul." Kell took a deep, burdened breath before proceeding. "I have a message. Dark times are ahead."

"That I know," said Wilbur in a tone of futility. "It is my daily prayer for Jor'el to fulfill his promise quickly."

"We both know Jor'el will do so in his time. Until then, be strong and have faith."

The anguish of worry joined with the weight of the news made Wilbur sit on the front pew. "I am too old to endure much longer. My strength fades—though my faith remains," he added.

"Which is why I am here. Jor'el has chosen your successor."

Wilbur's worry turned to imploring, almost on the verge of tears. "Please tell me it is not Odell!"

"No, it not Odell," replied Kell with reassurance.

Wilbur sagged in relief. "Who?"

"Even now, he senses his calling, yet battles within himself. When the time comes, you will know him." Kell raised his right hand, which remained clenched at his side in holding something. "Jor'el sends this for safekeeping." He opened his fingers. In the palm of his hand lay an amulet attached to a chain.

Wilbur took it to examine both the chain and amulet. The gold chain appeared old and the amulet an odd shape with an oval knotted appendage. "I don't recognize the symbol. What is it?"

Kell shrugged. "It was forged in the heavenlies. For what purpose, I am ignorant. However, like your successor, you will know what to do with it when the time comes. For now, keep it safely hidden."

Wilbur placed the amulet under the neck of his robes. When he withdrew his hand, he patted the robe just above his heart. "It will be safe."

"There is one more thing, though it will not be easy in Berk's current state of mind. You must go to Waldron and warn him of the danger to come if he doesn't change his ways."

Wilbur's face showed the inner conflict at the instruction. "To approach him without being summoned is dangerous."

"It is Jor'el's instructions," insisted Kell.

"Oh, I do not say that to suggest I will not obey. Merely wondering out loud if I have the strength to complete such a perilous task."

"Be of good courage, Wilbur. Strength will be given you, and your faithful service will be rewarded."

"In the heavenlies, you mean." Seeing Kell's compassion, Wilbur smiled as he added, "I do not fear death. It is but a transition."

Kell nodded with understanding. "When *that* time comes, speak only of my visit to your successor and Sir Niles." He warmly smiled. "Blessings upon you, dear Vicar." This time, Kell disappeared in the white light of dimension travel.

When Kell reappeared in the forest surrounding the Temple, he sensed the presence of multiple individuals. He drew his sword.

"Easy, Captain," said a female.

Kell relaxed at seeing two fellow Guardians: Zinna, a female archer with bright russet eyes, and Jedrek, a warrior with clear amber eyes. Both were blonde haired with Zinna wearing hers in a thick braid. A longbow and quiver hung slung across her back.

"What are you two doing here?" Kell demanded.

"Gresham told us you headed north, so we followed." She smiled.

Kell's annoyance showed in the slamming of his sword in the sheath. "I didn't leave a trail *to* follow."

Zinna's smile widened. "It isn't hard to guess where you would go when heading north. You are in charge of the Region of Sanctuary."

Kell turned to Jedrek. "You haven't answered me."

The warrior spoke with grave concern. "The sense has turned ominous in the Delta. It has something to do with Zared, but I can't clearly discern what?"

"First Midessex, now the Delta," Kell mused under his breath.

"*And* the South Plains," stressed Zinna.

Kell questioning glance prompted her to continue.

"That dark and familiar sense of doom."

"I think this confirms Dagar has found a way to unleash his power again," said Jedrek with dreaded certainty.

Kell didn't answer. Instead, he turned his attention to the Temple of Providence. Jedrek and Zinna waited, respectful of the captain's focused concentration. Kell remained silent for longer than expected.

Jedrek broke the silence to ask, "Will Jor'el send us aid to stand against this new tide of darkness?"

Kell looked directly at them to reply. "No."

"We are only twelve! Surely, he won't abandon—" Zinna began in disturbed protest. She stopped when Kell placed a hand on her shoulder.

"Regardless of numbers, we do our duty."

"Of course. I'm just concerned for the mortals. There aren't many faithful left to withstand the Dark Way."

"There will be enough. It is those remaining we must aid and protect."

Jedrek snarled in anger. "Then Dagar has won—"

"No!" Kell's golden eyes flashed with intensity. Jedrek and Zinna recoiled at his forcefulness. Kell softened his tone to encouragement. "Dagar has been defeated before, and will be again."

"As you say, Captain," Jedrek spoke in a weary voice of uncertainty.

No need to speak further on the matter. Dejection seemed the order of the day, thus Kell said, "Return to your provinces and keep watch. Any confirming sign of the Dark Way, alert me immediately."

They made the Guardian salute before going their separate ways.

Kell headed due west from Temple. Again, he covered great distances in a short period of time. He stopped at the foothills of the mountain range that ran from the Highlands to the Lowlands. It served as the natural border between several provinces included the Region of Sanctuary and the North Plains.

Instead of crossing the mountains, Kell found an alcove in the rocks near the border marker. He drew his sword and sat to assume the Guardian meditative position with legs crossed, sword on his lap, hands on knees and eyes closed. With his senses, he reached out in search of several essences. He flinched after each contact. Finally, he exhaled and rubbed his eyes at the energy drain. He hoped no one other than the individuals sensed him.

Hearing something nearby, Kell stood with his sword ready. She appeared from around an outcropping. He grinned and he put up his blade.

Mona stood six inches shorter than Kell at seven feet. Aquamarine eyes beautifully complimented her rich dark brown hair. She wore breeches and tunic, armed only with a dagger. "You summoned me, Captain?"

"I have a task for you. One that is dangerous, but greatly needed."

"Who? And when?"

"Return with me to the Temple so we can speak privately. I took a risk summoning you as I did."

⁂

Two torches provided light in the secret vault underneath the Temple. Kell stood before Mona, who sat on a bench lining two walls to create an "L" shape. She stared at the floor in deep consideration.

He spoke with unction. "I would not ask, if it were not vital."

She simply nodded.

The others Kell contacted where also present: another warrior and a physician. Second-in-command of the Guardians, Armus had a more muscular physique than Kell. His bright chestnut eyes showed alertness for duty. Eldric, the prime physician, stood the same height at Mona. His violet eyes showed wary skepticism of the plan.

Eldric questioned Kell. "Is there is no other way?"

Frustration came out in the captain's reply. "Do you really believe I haven't considered other options? That I would carelessly place another Guardian in jeopardy?" He then added with emphasis, "We need intelligence!"

Armus took hold of Eldric's shoulder to speak. "Mona isn't going alone. We will *all* be vulnerable by taxing our energy force."

Mona approached Eldric. "I depend upon you to keep her safe so I can freely act in her place. If not …"

"I will! As long as these two maintain security." Eldric jerked his thumb at Kell and Armus.

Exasperated, Kell looked to the ceiling. "Why didn't you leave Phoebe instead of *him*?"

"Because someone needs to keep *you* in check, Captain," retorted Eldric.

Mona coughed aside a laugh. Armus cleverly used a hand to hide his smile.

Kell scowled. "We act immediately! There can be no delay."

"We should tell Gresham," said Armus.

Kell nodded. "Ay. Although being here gives us added strength, we don't need to arrive in dimension travel and possibly alert the enemy to our presence. We'll proceed on foot, contact Gresham then execute the plan."

Chapter 4

NILES REMAINED WITH AKILLES. BEING A TRAINED JOR'ELLIAN, he knew how to conserve energy by not worrying unnecessarily, which tended to drain stamina. He kept his prayer and meditation focused on Akilles, and did not allow his mind to become distracted by the broader situation. Things requiring his attention would be dealt with in due course.

Shortly after dawn, Gilby returned. "Good morning, Sir Niles. Did you come to fetch the Prince for his morning exercises?"

"I never left."

Akilles woke at hearing voices. "Morning already?"

Niles chuckled. "Ay."

"Shall I draw a bath or wait until after exercises, Highness?" asked Gilby.

"Morning exercises can be delayed. If His Highness permits, I will retire to freshen up and we can begin after luncheon," said Niles.

"Retire?" asked Akilles.

"He stayed the entire night," said Gilby. The valet laid out Akilles' clothes for the day.

"At your age, you must be tired after staying up all night," said Akilles innocently.

Niles cocked a contrary eyebrow. "My training has conditioned me to remain awake for up to three days. Teaching a lesson after a sleepless night will not be difficult. I simply want to take a bath and change into a fresh uniform. "

"I didn't mean it as an insult, rather concern for your age."

"Since life expectancy is one hundred and twenty to one hundred and fifty years, being sixty, I am in the prime of life."

Akilles rose from the bed. "My father is only in his forties and looks older than you."

With a sober sigh, Niles said, "Ill health plagues the King, not age."

Akilles spoke to Gilby. "A bath now, then breakfast. Sir Niles can retire. I don't want him to become ill due to lack of sleep." He flashed a teasing smile in Niles' direction.

"Expect a extra vigorous afternoon session for taking the morning off," said Niles in wry retort.

Gilby laughed but quelled it at Akilles' thwarted frown.

Niles went to his quarters located in the upper gallery near the front entrance to the main building. Upon entering, he discovered a dark-haired young man asleep in a chair beside a small table. He wore the same uniform without the blue trim. A lone candle had burned out, as told by the amount of wax around the holder and some on the table.

Niles shook him by the shoulder. "Colin."

Colin woke with a start. "Oh, Pappy. What time is it?"

"Morning. How long have you been waiting?"

"Since midnight, I think. Or whenever the banquet ended." Colin rubbed his aching neck due to the uncomfortable sleeping position. He rose, stretched and yawned. At twenty-two, he resembled his father only with hazel eyes instead of blue. He stood as tall as Niles. He ran fingers through his dark brown hair to put it in place. "Where have you been?"

"With Akilles." At a refreshing table, Niles removed his surcoat to roll up his sleeves. He poured water into a basin to wash his face.

"All night? Why?"

Niles didn't immediately answer, as he tended to his morning toiletry. He splashed water on his face then toweled dried off. "At the queen's request," he finally replied then examined his beard. It needed a trim so he prepared the razon using a strap for sharpening

Colin tried to stifle a yawn. "Sir Abner thought it strange you weren't at the banquet."

Niles looked at Colin by way of the mirror. "You spoke to Abner last night?"

"Ay, which is why I came to your room in search of you." Colin moved closer to continue. "He wishes to speak to you at the earliest possible convenience."

Niles paused in shaving to glance along his shoulder at Colin. "Did he say why?"

"No, but he appeared disturbed during our brief exchange."

Niles frowned in thought before speaking again. "Fetch us breakfast while I finish shaving. I'll find Abner when we're done."

"What about sleep? Seeing as you've been up all night with the prince."

Niles looked crossly at his son. "You're the second person to insinuate I need sleep. At my age, I can tell when I need rest and don't."

Colin snorted a chuckle. "At your age you can also be cantankerous." He threw his hands up in surrender at the fatherly scowl. "Very well, I'm going. Just stay awake long enough not to cut your throat." He hurried out the door.

Cleaned and fed, Niles went to find Abner. Normally, visiting lords stayed in the guests' quarters. However, Abner left a note with his trusted valet. In a quiet corner, Niles paused to read. Afterwards, he stuffed the note in his pocket. He returned to his room to fetch a cloak and riding gloves.

In the stables, busy grooms rushed around. Although Niles intended a short sojourn from the castle, he learned a day of riding had been planned. Rather unusual that he wasn't informed of the King leaving Waldron. He could tolerate being separated from Berk within the confines of the castle, but not outside. Perhaps that's why Abner wanted to see him, to inform him about the ride. Being unsuccessful, Abner left a note about the location.

"Have you see Sir Abner?" Niles asked the head groom.

"He and Sir Gordon left."

"When?"

"About fifteen minutes or so."

The answer made Niles tug on his lip in befuddlement. Rather than go with the excursion they must have gone on ahead to await him.

Instead of pulling the grooms from their task, Niles saddled his horse. Once out the gates, he urged the animal into a gallop to head southeast toward Lake Alewin. Within thirty minutes, he reached the specified place. He didn't see Abner or Gordon only two horses tethered to a fallen log. Cautious, Niles dismounted to tie his horse to a low tree branch. He held the hilt of his sword to approach the horses.

"Hello? Sir Abner?" Niles stopped at hearing the rustling of footsteps.

"Ah, Niles. You got my note." Abner appeared with Gordon.

Niles relaxed, but remained curious. "Why didn't you wait for the King?"

"What do you mean?"

The answer puzzled Niles. "You don't know about the excursion?"

Abner shrugged and sent Gordon a conferring glance. "No. We wanted to find a private place to speak with you."

"What better place then out in the open? Nowhere for spies with big ears to hide," said Gordon.

The explanation didn't satisfy Niles' concern. "The grooms were extremely busy when I reached the stables. Something about an excursion."

"I thought you said Berk isn't riding much these days due to his health?" asked Gordon.

"He's not, which is why I find this odd."

Abner laid hold of Niles' arm. "We don't know about the activity in the stables. Our intent is to speak privately." He indicated another log beside where the horses were tethered. They sat.

"I know something unsettling transpired between the Queen and Zared," said Niles.

"That's putting it mildly," groused Gordon.

Niles sat up straight, irate at the implication of the comment. "He dared to be so bold as to insult the queen in public?"

"Not Zared—Berk."

"At Zared's prompting," added Abner. "He mentioned the Queen's recent *misfortune* when speaking of dancing."

"A late miscarriage is not a *misfortune!* It's a tragedy," rebuffed Niles.

"Misfortune was Zared's word, not mine," insisted Abner. "Berk deferred the first dance to Zared, which forced Myla to comply."

Gordon shook his head with heavy frustration. "I don't know how she tolerates it. Before, Jor'el, I could never treat a woman with such contempt. Certainly not the mother of my future children, whoever she might be."

Niles grew somber. Gordon's words hit hard due to recent personal pain. "They are to be cherished while they are with us."

Gordon regretted his words. "I'm sorry, I didn't mean to upset you."

Niles half-smiled. "It's me. I still miss Rhonda."

"Although unexpected, she gave you a son to be proud of," said Abner.

"Ay." Niles smiled at the statement and shook off his somberness. "Now back to the matter at hand."

Abner continued. "From what we observed, the dance went as well as can be expected. Until Zared spoke, that is. He made reference to Myla's distraction in missing several steps."

"We were paying close attention," Gordon said.

"Ay," agreed Abner. "We suspected Zared would try to pull something—and he did by linking this distraction to his earlier reference of the misfortune."

"That's when Berk spoke about her inability to bear more children."

Niles stirred with anger.

"Zared made a feeble attempt to sway Berk by saying how he has been blessed with four sons yet questioning the health of the youngest," said Abner.

This piqued Niles' interest. "Is there something wrong with Delwin? Something I've not been told?"

"Not that we heard. He appears to be a healthy, active boy. Then again, we're bachelors and not the best at determining such things. "

Niles reflected on what Myla told him about Delwin growing tired and going to bed before dinner. Was the fatigue natural? He then asked, "Did Zared say anything specific about Akilles?"

"How he hoped the young man remained whole and hearty," replied Gordon.

Niles suddenly understood. "She believed it a veiled threat."

Abner snorted a huff. "I don't think there was anything veiled about it, certainly not the way he stared at her."

"And grabbed his collar while doing so." Gordon demonstrated by clenching the neck of his doublet.

Niles watched with troubled interest. Myla mentioned Zared's same action. "Berk didn't take exception to Zared speaking so brashly about his heir?"

"No! He chided Myla about her family's inferiority jeopardizing the health of his sons. That's when she left," replied Gordon.

Incited, Niles bolted up. He took a few brisk steps from the younger lords.

Abner spoke a word to Gordon, who moved to the horses while Abner approached Niles. He spoke low and confidential. "You must act with discretion where Myla is concerned. You can't allow your relationship to become known."

Niles glared at Abner with intense warning. "Who told you?"

With noble pride, Abner squared his shoulders. "No one. Have you forgotten your great-grandmother was from the house of Garwood?"

Niles' anger turned to surprise at the revelation.

"You didn't know?" asked Abner to the change in countenance.

"No." Niles lowered his voice. "Is that why you sought me for instruction in arms as a lad? Because of our family connection?"

Abner smiled. "Ay. Although, I'm surprised you didn't know considering your vast familiarity with history and lineage."

Niles brows leveled in serious reflection. "My great-grandparents lived during the time of Segar, a very unstable period. With too many illegitimates running around seeking the crown, a single wrong word and—" He made a motion of cutting off one's head.

"It's no different now. We need to keep our tongues," said Abner grimly.

"Ay." Niles steered Abner to where Gordon waited with the horses. "Thank you both for taking the risk to tell me. Now, I must return. Will you continue riding for a while longer?"

"Ay. We'll leave an appropriate amount of time between returning so as not to arouse suspicion," replied Abner.

Niles arrived back at Waldron to discover the activity in the stables had quieted. The grooms grumbled when taking charge of his horse. No surprise. Constant shifting sentiments around Waldron became commonplace, as Berk's temper tantrums were increasingly disruptive. Servants rarely voiced protest or objection, rather displayed silent vexed attitudes when going about their work.

To satisfy his curiosity for the mood change, Niles stepped inside the stables. Horses that earlier wore saddles, now contently stood in their stalls without tack. He could well imagine the scene created by the cancelling of a hastily called outing. An erratic King made for difficult working conditions.

After he emerged from the stables, a voice hailed him.

"Sir Niles!"

Upon spying Zared, Niles assumed a braced posture. "My lord."

Zared made a quick survey of Niles' attire. "Where have you been? Out joy riding?" Disdain crept into the question.

Niles' ire flare yet kept his voice neutral. "I was told the King left Waldron on a pleasure ride. I hurried to find him, for his protection, as is my sworn duty."

Zared made a dismissive wave. "The ride was cancelled, so you rode off for nothing, thus leaving your post."

"Hence, my prompt return." Niles gave Zared a hasty bow. He moved in the direction of the main building.

"The King is not in need of your presence this day," Zared called.

Niles pulled up. "Why is that, my lord?"

Zared flashed a thin smile. "It should be obvious. He grows tired of being smothered by you."

Niles moved to confront the baron, who stood three inches shorter than him. "Doing my sworn duty is hardly *smothering*."

Zared became angry. His hand moved in a gesture of contempt. "Don't raise your voice to me, knight!" The action ended with touching the collar of his doublet. "I am a nobleman and member of the Council. If anything *you* answer to me!" He stared intensely at Niles. "Until you are summoned, remain confined to your quarters! In fact," he added in a more conciliatory voice, "go rest, get some sleep. You look in need it."

Staring at Zared, Niles suddenly felt all his combativeness soothe into compliance. "As you say, my lord." He bowed. He went straightway to his chamber. Niles didn't even remove his sword when he laid on the bed and fell asleep.

Zared entered the King's study to shouting. Berk kept repeating the same phrase. "He is incompetent!"

Lord Patrin attempted to calm him. "Sire, you mustn't upset yourself so much."

"Incompetence! I'm surrounded by incompetence!"

Patrin stepped in front of Berk. "Sire—"

Berk tossed an arm about Patrin's shoulders. His voice filled with affection. "Ah, Patrin, my only true and loyal friend."

"I'm honored you feel that way, Sire."

"Would I have allowed you the privilege of naming your son after me if I thought otherwise?" Berk laughed at his own question then answered it. "Of course not! Such an honor is reserved for members of the royal family. That is how much I think of you, my dear Patrin." He spotted Zared. "Ah, baron. Any news of our wayward knight?"

"I'm afraid he has yet to return, Sire."

Berk so forcefully moved from Patrin that he practically shoved his friend. "He compounds his incompetence with dereliction of duty!"

"Sire," began Archimedes, the other individual in the room, "you have practically banished Sir Niles from your presence. If you send for him, he will come."

Berk flashed a mocking smile. "So like Jor'ellians to stick together. However, you are deceived, Archimedes."

The First Jor'ellian didn't take the slight well. "With all due respect, Sire, I differ on being deceived. Jor'ellians are bound by the same oath to Jor'el and to his appointed king. Niles would never break his oath. If he left Waldron, it was in search of you, thus showing his ignorance of the cancellation."

"You dispute the King?" demanded Zared.

Archimedes turned upon the diminutive lord. "I defend a fellow Jor'ellian whom the King has wrongly insulted."

"Get out!" Berk bellowed with rage followed by more complaints of incompetence.

"Now, see what you've done?" Patrin accosted Archimedes. "I just calmed him." He seized Archimedes by the elbow with the intent of escorting him out. Being strong from years of knightly training, Archimedes was not easily moved. Patrin continued his argument. "If you don't leave quietly, he might do something rash."

"My oath to Jor'el compels me to remain and—"

"Take your silly knight's oath and leave!" shouted Berk.

"I'm not solely a knight, but also a priest, as told by my rank of First Jor'ellian."

"Knight! Priest! It's all the same silliness."

"Sire, you don't mean that," said Archimedes in warning.

Berk boldly confronted Archimedes. "Do you think it an oversight that Wilbur wasn't summoned along with the rest of the Council? Hah!"

He huffed in loud scoffing. "This is what I think of your oath!" He jerked the chain of office from around Archimedes' neck, threw it to the floor and stomped on the medallion.

Every sinew and muscle in Archimedes' body tensed with outrage. His fury came forth in the challenging tone. "Pray you don't regret your actions against Jor'el."

Berk went to strike Archimedes, but the First Jor'ellian anticipated the attack. With a crushing grip, Archimedes held Berk's arm at bay while staring mercilessly at him. When Berk recoiled, Archimedes snatched up his medallion and marched from the room.

In hurried steps, Archimedes made his way to the stables where he accosted a groom. "You there? How long ago did Sir Niles leave?"

"He returned."

The answer surprised Archimedes. "When?"

The groom shrugged. "Perhaps ten minutes or so."

Archimedes pursed his lips in thought. "Did you see which way he went?"

"Toward the main building."

"After speaking to Baron Zared," chided a second groom.

More surprise. "He spoke to the baron?" asked Archimedes.

"Ay. Rather contentious, if you ask me."

Something wasn't right. Zared said Niles hadn't returned. Why didn't Niles come to the study? Surely he would confront Zared's lie. Archimedes returned to the main building to begin a search for Niles.

After nearly thirty minutes of inquiry, Archimedes went to the upper gallery. The chamber of the King's Champion was located on the same level as the King's study, and the last logical place left. Receiving no response to his knock, Archimedes entered. Dressed and armed, Niles lay on the bed face down. Fearful of the reason, he seized Niles in an attempt to rouse him.

"Niles!" Upon hearing groaning and seeing sluggish movement, Archimedes grew more forceful. "Wake-up, man!"

Niles rolled over to make defense at the manhandling. Surprise turned into confusion. "Archimedes?"

"What are you doing in bed fully clothed and armed?"

"Huh?" Niles' befuddlement intensified. "How did I get here?"

"I think you know the answer to that question," chided Archimedes.

Niles sat up. He didn't rise to his feet for feeling dizzy. He held his head. "No, I don't. The last thing I remember is talking to Zared."

"At the stables."

Niles looked curiously at Archimedes. "How do you know?"

"Because I went looking for you after he reported to the King that you hadn't returned."

Niles rubbed his eyes. "Why would he say that after we talked?"

Archimedes sat beside Niles. "That's what I want to know, and why I came to find for you."

Niles earnestly regarded Archimedes. "Upon my oath, I have no idea why he would lie or how I ended up in bed."

Archimedes made a nod of ascent. "Tell me what you remember, and perhaps together we can determine what happened."

Niles took a moment to recall. He tossed a cautious look to door then switched to the Ancient language. He kept his low voice. "I thought Berk left Waldron without me, so I followed. When I discovered he wasn't where I had been told, I returned. I spoke to Zared at the stables and then you woke me. What transpired between then and now, I don't know. In fact, what time is it?"

Archimedes replied in the Ancient. "Almost an hour since you returned. Can you recall anything of what was said between you and Zared?"

"Aside from insults?" Niles groused. "He told me the King is tired of my *smothering*, to which I took great offense. Doing my duty is hardly smothering. He spoke disparagingly of my vows while extolling his position as a noblemen and Council member ..." While speaking, Niles' hand moved in mimicking Zared reaching for the neck of his doublet. This made him pause with sudden realization.

Archimedes noticed the change. "What?"

"Something others remarked on seeing that I witnessed for myself during our encounter. Zared tends to grab the collar of his doublet and hold it when making a point." Niles then made another comment on something he noticed. "Where's your medallion?"

Archimedes snarled in anger. "In a fit of rage, Berk tore it from my neck and stomped on it! He denounced the Jor'ellian oath as *silliness*. He admitted to slighting the Vicar by not inviting him with the rest of the Council."

"Oh, no," murmured Niles. "Turning on me due to Zared's influence is one thing, but insulting you and the Vicar is wrong. Heaven help him." He pleaded and glanced to the ceiling.

Archimedes laid hold of Niles arm to get his attention. "If Berk continues on his course of defaming Jor'el, I don't think heaven will help him."

"That is my greatest fear. For then, how do I keep my oath to protect him?" argued Niles.

"Our oath also binds us to defend the honor of Jor'el. If a choice must be made, for whom will you decide?"

"Hence my dilemma. Will Jor'el allow me to break my oath to protect his appointed king in defense of his holy honor?"

Archimedes grew silent, which prompted Niles to question him.

"As First Jor'ellian, could you break your oath to the King?"

Archimedes spoke with dreaded certainty. "The *King* broke the oath when he accosted me and spoke against Jor'el." He tugged at his collar. "Do not be surprised if he does the same to you, King's Champion."

Disturbed, Niles chewed on his lower lip. He spoke with unction, mindful of his volume. "Something dark compels him, I'm certain of it!"

"We both know there is only one *darkness* that can so change a man."

Fearful, Niles seized Archimedes' arm. "Do you think it influenced me? For how else could I lie in bed without memory or be kept from my duty?"

Archimedes' brows knitted with uncertainty. "That would mean Zared …"

Niles interrupted Archimedes. "What has been the target of his ridicule?" He tapped at Archimedes' collar. "You just said only one darkness …" He didn't finish for seeing Archimedes understood.

"We need proof, which means proceeding very carefully."

A loud bang and crash came from outside the door. Both Jor'ellians rushed from the chamber ready to draw their weapons. They discovered five-year-old Delwin lying on his back at the base of a statue suit of armor. Broken pieces of something littered the floor. Akilles ran from the end of the hall to Delwin. Relieved at discovering the source, Archimedes and Niles joined Akilles.

"What happened, little prince?" Niles asked, now speaking Allonian.

Upset, Delwin sniffled. "I wanted to show Father what I made, but I fell and broke it."

"You weren't paying attention and ran into the statue," said Akilles.

Although the simple statement was not a rebuke, Delwin sobbed.

"Now, don't cry. I'll help you put it back together then we'll take it to Father."

After gathering the pieces, Niles and Archimedes spied Zared and Patrin when they emerged from the King's study. For a moment, the four men stared at each other. Delwin focused on his broken project. Akilles noticed the tense visual exchange.

"Sir Niles?" asked Akilles.

Niles flashed a distracted smile when shifting his attention to his charge. "Return to the family salon for repairs."

Akilles didn't appear convinced so Niles began to usher him and Delwin in the opposite direction of Zared and Patrin.

"Sir Niles!" Patrin called.

Archimedes intervened to escort the Princes away. Delwin went willingly while Akilles hesitated. He received a prompting nudge from Niles to leave.

"Did you hear me, man?" Patrin demanded, his voice closer.

"I did, my lord. However, what needs to be said is best done between adults and not to the terrorizing of children."

Patrin turned red-faced. "How dare you?"

Niles stood his ground. "My duty is to protect the royal family."

"A fine job you are doing by riding off and leaving them vulnerable," scolded Zared.

"A find job you did by wrongly reporting to the King that I had not returned after we spoke at the stables." Niles felt the hard sting of Zared's slap.

"Let that be a lesson in accosting your betters!" Zared made the same earlier gesture in reaching for the collar of his doublet.

Incited by the action, Niles commanded in the Ancient, "*Stad! Ni dean imich!*"

Shock registered on Zared's face when his hand stopped inches from his collar. Fury quickly replaced surprise. Zared turned on heels and marched away.

Niles' intense glare found Patrin. The lord recoiled a step yet maintained some dignity in withdrawal. Niles did not change his focus from the departing lords to Archimedes' return though he spoke in the Ancient. "Is that proof enough? My command stopped him."

"I think you tipped your hand," warned Archimedes.

Niles sharply turned to Archimedes. "Did you not sense the evil?"

"Ay, which is why I returned." Archimedes took Niles by the elbow to steer him away.

At the corner to the royal wing, they found Akilles and Delwin waiting. The older Prince appeared anxious. Delwin sat on the floor more interested in his broken project.

"Why did you command the baron to stop?" asked Akilles.

Niles didn't immediately answer Akilles rather spoke to Archimedes in Allonian. "See to Delwin while I speak to His Highness."

"Come, little prince. I know how to fix it."

"You do? Oh, good." Delwin gathered the pieces. He eagerly accompanied Archimedes, chattering about his project as they left.

"Your chamber." Niles motioned Akilles to proceed. Once at the room, Niles spoke a word to a Jor'ellian on guard before shutting the door. "I suppose I should be glad you are learning the Ancient so well as to understand."

Akilles sheepishly admitted, "I only heard *stad* for stop. Did you say that because he was going hit you again?"

"If he had struck me a second time, he wouldn't be standing. And I would be within my rights to defend myself."

"How? He's a lord and you just a knight."

"Despite the difference in rank, Jor'el's book of Verse teaches against unwarranted violence. I did nothing to provoke the attack in the form of intimidation or threatening physical harm. What I *did* is confront the baron for lying to your father concerning me. Another part in Verse speaks about standing up for the truth in the face of falsehood."

"Why would he lie about you?"

Niles pursed his lips in consideration of his answer. "That is a bit more involved than you need to know at present."

Akilles became offended. "I'm not a child! I'll be thirteen in two months, and will take my place at court as the Prince Royale, heir to the throne."

"When you are officially installed as such, I will speak to you as man to man! Until then you are my pupil in studies and my charge in duty."

Akilles threw up his arms in exasperation. "You are infuriating! No wonder my father has little patience for you."

His temper exhausted, Niles caught Akilles by the arm. "I'm trying to keep you safe!"

The passionate outburst surprised Akilles. "From what?"

"Forces you have no knowledge of." Niles took Akilles by the shoulders to look directly at him. "You *must* trust me, Akilles. For as Jor'el is my witness, I only seek your good."

Akilles swallowed back discomposure at the urging. "I believe you."

Niles flashed a smile of relief. "Whatever you do, avoid Zared as much as possible."

"I'll try."

Satisfied, Niles took a deep breath to change his mood. "Now, since you insist, we shall have a lesson in the Ancient."

Akilles rolled his eyes. "*Ay, maighstir.*"

Chapter 5

GRESHAM JOINED KELL, ARMUS, MONA AND ELDRIC ON A HILLTOP overlooking the castle plain. He listened intently even when Kell spoke in conclusion.

"We depend upon you to alert us for any trouble."

"I think you would sense that before me. Whatever is happening is coming from Waldron." Gresham gestured toward the castle.

"It doesn't hurt to have eyes and ears on multiple fronts," said Armus.

"A few more swords wouldn't hurt either," countered Gresham.

"We deal with it as we can." Kell nodded to the others as a signal to begin. He brought his hands together, bowed his head and spoke a low command in the Ancient. Soon, he took on a more mortal appearance by shrinking a little over a foot in height and wearing a royal soldier's uniform. He retained his facial features with black hair, only his golden eyes turned to a mortal yellowish hazel.

Eldric, Armus and Mona mimicked Kell. Armus also wore the uniform of a royal soldier. He stood the same mortal height as Kell. His eyes became a dull brown. Eldric's eyes turned dark blue while his clothes became those of a male servant. Mona's eyes turned greenish-blue, and her clothes that of a female servant. She remained the shortest of the group at around five and half feet. Each showed signs that the transition into mortal form wasn't easy. This caused Gresham concern.

"Are you certain everyone can keep cover until this is done?" he asked.

"Jor'el willing," said Kell.

"Doesn't sound reassuring," groused Eldric.

"If you need reassurance to do what you were created to do then maybe you should back out—now!"

Momentarily stymied by Kell's rebuke, Eldric said, "I meant you didn't sound sure, not Jor'el—oh, never mind," his voice trailed off when he realized how flimsy he sounded.

Kell grabbed hold of Eldric while Armus held onto Mona. They moved from the hill toward Waldron. Eldric and Mona behaved like struggling captives.

"Hello, the gate!" called Kell.

They paused to be recognized by the soldiers on the rampart.

"What have we here?" asked a soldier.

"Two indentured servants attempting to run away," replied Kell.

The soldier made a sarcastic scoff. "Can't have that, now can we? Open the gate door," he called down to the gatekeeper.

Once inside, the soldier from the rampart met them in the courtyard. "Take them to guardhouse."

"No, the steward said he wanted to deal with them *personally*," said Kell with emphasis.

"Apparently, they made a fool of him," added Armus.

The soldier caustically smiled. "They'll wish they went to the guardhouse." He motioned for them to pass.

Knowing the castle from when originally built, Kell and Armus brought Mona and Eldric around to the back of the main building. Instead of entering, they made a quick detour to a secluded spot deep in the shadows between buildings.

"Time to act," Kell said to Mona.

She closed her eyes. After a brief moment, her eyes snapped opened. "She's in the family wing."

They entered the nearest door down from the kitchen. This led to the rear hallway.

"Oh!" cried a startled woman. She wore a fine dress showing her status of high rank in the household. She carried a tray with a teapot, cups and some pastries.

To avoid trouble, Kell seized the woman while Armus took the tray.

"The Queen—!" she began in protest.

"Caidil!" Kell said. She immediately fell asleep in his arms.

"This room appears to be a storage closet," said Eldric.

"Sleep until I wake you," Kell spoke in the woman's ear. He gently placed her in the closet and shut the door.

"Let's hope no one finds her," said Mona.

Kell spoke another command and flicked his wrist. A lock clicked. "No key will open it, only my command."

"I think this is your way to Queen." Armus handed Mona the tray.

"Don't follow too close," she told them.

With tray in hand, Mona headed up the back stairs to the family wing. The others maintained a respectful distance.

Mona directed her steps to the salon. Upon entering, she discovered the Queen was not alone. Two ladies-in-waiting and five-year-old Delwin also occupied the room. The boy played contently with some toys. The women did needlepoint using hand-hoops while Myla sat before a large stand to do her work.

"Your tea, Majesty." Mona set the tray on a small side table.

"Where is Isobel? I sent her to fetch the tea," asked Myla.

"Indisposed, Majesty. However, she didn't want you to wait."

"I wasn't aware she felt ill."

Mona prepared the tea. "I can't say, Majesty. I only know what she told me." She handed Myla the teacup. She caught the Queen's eye and smiled.

The brief exchange made Myla curious. "Do I know you? You seem familiar."

"Being a servant, we have not been formally introduced. But I'm sure you've seen me around, Majesty." Mona again smiled. She stepped back to let Myla enjoy her tea.

For a moment, Mona watched and waited. The problem was how to act with so many others in the room? She shifted her focus to Delwin. Shortly, he grew agitated then injured his hand on a toy.

"Delwin?" Myla nearly spilled the tea she set on the table to rush to her son.

"My hand!" he sobbed.

Myla took hold of his small hand for examination. "It doesn't look bad."

"It hurts."

"Because he is tired," said one of the ladies in a hinting tone.

Myla gave him a motherly frown. "Did you have your nap today?"

Delwin shook his head and sniffled.

"Well, your hand is fine, but you need to rest."

"I'll take him, Majesty." The lady who spoke came to take Delwin.

"No, I will. You can stay with him after he's fallen asleep."

Myla headed for the door. Not the outcome Mona hoped for. When the gap grew between Myla, the women who spoke and the second lady, Mona acted. She blocked the second lady's path to shut the door.

"What are you doing?"

In an instant, Mona reverted to her Guardian self, grabbed the woman and placed a hand over her face. The woman swooned just as Mona shape-shifted into her likeness; that of a forty-year old with light brown hair and green eyes.

Eldric, Armus and Kell rushed in. Armus held the door shut to keep anyone from entering.

"We sensed your shift. She isn't the Queen," said Kell.

"No time to explain. Just keep her hidden like you're supposed to!" Mona said to Eldric.

Armus opened the door for Mona. He and Kell followed her, yet kept a discrete distance while she rushed to catch up to the Queen.

Myla noticed Mona join them at the door to Delwin's chamber. "Wilma? You look flush."

"Sorry, Majesty. I tripped over one of the prince's toys when leaving thus ran to catch up."

In the armory, Akilles practiced with a quarterstaff. Under Niles' watchful eye and barking commands, the prince responded. Each time Akilles held the staff incorrectly, Niles made adjustments in his position and the process began again. Not until Akilles' successfully completed the exercise without a mistake, did Niles allow him a moment to rest.

"Your form and quickness is improving," said Niles.

Akilles finished a drink then replied. "I prefer the staff to the sword."

"You need to be proficient in all forms of arms."

Akilles took another drink. "Which weapon do you like best?"

Niles grinned. "Any one that helps in my duty." He stopped Akilles from taking a third drink. "Time for the sword."

Akilles rolled his eyes.

A servant entered. "Your Highness, the King sends for you."

Akilles grinned at Niles. "The sword will have to wait." He quickly donned his doublet. Niles moved to accompany Akilles.

"He didn't send for you, knight," said the servant tersely.

Akilles scolded the servant. "Since when does the King's Champion need a summons to see the king?"

The man grew apologetic. "Highness, I merely convey the King's wishes. He sent for you, with specific orders that if you were with Sir Niles, to come alone." He emphasized *alone* in speaking toward Niles.

Seeing Akilles' uncertainly, Niles reassured him. "I shall accompany you to the study—" When loud contrary cough interrupted him, he cast a stern glare to the servant to add, "and wait in the hall!"

They began to leave when the royal jeweler met them at the threshold.

"Sir Niles. I completed the new chain for mounting the medallion."

"Now?"

"It will only take a few moments to attach it."

The servant slyly smiled in triumph. "You wouldn't want the King to find you without your medallion, knight."

"Maybe we should wait," said Akilles.

"No, don't give your father any reason to become angry. I'll be along shortly." Niles nudged Akilles to leave.

Akilles continued his trek to enter the main building. He barely took two steps from the door when he met Zared.

"Highness." The baron made a partial bow, during which he held the collar of his doublet. "You look rather piqued today. Are you well?"

As Akilles stared into Zared eyes, a knot tightened in his stomach. "I—I'm well. Why do you ask?"

"I know how hard Sir Niles works you. Endless lessons and repetitive exercises." Zared moved closer to lay a hand on Akilles' shoulder. "I don't want him to overtax your health."

The stomach knot turned into queasiness. "He … he's not."

"Then why are you so nervous? Are you tired? Ill, perhaps?"

Akilles swallowed back an abrupt rise of stomach bile. He didn't feel ill a moment ago, so why all of a sudden? He turned from Zared to compose himself.

"Oh, dear, he has made you ill," said Zared with certainty.

"No!" Akilles quickly turned back to Zared. The eyes again! So intense and sinister that he recoiled in fear when Niles' warning echoed in his mind; *whatever you do, avoid Zared as much as possible.*

"Highness?"

"Stay away from me!"

"Why?" Zared asked in an unusually calm voice.

"Here now. Is something wrong?" Patrin arrived.

"Sir Niles went too far in training, and the Prince is ill as a result," said Zared.

"No, no, that's not true!" refuted Akilles.

"Then why are you shaking?"

"I'm not!" Akilles squared his shoulders in an effort to regain his self-control.

"But you are, Highness," said Patrin.

"Am I?" Akilles glanced to his hands. Indeed, he trembled. Where did this overwhelming fear come from? Feeling Zared take hold of his arm, Akilles jerked away in defense.

"Let us take you to your room so you can rest."

"No, my father sends for me. I can't keep him waiting."

"You should be more rested and in command of yourself before seeing the King," said Patrin.

When Patrin reached for him, Akilles bolted from them. The encounter proved physically and emotionally unsettling but why? Even recalling Niles' warning, he had difficulty understanding what just happened.

Atthe door to his father's study, Akilles paused to catch his breath and calm his racing heart. That became difficult upon hearing his father bellow some unintelligible words. Did the delay make him angry? There was only one way to find out. Taking a deep breath, Akilles motioned the soldier on duty to the door.

"Come!" said Berk in sharp response to the knock.

The soldier entered and announced, "Majesty, His Royal Highness is here."

"Send him in!"

Akilles clenched his fist to keep from shaking. This fear was brought on by his father's temper. He proceeded with all formality. "You sent for me, Sire?"

"What took you so long?"

"I was in the armory, and paused a moment to become presentable."

Berk sneered. "And your tutor? Is he not presentable?"

Akilles knitted his brows with confusion. "We were told you only summoned me, and not Sir Niles."

"The man is arrogant and insufferable! He slights me at every turn."

"How is it slighting if you didn't summon him?"

"You defend him? To me your father and King?"

"No, I just don't understand your anger toward Sir Niles."

Berk waved him off. "You're just a boy, you don't understand anything."

Akilles wisely let the insult pass. "Sir, why did you send for me?"

"To inform you that Baron Zared will see to your instruction from now on."

Akilles paled at the statement. "What? No!"

"No?" repeated Berk, his temper flaring. "You dare dispute my command?"

Akilles fought to maintain his composure. "Sir Niles is Jor'el's chosen to be the King's Champion and—"

"Do not use that name in my presence!"

"But *he* won his position, and is a renowned Jor'ellian Knight."

"Not Niles! I mean *him!*" Berk motioned toward the ceiling.

In utter shock, Akilles stared at his father. "Jor'el? But he is the Almighty. Creator of all things."

Berk snarled with intense irritation. "Zared is right! Niles has polluted your mind with nonsense." He seized Akilles' arm, scaring the lad. "The sooner this foolishness is rooted out of you the better! Now go!" Berk practically tossed Akilles into the hall. "Find Zared to begin your instruction immediately, and hopefully see reason."

Dumbfounded, Akilles stared at the slammed door. This was too much for his mind to understand or reason. "Marmi." He hurried to find his mother.

After Delwin fell asleep, Myla and Wilma/Mona headed back to the salon. Wilma/Mona noticed Kell and Armus standing guard at the end of the hall like any royal soldier on-duty. She hoped this meant Eldric had the real Lady Wilma safely hidden. The room was empty. Good.

Since assuming Wilma's persona, Mona got the sense from the mortal's essence that she was the most trusted of Queen Myla's ladies. This might work better, since she could freely observe rather than experience Myla's emotions.

They just resumed their pastime of needlework when Akilles burst into the room. He pushed so hard that the door slammed behind him.

"Marmi!" He was flushed, his worried expression bordered on fear.

"Akilles? What is wrong?"

Before Akilles replied, there came a knock on the door followed by Niles' voice. "Majesty?"

Akilles rushed to open the door. He pulled Niles inside and shut the door. Niles wore his medallion on the new chain.

"I thought you went to see the King?" Niles asked Akilles.

"I did, but he said things I can't understand." Akilles spoke in hurried concern. He turned to Myla. "Marmi, he is so changed. I don't know what do."

"Calm down and tell us what happened." She motioned him to the footstool of her chair.

Akilles sat perched, his movement agitated. "He said Baron Zared is to be my new tutor, and practically cursed Sir Niles."

Hearing Zared's name made Myla glance anxiously to Niles, which prompted him to speak.

"What exactly did he say?"

"He called you *arrogant* and *insufferable* when you didn't come. I told him the servant said you weren't summoned. But that's not the worst." Akilles turned back to Myla. "He denounced Jor'el by calling the Almighty—*nonsense* and *foolishness*. He said the sooner Baron Zared got me to see reason the better."

Their reactions were measurable. Myla gasped in horror while Wilma/Mona winced in distress. Niles grabbed the hilt of his sword to steady his anger.

"Are you certain of this? Answer me carefully, Akilles," said Niles.

Akilles stood to face Niles. "As Jor'el is my witness, it is true. My father, who once worshipped the Almighty, now considers him foolish nonsense! And wants me to change my belief!" He quickly sat back on the footstool to plead with Myla. "Marmi, what should I do? In my heart,

I can't do as Father wants, not about Jor'el. And after speaking to the baron, I *won't* be subject to him!"

"Was Zared with you father?" she asked.

"No, I met him on the way to the study. He thought I looked tired." Akilles glanced to Niles. "He insisted your training overtaxed me, and is a threat to my health. But I felt fine, until talking to him made me sick to my stomach!"

"You felt ill?" asked Wilma/Mona. Until now she had been an observer, but Akilles' statement made her curious.

"Ay. It came on suddenly. I thought I would retch in the hallway."

Niles touched Akilles' shoulder to get his attention from Wilma/Mona. "Tell me, did Zared hold onto the neck of his collar?" He made the gesture.

Akilles thought for a moment. "I believe so, but it was his eyes! There was something ... sinister ... cold and frightening. Patrin arrived and tried convince me to retire, but I didn't want to make Father angry so I went to the study. I almost wish I hadn't!" He became downcast.

"You did right by responding to your father, the King."

"Indeed," agreed Myla. "Not going would have made him angrier."

"What can I do, Marmi?"

Myla held Akilles' hand in a gesture of encouragement, but it was Wilma/Mona who replied.

"Pray for strength and guidance. Jor'el already knows what you need, so don't be afraid to ask." She softly grinned.

Myla fondly spoke. "Dear Wilma, always the voice of faith and trust."

Wilma/Mona spoke with a tone of certainty. "I know Jor'el will never abandon the faithful, no matter what other mortals may do."

Niles cocked his head in regard of Wilma/Mona. "That's an interesting phrase in referring to other people as *mortals*."

Wilma/Mona lightly blushed at the miscue. "Well, with Jor'el being immortal and eternal, what are we but mortals?" She tried to pass if off with a chuckle.

Myla made a teasing laugh. "She's being spending an awful lot of time with Archimedes. There might be something in the future."

Niles guffawed with a good belly laugh.

Wilma/Mona's blush brightened with embarrassment at the humor. Truly, Mona sensed Wilma had deep affection for Archimedes.

Akilles sighed with frustration. "At least *she* has a choice!" He waved a hand at Wilma/Mona. "I'm supposed to do what I'm told."

Niles' humor ceased to speak to Myla. "It may be time."

Myla somberly nodded.

"Time for what?" Akilles asked at their exchange.

Myla tugged on Akilles' hand to get his undivided attention. She leaned forward to speak confidentially. "To go to the Fortress, where you can complete your training and studies in peace and safety."

Akilles noticed the great angst on her face. "Do you think I'm in danger here?"

She caressed his cheek and fought to contain her anxiety. "After your encounter with Zared, I believe you know the answer to that question."

Akilles shook his head in refute. "I don't want to leave you. What about my brothers?"

She stopped his protest with a hurried explanation. "Hear me, Akilles! You are the eldest, the heir. Once you turn thirteen, you will be a greater threat, for on that day, you can legitimately take the throne without consent or interference."

Niles moved beside Myla's chair. "She's right, my Prince. Zared wants to influence you before then, and eliminate your faith ... "

Myla seized Niles' hand to stop his speech.

Akilles stood to ask Niles, "Will you go with me?"

Niles smiled. "That is the plan."

Akilles swallowed back his emotions. "When?"

"As soon as we can arrange it. For the time being, act as if you are following Zared's advice. Go to your room and rest. Trust Jor'el, and us."

Myla nudged Niles' arm. "Go with him. You must act as if this is news to you."

"I'm sure Zared will relish telling me," he spoke with bitter sarcasm.

After the door closed on Niles and Akilles' departure, Wilma/Mona sat on the footstool. "Courage, Majesty."

Myla's smile quivered. "Dear Wilma, what would I do without you?"

"The same as you do now, trust in Jor'el. He is with you. And with your son." Wilma/Mona glanced at the door. "Despite his impulsiveness, he has deep faith for one so young."

"I credit Niles for that. He helped me when we were children."

"How so?"

Myla looked curiously at Wilma/Mona. "You know why."

Mona searched Wilma's memory to understand Myla's retort. She smiled when discovering the answer. "I thought you meant something else." She lowered her voice to continue, "Tell Akilles of the relationship just before they leave. I'm sure it will be of great comfort to him."

There came a knock at the door followed by a male voice. "Majesty? May I beg a brief audience?"

Myla whispered in dread. "Zared! What could he want?"

"To gloat, no doubt," chided Wilma/Mona, her ire riled.

"Majesty?" inquired Zared.

"Brace yourself," said Wilma/Mona.

"With you as back-up." Myla nodded toward the door.

Wilma/Mona admitted Zared. "My lord, *Her Majesty* has only a moment to give you." Her displeased gaze conveyed her meaning clearly.

"You are in rare form this day, Lady Wilma." Zared returned her provoking glare. His hand touched the neck of his doublet.

A cold, eerie sensation made Wilma/Mona flinch. Zared must have noticed, for his expression turned to marked caution. When he showed curiosity, she moved to stand beside Myla's chair.

"You wish to speak to me, my lord?" asked Myla. Although she remained seated, she assumed a posture of regal dignity.

Zared bowed. His hand remained on the collar. "It is on behalf of the King that I convey his wishes regarding His Royal Highness."

"That you are to replace Sir Niles as his tutor."

Zared reacted in surprise at her knowledge. "Indeed, Madam. May I inquire how you learned of this?"

Myla wryly smiled. "I'm not ignorant of my husband's decisions."

"No, of course not. However, the King instructed me to inform *you*. May I inquire how you came to hear the news before my arrival?"

"You may not."

Zared didn't take the refusal well. "Madam, if there is a spy or informant that defies the King's wishes—"

"Spy? Informant? Truly, sir, you go too far as to insult my household! Has your newfound position gone to head your already?"

In an angry gesture, Zared clenched the fringe of his collar. "Madam—!"

Immediately sensing a cold surge of power, Wilma/Mona stepped between Zared and Myla. "You dare accost the Queen with your continued insolence?"

Zared didn't reply, rather stared intensely at Wilma/Mona. This time, Wilma/Mona stood her ground, roused to defense by what she sensed. She matched his intensity, which made his expression alter between rage, confusion and finally indignation. He stormed from the room and slammed the door behind him.

Curious, Myla's attention went from the door to Wilma/Mona. "What did you do to make him leave so abruptly?"

Wilma/Mona didn't answer. She had much to consider before speaking.

"I don't think I've ever seen you so forceful," continued Myla.

"All I did was step in to defend you."

"Well, maybe you should do that more often." Myla chuckled.

A quick smile came and went, as Wilma/Mona was still distracted by the encounter with Zared. She suddenly swayed and caught a nearby chair to keep from swooning. Not good. The energy needed to maintain mortal form grew taxing.

"Wilma?"

"A slight dizziness."

"You look awfully pale."

"I need to lie down…" Wilma/Mona didn't wait for Myla's permission, rather hurried from the room. Kell and Armus must have sensed her distress. They ushered her into a small room around the corner. Armus helped her to sit while Kell locked the door. Mona reverted to her Guardian form.

Eldric moved from the sofa upon which lay the real Lady Wilma to help Mona. "What happened?" He examined her for wounds or injury.

"I'm not sure. After my encounter with Zared, I felt weak and unable to maintain my shift." She glanced to Kell. "I believe he is connected to the Dark Way."

"We sensed evil. Rest a moment—"

Lady Wilma moaned as if waking. Eldric hastened to the sofa, placed a hand on Wilma's head and spoke. She grew still. "We must leave. She'll be awake shortly."

"I don't know if I can take on a mortal façade," said Mona, weary.

Kell knelt beside the chair. He took Mona's face in his hands to look her in the eye. He repeated several phrases in the Ancient. Mona transformed into the same servant persona as when they arrived. Kell blinked in pain. Armus helped him stand.

"Are you all right?" Eldric asked the captain.

Kell waved him off. "We'll need strengthening tonics when this business is done."

"I brought extra for that purpose."

They headed for the door when Mona spoke. "Wait." She moved to Wilma, placed her hand on the woman's forehead. "Remember the encounters, but nothing of your absence. Help the Queen, Prince Akilles and Sir Niles. Oh, and tell Archimedes how you feel." She smiled.

"What did you mean by all that?" asked Kell.

"I'll tell you when we are safely away."

During their exit from the castle, the Guardians paused by the closet where the woman slept. Kell whispered into the lock. It clicked and they heard movement from behind the door. Quickly, they headed toward the postern gate.

Once again, Kell took hold of Eldric and Armus held Mona. Only this time, it was to conceal their movement. Both Kell and Armus spoke the Ancient: *"From mortal eyes veil our frame until we reach safety."*

They walked past the royal guards without a blink of recognition or word of acknowledgement. Not until they reached the safety of trees did Kell and Armus release Eldric and Mona.

Even for the captain and lieutenant, the use of power proved draining. Almost immediately upon reaching the rendezvous, all reverted to Guardian form. Mona collapsed to her knees in exhaustion. Eldric knelt beside her, he too unsteady. Armus and Kell sat on a log for a moment of recovery.

"I supposed you need this." Gresham held out the satchel to Eldric.

"Did you bring any water?"

"He didn't, but I did," said a female.

Armus and Kell rose to make defense. They relaxed at seeing Wren, a Guardian huntress. Her long auburn hair hung loose, the bright green eyes glinted with humor at their reaction. A crossbow and quiver were slung across her back. She carried a large flask.

Gresham smiled at their reaction. "You said extra eyes and ears would help."

Armus didn't argue rather sat back on the log.

"Tell us what happened," Kell spoke to Mona.

While Eldric prepared the strengthening tonic, Mona recounted her time as Wilma. She only paused in speaking to drink when from the flask when passed around to those who entered the castle.

"Finish it. You need more than the rest of us," said Eldric.

She didn't immediately comply rather concluded her report. "I'm convinced Zared is the source of the Dark Way. Rather the conduit for Dagar."

"Did you see the talisman?" asked Kell.

She drank the rest of the tonic before answering. "No. But the overwhelming cold sense of evil felt like the Dark Way. Even disguised in mortal form, he backed down when I stepped in to defend the Queen." Mona grew disconcerted. "The look on his face ... like he recognized me. As if he could see past my persona."

The statement drew everyone's attention

She continued, "Immediately upon Zared leaving I got weak, on the verge of losing my shift. That's why I left so abruptly."

"We sensed evil, and were coming to help when we saw you exit the room," said Armus.

"Is that why you're convinced Zared commands the Dark Way, because of his recognition?" Wren asked Mona.

"Ay. Only the most astute Guardian can sense a shape-shifter. In this case, a Grand Master of the Dark Way with access to power beyond normal mortals."

"He *must* have Dagar's talisman somewhere on him. It's the only way to command such power," chided Armus.

Mona finished the tonic. Her hand moved in lowering the flask thus brushed the neck of her doublet. Her eyes widened in recollection. "He does! Only hidden." She tugged at her collar. "Niles asked Akilles if Zared held his hand here. Zared did the same the entire time he spoke to Myla."

Armus said to Kell, "You need to warn Jedrek to be on the lookout for Dark Way activity in the Delta."

"He already suspects a connection."

"Well, this confirms it."

"What can we do about Myla's fear for Akilles?" asked Mona.

Kell thought for a moment. "You said she and Niles have a plan, so let's make certain it happens. Other than that, we'll be doing good to keep the Dark Way threat to a minimum."

"Doesn't sound like much," said Eldric.

This time Kell didn't rebuke the physician. Instead, he sighed and nodded. "When both of you are ready, return to your provinces," he said to Eldric and Mona. "You too, Wren." Kell drew Armus away to speak privately. "Go immediately to the Temple as Finn and *discreetly* escort Wilbur to Waldron. Tell him Captain Seul sent you, he'll understand."

"What are you going to do?" asked Armus.

"Remain with Gresham. The greatest danger is here." Kell's black brows levelled with uneasiness. "Be mindful of Odell. He is an ambitious mortal of dubious motivation."

"What makes you say that?"

"He entered the priesthood late in life, age thirty in mortal years. He quickly rose through the ranks to become the Temple Headmaster then Wilbur's personal assistant six years ago." Kell shook his head with consideration. "Every time I've seen him, there is something unsettling I can't quite discern."

The statement intrigued Armus. "Have you spoken to Odell as well as Wilbur?"

"No. During the few times I've been permitted to approach Wilbur, I'm struck with uneasiness simply at the mention of Odell. Wilbur pleaded with me that he not be named as successor."

"That's telling," mused Armus.

"Ay, which is why I need *you* for this task," said Kell pointedly.

Armus wryly smiled. "Knowing the reason isn't necessary, just helpful."

Chapter 6

Troubled, Akilles restlessly moved about his chamber. He went from lying on his bed, to sitting in a chair and finally pacing.

"You'll wear yourself out," Niles commented.

"How can you be so calm after what happened?" asked the agitated Prince.

"Because I trust Jor'el. So should you."

"I do! I just wish I could understand what changed my father's attitude. We used to sit in Chapel together, visit the Temple on holidays. Now, he is mean and angry. Why?" he asked with desperation.

Niles sighed, long and deep. He and others wondered the same, but always came to the same conclusion involving Zared. He hesitated to reveal too much. "That is a question only he can answer."

Akilles shook his head with insistence. "You and Marmi know something you're not telling me. Why else make the plan?"

Niles drew close to Akilles and spoke in warning. "Do not speak so loudly. What we told you is private."

"I swear, I won't tell anyone. But why make the plan?" he repeated in a lower voice. "Surely, I have a right to know," he added at Niles hesitancy to speak.

Niles drew Akilles to a far corner of the room away from the door and windows. "There is too much to explain, save to say Berk's turning from Jor'el is cause for great concern on many levels. Not solely for his own soul, but also as king. People look to him for an example of faith." He paused with pensive reflection. "Alas, his denouncement shows how much the influence of *others* has changed him."

"I know you mean Zared, but what others?"

For a moment, Niles wondered if he said too much. However, Akilles wouldn't be put off.

"I *need* to know if I'm to be careful in how I act or what I say around people."

Despite being very astute, Akilles was still a boy, though not for much longer. Niles replied with discretion. "The one with him during your encounter.

"Patrin?" asked Akilles with some confusion. "He's Father's dear friend. He even named his son in honor of him. Why does he concern you?"

"Just like your father, Patrin has changed. He is suddenly attached to Zared in everything when before Patrin avoided him." Niles pursed his lips, reconsidering the conversation. "Truly, Akilles, there is much beyond what you can understand right now. Forces that are at work—"

"The Dark Way."

Surprised, Niles stared at Akilles. "What makes you say that?"

"Verse speaks of the Dark Way, and the great enemy. You have mentioned it during my lessons. Vicar Wilbur preaches about it during the commemorative services at the Temple. I am able to comprehend what I hear and read!" Offense crept into Akilles' voice.

Niles lightly chuckled with relief. "Of course you are. I just thought maybe you encountered something recently that you failed to tell me."

"No." Akilles grew sheepish. "I can't keep anything from you, which is probably one of the reasons my father wants to separate us."

Niles smiled with affection. "You are remarkably intelligent and intuitive. I've been blessed to be you tutor all these years."

"Now that will end!" Akilles' earlier upset returned.

"Only for a short time," Niles said with encouragement. "Yet your trust and faith in Jor'el will be tested. Remember all I have taught you about the Jor'ellian Code. Believe the Almighty's words and you will succeed."

"Highness?" came a call and knock on the door. "It is Baron Zared."

Akilles balked so Niles took the Prince's face in his hands to get his attention from the door. "I may not be your tutor any more, but as the *King's Champion*, I'm *not* leaving Waldron. I will still be here, waiting and watching for the right time."

Akilles relaxed, even smile. "Ay."

"Highness?" Zared called again.

Niles' tone turned sarcastic. "Now to play our parts." He answered the door. Zared immediately scowled at sight of him.

"What are you doing here, knight?"

"Where else would I be? If I'm not with the King, I am with my pupil," Niles casually replied.

"*That* has been remedied," Zared hissed before proceeding further into the room. He assumed a pleasant smile and bowed to Akilles. "Your Royal Highness." The motion brought his hand to his collar.

Akilles flinched at the movement. A warning wave from Niles made him relax. At least, he didn't show fear, rather guarded. "To what do I owe this visit, my lord?"

"Surely the king informed you of the new arrangement?" It was more a statement than question.

"He did."

"Then why is Sir Niles here? If I may be so bold as to inquire?"

"Bold is something you are, my lord."

Niles fought a smile at Akilles' well-placed retort. He stiffened when Zared took exception to the rebuff and clenched his collar. Niles acted to avert Zared's attention. "Why do you object to my presence, my lord?"

It worked. Zared changed his focus to Niles. "That should be obvious, knight! Your services are no longer required in regard to the Prince's education."

"The *safety* of the Prince still falls within my duties as the King's Champion in protecting the royal family."

Zared's knuckles turned white in clenching the collar. The eyes narrowed with intensity at Niles. This caused Niles to brace his feet in a defensive posture and boldly return the glare.

"State your purpose in coming," demanded Niles.

"To tell the Prince that his new instructions begin tomorrow."

"You have discharged your purpose."

Zared's jowls clenched. He turned to Akilles and made a short bow. "Until the morrow, Highness."

Niles remained in his defensive stance, as his gaze followed Zared's departure. The door slammed for effect.

"He clenched his collar like you mentioned earlier," said Akilles.

Niles didn't respond, preoccupied with consideration.

"Why would he hold his collar like that?" continued Akilles.

"I'm not sure. It seems to embolden him."

"I think he's totally boorish."

Niles snorted a chuckle. "Since you are free from his *boorish* presence for the remainder of the day, rest. Read. Or whatever you like, only stay in your room."

"Why?"

"So I know where to find you," he retorted with sarcasm.

Akilles rolled his eyes. "It'll be boring."

"Better boring than with Zared."

"Ay," Akilles grunted in agreement. "What are you going to do?"

"Find out the reason for this change." Niles grinned when struck with a thought. "I know just the person to stay with you." He moved to a bookshelf, found what he wanted and handed it to Akilles. "Read this until he comes."

Akilles frowned at seeing the title, *The Manual of Superior Swordsmanship*.

"Read!" Niles tapped a finger on the cover then left.

Niles made his way from the family wing to the barracks on the rear wall. After a brief conversation with the sergeant on duty, he went to the armory. In a back room, Niles spied his quarry with others inspecting various pieces of armor.

"Colin." Niles used a finger to beckon his son from the others.

The young man spoke a word to his comrades before joining his father near the door. Niles steered Colin to a quiet place in the courtyard.

"Go, and stay with Akilles. He is in his chamber waiting for you."

"Is something wrong?"

"Indeed," chided Niles. "By order of the King, Zared is his new instructor."

"What?"

"Keep your voice down." Niles cautiously glanced around, but no one seemed to hear or paid them any attention.

Colin obliged by lowering his voice. "Why did he do that?"

"I intend to find out. Zared said instruction would start tomorrow. This gives me time to investigate; only I don't want Akilles to be alone."

"Consider it done."

Niles waited until Colin entered the main building before directing his steps to the Chapel. Even in the peak of the day, the Chapel was not well lit. Some daylight filtered through the high windows, casting long shadows into the darkened room. The candles on the altar had burned to the wick. Frustrated, Niles approached the altar to search for new candles

"Here now, what are you doing?" The Chapel priest accosted Niles.

"The better question is what are you doing? Altar candles should never be allowed to burn out! Fetch more and light them immediately."

"Who are you to give me orders?"

"One who has more respect for Jor'el than you! Now where are the candles?" demanded Niles. He began searching again.

"Your authority doesn't extend in here, knight!"

"Mine does." Archimedes made his way from the threshold to the altar. "First Jor'ellian, if you have forgotten my rank."

"Will you dispute him also?" Niles challenged.

The priest muttered under this breath, "I'll get the candles," and scurried off.

After the priest left, Archimedes spoke. "I heard what happened. I thought to find you when I noticed you enter the Chapel."

"News spreads fast," groused Niles.

They stepped aside when the priest returned with new candles. He tossed them a nasty side-glance while replacing then lighting the candles. When finished, he went to a side room.

"How did he ever make priest?" complained Niles.

"Becoming a priest is one thing, staying faithful and true is another. Sadly, weakness of faith under harassment has been the downfall of many," Archimedes spoke with lament.

"I fear it will get worse with the King's growing hostility."

"Given the circumstances, you lasted longer than I expected."

Niles ignored the dry humor to step closer to Archimedes. "Not just me. Berk *again* called the Almighty foolish nonsense."

Archimedes straightened to his full. "When?"

"Earlier today. Akilles said Berk hopes Zared will drive the foolishness out of him and make him see reason. It greatly upset the lad. Myla, myself and Wilma tried to be reassuring." Niles grinned at seeing Archimedes interest when he mentioned Wilma, so he continued. "Wilma spoke with staunch resolution that Myla contributes to spending an awful lot of time with *you*."

"What of it?"

Niles laughed at the protective reaction. "Nothing, my friend. However," he grew serious, "if there is an understanding, you might consider a way to secure her from what could come ... and soon."

Archimedes grew thoughtful.

"For Akilles' sake, I intend to learn if what we fear is the *reason* Berk means."

"That won't be easy."

Niles scratched at his beard. "Are Abner and Gordon still here or did they leave like some others?"

"No one has left yet. Berk has called for a *high* banquet by week's end. Such preparations usually take longer, so four days will be hard enough on the staff."

Nile cocked a curious brow at the news. "Do you know the reason for this?"

"No. Abner and Gordon might."

Niles' eyes narrowed in contemplation. "We will need to enlist their aid."

Archimedes spoke to contrary. "It will be dangerous for them to spy on Zared and the King."

"Who said *spying*? Merely keeping open eyes and ears. Besides, Abner and Gordon are Jor'ellians."

"They are also on the Council. Zared has proven his disdain for you and would become suspicious if he sees you speaking to them."

Niles flashed a cunning smile. "Archimedes, my old friend and comrade-in-arms ..."

"Stop!" Archimedes raised a hand. "Every time you say that, there is a scheme behind it."

"Tell me, why did you come looking for me when you heard of my misfortune?"

Archimedes scowled with resignation. "When do you want to meet?"

"Midnight. The armory cellar."

To pass the hours, Niles busied himself with various tasks. He pretended to inspect the guards and struck up idle conversation. He hoped to stumble upon some scuttlebutt or chatter learned from gossiping servants or indiscrete nobles. Instead, he discovered the disgruntled attitude among the soldiers appeared to be growing. The older ones remembered life at Waldron before Zared arrived six years earlier. Some even further back when Berk's father, Rogan, ruled over fifteen years ago. Niles recalled to when he earned his title of King's Champion.

Rogan told Niles he secretly rooted for him against Archimedes during the tournament. Of course the King was supposed to be unbiased, but Rogan liked Niles. For all his faults and weakness, Rogan did the best he could in ruling.

When Rogan unexpectedly died, Berk inherited Niles in his position of King's Champion. One of Berk's first acts was to order a new tournament in hopes of unseating Niles. It didn't work. Niles defeated all challengers. Why Berk objected to Niles still remained a mystery. It could simply be the natural reaction of a son wanting to be free from anything attached to his father's reign.

This sounded reasonable since Berk even rejected the bride Rogan chose. The noble family tried to reason with him, but with Rogan dead, Berk's word became law. It surprised everyone when he chose a bride from among the merchant class. Myla caught his attention while on holiday in the Northern Forest. He flirted with her, wooed her and finally won her father's approval. Then again, what father would refuse the King and the chance to enrich his station?

Like all things, Berk's fancy faded after Akilles, Blaine and Calder were born. This cooling of the relationship happened shortly after Zared assumed lordship of the Delta six years ago. This caused some to speculate about Delwin's parentage, but Berk acknowledged the newborn as his son.

While trying to keep occupied, Niles resisted the urge to visit Akilles. Whereas his relationship with Berk deteriorated over the years, he felt a special affection for Akilles. The boy responded to him when it mattered most. Seeing Akilles upset caused Niles' personal angst. He managed to stay away knowing Colin would be diligent to remain with Akilles. At least he and his son were close, both in kinship and dedication to duty. He couldn't imagine turning his back on Colin or Colin rejecting him. It seemed unthinkable and unnatural.

"Unnatural," Niles muttered to himself. He now sat in the armory office. The darkness outside the window showed the lateness of the hour. A solitary lantern illuminated the room while a small brazier gave off warmth. *Ay, what is happening feels unnatural.*

Niles closed his eyes to pray in the Ancient. "Jor'el, grant me wisdom and discernment to discover what is driving Berk to denounce you. By what manner of persuasion Zared is using ..." He stopped and opened his eyes. Worry filled his features. He removed the chain from around his neck to stare at the medallion. "Is it truly the return of the old enemy?

Are we enough to counter any attempt?" He clenched the medallion, closed his eyes and bowed his head. "Jor'el, give me strength."

"*Tangiel.*"

The voice made Niles bolt to his feet. Archimedes stood just inside the rim of candlelight. Niles scowled. "You should know better than to startle me."

Archimedes wore a teasing grin. "How else would you know the others are waiting?"

Niles placed the chain around his neck. He grabbed the lantern and left with Archimedes. They proceeded to the old door at the back of the armory. Niles handed the lantern to Archimedes then produced the key from his doublet pocket.

"I assume you locked it before fetching me," he snickered.

Archimedes simply smiled.

Click! The lock opened. Once inside, Niles locked the door. A stairway led further down into the cellar. Archimedes held the lantern high to light the descent. The soft glow of light from the cellar grew brighter upon nearing the bottom.

Abner and Gordon sat at a small table upon which was another lantern. Both dressed against the cold. Gordon rubbed his gloves hands together for warmth.

Archimedes set the second lantern next to the other when he and Niles joined them.

"Thank you both for coming," said Niles.

"Archimedes said it was urgent," said Abner.

"That is understatement." Niles looked earnest at the lords. "Have either of you encountered Zared today?"

"Briefly," said Gordon.

"And with Patrin," added Abner. "Why?"

"Did he say anything?"

Gordon and Abner exchanged conferring glances. "Nothing that seemed out of the ordinary, if that's what you mean?" said Abner.

"Well, he did act extra smug," said Gordon.

"True. He and Patrin enjoyed whatever they were discussing when we crossed paths," agreed Abner.

"When was this?" asked Niles.

"After supper. Has something happened that made you want to see us?"

Niles proceeded to tell them of Berk informing Akilles' about the change in tutor along with the subsequent arrival of Zared to Akilles' chamber.

Abner scowled in anger while Gordon stared with surprise at Niles.

"He is to replace *you*? Why?" Gordon asked.

"I intend to find out. In the meantime, I sent Colin to stay with Akilles. Zared might not approve of the assignment, but he can't order Jor'ellians, only myself, Archimedes and the Vicar have such authority."

"If Zared tells Berk, he might forcefully relief Colin of duty," warned Abner.

"I'll deal with that if necessary."

Gordon shook his head, still trying to digest the situation. "I hardly think you taught nonsense," he said to Niles.

"*Nonsense* was the king's word in reference to Jor'el," said Archimedes in a tight voice of offense.

"What made him say that?" asked Gordon with concern.

Niles replied with heavy emphasis. "It's worse than you think. Akilles heard Berk *denounce* the Almighty while saying he hopes Zared will help Akilles see *reason*."

"When Berk confronted me, he ripped off my amulet, threw it to the floor and stomped on it!" chided Archimedes.

Stunned, the Abner and Gordon sat momentarily mute until Abner murmured, "Merciful heaven." With guarded anticipation, Abner asked Niles, "What does he mean by *reason*?"

"That is what I'm hoping to discover while praying it is not what I fear."

Abner held Niles' gaze for a long moment. His expression showed dreaded comprehension.

"Abner?" Gordon prodded his friend to get his attention, "Does he mean—?"

"Ay. The Dark Way," Abner could barely speak the thought.

Gordon closed his eyes, his face screwed with anguish.

"Have no fear, my lord. The Almighty will defend his own," said Archimedes.

Gordon shook his head. "Not fear, rather distress that our precautions have turned into a necessary reality."

"What precautions?" Niles asked.

Gordon took a deep breath before explaining. "My father became concerned by Zared's growing influence—that he *would* sway Berk away from Jor'el and all the House of Tristan stood for. We often discussed ways to protect our family should the worst happen. He died just as we implemented our plan. A month ago, I completed it." He sat forward to use his fingers to draw on the table. "We built—"

Niles seized Gordon's hand. "No! Keep it secret for now. We may need to make use of it in the near future, but not a word of this is to leave the room."

"Upon my word as First Jor'ellian, I will be silent," said Archimedes.

"You know our trustworthiness otherwise you wouldn't have summoned us," said Abner to Niles concerning he and Gordon.

"Trust can be lost if what is suspected turns out to be true!"

"Easy, old friend," Archimedes warned Niles. "We are Jor'ellian brothers," he motioned between himself, Abner and Gordon. "Our oath guides us."

To calm his temper, Niles took a deep breath and slowly exhaled. He looked at Abner and Gordon. "Your word will be enough."

Gordon stood. "Before Jor'el, I reaffirm my Oath. I will help you uncover the truth and protect the royal family."

Abner also rose. "As our Oath so states, we protect our brothers to the death." Together, he and Gordon made the Jor'ellian salute.

Niles returned the salute. "Archimedes told me Berk ordered a high banquet. Do either of you know why?"

"No, just given instructions to remain," said Abner.

"For a state affair, you should be there," said Gordon to Niles.

"Oh, I will be, whether Berk approves or not. It is protocol. However, if you learn anything before then, contact Archimedes. If seen with me, it could arouse suspicion. He and I keeping company, is expected." He flashed a droll smile at hearing Archimedes huff then added to the First Jor'ellian, "Make certain they reach their quarters safely. Gentlemen." He picked up a lantern and left.

Chapter 7

ARMUS DIMMED THE LIGHT FROM HIS ARRIVAL IN THE TEMPLE vault. Even though he didn't expect any mortals to be in the undercroft, the assignment called for stealth. He took a moment to relish the sense of full power enlivening in his spirit and body. He brought his hands together, bowed his head and spoke the Ancient. Again, he took on a mortal persona, only this time in the guise of a Jor'ellian Knight commander. He stood tall for a mortal at six feet four inches, still brown haired and brown eyed. He carefully left the vault to make his way upstairs in search of Wilbur.

In the hallway to the Vicar's chamber, Armus encountered servants scurrying about. He heard orders that alerted him to preparations for departure. He arrived just in time. Entering the Vicar's room, he spied Wilbur with his assistant Odell, who made strenuous objections.

"My lord, you can't go to Waldron. It's too hazardous to your health, not to mention the King is hardly interested in seeing you."

Wilbur replied with restrained gruffness. "This is something I must do so please stop interrupting my preparation."

Odell didn't heed the advice. Instead he grabbed Wilbur when the Vicar began to move off. "Let me go instead."

"No!" Wilbur attempt to remove Odell's hand, but the younger priest remained persistent in his hold.

In witnessing the argument, Armus sensed something amiss. He intervened. "My lord Vicar." He made the Jor'ellian salute. "I am here to lead your escort."

Upon receiving attention, Armus studied each mortal. Whereas Wilbur appeared glad of the interruption, Odell sneered with irritation. In response, Armus' intense disapproving look went from the assistant's face to Odell's hand still holding Wilbur's arm. The silent rebuke had the intended effect. Odell balked and released Wilbur.

Odell tried to recover his momentary discomposure by asking, "Commander...?" searching for a name.

"Finn," replied Armus.

"Well, Commander *Finn*, I don't recognize you. Under whom do you serve?"

"I'm newly assigned to the Temple by Captain Seul."

The answer didn't satisfy Odell while Wilbur smiled with understanding and said, "Your service is appreciated, Commander. You see, Odell, I'll be in good hands."

"I'm going with you," Odell argued.

"That won't be necessary," said Armus firmly.

"I will decide what is necessary concerning the Vicar's well-being, knight!"

"Odell!" Wilbur jerked on Odell's arm to get his marked attention off Armus. "You wrongly rebuke Commander Finn."

"I am your personal assistant thus responsible for your care."

"As such, I need you to stay here! To look after things while I am gone," Wilbur stoutly rebuffed. When Odell scowled in disagreement, Wilbur continued. "You just said how Berk won't be happy to see me. One of us *must* remain to ensure the continuation of service to Jor'el."

To this counter-argument, Odell's attitude softened. "I concede your point."

"Good. Now, I will continue my preparation while you see to duty here."

Armus added his prompting for Odell to depart by motioning to the door. Odell stormed out.

"Close the door, so we can speak privately," said Wilbur. After Armus complied, Wilbur smiled at him. "Clever use of the Ancient word *finn-seul* for *legends*. However, you are not the *one* who charged me with the task at hand."

Armus returned the smile. "No, but I will see you safely to your destination."

In the Temple courtyard, the escort assembled. This included ten Jor'ellians, several pack horses, a supply wagon and a two-person carriage pulled by a large draft horse. Odell beckoned to a Jor'ellian Knight among those assembled.

"Lieutenant Markes!"

The grey bearded knight made his way to Odell. "Ay, Headmaster?"

"Apparently, you are no longer in-charge of the escort. A Commander Finn will be assuming that role."

Markes considered the name. "Commander Finn? I don't think I've met him."

"I didn't recognize him, although he said Captain Seul assigned him the task."

"The captain's name is familiar."

Agitated, Odell tugged on his fingers. "All the same, I'm not sure I trust his sudden appearance."

"Why? If he's a Jor'ellian and assigned by Captain Seul . . ."

"Because I don't trust anyone I don't know with the Vicar's safety! I want you to keep an eye on him."

Markes took note of Odell's tense features. "Very well, Headmaster."

"And, Lieutenant," began Odell with harshness directed at Markes, "if he does anything to jeopardize the Vicar, take care of him … *permanently.*"

"Permanently?" repeated Markes, uncomfortable with the implication.

Odell squared his shoulders, eyes narrow. "You question me, Lieutenant?"

Markes balked with uncertainty. "No, Headmaster." He slapped the hilt of his sword in military acknowledgement.

"Odell!" he heard the familiar voice of Wilbur call.

"Say nothing of our discussion," Odell warned Markes in a low hasty tone. He then donned a calm expression. "Just giving last minute instructions since Commander Finn will be taking over the lead from Lieutenant Markes."

Markes gripped the hilt of his sword. He stood ramrod straight at attention. "Commander." He made the Jor'ellian salute to Armus, who returned the gesture.

"At ease, Lieutenant." Armus spoke with pleasant tone and kind grin.

When Markes looked at Armus, his rigidity relaxed into a small smile. "Everything is ready for departure, Commander. Vicar, I put some extra cushions and blankets in the carriage for you. Winter seems to be coming early."

"Thank you, Markes," said Wilbur. "Let us gather in prayer before departure."

Markes summoned the Knights for prayer and to inform them of the change. "By order of Captain Seul, Commander Finn will be leading the escort."

Armus simply nodded to the introduction.

"Let us pray." Wilbur paused a moment for the Jor'ellians to remove their headgear before proceeding. "Gracious Jor'el, we thank for this unexpected opportunity, and pray you will grant favor to our travels. Open the eyes and heart of the King to receive your message. Watch over our brothers remaining here. We ask all this in accordance with your will for this venture. Tangiel."

"Tangiel," the others echoed.

"It'll be just few moments delay while another horse is saddled for the Commander," Markes said to Wilbur.

"It will take me that long to get comfortable," Wilbur chuckled.

"Allow me." Armus took hold of Wilbur's elbow to escort him. He aided the aged Vicar into the carriage. "Be sure to bundle up, keep the window closed and curtains drawn. No need to tip our hand too soon."

"Leaving the Temple won't alert Zared's spies to my departure?" Wilbur spoke in a good-natured challenge.

"Without clear visibility they could mistake the passenger for Odell," Armus lightly retorted. He placed a blanket over the Vicar's lap.

Instead of accepting the humor, Wilbur sighed, heavy and weary.

"Courage. All will play out as it should."

Wilbur nodded. "Thank you."

"No, thank you, for dedication and obedience," Armus spoke with sincerity.

Markes approached. "Commander, your horse is ready."

"Thank you," he said to Markes then to Wilbur, "I'll inspect the wagon and then we'll leave." Armus closed the carriage door. He spoke to Markes as they headed to the wagon. "What supplies are packed?"

"The Vicar's tent, food and all that is needed for travel."

Armus lifted the canvas to look underneath. "No plans to stop at inns along the way?"

"No, and I'm surprised Captain Seul didn't tell you why."

Armus paused in his inspection. "You mean about the Vicar tiring easily or that people aren't too kind when he appears? I'm better informed then you think, Lieutenant," he said stoutly, then softened his tone at Markes' embarrassment. "I meant are there no plans to stop and resupply?"

"Oh, ay!" said Markes, eager to redeem his earlier blunder. "There is farm a mile before the Pass of Peace where we obtain what is needed before entering Midessex. The farmer is very generous, if you understand my meaning."

"I understand all too well how few faithful remain." Weariness crept into Armus' reply. When his tone made Markes curious, Armus went to his horse. Once mounted, he moved to the head of the escort. Lieutenant Markes rode to his right. "For Jor'el, for Allon," he spoke the Jor'ellian motto.

"For Jor'el, for Allon," the Knights repeated.

Leaving the compound, Armus prayed for the added strength to remain in his covert role. The further they traveled from the Temple; he knew his power would diminish back to half. Unlike the quick trip to

Waldron, this persona would have to last at least a week. It normally took four days to reach Waldron, and who knows how many more if Wilbur's health impacted their travel.

In the past, remaining in mortal disguise was easy. Alas, nothing had been *easy* the last four hundred and ten years! However, the last twelve months an ominous sense of foreboding made the Guardians' tasks even more difficult. Whatever reason Kell gave Wilbur for this journey dealt directly with the rising menace. Armus would make certain nothing interfered.

Armus carefully glanced to his right. Something about Markes didn't set well. He acted antsy, even stressed when around Odell, but then relaxed after Armus spoke to him. As for Odell, the argument between him and Wilbur helped Armus understand Kell's reservations regarding the Headmaster. Fortunately Odell remained at the Temple while Markes travelled with the escort. At first opportunity, Armus would make better assessment of the middle-aged lieutenant.

<hr />

By nightfall they reached the customary camping area, or so Markes informed Armus. It laid a half-mile off the main road in a sheltered grove with a good size creek.

After issuing orders for encampment, Markes told Armus, "Mid-morning tomorrow, we'll reach the farm to resupply."

Armus frowned in consideration. "We passed two inns before stopping here. Even those in the Region of Sanctuary are ill-disposed to housing the Vicar?"

"Not entirely. When Berk issued edicts against the Fortresses, the Vicar thought it prudent to spare people any trouble that could come from giving him shelter."

"Hence the camping supplies, while discretely calling upon those he can trust," said Armus in summation.

"Exactly," droned Markes. "Captain Seul …"

"Told me everything I needed to know! I simply want to gauge your knowledge and understanding of the situation, Lieutenant."

"Captain Seul is the one who suggested the camping idea to the Vicar. That's what I was about to say," countered Markes.

Armus studied the grey bearded lieutenant. While Markes withstood the scrutiny, Armus again noticed conflict behind the lieutenant's gaze. "Continue with your duties. Inform me when the Vicar's tent is complete." He didn't wait for a reply and headed for the carriage.

Wilbur had drawn back the curtain. "You're hard on Markes."

"I will test everyone with probing questions," said Armus.

Wilbur grinned. "You'll find most are dedicated. They have to be considering the current disdain toward Jor'el."

"The situation could also make *mort-* ... *men* turn," Armus corrected himself in mid-sentence.

Wilbur lowered his voice. "Which is why *you* are here, Commander Finn, to ensure my safety if—Jor'el forbid—such should happen."

Armus regarded Wilbur with a hint of admiration. "You have no fear."

Wilbur grinned. "Death is but a transition to a better life with Jor'el in the heavenlies."

Armus fought a grin. "I need to keep you alive to complete your task."

Wilbur chuckled and patted Armus on the shoulder. "You will. Now, for some food before retiring."

Armus aided Wilbur to the tent where a few last minute items were arranged for the Vicar's dinner. While Wilbur ate, Armus made certain the area outside the tent was clear of anything that could be used for concealment. Satisfied, he paused at the front entrance when Markes emerged.

"The Vicar is retiring." With sadness, Markes glanced to the tent.

"Something wrong, Lieutenant?"

"He only ate a little bit. Certainly not enough for what lies ahead."

"Sometimes those with much on their mind only eat enough to quiet the stomach."

Markes was slow to turn from the tent. Instead of continuing the discussion, he asked, "Normal nightwatch protocol, Commander?"

There was a brief pause in answering, as Armus attempted to discern the source of uneasiness about Markes. "Do you think this calls for *normal* protocol, Lieutenant?"

"No, but unless you have specific instructions from Captain Seul, I thought it best to inquire."

"Secure the perimeter with six Knights on duty. Rotate four of them every two hours to rest. I will be inside with the Vicar."

Markes saluted and left to carry out the orders.

Armus quietly entered so as not disturb Wilbur. Even in mortal persona, he didn't require sleep. He drew his sword and sat in a chair. Normally he would take-up the Guardian meditative position, but he had to maintain the façade. The chair would serve with the sword resting across his lap, hands on top of the blade only his eyes remained open. Whatever disturbed him about Markes, he didn't want the lieutenant to enter and assume he had fallen asleep.

The night passed without incident. Upon hearing the noise of activity, Armus gently woke the Vicar.

"Good morning, my lord."

Confused, Wilbur spoke. "Morning? I must have slept deeper than intended." At Armus' smile, Wilbur recanted with slight embarrassment. "No, I suppose I shouldn't be surprised with you here."

Armus chuckled. "I'll fetch you breakfast. Only this time, you will eat better than last night."

Wilbur did as Armus instructed and ate a hearty meal. With the Vicar secured in the carriage and everything packed, the escort continued.

"We'll reach the farm by mid-afternoon," Markes informed Armus.

"With or without stopping to eat?"

"With."

"How far is the Midessex campsite from the Pass?"

"Two miles."

Armus considered out loud, "The Pass is four miles with distance on either side for a total of seven miles." He shook his head. "We won't stop. Have Chalmers place two slices of roast venison, small loaf of bread and some cheese on a plate for the Vicar to eat as we travel. The others can eat whatever they can handle as we ride."

"But the Vicar will need to rest," insisted Markes.

"Too risky. He can sleep in the carriage. See to it, Lieutenant."

The reply didn't set well with Markes, as told by a deep frown and rough turning of his mount to carry out the orders.

Armus didn't look back. Although he couldn't fault Markes about his concern for Wilbur, the uneasiness from the lieutenant intensified during the exchange. Ever so slightly, Armus extended his heavenly senses. He didn't direct them at Markes in particular, rather searching for any nearby danger. Despite the rising perception of evil, the Region of Sanctuary experienced more peace than the other eleven provinces.

After ten minutes, Markes returned to his customary position of riding to Armus' right. If Markes waited for Armus to inquire about the dispensation of his order, he didn't. Armus continued in his part of a Jor'ellian Commander. Once an order was given, it was expected to be fully carried-out.

At length, Markes spoke in a begrudging matter. "It seems the Vicar *agrees* with your intention of continuing to the farm without stopping."

Armus simply nodded.

The ride continued without much discussion between Armus and Markes. The only interruption came when a Knight arrived and offered them some thinly carved venison placed between two slices of coarse bread. Armus noticed Markes screwed up his face in displeasure while eating.

"Something wrong, Lieutenant?"

Markes heaved a shrug. "I never liked the priests' bread. Too grainy."

Armus took a bite to do his own tasting. With level brows, he spoke with lament. "I heard that a long time ago, only the finest flour was used for baking at the Temple. But you're right, this isn't it."

"Finally, something we agree on," Markes murmured under his breath.

Armus heard. "Lieutenant, are you angry that I replaced you?"

Surprised by the question, Markes swallowed so hard that he coughed to recover. "No, Commander!"

Armus cast a harsh side-glance to Markes. "Really? You acted tense with Headmaster Odell."

"Odell? Oh, no, all he did was inform me of the change," Markes said in his attempt to deflect the uncomfortable subject. He even flashed a quick unconvincing smile. "Nothing more."

"Then why so nervous?"

At the challenge, Markes managed to regain his composure. "I'm not nervous, Commander. Merely concerned for the Vicar's well-being."

Armus looked directly at Markes. "As am I, Lieutenant. And perhaps for longer than you."

The statement puzzled Markes. "You can't be more than thirty years old. Younger than I am."

Armus tried to cover his miscue. "Since my youth I have been concerned for the Vicar, along with anything pertaining to Jor'el."

Markes didn't appear convinced.

Armus turned forward to continue the ride in awkward silence. Over the centuries when situations called for going undercover, the sad state of Allon and the mortals hit so deep that an unguarded comment slipped out. *Jor'el, help me keep my tongue from further indiscretion,* he silently prayed.

⁕

The farmer proved to be as generous as Markes reported. While they loaded supplies, the Vicar partook of a special meal cooked by the farmer's wife. Wilbur insisted Markes and Armus join them. Comments by the mortals told Armus that the food far exceeded anything currently prepared at the Temple and Fortress. During good times of the past, Armus dabbled in cooking as a hobby. Back then, mortals and Guardians shared everything. Such remembrances made the present reality of being nothing but obscure legends painful. He fought to keep personal dejection from being visible during the meal.

They just completed dessert when Armus spoke. "We really need to press on and travel the Pass before sundown."

Wilbur sighed in weariness, which prompted Markes to counter Armus. "The Vicar is in need of rest. We should remain here tonight and continue tomorrow."

Armus assumed a braced posture at the dispute, but before he could reply, Wilbur spoke. "No, Commander Finn is correct. While this was a delicious and welcomed repast, it is a pressing journey."

"Vicar— " began Markes in dispute.

Wilbur took hold of Markes' arm to stifle the objection. "Your concern is appreciated, but we will continue."

Markes flashed a disgruntled glance to Armus then recanted to Wilbur. "As you say, Vicar. *I will* help you to the carriage."

Armus' jowls tightened, but he didn't intervene when Markes escorted Wilbur. Outside, Armus called for the escort to assemble.

Again the ride continued in uncomfortable silence between Armus and Markes. The mortal lieutenant's opinion of him didn't trouble Armus. Instead, he was uneasy about the tension he sensed from Markes. It came forth in combativeness and muttered annoyance. The questioning of a superior officer in the Jor'ellian ranks became commonplace since Berk was crowned. The King turning from Jor'el and subsequent actions against the Fortresses led many Jor'ellians to abandon their vows, along with a serious decline in recruits. Despite Markes' attitude, Armus hoped the journey would pass uneventful.

His hope materialized in passing of another peaceful night in Midessex. However, in the wee hours of pre-dawn, Armus emerged from the Vicar's tent. Something didn't feel right. Nothing alarmed the mortals since the Knights had not begun to stir.

A sentry approached. "Should I wake the others, Commander?"

Though a bit distracted, Armus answered, "Ay." He moved to the edge of camp facing south toward Waldron. His eyes narrowed, and the brown hue brightened in concentration. For a fleeting moment he sensed danger, then a sudden repelling force made him take a step back, breaking his focus. He rubbed his eyes in momentary pain.

"Commander?" asked Markes.

Armus didn't immediately answer, still recovering. Markes grabbed him. Armus stiffened at a feeling of threat. Intense eyes turned harsh upon Markes. The mortal lieutenant immediately released him, befuddled by intimidation.

Markes barely found his voice to inquire, "Is something wrong?"

Miffed by the unintended effect upon Markes, Armus regained his composure. "Just preparing for what awaits us at Waldron."

Markes didn't reply.

Armus scowled in annoyance at another miscue. "Break camp while I tend to the Vicar."

Within the hour, the escort again moved south. This time they rode in silence because Armus used his heavenly senses to search for any lurking danger. He couldn't bother with small talk or Markes' disgruntled attitude. Whatever he felt required his full attention.

Being in Midessex, Armus considered seeking out Kell's essence to alert him to possible trouble. However, that meant taking his focus off any possible nearby menace. He hoped Kell sensed what he did and already proactive.

Hit with a sudden awareness of immediate danger, Armus jerked his horse to a halt. Then it happened! Deafening howls accompanied by ear-piercing screeches. From both sides of the road a pack of wolves rushed them. Out of the trees came winged reptile creatures.

Armus drew his sword and shouted, "For Allon, for Jor'el!" He turned his horse around to issue orders, "Protect the Vicar at all costs!"

Arriving at the carriage, Armus leapt from the saddle. It was easier to deal with the wolves and creatures on foot than astride a horse. Though in disguise, he would use any power necessary to keep Wilbur safe.

Upon first glance, the wolves appeared normal, but when one jumped at him, Armus felt unusual strength knock him backwards into the carriage. He dropped his sword to catch the wolf's head. He held its jaw from closing upon his neck.

"*Bi Jor'el's luths neart!*" Armus summoned his strength to break the wolf's neck. He tossed it aside. The dead wolf hit the ground with a hard thud. Armus breathed heavy at the exertion of power, only he couldn't take time to recover. He snatched up his sword when more wolves surrounded the carriage.

"What—?" Wilbur opened the curtain.

"Stay inside!" Armus roughly closed the curtain. He slashed a wolf, the blade ripped deep into its hide. It yelped and briefly retreated. Such a wound should have sent it scurrying back into the woods.

At that moment, Armus noticed the unusual size of the wolf's haunches and unnatural red eyes with black slits. These were no ordinary wolves! When it leapt at him, Armus sidestepped. He again called on his power and cleaved the wolf in half.

At a brief pause in the attack, Armus took stock of the Jor'ellians. A few were wounded, but they appeared to be holding their own. Markes became unhorsed by a winged reptile, but made a quick response that beheaded it. Markes glared with deadly intent at Armus. Hopefully it was just a reaction to battle. Armus didn't have time to discern the mortal's meaning when he heard ear-piercing screeching.

Two winged reptiles came at him. When Armus clobbered one aside, the sharp teeth tore his left sleeve yet missed flesh. Before a second one reached him, an arrow downed it in mid-leap. Armus snatched at glance in the direction the arrow came. Wren hid among the trees. Three more wolves attacked him.

Swoosh! Thud! An arrow impaled one wolf in the back of the head, killing it instantly. Armus dealt a serious wound to another while moving out of the way of the third. Upon an outcry, Armus whirled around to find the wolf on top of Markes. With dagger in hand, Markes tried to fend off the wolf.

"*Air'falbh!*" Armus swung his sword and sent the wolf flying off Markes. The mortally wounded wolf barely hobbled to the side of the road where it collapsed, dead.

Stunned, Markes raised himself off his back onto his elbows. He blinked in fright when Armus held his hand out to help him up. "You saved me," he stammered.

"That's what Jor'ellians do. Up man." When Markes grabbed hold, Armus practically pulled up to his feet. He looked around. Seven wolves and four winged creatures lay dead. "The attack seems to be over. At least for now."

Still stupefied, Markes almost blathered. "I don't know what to say."

"See to the men while I check on the Vicar." Armus nudged Markes on his way. He again looked carefully to Wren. She shrunk back into the forest. Couldn't leave evidence. He yanked out the arrows from the wolf and winged reptile. Holding them between both hands with his back to the escort, he whispered, "*Bi falbh!*" The arrows disappeared. He took a deep breath of recovery before approaching the carriage.

"Vicar, are you hurt?"

Wilbur pulled back the curtain. "No, I'm fine. What about the men?"

"Markes is taking an accounting." Armus lowered his voice. "Those weren't normal creatures. The wolves were altered and … *kelpies*," he said with dread.

"Merciful heavens," Wilbur muttered under his breath.

"We will take extra precaution tonight, and only rest for a few hours. The sooner we arrive at Waldron, the better."

"That's an interesting way of putting it," Wilbur wryly said.

"Better a known danger than unknown."

Wilbur understood. "You know best, Commander."

Markes arrived. He couldn't look directly at Armus when making his report. "Commander, Lennox and Finlay sustained serious wounds, but capable of traveling. Emmett's horse was killed."

"See their wounds are properly treated before we continue. Have Emmett help Cleary in driving the carriage."

Markes saluted and left.

Moving off by himself, Armus closed his eyes and carefully stretched out his senses to contact Wren. They needed a safe place for the night. He quelled a smile and opened his eyes. He found his horse where it wondered off to graze. He rode to the front of the carriage. Emmett joined Cleary on the driver's seat.

"Fortunate you weren't injured when your horse was killed," he said.

Emmett replied with grief. "I rode Baldwin since my youth. I thought about retiring him before this journey. Now, I wish I had."

Not much Armus could say to help the mortal's grief, so he didn't address it. "We'll make camp early. There is a sheltered hollow a mile from here."

In heavy silence, they continued. Occasionally, Armus caught glimpses of Wren, who covertly led them to the campground.

Armus dismounted. "No tent. We won't be staying the entire night. The Vicar will sleep in the carriage. Eat and take what rest you can."

Markes offered no dispute to the order. Instead, he joined the other Knights in following Armus' instruction. Several times, Armus caught Markes' disconcerted regard of him. The mortal's attitude had certainly changed.

While the others ate, Armus stood on the edge of camp facing southwest.

"C—Commander Finn," began Markes, very awkward and unsettled.

Armus tried to catch Markes' eyes to read the mortal. Unsuccessful, he replied in a placid tone. "What is it, Lieutenant?"

"I have a confession to make."

"That's usually done to a priest."

"No! It's what I nearly did to you that I must confess."

"Oh?" When Markes' discomposure turned to trepidation, Armus placed a hand on the mortal's shoulder. "You have nothing to fear."

Markes met Armus' compassionate gaze. "But I do! I nearly did the unthinkable. Something that goes against the Jor'ellian oath!"

Armus took hold of Markes by both shoulders. "You can tell me without fear of reprisal."

Markes' eyes grew misty with regret. "When you knocked the wolf off me, I wasn't coming to help you I—I was coming to kill you."

A startling confession indeed, so Armus asked, "Why?"

"Odell told me if I suspected you of meaning harm to the Vicar that I was to take care of you ... permanently!" Having broached the subject, his words came spilling forth. "I questioned him because it is wrong to take the blood of fellow Jor'ellian. But when you acted in ways I thought *would* place the Vicar in jeopardy, I reconsidered. Then you saved my life. I had to tell you the truth no matter the consequences. I dishonored my vow and am disgraced in the sight of Jor'el and my comrades." Markes hung his head on the verge of tears.

"Look at me, Lieutenant," said Armus in quiet command. Markes complied. Beyond the mortal's watery gaze, all the combativeness and uneasiness he sensed became replaced by true remorse. "You felt caught between two difficult choices. A Jor'ellian is to obey his superiors, which include the Vicar and Fortress Headmaster. Only this time, obeying Odell went against your Oath."

"Ay," said Markes with a shaky voice. "I'm sorry, Commander. I should have been honest when you confronted me about Odell." He choked back his emotions in coming to attention. "I will accept whatever punishment you decide."

At present, this wasn't a decision Armus wanted to make. The journey took precedence. However, a breach in Oath and duty could not be ignored. Armus glanced back to camp before speaking. "I said such confession is done to a priest. Speak to the Vicar. Then we shall see what punishment is warranted."

"Ay, Commander." Markes saluted.

Armus watched Markes. After a brief exchange with Wilbur, Markes entered the carriage. Armus' attention became drawn to the left. He muttered the Ancient before he made his way to just inside the tree line. He grinned at Wren. "Good shooting. Thanks."

"I had to do something. I tried to stop the wolves before the attack, only my commands proved useless. I didn't know about the kelpies."

"Those were no ordinary wolves."

"I still tried to stop them," she groused. "How goes it with Wilbur?"

Armus didn't immediately answer rather sat on a log. He rubbed his neck with fatigue. "Using my power when in disguise is tiresome."

"I'll mix a strengthening tonic."

"I can't be gone too long."

She took what was needed from her pouch. "It will only take a moment. Besides, you need strength to keep up the mortal façade." He didn't argue so she quickly mixed the ingredients in her leather flask. "Take it." She handed him the flask. "Drink some now then the rest over a couple of days. It's not much, but it should help."

Armus took a long drink. "They will wonder where I got this." He spoke about the flask.

Wren smirked. "As if you couldn't find a place to hide it on your uniform."

He chuckled. "I better return. Tell Kell what happened. I'm sure he'll be interested to know about the altered wolves and kelpies."

"Kell sent me to keep watch. He thought you might need help."

Armus grinned. "*He will* want to know about the attack."

"Ay, once you reach Waldron. Until then, I'm your shadow." She flashed a stubborn smile.

Chapter 8

WREN WASN'T THE ONLY ONE COVERTLY FOLLOWING WILBUR'S retinue since it arrived in Midessex. Tall and wiry, he dressed in all black with a bow and quiver of arrows slung across his back. He kept a safe distance to avoid being detected. Bright slate blue eyes narrowed in watching the chaotic action of the attack. The defeating of the wolves and kelpies surprised him. Not good! He waited until the group travelled out of sight before racing to the scene.

He inspected each dead wolf and kelpie. Two kelpies were beheaded while one wolf cleaved in half. He paid particular attention to the divided wolf. It had to be one powerful mortal. Another wolf and kelpie had deep puncture wounds at the base of the skull, but no sign of arrows. These could have been made with a blade only it had to be thin and precise to kill. He vacillated about whether to continue his clandestine pursuit or report the failed attack. Knowing Dagar, he chose the latter.

With tremendous speed, he ran due west. He covered the normal two-day mortal journey to the overgrown ruins of Ravendale in three hours. He thought to rest before attempting to bridge the transverse to the nether dimension, but became alert to another presence. His armed bow was up and ready. He held his fire when a red-haired Shadow Warrior appeared.

"Tor," he huffed and lowered the bow.

"Carvel. What are you doing here?" demanded Tor.

"The attack failed."

"What?"

Carvel hurried an explanation to forestall Tor's temper. "I'm not sure what happened. I followed the plan exactly. I waited until they were out of sight to inspect how each was killed."

Tor seized Carvel, and in white light, they disappeared in dimension travel. Carvel felt a bit lightheaded when they reappeared in the Nether Cave. The main audience cavern was furnished with a wrought iron tripod basin and altar containing images of ravens alongside man-like dragon statuettes.

"Wait here!" Tor ordered.

"Are you sure this is a good idea? I mean, I'm supposed to follow them." Carvel tried to keep any nervousness from his voice.

Tor's intense snarl was enough to still further protest.

Carvel waited, anxious. Since succumbing to reconditioning, he took command of the Shadow Archers. Every once in a while, Dagar sent him on a solo mission requiring the stealth of an archer. Only one time did a mission fail and that lead to more reconditioning, something he tried very hard to avoid since. Hearing the echoing of footsteps, Carvel came to attention. He wouldn't cower when facing Dagar.

The Guardian Master of the Dark Way appeared every inch a cunning, ruthless warrior. Mahogany eyes stood in marked contrast to his sun yellow hair. While the Shadow Warriors and Archers wore black uniform with scarlet trim, Dagar wore the opposite, a handsome scarlet suit trimmed in black.

Dagar stopped before Carvel with Tor standing behind him. Both Warriors stood six inches taller at seven and half feet. Dagar's eyes narrowed. "Carvel. What is this I hear about the attack?"

"It failed, and I went investigate why?" Carvel boldly replied.

"Did you discover the answer?"

"I'm not sure," began Carvel, thoughtful. "The escort consisted of ten Jor'ellian Knights, yet they killed seven wolves and four kelpies. Only a couple of Knights sustained wounds."

"The plan called for twelve wolves and six kelpies."

"The other wolves ran off after being wounded. I tried to get them to regroup, but they refused. Only four kelpies responded to my commands." Carvel shrugged with befuddlement. "I don't know why two kelpies went off on their own. Still, that number should have been more effective against the Knights."

"You mentioned inspecting how the beasts were killed," said Tor.

Curious, Dagar folded his arms to await Carvel's answer.

"A few had questionable wounds."

"Meaning?" demanded Dagar.

"One wolf was cleaved in half, and another killed by a puncture wound to the base of the skull. I found the same puncture on a kelpie. No signs of exit wounds or arrows. Could have been a thin blade, but it needed to be a precise thrust."

Dagar tugged on his lower lip. "Although Jor'ellians are skilled, I don't know of any mortal so powerful as to cut an altered wolf in half."

Carvel shook his head in adamant dispute. "I sensed no other presence." Then he added as an afterthought, "Though, a large mortal appeared to be in command."

"Describe him."

Carvel searched for the words. "Nothing really unusual, except he stood a few inches taller than the others. Again, I didn't sense another essence." When Dagar glowered at him, Carvel spoke in defense. "It is said Jor'ellian swords are specially forged. Besides, even altered creatures can be killed."

"He has a point," said Tor.

Dagar only briefly looked at Tor before returning to Carvel. "Perhaps some reconditioning will further jog your memory."

"I did as you asked!" insisted Carvel, trying not to sound shaken. "Rather than pursue, I came to provide intelligence." Seeing Dagar's continuing glare, Carvel continued more forcefully. "You need me to command the Archers. If reconditioned, I won't recover in time. What are a few beasts compared to a successful coup?"

Dagar's expression changed to a warped smile. "Well said. You've grown more confident. I don't recall you being so assertive when serving under Armus."

Carvel flinched at the painful reminder of his past duty. "There wasn't any need."

"So you just went along with what he said," Dagar scoffed. "Hardly behavior befitting a commander to cower before a superior. Now," he flashed a goading smile, "you know what true power feels like thus are able to speak with conviction."

Carvel grew suspicious. "Then why threaten me with reconditioning?"

Dagar guffawed with a cynical laugh. "To test you, of course." He tossed an arm about Carvel's shoulders to steer him from the chamber. "Come. Griswold has ten new recruits for your inspection."

They left by way of an earthen tunnel that ended in the reconditioning chamber. The cavernous room rose one hundred feet high by fifty feet wide. Around the central portion of the chamber, were multiple levels reached by narrow stone steps. Cages and carved out cells were scattered throughout the cavern. Guardians of different genders and castes occupied the cages and cells. Some appeared whole, while others in various stages of suffering. Shadow Warriors stood guard at various stations around the chamber. Dagar, Carvel and Tor made their way to the central part of the cavern.

Two ranks of five archers assembled. Their forest clothing badly soiled and torn yet identified their caste. In front of the archers waited Griswold, a massive Guardian whose bulk and fierce features made even the most stouthearted Shadow Warrior cringe. Despite standing seven feet tall, the archers appeared puny next to Griswold.

"Ten more for your ranks." Dagar motioned toward the archers. "Can you have them ready to march?"

"If they're not ready, I'll shoot them," said Carvel, cool and dispassionate.

Dagar loudly laughed and thumped Carvel on the back of the shoulders. He calmed his laughter to indicate a particular archer. "On the back row, you'll find a very interesting recruit. Ashby, Vidar's final protégé."

Carvel followed the indication. "Step forward." He waved.

Ashby complied. His uniform showed the most wear and tear of the recruits. The mess of dark brown was hair unkempt. Bright amber eyes appeared fatigued, though steady in their gaze.

"Dagar says you were Vidar's final protégé."

Ashby nodded. "I was among the last group of Guardians created."

"How did you feel being assigned to the Premiere Archer?"

Ashby scoffed. "You mean the last one picked. Vidar took pity and volunteered when all other assignments were made."

Carvel shrugged at the scorn. "Still, many would have eagerly traded places with you to learn from him."

More malice came forth from Ashby. "The only thing my lessons from Vidar gained me is a trip here along with extra reconditioning."

"Then I'm sure you won't mind telling him that," said Dagar.

"Vidar is here?" asked Ashby with mild surprise.

Dagar wickedly smiled. He made a hand gesture to show the direction. When Ashby turned, Dagar immediately took the opportunity to escort the archer across the chamber. Carvel and Tor went with them. Through a maze of cages and implements of reconditioning, Dagar led Ashby. They paused before a carved out cell in a darker portion of the chamber.

"Vidar! You have a visitor," snapped Dagar.

From the back of the cell, Vidar emerged. The Premiere Archer of the Guardians appeared a bit disheveled, his face dirty yet unmarked. Copper eyes grew wide with surprise. "Ashby?"

"Hello, Vidar," Ashby chided in a tone of mockery.

Confused by the combative manner and Dagar's presence, Vidar asked Ashby, "What is going on? Why are you here?"

Dagar replied in a much too sarcastic manner to be sincere. "Can't you tell? Ashby wants to thank you for all your lessons … before he joins my ranks!"

Disturbed by the implications, Vidar confronted Ashby. "Is he speaking the truth? Have you turned?"

"Better to make my own choice than being the last one picked!"

Carvel smiled and clapped Ashby's shoulder. "What would you say to being First Lieutenant of the Shadow Archers?"

Ashby's snickering gleam passed from Carvel to Vidar to reply, "Gladly."

Furious at the taunting display, Vidar scowled at Ashby.

"Come, Lieutenant, we have recruits to whip into shape," said Carvel.

Satisfied, Dagar and Tor left with Carvel and Ashby.

Elgin, a vassal and Vidar's cellmate, came alongside him. He spoke with sympathy. "I'm sorry."

Vidar's jowls flexed between anger and painful regret. "Some protégés just don't live up to their potential."

"I'm sure you gave him as much encouragement as you did Wren and others."

Vidar grinned at Elgin's mention of Wren.

"Ay, Wren is still loyal," said a voice from the next cell.

Vidar turned to the speaker, Mahon, a blond-haired youthful Guardian warrior. "Same as you do Avatar credit," he said in reference to Mahon's mentor.

"I wonder what Carvel meant by whipping the other archers into shape?" said Cyril, a warrior and Mahon's cellmate. Unlike Mahon, Cyril appeared older with white shoulder length hair.

"More than likely another one of Dagar's schemes," groused Mahon.

Vidar moved to the sidebars to speak confidentially. "Which means, he hasn't fully succeeded in seizing total control of the kingdom."

Mahon and Cyril understood. Both grinned. "I'm sure Avatar had something to say about that," snickered Mahon.

"He, Kell and Armus," added Cyril. "If the High Trio gets wind of Dagar's latest plan, we may not be here much longer."

"May it be so!" Elgin eagerly said. "I don't know how much more I can take."

Vidar held Elgin's shoulder. "It is by Jor'el's strength we endure, not our own." He pointed toward the chamber. "Those who succumbed have forgotten that. As long as we cling to the Almighty, we shall manage until Kell comes. And he *will* come to deal with Dagar."

"Ay, remember when I relayed Kell's message?" began Mahon. He then quoted Kell, *"Tell the others, they are not forgotten. I will come for them when I can, and on that day every Guardian and mortal who has suffered will be avenged."*

"Let us pray Dagar fails again with whatever scheme is attempting, and that our day of rescue is soon," Vidar said.

Elgin grinned. "Ay."

Chapter 9

LATE INTO THE NIGHT, COLIN SAT IN A CHAIR BETWEEN THE DOOR and the bed where Akilles' slept. He understood his father's fondness for Akilles. He was very intelligent with a keen awareness of circumstances beyond his years. He also exhibited the natural tendencies of youth, with acts of reckless impulsiveness. Since taking charge of Akilles, Colin watched the Prince grow more agitated. Knowing Zared as the source of Akilles' disturbance, Colin tried to counsel and sooth him when in private. Intervention during instruction would further inflame the already tense situation. Colin became alert at a stirring coming from the bed.

Akilles sat up in bed. "Sir Colin!"

He rushed to the bed upon hearing distress. "I'm here, Highness."

Akilles' face glistened with sweat and his breathing labored in fright. "I had a terrible dream."

Colin sat on the bed. "Try to calm down."

Akilles vigorously shook his head. "His eyes! I can't get them out of my mind."

"Who?"

"Zared!" Akilles became upset to the point of tears.

Colin took hold of Akilles. "Focus on me and recite the Creed." Colin did the same as Niles by beginning the phrases for Akilles to repeat. It took reciting the Creed twice before Akilles calmed down. "Better?"

"I think so." Akilles flashed a small smile. "I hoped he would send you."

"You didn't know?"

"No, just to read until the one he sent arrived. I'm glad it was you."

"Because I'm his son?"

"In a way." Akilles became downcast.

"And?" Colin gently probed.

Akilles shrugged with uncertainty of answering.

Colin lifted Akilles' chin to look at him. "You can trust me, Highness."

"I know. It's just ..." At first he hesitated then emotions spilled forth. "You and he act like father and son. You believe the same things. Think the same. It used to be that way with my father. Now—" Akilles became angry. "*He* interferes, and I can't stop him!"

"You mean Zared."

"Ay! And that was my nightmare. No matter what I tried, I couldn't stop him and help my father. Now, he's my tutor!"

Colin's brows furrowed in listening to the troubled prince. "We can't always help others when they make bad choices. All we can do is pray for a good outcome."

"See! You even talk like Niles."

When Akilles wept, Colin held him. The situation proved difficult for grown men. He took the lad's face in his hands. "You must trust Jor'el that there is a reason. One that will help your father to realize the truth."

Akilles sniffled back tears. "What about Zared? How can I continue to listen to him?"

Colin slyly grinned. "*Listening* to someone doesn't mean you agree with what is said. You know the truth. You know what is right. Words going in here," he touched Akilles' left ear, "do not have to travel here." He tapped a finger on Akilles' chest over the heart. "You don't need to take to heart Zared's instructions. Only appear to *listen*. Or, as my father said when I was your age, *let something go in one ear and out the other.*"

Akilles smiled. "He also accused you of not listening?"

"Frequently." Colin laughed. "In this case, he would give you the same advice. Put your mind on the task, but keep your heart for Jor'el."

Akilles appeared to be in agreement then frowned. "It will be difficult."

"Nothing worth doing is ever easy. Keep the faith, trust Jor'el, and he will strengthen you." Colin rose to ease Akilles back onto the pillows. "Now, rest." He placed a gentle hand on the prince's forehead. "Sleep in Jor'el's peace."

Colin didn't leave the bedside until he heard the rhythmic breathing of sleep. Disturbed and concerned, Colin went to the sofa where he knelt to pray. He began by reciting the Jor'ellian Creed in a low voice. He needed wisdom and discernment to continue to help Akilles.

Startled by a sound, Colin sat back on his heels. The dim light of dawn filtered through gaps in the window drapes. Morning! Granted, his prayer took him deeper than intended, but to fall sleep? He stood at hearing movement then relaxed at seeing Gilby.

"Good morning, Sir Colin," the valet simply greeted him.

"Gilby." He intercepted the valet when the man moved toward the bed. "Let him sleep a little longer. He had a nightmare."

"I would gladly do so, only Baron Zared is very insistent His Highness be ready to being instructions shortly after dawn."

Colin made a low throaty growl of annoyance when the valet approached the bed to wake Akilles.

"Highness," Gilby began. "It's time to wake-up and start the day." Akilles was not agreeable in waking up so Gilby nudged his shoulder. "You should not keep Baron Zared waiting."

Akilles' eyes snapped open. "Zared!" He stared wide-eyed at Gilby. "No, this is how it started!"

The valet appeared confused. "How what started, Highness?"

Colin swiftly approached the bed. "Easy! This is not the dream. It is really morning."

Akilles' focus shifted between Gilby and Colin, ending on Colin. "Morning?"

"Ay. Time to do what we discussed. *Misneach, mo prionnsa,*" Colin added in the Ancient.

"Ay, courage," Akilles repeated. He rose and just finished dressing when Zared arrived.

"Sir Colin? Why do you insist on remaining with His Highness?" Zared did not hide his displeasure.

"Because it is my duty."

Zared waved with impatience. "We shall see about that!"

"Is that a threat, my lord?" asked Colin in a harsh, commanding tone.

Instead of answering, Zared pointed toward the door. "Your presence grows tiresome. As of this moment, you are relieved of duty. Now, get out."

"You have no authority to dismiss me. My orders come directly from the Vicar, the King's Champion or First Jor'ellian. Until I hear from one of them, I remain." Colin casually placed a hand on the hilt of his sword.

"You are as impertinent as your father!"

Colin didn't reply or move from his assumed position.

"I want Sir Colin to remain. He knows the Jor'ellian fighting positions, and has been of great help during private practice," said Akilles. He fumbled over the last words *private practice* when he realized he spoke too much.

Zared scolded Colin. "Private lessons? Now there you go too far! *I am* His Highness' tutor, not you."

"I merely aided the Prince when he had difficulty with your techniques," Colin shot back.

Zared tempered his tone to Akilles. "My new techniques are better suited for your position, Highness."

"How better? Jor'ellians know the fighting secrets of the Guardians."

Zared burst into laughter. "Guardians? Don't you mean *legends*? Myths? How can myths have superior techniques? No, my Prince, what I teach you are real fighting stances, not based upon folk tales."

Colin stiffened at the denouncement. "Beware, my lord, your words are offensive."

Zared accosted Colin. "Can you prove the existence of these *legends*? Have you actually seen a Guardian?"

"No. Nor have I seen Jor'el, yet he exists," Colin spoke in stout rebuttal.

"We waste time arguing nonsense."

"Nonsen—? Akilles began to speak.

Colin made a curt warning shake of his head to Akilles, one that Zared didn't witness. Akilles clamped his mouth shut.

"I will teach you to discern the difference between reality and nonsense. Something Sir Niles failed to do." Zared began to steer Akilles from the room.

"Now? Before breakfast?"

"You have not eaten yet?"

Colin intervened. "No. After a troubled night, His Highness didn't wake until late." He stepped in front of Zared and Akilles. "I shall bring him to the armory after breakfast. You wouldn't want him to become fatigued during training, now would you?"

Zared flashed an intimidated gaze up to Colin. He bowed to Akilles. "After breakfast, Highness." The door closed upon his departure.

An hour and a half later, Colin brought Akilles to the armory. Zared greeted them with impatience.

"That was a long breakfast," he chided to Colin.

"With banquet preparation, it took longer than usual for the food to arrive." Colin patted Akilles' shoulder, to which the Prince responded by speaking to Zared.

"I'm ready, baron."

A flicker of a grin appeared that vanished when Zared spoke to Colin. "I may not have the authority to dismiss you, *but* I do have *authority* from the King to instruct His Highness. From now on, I will do so in private. Wait here, Knight." He ushered Akilles inside and slammed the door.

Colin caught sight of his father walking to the main building. "Sir Niles!" he shouted. Niles changed his course to approach Colin.

"How goes it with Akilles?" asked Niles.

Colin drew Niles a few steps from the armory door to speak privately. "Rough, as you probably suspect. Zared is very forceful. I try to counter him when and where I can only Akilles is very agitated by the situation."

"I hope that after the banquet, Zared will leave with the others and tend to winter preparations."

"Have you learned why Berk called the high banquet?"

Niles shook his head. "Not yet. Berk is not only combative, but also cagey whenever I'm near. I know he is up to something. No doubt due to Zared's corrupting influence." His regard of the armory turned fretful. "Stay as close to Akilles as possible tonight."

"That will be no different than other nights," said Colin with a grin. "I have been able to stay with him every day and night since you gave me the task."

Niles smiled at news. "Excellent. I thought Zared would have Berk physically relieve you."

"Maybe Zared doesn't consider me as much of a threat as you."

"Don't count on it," snickered Niles. "I'm certain he's more interested in the banquet. Speaking of which, I must go prepare." He clapped his son on the arm, a look of pride before he departed.

Inside the armory, Akilles shrugged off Zared's hold. "You may have my father's permission to instruct me, but not to touch me!"

A sarcastic smile appeared in regard of Akilles. "Highness, you misunderstand. I offer you guidance."

"So did Sir Niles."

Zared's caustic smile showed he fought to keep his temper. "Let us not discuss him. There are more important matters for you to learn." He took a step closer to the Prince, eyes intent in their focus.

Akilles recoiled a few steps. Fear crossed his face.

"Something wrong, Highness?" asked Zared with nonchalance.

Akilles stood his ground and spoke with confidence. "No."

Zared clicked his tongue and shook his head. "Alas, the sway of old folk tales have made you wary. That should not be. One who is enlightened has nothing to fear."

Akilles raised his chin with pride. "I'm not afraid."

"No?" Zared tried to act casual. His right hand scratched his chin. "Jor'ellians base their techniques on fables. There is no manual, nor is anyone outside the Jor'ellians permitted to teach their method. Why do you suppose that is?"

Akilles started to answer, but unable, so he shrugged with ignorance.

"I'll tell why. To keep the secret that no such beings ever existed."

"You mean no Guardians?"

"Exactly." Zared motioned to the door. "Even Sir Colin admitted he has never seen a Guardian."

"He also said he has never seen Jor'el, yet the Almighty exists. You can't deny that."

Zared looked directly at Akilles. His right hand slipped from his chin to the collar of his tunic. "Does Jor'el really exist?"

Akilles visibly shivered. "No!" he murmured and turned away.

"Indeed. You are correct. Very good for your first lesson."

"I didn't mean about Jor'el," stammered Akilles. He dared a glance to Zared.

"What did you mean, Highness?" Zared continued staring at Akilles.

When the baron's hand clenched at his collar, Akilles balked. "What are doing? Stop that!" he spoke in trembling command.

"Stop what? I'm only asking a question, Highness."

"That!" Akilles pointed at Zared. "Your hand."

"My hand isn't doing anything, Highness." He held up his left hand.

"No! This hand." Akilles reached to move Zared's right hand.

Zared snatched Akilles before he grabbed the collar. "No need to get physical."

"Move your hand away!" Akilles jerked from Zared. He again reached to remove Zared's right hand from the collar.

This time Zared acted more forcefully to fend off a determined Akilles. The brief wrestling of hands tore Zared's collar. Something cold became tangled in Akilles fingers. When he pulled to withdraw his hand, it appeared. Akilles gaped in seeing the black octagon-shaped amulet. Zared immediately clouted Akilles, who cried out when he fell sideways to the floor.

Zared snarled maliciously at the startled lad. "You will forget what you saw or suffer the consequences!"

"Highness?" shouted Colin.

Hearing the voice and rushing feet, Zared hid the amulet under his shirt. He assumed a calm tone when Colin arrived. "A little demonstration of a new wrestling move."

Akilles' discomposure contradicted Zared's statement.

"I think His Highness has had enough of this lesson," said Colin. He reached to help Akilles stand when Zared turned him aside.

"It will be enough when I say it is enough, Knight!"

Colin didn't take well to the manhandling and seized Zared.

"No!" Akilles scrambled to his feet. "Let him go."

Colin hesitated at first.

"Please, Sir Colin."

Colin shoved Zared away. "Perhaps, if you demonstrate this *new* move against me, His Highness will be able to observe your technique."

Zared glanced up and down as at Colin, who had a three-inch height advantage. "I believe a recess is in order." He then said to Akilles, "Until this afternoon's lesson, Highness." He hurried from the armory.

Colin's focus went from the departing Zared to Akilles. "What happened?"

Akilles couldn't bring himself to speak rather rushed out of the armory. At a brisk pace, Colin followed. Akilles entered the rear of the main building and climbed the backstairs to his room.

"Leave me!" Akilles snapped at Colin. He slammed the door.

Reaching for the handle, Colin heard the lock click. "Highness?" No reply. "Why lock the door?" He jiggled the handle. "Akilles!" Again there was no reply. "I can be stubborn too. I won't leave until you let me in." Crossing his arms, Colin leaned against the door to wait.

The Queen approached. Lady Wilma accompanied her. "Sir Colin? Is there a reason you are standing outside my son's door?"

"The Prince locked me out."

"Why would he do that?"

Colin learned closer Myla to speak privately. "He is very upset by an encounter with his new *tutor*," he spoke with discretion. "Only he isn't inclined to confide in me."

Displeased by the report, Myla knocked on the door. "Akilles. I know you're in there. Unlock the door."

They heard movement from inside then the lock *clicked*. Colin opened the door for the Queen to enter.

"See we are not disturbed," Myla instructed Wilma before entering.

Colin shut the door after he and Myla entered. Akilles' posture and expression told of great disturbance.

"Sir Colin informed me that you refuse to tell him what happened with the baron. You even locked him out of your chambers. Not a very respectful way to treat a Jor'ellian," said Myla.

"I wanted time to think! Not to be disrespectful," chided Akilles.

"There isn't much time until your next lesson, so take advantage of the break," said Colin.

Akilles bit his lower lip, obviously considering what to say.

"You have nothing to fear," Myla added her encouragement.

"You are the Queen! You don't have to listen to *him*. Father made him my tutor!"

Myla grew concerned. "What is this?" She touched his left jaw. "A bruise?"

"The Prince was on the floor when I arrived. A wrestling move, or so the baron claimed," said Colin with disbelief.

Myla understood. "Come. Sit and tell us everything." She led him to the sofa only he refused to sit. "Wilma is at the door. We will not be disturbed," she said with an encouraging smile.

"*Fois, Akilles. Fois,*" Colin soothed. "*Suidh.*"

Akilles followed Colin's instruction and sat.

"Now, what happened?" she asked.

Akilles looked up at Colin. "His eyes were just like in my dream! He kept staring at me. He scorned Jor'ellians for believing in old folk tales about Guardians. But that's not all!" Upset changed to fury. Akilles sat perched on the edge of the sofa. "He questioned Jor'el's existence! He thought I denounced Jor'el when I answer a question in the negative, but I didn't!" he quickly added. "My response was about his hand movement." He demonstrated. "He held his collar. You and Sir Niles spoke about it," he said to Myla. "When I saw it, I told him to stop. He didn't listen. When I tried to remove his hand, he shoved me away."

"Is that when you received the bruise?" she asked.

"No. I tried again, only the collar ripped, and a chain became caught in my fingers. That's when I saw it!" He held up his hand in demonstration.

"What?"

"It! An amulet he wears tucked underneath." Akilles tugged at his collar in emphasis. "That's when he hit me and I fell to the floor."

"The wrestling move," groused Colin while Myla become irate.

"He dared to strike you? The Royal Prince?" she spoke with anger.

"He commanded me to forget what I saw. I can't! It felt as cold and frightening as his eyes." Akilles rubbed his arms like warding off a chill.

"Can you describe this amulet?" asked Colin.

Akilles' brows furrowed with recollection. "Black and silver with a number of pointed sides. It had a black bird in the center. A raven, I think. I'm not sure. I didn't see much before he hit me."

Myla kindly stroked Akilles' hair. "I can understand you being upset, yet that is no reason to lock the door on Sir Colin."

Akilles' shrugged. "I just wanted time to think. I'm sorry, Sir Colin."

"Apology accepted, Highness." Colin kindly smiled.

Akilles spoke to Myla. "What do I do now?"

"Use his own excuse against him," began Colin slyly. "He said you *fell* when he demonstrated a wrestling move. We shall claim the *fall* resulted in an injury that prevents you from participating in any further lessons today."

"I don't think he will even consider anything else today with the banquet scheduled at four o'clock," said Myla.

"Isn't that rather early?" asked Colin.

"A bit. However, it does allow for Akilles to get some extra rest."

"Today. What tomorrow or the day after?" insisted Akilles.

"One day at a time, my Prince. For now, rest." Colin fetched a book from the side table. "Read." He smiled when handing Akilles the book.

Akilles rolled his eyes at seeing the same book Niles gave him. "This is so boring! I fell asleep after three chapters."

Colin chuckled. "You read further than me. I didn't make it through the first chapter."

Myla kissed Akilles' cheek. "You're in good hands with Sir Colin." She smiled at Colin and left.

"Do I really have to read?"

Colin pursed his lips in sarcastic consideration. "Only if you want to learn about Jor'ellian techniques."

"Baron Zared said there was no such book."

Colin huffed a contrary laugh. "Zared doesn't know anything about Jor'ellians."

Akilles opened the book. "Where are these techniques?"

"Start at chapter five and read through chapter twelve."

Akilles made himself comfortable on the couch. He eagerly turned the pages to find the spot to start reading.

Colin took up position between the couch and the chamber door. He wanted Akilles to be occupied while he considered the situation, specifically Zared's amulet. He knew his father would be occupied with banquet so speaking to him was out of the question. He thought of another person. Unfortunately, he too may be engaged for the evening.

The only way to find out would be after Akilles fell asleep and he could make arrangements to leave. For now, he waited.

Patrin entered the guest chamber Zared occupied. Zared wore a shirt, no doublet, and in a foul mood. He snapped commands to his valet and shoved the man out the doors.

"Go! Do as I said." He slammed the door shut.

"Obviously something has happened," Patrin calmly said.

"The brat!" Zared snatched a clean shirt off the bed where the valet laid. "He ripped my collar, which revealed the talisman."

"How did he manage that?"

Zared shook his head while he tucked the shirt in his pants "It doesn't matter. What matters is he has seen it!" He glowered. "I'm not sure if my command to forget took hold. *Colin*'s arrival prevented any further instruction."

"Colin? How did he—?"

"Niles, of course! He sent his son to take his place in *guarding* the Prince."

"Why didn't you dismiss him?"

Zared snarled. "He claimed I have no authority, as his orders come only from the King's Champion, First Jor'ellian or Vicar."

"Berk would say otherwise in regards to his son."

Zared frowned in consideration. "I don't know that I want to involve Berk right now." His face broke into a cunning smile. "After tonight, I *will* have authority to command anyone!" He tapped the talisman. "Fortunately, Colin didn't see it. However," he said with new brooding, "the brat's discovery makes it imperative we accelerate our plans. He could blab about it."

"How do we do that?"

"*We* leave after the banquet."

"Leave? Just like that?" Patrin snapped his finger.

"You know the banquet will set everything in motion."

The answer didn't satisfy Patrin. "What will you tell Berk? It took a lot of persuading to call this banquet."

"I'll have Japeth come with a supposed note telling of sudden crisis in the Delta. You will come to help."

"He might ask why, since the South Plains is far removed from the Delta."

Zared held up the talisman. "He wouldn't question us." He made certain the talisman was secure under the collar. "Now, go! Prepare, for the banquet and departure."

Chapter 10

B Y MID-AFTERNOON, BANQUET PREPARATIONS WERE NEARLY FINISHED. While servants scurried about tending to last minute details, Niles began his customary inspection of the Great Hall. He scrutinized seating arrangements, access in and out of the Hall and for anything that could be a potential threat or help to understand the need for the banquet.

Niles noticed Cedric among the pageboys receiving instructions from the head butler. His attention became diverted to the exit when Alvin arrived. He appeared anxious in movement. Alvin even snapped at several maids placing intricate decorations on the high table. Not normal behavior for the affable Alvin. Niles decided to speak to him. Perhaps he could provide insight into the event.

Upon approach, Niles noticed further evidence of Alvin's jitteriness by the expression on his face. "Alvin."

The chamberlain flung up his hands. "Not now!"

"Then when?" asked Niles, not accepting being put-off.

"I—I don't know...later!"

Niles stopped Alvin from leaving. "No, I think this is the best time. You're unusually agitated."

Alvin pushed past Niles to exit the Hall. Niles followed. Indeed something upset Alvin. In truth, Alvin's manner had grown more irritable in the last year with Zared a frequent visitor to Court. For the last three months the baron practically lived at Waldron. In many ways, he usurped Alvin's duty to the king.

Niles caught Alvin by the arm and drew him into an alcove. "*Now*," he insisted. When Alvin hesitated, Niles pulled rank. "As the King's

Champion, if there is something I should know about this banquet, you would be derelict not to tell me."

Alvin yielded to the argument. He spoke with discretion. "A last minute change that is highly unconventional. You know high table is only for the royal family, correct?"

Niles simply stared at Alvin, the answer obvious.

"And that *high* banquets are reserved for royal family celebrations such as a birth or marriage."

Niles grew impatient. "Tell me what I *don't know.*"

Alvin whispered, "Baron Zared is to sit at the king's *right hand.*"

Niles straightened in surprise, his brows narrowed. "Are you sure?"

"The King himself told me!"

"Did Berk say why?"

"No! And wouldn't tolerate any questions."

Before Niles could inquire further, the head butler called for Alvin. Niles left the main building by way a rear door. He needed to consider the news. He weaved his way through the busyness of the courtyard to head for the Chapel.

At one point, Niles stopped to allow a loaded wagon to pass. He noticed Archimedes the same time the First Jor'ellian saw him. Niles made a discrete beckoning gesture before continuing his course to the Chapel. Niles didn't pause in his trek to enter a back room. He wasn't alone for long when Archimedes arrived.

"Make sure the door is locked," said Niles.

The request alerted Archimedes to the need for privacy. He complied. "You learned something?"

Niles switched languages to the Ancient. "Perhaps a key to solving the mystery of this banquet." He looked directly at Archimedes to say, "Zared is to sit at the king's right hand."

Archimedes' reaction mirrored Niles from earlier. He too spoke the Ancient. "Are you certain?"

"Alvin said Berk personally informed him of the arrangement."

Archimedes took a moment to contemplate the news. "Why?"

"Alvin didn't know." Niles began to reason out loud. "Can't be a marriage because the king has no female relative to give Zared for a wife. Patrin is the one who received permission to name his son after Berk."

Archimedes titled his head to the contrary. "Undoubtedly, Zared has something in mind."

"Of course. I'm just trying to discern his objective."

In a sudden voice of worry, Archimedes said, "Akilles—"

"Safe with Colin, whom I spoke to earlier. He said Akilles is managing as well as can be expected."

"Doesn't mean something can't happen between now and tonight *if* Zared's objective is to replace him as heir."

Niles features turned deadly. "Zared so much as thinks to harm Akilles, he will answer to me!"

"You'll be at the banquet," countered Archimedes.

"So I'll know what is happening!" Niles stoutly rebuffed.

Archimedes cocked his head with consideration. "All the same, I'll assign a few *extra* Jor'ellians to watch the Prince's chamber tonight."

Niles flashed a wry smile. "I hoped you would say that."

Archimedes became suspicious. "Then why didn't you simply ask me for more security instead of scaring me with concern for the Prince?"

"Because I share that concern…deeply!"

Archimedes took a deep, calming breath. "Let's pray Jor'el will help us this night."

"Tangiel," said Niles in hearty agreement.

"Now, I'll leave first. Wait a few moments."

Niles allowed five minutes to pass between Archimedes' departure and when he left the Chapel. The banquet was scheduled to start in four hours. While he wanted to visit Akilles, his first duty was to the King. Not that he doubted Archimedes or Colin; he simply wanted to see the boy for himself.

Niles made his way to the King's study. He could hear voices, but at a reasonable volume and not the shouting that had become common of late. Upon entering he found the King's Secretary and Count Hagan, the royal treasurer and lord of the Lowlands, alone in the room.

"Where is the King?" asked Niles.

"Preparing for the banquet," answered the secretary.

Forty-year-old Hagan was not known for timidity, but at that moment he balked. "I came to get approval for these bills from the grocer and wine merchant."

A bit confused, Niles asked, "Can't it wait until tomorrow?"

"These are for the banquet. They are awaiting payment because last time the King delayed two months causing them great hardship." Hagan held them out to Niles. "Give them to the King when you attend him."

Niles became cross. "You're not passing this responsibility onto me." He pushed the papers back.

"Then at least escort me to the King. As a Knight, I expect protection."

"From the King? We'll be lucky if he doesn't throw us out. No, let it wait until tomorrow morning. If the banquet is a success, he will be in an agreeable mood."

"That is what I told him!" argued the secretary.

"What about the grocer and wine merchant?" demanded Hagan.

"Let them enjoy the King's hospitality by dining with the Jor'ellians or royal guards." Niles smiled. "A night of good food and drink may put them in a better mood also."

"There!" The secretary motioned to Niles while speaking to Hagan. "Sir Niles agrees with me. That should convince you."

"I don't know."

"Who is more acquainted with the King's moods than the King's Champion?"

"Baron Zared!" Hagan shot back. "I'll take this up with him since neither of you see the problem." He marched from the study.

The secretary looked hapless. "I tried, I really did."

Niles simply patted the man's shoulder in understanding. He left the study to head for the King's chamber. It disturbed him to witness how

Zared's influence affected daily life at Waldron. If he managed to gain unfettered access to the royal treasury, there is no stopping what he could do! Bribes, rewards, gain control of key policy decision or any number of nefarious objectives.

Entering the family wing, Niles spotted two Jor'ellians near Akilles' room. *A good start,* he thought. He waited at the door to the King's room while the guard announced him. Once he heard his name, he entered. Berk appeared pre-occupied with being fitted for a suit and made no comment to Niles' arrival. That was until Berk looked at him by way of the full-length mirror.

"Ah, Sir Niles. How go the preparations for the banquet?"

"Well, Sire. Everything appears to be in order. Although, there is a peculiar seating arrangement." He said with purpose and watched for the reaction.

Berk laughed. "That will be remedied tonight so you needn't concern yourself about it."

"Sire, your welfare is my upmost concern."

For a moment, Berk stared at him using the mirror. "Return to the Great Hall."

"My place is with you, Sire."

"You place is where *I* say it is!" Berk made an abrupt wave, which jerked his arm away from the tailor working on the suit.

Rather than pursue the argument, Niles slapped his sheathed sword, bowed and withdrew. *Well, at least I'm not banished from the banquet,* he thought with some consolation.

The time passed slowly for Niles. He walked the Hall at least a dozen times inspecting everything over and over again. He did enjoy a quick meal sent to him by Alvin. He would not sit during the banquet rather wait in his customary place behind the King's chair.

Nobles and guests arrived at the appointed time, and all hoped for good seats. Naturally rank and relationship to the royal couple played a part in their proximity to the high table. The head butler instructed the nobles and assigned a pageboy as escort. The royal herald announced them when they passed him to take their seats.

A hard nudge on the arm diverted Niles' attention from the nobles. Once again Alvin wore a discomposed expression.

"There's been another change," Alvin said in a low hasty voice. He moved toward a far corner with Niles. "Lord Patrin is to sit at high table to the left of the Queen! Two noblemen of low rank sitting at high table is extremely unusual."

Niles lips pressed together at this latest development. "Not with the way Zared has been acting lately," he groused. Thoughtful, he turned his attention to the activity of arriving guests. He then asked Alvin, "Have you sent your wife and daughter to town?"

"I was about to when word came of Patrin."

For a moment, Niles' gaze lingered on Cedric. The boy finished escorting a couple to their places. "Send Cedric also."

The suggestion surprised Alvin. "Why?"

Niles turned to Alvin. "You just said how *unusual* this is."

Alvin followed Niles' indication of Cedric. "He'll be disappointed."

"Better disappointed than caught up in whatever is planned for this evening."

Alvin sighed with resignation. "I'll give a plausible excuse." He made his way to the head butler.

At a pause during the introductions, Niles witnessed Alvin speak to the butler. There appeared to be resistance, but the butler yielded. Alvin then found Cedric. When the boy began to object, Niles made his way across the floor.

"Sorry to see your first banquet cut short?" asked Niles.

Puzzled, Cedric asked, "You know?"

"Remember what we discussed last time in regards to dinner?"

Cedric flashed abased eyes at his father then back to Niles. "Ay."

"Ease your father's mind by escorting your mother and sister. Also as a personal favor for me." Niles winked at Cedric, and jerked a thumb at Alvin.

"What exactly do you mean *personal favor*?" asked Alvin, suspicious.

"So I don't have to endure your long face all night. Knowing they are in good hands with Cedric, you can face the night with a smile." Niles made a cheesy grin.

Cedric laughed then stopped for his father's benefit. "I'll go."

Alvin and Cedric left the Hall.

Abner and Gordon were among the last to arrive. As common practice, bachelors came after married nobles and sat together. Niles thought to approach the young nobles, only reconsidered it when Archimedes arrived. The First Jor'ellian also occupied a station near high table. Niles decided to say a word to Archimedes about the second change. Yet before he could approach Archimedes, trumpets sounded for the royal arrival. He assumed his customary place.

After the last blast, the herald pounded the floor with the golden staff. "All rise! His Majesty King Berk, Her Majesty Queen Myla," there was the briefest of pauses, but noticeable when the herald continued, "His Lordship Baron Zared and His Lordship Lord Patrin."

Hearing Patrin's name, Archimedes shot a harsh questioning glance to Niles. The King's Champion heaved a hapless shrug.

Zared and Patrin followed the royal couple in walking from the rear of the Great Hall to high table. Curious, wary and angry glances came from the crowd. Upon reaching high table, Zared and Patrin stopped beside their respective chairs.

The lead butler and Alvin held the chairs for the King and Queen. Berk appeared rather pleased as he helped Myla to her chair. This was something he hadn't done in years. When Berk sat, he motioned for Zared and Patrin to sit. The crowd remained standing. Berk nodded to the herald, who in turn pounded the staff twice. The nobles sat. A heavy silence filled the Hall.

Berk's gaze swept over those assembled. He wryly smiled. "No doubt this new arrangement appears unusual. However, it will be common from now on."

The nobles appeared perplexed and guarded, though none spoke.

Myla broke the uncomfortable silence. "Perhaps if you explain, we will all be enlightened."

Niles straightened at Myla's question. She too was ignorant of the reason.

In the courtyard, the Vicar's retinue arrived. His appearance caused anxious chatter among the grooms. Armus dismounted to aid Wilbur from the carriage while Markes took exception to the grooms' reactions.

"Stop gawking and tend to your duty!" Markes ordered them.

"If you please, sir," began one brave groom. "The Vicar may wish to retire, as the King is at high banquet and unavailable until the morning."

"Did you say *high* banquet?" asked Wilbur, wary yet curious.

"Ay, my lord Vicar."

Wilbur glanced to Armus. "It appears we arrived just in time."

Armus reached into the carriage for the Vicar's robe of state. He placed it over Wilbur's shoulders. He then retrieved the staff of Jor'el, a tall slender gold rod with the head of an eagle.

"Lead on, Lieutenant," Wilbur instructed Markes. "Commander, lend me your arm."

Armus kept pace with Wilbur, as the first few steps were stiff due to riding in the carriage. By the time they entered the grand foyer, Wilbur moved more easily.

At the entrance to the Great Hall, Markes argued with the herald.

"Is there a problem, Lieutenant?" asked Armus.

"Commander, this *man* is refusing the Vicar entry," chided Markes.

"Commander, I am merely following the King's orders not to be disturbed while the banquet is in progress," argued the herald.

"The King cannot refuse me," said Wilbur pointedly.

The herald became conflicted in compliance.

"Announce the Vicar," Armus sternly said, his eyes intense on the herald. "Announce him!" he ordered when the man hesitated.

The herald spun on his heels. He marched to his position at the end of the Hall opposite high table. Berk was replying to Myla's question.

"I will most gladly explain—"

"Sire!" the herald shouted.

"What is it?" Berk demanded at the interruption.

The herald pounded the staff and announced, "His Lordship, Wilbur, Vicar of Jor'el!"

The reaction was measureable with vocal gasps or comments. Niles and Archimedes moved forward to stand before high table, not in protection of the royal couple rather in reverence to the Vicar. They remained bowed at waist, as a disguised Armus escorted Wilbur from the rear of the Hall. Markes followed them. Those favorable to Wilbur mimicked Niles and Archimedes in rising to bow, this included Abner and Gordon.

Zared clenched the collar of his doublet. He sent a glowering sneer to Patrin. The latter seemed leery. This prompted Zared to address Berk. "I do not recall Your Majesty summoning the Vicar."

"I did not!"

Wilbur stopped his advance to speak. "My service to Jor'el supersedes that of any earthly king. It is on behalf of the Almighty that I have come."

Berk's temper appeared ready to explode when Zared again spoke.

"You insult Jor'el's appointed king?"

"The King insults Jor'el," Archimedes replied. He moved to stand beside Wilbur. "My lord," he acknowledged the Vicar.

Zared snarled with warped smile. "With what the King has to announce, Allon will be changing from the archaic to the enlightened." He gave Berk a nod of encouragement. "Sire, perhaps it is advantageous that the Vicar is here to witness the new direction."

During Zared's intervention, Berk regained his composure. "Indeed." He addressed Wilbur. "As of tonight, Baron Zared is our Grand Master, responsible for guiding the kingdom in a new age of enlightenment denied us by other *spiritual leaders, becoming,*" he voice turning emphatic, "second in authority to me. And *I* shall be the supreme."

Wilbur flushed, red-faced with fury, but Armus reacted first. He took several steps toward the high table to speak. "You would usurp the Vicar of Jor'el?"

Berk's temper exploded. He pounded the table with his fists. "I usurp nothing! I am king!"

"What of him?" Armus' outrage continued as he motioned to Zared. "You dare make him responsible for Allon's spiritual leadership?"

Zared bolted to his feet. He clenched the collar of his doublet. Angry eyes narrowed upon Armus. "Who are you to question the King?"

Armus locked eyes with Zared. The brief exchange made Armus flinch, not with intimidation, rather in pain at a drain of energy. Wilbur took hold of Armus in a gesture of warning. Archimedes also came alongside Armus, though a bit curious of the Commander. Armus nodded to Wilbur and retreated a step. Archimedes remained with Wilbur. The energy drain wasn't enough to endanger his cover, but it did concern him as to the source. Armus watched Wilbur confront Berk.

"You take more upon yourself than is advisable."

"I take what is my right! Baron Zared will be Grand Master with Lord Patrin as Regent should anything happen to me before my heir comes of age."

Myla gasped in surprise at the second announcement. "Regent? Patrin? I am Queen, and Akilles my son. By right Regent is my duty."

Berk's wrath focused upon Myla. "It is *my* decision to bestow the title on whom *I* choose!"

"You overstep your bounds," Wilbur scolded.

When Zared focused his furious gaze at the Vicar, Abner quickly asked, "What about the Council of Twelve?"

Berk motioned Zared to sit. A jeering smile crossed Berk's lip in replying to Abner. "Did I forget to mention the Council? Well, I assure you, Sir Abner, it was not an oversight. The Council no longer exists. It is immediately *dissolved!*"

Shouts of protests and objections erupted in the Hall.

"Restore order!" Berk shouted at Niles, only Niles didn't move. "Didn't you hear me, man?" Unable to get a reply, Berk shouted, "Captain of the Guards!"

The herald repeated the shout for the royal Guards.

Wilbur pounded his staff to get attention. When the crowd began to grow quiet, he spoke with authority. "Hear me and take heed, Berk, Son of Rogan, Son of Tristan! Jor'el sends a warning. Continue on this course of abandoning the heritage passed down by your forefather, and you will forfeit your place in the royal lineage! Jor'el will not be mocked." He pointed to Zared, "This creature will be the ruin of you!"

Outraged, Zared jumped to his feet and grabbed his collar. When his eyes met Wilbur, the Vicar winced. With grit and determination, Wilbur stood his ground, but only as much as an old man could.

A cold sense of evil stabbed at Armus' spirit. When Wilbur swayed, he seized the Vicar to keep him on his feet. Markes also came to support Wilbur. Archimedes moved between Zared and Wilbur ready to draw his sword.

Niles rushed to Wilbur. The Vicar appeared on the verge of swooning. "You need to leave, my lord," he urged.

Royal Guards hurried into the Hall. Chaos ensued when people panicked in an effort to leave. Soldiers started to corral everyone.

Armus spoke the Ancient under his breath. He and Markes aided Wilbur from the Hall. They passed the soldiers without harassment.

Once in the courtyard, Markes marveled. "They didn't stop us."

"Jor'el is with us," Wilbur whispered, the strongest voice he could manage.

"Take him and leave Waldron immediately!" Armus ordered Markes.

"What are you going to do, Commander?"

"Never mind me. Get the Vicar to safety." Armus then summoned the Knights. "Jor'ellians! Secure the Vicar. Return to the Temple!"

"Commander ..." began Wilbur in a weak voice.

Armus spoke with gentle reassurance. "You have discharged your duty. Go in peace." He allowed a brief brightness in his eyes to bolster the Vicar.

Wilbur managed a small smile before Markes helped him into the carriage.

Armus watched, ready to ensure the group left safely. He swayed and held his head at feeling an overwhelming depletion of strength. Not good! With unsteady steps, he hurried toward the postern gate. He stumbled sideways into some barrels. From under his tunic he removed the flask Wren gave him. He uncorked it. Empty! He drank the last dose before reaching Waldron. The overwhelming sense of evil exhausted his energy. He had to get to safety before he lost his shift!

"Run unseen!" he spoke the Ancient. He raced to the gate. "Open!" The guards on duty didn't react when Armus ran through an open gate. It shut behind him. He barely reached the trees where he blacked out.

Chapter 11

ONCE WILBUR LEFT, NILES RETURNED TO HIGH TABLE. "Come, Sire, Majesty!"

"What are you doing?" Berk demanded.

"Escorting you and the Queen to safety from this chaos," Niles stoutly replied.

"I gave you an order to restore the peace, which you ignored!"

"Only after you are safe! Which is my first sworn duty."

"I'm staying!" Berk stubbornly remained in his seat.

Myla took hold of Niles' arm to leave. He escorted her out a rear door to the servants' corridor.

Archimedes stopped a soldier from accosting Wilma. "Leave off!"

"We are restoring order," argued the solider.

"That doesn't require manhandling the Queen's lady!" Archimedes forcefully removed the soldier's hold of Wilma. His interruption stopped any further action. The soldier left.

Wilma smiled in gratitude, which faded at seeing Myla's chair empty. "The Queen!"

Archimedes made a quick survey of the Hall. "Probably Niles. Come. Let me take you out of here."

"What is happening?" she asked when leaving by same back door.

"The fulfillment of Zared's plans." They moved down the rear corridor to the back staircase. "After the Vicar's visit, it will get worse. Zared will use his newfound authority against Wilbur."

"What can we do?"

"Other than prayer, not much."

At the top of the stairs, Wilma tugged on Archimedes to draw him into an alcove. She spoke in the Ancient. "You are First Jor'ellian. Go to the Temple and help Wilbur. He looked so feeble against Zared."

He gazed affectionately at her. "Helping him means leaving you."

Wilma kindly smiled, and lowered her voice. "There is a plan, remember?"

"Only now there is a new danger," he spoke with emphasis.

"A danger more to others than to us."

Her continuing argument made him fretful. "Not if our secret is discovered. Zared could use you against me, and I would be the worse for it."

Wilma tenderly touched Archimedes' face. "What if I told you there is another you must protect. One for whom, the future depends upon you acting?"

"Who?"

Her smile widened with pride. "Our child, dear husband."

Briefly stunned mute, Archimedes fought against excitement at the news. "You are with child? When were you going to tell me?"

"Tonight, when we met afterwards." As he kissed her hands, she spoke with urgency. "Do not shirk your duty. Those who love you, depend upon it."

Archimedes grinned, both happy and poignant. "I will escort you to the Queen so you can maintain *your* duty. I will learn the aftermath of all this upheaval before making arrangements to leave."

At the Queen's chamber, they found Myla alone.

"Majesty, are you well?" asked Wilma.

"For now. What of you, dear Wilma? The excitement did not overtax you, did it?" Myla spoke with concern.

"No." Wilma warmly glanced at Archimedes, who appeared wary.

"Your secret is safe, Lord Archimedes," said Myla.

"I'm just surprised, Majesty."

Myla lightly chuckled. "A woman knows."

Archimedes simply nodded. "May I inquire if Sir Niles aided you?"

"He did." Her tone turned to annoyance. "Apparently, Berk insists on continuing the banquet. I declined citing upset, but Niles is recalled."

"Rather unusual," mused Archimedes.

"This whole evening is *unusual*," chided Myla.

"Indeed, Madam. This warrants investigation. Before that, I will assign more Jor'ellians to make certain the royal chambers are undisturbed." He bowed to Myla and smiled at Wilma on his way out.

Archimedes just passed Akilles' room when Colin emerged. "Lord Archimedes."

"Ay?"

Cautious, Colin leaned closer. "I must speak with you on an urgent matter."

Archimedes wryly grinned. "What of your father? A problem he can't solve?"

Colin let the humor slide to speak with sobriety. "This *can't* wait until the banquet is over."

Archimedes took note of Colin's seriousness. "What is so urgent?"

Colin switched to the Ancient and kept his voice low. "Have you ever heard of a multi-sided black and silver amulet with a raven on it?"

Archimedes drew to his full height with dreaded surprise.

"Have you?" Colin insisted when Archimedes didn't reply.

"To the Chapel!" Archimedes snapped.

Colin said a quick word to the Jor'ellians guarding Akilles' chamber before he hurried after Archimedes. With long hurried strides, Archimedes led Colin to the Chapel.

Barely inside, Archimedes accosted Colin, though he continued speaking in the Ancient. "What made you interested in this amulet?"

Colin cast a watchful glance around the Chapel before replying. "It is reported that *the baron* wears one. I need to know what it is."

Archimedes' brow leveled in worry. "Who made the report?"

Colin shook his head. "For security, I'd rather not say."

Archimedes momentarily stared at Colin. "You don't have to. I can guess since I know your assignment."

"What about this amulet?"

With a heavy sigh, Archimedes said, "By the description, I have a suspicion regarding its origin. Fortunately, there is a way to confirm or dismiss it." He added with deadly earnest. "*You* must gird your heart if I think is confirmed. Do you understand?"

"Not completely—*yet* I will not waiver."

"Good. You'll need your father's stubbornness."

They moved from the entrance to a side table near the altar. Archimedes used an altar candle to light a lantern that sat upon the table. He led Colin through dark corridors to a back room. Once inside, Archimedes used a key to lock the door behind them. He handed the lantern to Colin. "Follow me closely."

In a far corner near a dusty bookshelf, Archimedes paused to look back at the door. "Hold the lantern up high, and close your eyes."

"Why?"

Archimedes would brook no question. "Because I said so!" He softened his tone at Colin's steady stare. "For your own sake. You can't tell what you don't see."

Colin did as instructed. He heard some scraping and a muffled thud.

"You can open your eyes now." On a pedestal in front of Archimedes, lay an open book. "Bring the light closer."

Colin looked over Archimedes' shoulder. "That's not the Book of Verse."

"No. It's one of two remaining Books of Prophecy."

Colin understood. "You didn't want me to see where it is hidden."

"It isn't a matter of trust, if that is your concern."

Colin grinned. "No, merely a statement of understanding."

Archimedes thumbed through the pages. Occasionally, he muttered the Ancient during his search. Suddenly, he slammed the book closed, which startled Colin.

"What did you find?"

Archimedes' voice barely rose above a whisper. "Confirmation. *It is Dagar's talisman.*" His eyes narrowed with dread. "Zared is indeed Grand Master."

Colin slightly recoiled at the statement of the amulet's identification yet puzzled concerning Zared. "What is a Grand Master?"

"Grand Master of *Enlightenment,* named to his position this night by the King. In history, a Grand Master commanded the Dark Way. Like Magelen once did."

"Magelen," Colin repeated with concern. "I've heard that name before, and with disgust."

"He was the Grand Master Tristan defeated to become king." Archimedes waved at Colin. "Your eyes."

Colin again closed his eyes while Archimedes returned the book to its hiding place. They departed the Chapel with hasty caution. Hasty in deliberation, but laced with caution to avoid being seen returning to the main building. Sounds of the banquet came from the Great Hall.

"Folly!" chided Archimedes at the noise. "We'll have to wait to approach Niles. Return to your charge."

"What will you do?"

"Pray." He nudged Colin on his way. With seething anger, Archimedes lingered in the Grand Foyer listening to the offensive celebrating. "Such an effrontery to the grace given this house."

The doors to the Hall opened. Several noble families filed out. Either the banquet was over, or they were retiring early. Archimedes caught sight of Abner and Gordon. The young men appeared grim. Small wonder. With deliberate steps Abner headed towards him with Gordon at his heels. Instead of stopping, Abner slowed his pace and spoke the Ancient when passing Archimedes.

"Some of the Council will meet tonight. Stay sharp." Abner didn't make eye contact with Archimedes, as he and Gordon proceeded to the main staircase.

Abner and Gordon went to Abner's chamber in the guest wing.

"How many do think will come?" Gordon asked.

"I suspect the usual opposed to Zared. Although, with this latest development, we must be cautious."

"Berk may have dissolved the Council, but it shouldn't stop us meeting ... as friends that is," Gordon added to Abner's sharp glance.

"Doing so tonight will cause suspicion. Unfortunately, there is no better time before we leave. Once away, there is no telling *if* meeting will be possible. Zared is acting quickly." Abner stopped at hearing one sharp rap on the door followed by two quick knocks. At the signal, he opened to admit Slater, Mather, Rafe and Jarrett.

Abner frowned. "Coming all at once is unwise."

"Together or separate, what does it matter?" challenged Slater, the fifty-five year old lord of the Northern Forest. "After tonight, anything is too late."

"This will make it more difficult to deal with the pirates," complained Jarrett. He and Rafe were middle-aged contemporizes. They commanded the naval forces protecting the East and West Coasts.

"Not to mention the mounting costs to lives, property and goods!" added Rafe.

"That is the least of our worries," chided Slater.

"Easy for you to say! You don't have to deal with the situation like we do."

Slater confronted Rafe. "Do you honestly think Zared cares about pirates or the resulting issues?"

"Gentlemen! Maintain a civil tone. We risk much meeting like this," came an unusual scolding from Mather.

"Mather's right," began Abner. "We need to keep our tempers. This new situation will affect everyone not just one or two provinces."

"How do you suggest we deal with it now that the Council is no more?" asked Jarrett.

"Though a harsh blow to our collective voice, it shouldn't impact our opposition," insisted Abner. "Whether here or at home, we can stand united in our support of each other, bolster Wilbur and do what is right for the kingdom."

A conciliatory smile crossed Slater's lips. "You speak wisdom that puts to shame those of us who are older and should know better."

"That was not my intention, my lord," said Abner in earnest apology.

Slater heartily patted Abner's shoulder. "Nevertheless, it is the result." He inquired of Mather, Rafe and Jarrett, "Gentlemen, what say you to Sir Abner's speech?"

"Ay," said Rafe and Jarrett in unison.

"Agreed," said Mather.

"Then I think, it is best we retire and keep contact to a minimum until we are away from here," advised Slater.

Rafe, Jarrett and Gordon departed. Instead of leaving, Slater shut the door behind them. He remained.

"Is something on your mind, my lord?" Abner asked.

"There is a more personal reason for my visit tonight." Slater motioned for Abner to a small sofa. "It's about Phyllis."

Abner grew anxious. "Has something happened to her?"

"No, no, nothing like that," said Slater kindly. "I mean in reference to this situation." He took a deep, contemplative breath before continuing. "As my only child, there is much to consider regarding her future."

Abner's anxiety turned to wariness. "We have an agreement."

"I'm not nullifying the agreement. You will marry her, only I think it is best to wait and not wed in the spring as planned."

"Why?" Abner tried to keep the anger from his voice.

"To see what Zared will do. He could move against the provinces."

"That should accelerate the wedding, not delay it. By marriage, the Northern and Southern Forests are united. We give mutual protection and aid."

Slater pursed his lips, worried and uncertain. "I'm concerned for her safety."

Abner sat up straight, offended. "You think I'm not? As a provincial lord and trained Jor'ellian, I'm very capable of protecting Phyllis."

Slater sat back against the sofa with pursed lips of consideration. "I realize that only these are worrisome times."

Abner's tone softened. "Let me help you ease that burden, as your son-in-law. And your friend."

With a fatherly smile, Slater regarded Abner. "Indeed, my dear boy, you are blessed with wisdom beyond your years, which is one of the reasons I agreed to the marriage." He patted Abner on the knee. "The wedding will go on as planned." He stood. "I bid you goodnight." He embraced Abner.

Chapter 12

ARUNDINE, THE FAMED COUNCIL HALL OF THE GUARDIANS, was once a hive of activity during their time of governing Allon. Since the Great Battle, it became hidden from mortals. Dense forest surrounded the six-sided structure while the once gleaming white marble façade became overgrown with vines, moss and weeds. A canopy of trees veiled the dome.

The interior was larger than expected by the exterior. Six pillars held up the dome with twelve marble chairs arranged in a semi-circle facing a slightly raised platform. A larger chair sat on the platform. Various sizes of colored marble tile created a floor map of Allon with the name of each province etched in gold. The same signs of nature's overgrowth appeared inside. Vines wound upwards on the pillars or hung from the ceiling.

Kell, Eldric, Zinna and Jedrek gathered around an unconscious Armus. He lay on the floor in front of the raised platform. Eldric became more determined in his effort to wake Armus and grabbed him by both shoulders. With hard shake, Eldric spoke in the Ancient.

"*Duigsh, Armus!*"

Startled, Armus' eyes snapped open. Lamplight temporary blinded him so he shielded his eyes.

"I told you I could wake him," Eldric spoke nonchalantly to Kell.

Confused, Armus asked, "Where am I?"

"Arundine," replied Kell.

His eyes adjusted, Armus noticed the lamps illuminated the Council Hall. "What time is it?"

"Still nighttime. You remained unconscious for an hour, which concerned me that you suffered some unseen injury."

141

"Kell, I told you it's simple exhaustion," insisted Eldric. "Granted *extreme* but just exhaustion."

Armus listened to the exchange still perplexed. "How did I get here? The last thing I remember is leaving Waldron."

"I brought you," began Kell. "I sensed you were in danger and went to help. I found you unconscious and reverted to Guardian form."

Armus groaned with fatigue. "What about Wilbur?"

"Wren is once again shadowing the retinue."

"Sit up so you can drink the strengthen tonic. I made it extra strong." Eldric helped Armus to sit up against the elevated platform.

Upon taking the cup, Armus noticed Mona, Zinna and Jedrek. "Did you need help getting me here?" he quipped before drinking the tonic.

Kell chuckled. "No. We're all curious what happened."

Armus downed the tonic in one long drink. His face screwed up in disgust. "You must find a way to make it taste better." He shoved the cup into Eldric's hand.

"Maybe after your second dose."

"Why two?"

"Because *he* wants you recovered quickly." Eldric motioned to Kell. "And with your size, one isn't enough."

"I thought drinking all of the tonic Wren gave me would be enough to keep my cover at Waldron. Unfortunately, that wasn't the case," groused Armus.

Eldric appeared curious. "It should have been sufficient."

Armus scowled to the contrary. "Not when I encountered Zared. He stared at me, as if he knew who I was, or least suspected. I felt a sudden drain of energy. That shouldn't happen with just a *mortal*."

Very curious, Kell asked, "Is that when you lost your shift?"

Armus shook his head since he drank the second tonic. He coughed down the dose. "Tasted worse than the first!" He continued his explanation. "Berk named Zared as *Grand Master*," he spoke the title with emphasis, "and gave him charge to guide Allon into a new age of *spiritual enlightenment*. Wilbur delivered Jor'el's warning to Berk then confronted

Zared. When Zared focused on Wilbur, a cold sense of evil alerted me to danger. I got Wilbur away and instructed the Jor'ellians take him back to the Temple. *That* is when I felt my cover fading. All I could was run."

"Grand Master like Magelen," chided Jedrek then said to Kell, "This confirms Zared has the talisman. *Spiritual enlightenment* can only mean the Dark Way!"

Kell made a slow nod. "All the signs are adding up, while the sense of danger is growing at an alarming rate." He put up a hand to stop Jedrek's protest. "In truth, it has been since the Great Battle."

"Did Wren tell you about the wolves and kelpies? We haven't encountered creatures of infrinn since Tristan became king," said Armus.

"She told us," said Kell with annoyance.

Armus blinked in recovery. "Oh, I nearly forgot! Berk also named Patrin as Regent instead of Myla, dissolved the Council and assumed *all* authority even usurping the Vicar."

Stunned, the others stared at Armus.

"Kell!" began Jedrek in strenuous objection.

The captain pursed his lips in regard of Jedrek. "Return to the Delta. Only be careful. The province could become the epicenter for whatever is being planned."

Armus stood. "He shouldn't go alone."

"I don't think you're recovered enough," said Kell in dispute.

"I feel better than when I woke. Besides, the Meadowlands lie between here and the Delta. He'll need back-up if what we suspect is about Zared is true."

Kell asked Eldric about Armus. "How long will it take for him to return to normal?"

"Since it's just exhaustion, a couple of hours at most."

"It takes six hours to reach Deltoria at a brisk pace, no extra energy needed. Armus will be fine before we arrive," said Jedrek.

Kell nodded. "Very well. Only use caution."

In the grey light of pre-dawn, Jedrek and Armus carefully made their way through the Delta marshes to Deltoria, the provincial castle. Unlike other structures enclosed for protection, Deltoria stood open and spacious. Known for recuperative spas and tepid climate, the vast wetlands teamed with a variety of fish and fowl.

Even from a distance, Deltoria showed its sprawling splendor. The numerous gardens were dormant during the winter season. Patches of grass remained. Thin pine trees rose tall and straight. The bitter cold winds from the north rarely came this far south. Since the temperatures generally remained above freezing, the sparkling pools and fountains flowed year-round. All contained the famed healing waters.

Due to the open landscape surrounding Deltoria, Jedrek and Armus moved slowly. They took advantage of the sparse cover in the form of rocky mounds, occasional brush or cluster of pine trees. True, they didn't want to be discovered by mortals, but an overwhelming coldness made them stop behind a mound of brush two miles from the castle.

"How can we feel it this far away?" Jedrek asked, disturbed.

"You believe Zared has Dagar's talisman," replied Armus.

"Kell said Zared is still at Waldron. He couldn't have returned home in a single day unless he had *unnatural* help."

"Shadow Warriors? They haven't been seen since Tristan was crowned."

Jedrek directed Armus' attention toward the distant castle. "Well, something disturbing is at Deltoria. If not Shadow Warriors then what?"

Armus' gaze narrowed in his view of the castle. "They would have to be here in large numbers for so strong a sense. Getting closer will reveal our presence." He frowned as he continued, "Only I don't know if I'm recovered enough to take on a second mortal persona."

"I'll go, you serve as back-up."

"It's risky alone if it turns out to be true."

"There isn't much of a choice," argued Jedrek. "We can travel a half-mile more, find a position for you to take up surveillance then I'll proceed to Deltoria."

When Armus gave an affirming nod, Jedrek took the lead. Coming from the north, they stopped behind a large embankment. It formed a channel for water to flow from a nearby spring to Deltoria. From here, the entire front of the manor became visible.

"This will do nicely," said Armus.

Jedrek removed his sword and dagger.

"What are you doing? You can't go unarmed."

"If I arrive looking like a soldier of fortune, I might be viewed with suspicion. As a simple traveler in search of food and shelter, I should be welcomed." Jedrek took a deep breath, brought his hands together, bowed his head and spoke in the Ancient. He shrunk in size to around six feet by standard measure. His uniform transformed into the clothes of a commoner. He exhaled and opened his eyes. The usual bright amber color changed to a dull brown.

"That wasn't as easy as it used to be," he complained.

"Now you see why we needed the tonics," snickered Armus.

"Stay alert." Remaining hunched over, Jedrek carefully moved along the embankment away from Armus to a knoll at the far end. A path curved around the knoll, making it more plausible for travel. He emerged from behind the embankment and onto the trail.

Jedrek tried to appear casual in approach of Deltoria. It wasn't how he felt. The disturbing coldness grew stronger the closer he got. He became distracted at movement on the west side of the manor.

A Guardian's eyesight far exceeded mortals. However, it proved a fleeting glimpse that disappeared around back. Jedrek judged them to be mortal males. He changed his course to follow since no common traveler would dare approach the front entrance. They always went to rear in hopes of obtaining food from a kitchen servant.

Nearing the western portion of Deltoria, Jedrek shivered, hard and unsettling. Winter weather didn't affect Guardians. No! This frigid sensation penetrated to the core of his being with the foreboding of evil! He paused to take a deep breath to regain his composure.

"Jor'el, give me strength to do what is needed."

Steeling himself against the sinister sensation, he proceeded. He heard the shouting of voices, the rattling of harness and a few neighing of horses. Even perceiving the presence of darkness did not prepare him for the startling sight awaiting him just around the corner of the building.

"Shadow Warriors!" Jedrek murmured in surprise. He quickly turned aside to recover his composure.

"You there! What are you doing here?"

Jedrek balked when a mortal soldier dressed in Zared's livery accosted him. "I'm just a traveler in search of food and shelter. I mean no harm!" he spoke in the most pitiful voice he could.

"Barlow! Who is this knave?"

Jedrek gaped when a tall, imposing being arrived. Recognition made Jedrek swallowed back the impulse to speak the name.

Barlow came to attention. "Commander Altari. I'm in the process of finding out."

Altari's cool grey eyes narrowed upon Jedrek, as if searching for the familiar.

Jor'el, don't let him recognize me! Jedrek's mind pleaded. He hung his head to avoid Altari's stare. He became startled when Altai jerked his arm. Maybe Armus was right. He should have at least kept his dagger.

"I only wanted some food! From the kitchen." Jedrek continued his pretense.

"Altari!" a voice called a moment before another formidable being joined them. His massive chest and shoulder could equal Armus, and with hands capable of crushing anything. A nasty scar ran from above his right eye and across the bridge of his nose to the left cheek.

Jedrek stiffened to contain any reaction at seeing Witter. He nearly lost control at seeing the talisman Witter wore.

"Some beggar wanting food." Altari roughly released Jedrek. This made Jedrek stumble backwards before regaining his balance.

"That can be remedied." Witter sent an unexpected blow to Jedrek's midsection. The force sent him backwards into the building. He fell to one side, clenching his abdomen.

Jedrek knew he couldn't stay down. He began to rise when a foot viciously kicked him in the side. Once more the force knocked him into the building. He hissed in pain. A hand reached down, seized him by the collar and pulled him up and off his feet. He tried to breathe under the crushing grip. Witter maliciously glared at him. He averted his eyes from Witter's scrutinizing gaze. He saw the talisman more closely since it practically hit his face.

"No," he muttered with disturbance.

"What did you say?" Witter demanded.

"No, please don't hit me again," he struggled to speak between gasping breaths for air.

"You're lucky to be speaking after my little slap."

"Slap?" Jedrek coughed when Witter's grip threatened to suffocate him.

"A slap you'll remember. You're not still hungry are you?"

Unable to speak, Jedrek shook his head. He did all he could to remain conscious. When Witter's face drew closer, Jedrek closed his eyes rather than look at the Shadow Warrior commander.

"You *won't* remember anything you saw here, will you?"

"No!" Jedrek managed to wheeze.

"Good, because if you do…" Witter didn't finish speaking instead he threw Jedrek into the wall.

Jedrek's back slammed flat against the wall. He struck his head, and gasped when the impact knocked the wind from his lungs. He took in large gulps of air to recover. Every inch of his body hurt. Out of the corner of his eye, he noticed Altari and Witter leave. He wasn't recovered enough to fight off the mortal soldier when jerked to his feet.

"You're lucky they left you alive." The soldier shoved Jedrek to leave.

Despite the almost debilitating pain of injury, Jedrek staggered off. At the corner of the building, he dared a quick survey of those assembled. When Altari turned, he ducked back.

The assault compromised his strength thus he stumbled in retreat from Deltoria. Not good! He had to reach the knoll before he lost the ability to maintain his cover. Fifty yards from safety, Jedrek fell on all fours. Weak to the point of collapse, he reverted to his Guardian form. He flinched when hands dragged him behind the knoll. Armus. Jedrek relaxed against the embankment.

"What happened? I felt danger and about to come when I saw you returning," said Armus.

Jedrek took a deep breath against the pain before replying. "Worse than we thought. We must leave the Delta—now!" He reached for Armus to help in move.

"Why?"

"No question ... just hurry!" Jedrek tried to stand, but couldn't. He doubled over in pain.

Armus placed Jedrek's arm over his shoulder with an arm around Jedrek's waist for support. Armus spoke the Ancient. He began running north, as fast as possible with an injured comrade.

Fortunately, the border to the Meadowlands lay only a couple of hours away. Once across the East Bendix River, Armus stopped inside a grove of trees to allow Jedrek to rest. Jedrek held his abdomen while gingerly sitting under a large evergreen.

"How did you get injured?" asked Armus.

Jedrek swallow back the pain to reply. "Summon Kell. He needs to hear this."

"No need. I sensed more trouble." Kell arrived and knelt to examine Jedrek.

"Did you bring any medicine or strengthening tonic?" asked Armus.

"No, but I can send for Eldric."

Jedrek shook his head. "Not yet." He looked squarely at Kell. "The Dark Way has returned in force. My injury is the result of a encounter with Witter and Altari."

Kell's jowls flexed with fury. Armus made a low growl of anger.

Jedrek continued. "Witter wears a talisman. They command at least a thousand Shadow Warriors. Some mounted on spirit stallions." He glanced to Armus. "That's what we sensed, the massive presence. Being at Deltoria, there is no doubt of Zared's involvement."

"Are you certain of the number?" asked Kell.

Jedrek shrugged, his features pale and weary. "I only had time for a quick assessment. Sensing my power compromised by injury, I didn't dare stick around any longer."

"It's a wonder they didn't sense you."

"Oh, they tried!" said Jedrek with certainty. "I thank Jor'el for going undetected and leaving in one piece." He coughed, which caused such pain that he doubled over. When he sat up, blood trickled out the corner of his mouth. His eyes shrouded on the verge of unconsciousness.

Concerned, Kell held Jedrek's face. "You suffered more serious injury than you want to admit. Perhaps, internal bleeding."

"Ay," he weakly agreed.

"There's an abandoned cottage two miles for here. I'll take him there while you summon Eldric," Armus said to Kell. Jedrek didn't balk or fuss when Armus carried him.

<hr/>

Ten Guardians assembled in the front room of the cottage. Along with Wren, Mona, Gresham, Zinna and Armus came Priscilla, a wind Guardian from the East Coast, Barnum, Valmar and Chase. In appearance, Priscilla was fair, wearing a flowing gown and unarmed. Barnum and Valmar were warriors. Barnum's bulk rivaled that of Armus. Valmar's white hair and violet eyes made him look older than the others. Chase was a sea Guardian renowned for his knowledge of the oceans and naval warfare. All listened intently to Kell's briefing on Jedrek's discovery.

Distressed by Jedrek's serious injuries, Priscilla sat in a chair beside the empty hearth. "Will he recover?" she asked in a muted voice.

"Eldric will tell us when he's done," said Kell.

"If he succumbs, will Jor'el send a replacement?" asked Chase.

Kell's features grew harsh at the question. "You should be more concerned for Jedrek's recovery than a replacement!"

Chase made a staunch rebuttal. "I didn't mean it that way! I meant, if for some reason we decrease in number, any of us—or all of us, will Jor'el send aid to the mortals?"

"He has a point," said Valmar.

Subdued, Kell remained silent for several moments. "I don't know," he said at length. "However, that should not be our primary concern. How to deal with this threat *is* where we need to focus on energies."

Eldric emerged from the bedroom where he treated Jedrek.

"Well?" asked Armus immediately upon sight of the physician.

"Fractured ribs punctured his spleen. I've been able to stop the internal bleeding, but I'm more concerned for the drain on his lifeforce."

"Won't strengthening tonics help?" asked Kell.

"To a point. You know what wounds do to a Guardian at full strength. We're at half-strength. Jedrek managed to maintain his façade at the cost of using valuable energy needed for recovery."

"Can you heal him?" asked Priscilla in shaky voice.

Eldric's expression showed both his desire to comply and hesitation. "Again, being at half-strength, I don't know if my lifeforce can take the energy drain." He raised a hand to still her counter-argument. "Under dire circumstances I would do so without hesitation."

Priscilla turned her pleading attention to the captain. "Kell?"

"This isn't dire. Not yet," said Kell, though he too appeared troubled.

Valmar brightened with a thought. "Eldric, how about using Highland berry sprigs?"

"What are those?" asked Wren.

"A plant that grows high in the mountains. Mortals use it for various medicinal purposes. They claim it does wonders for enlivening the spirit," explained Valmar.

Kell asked Eldric, "Could you incorporate these sprigs in your tonic?"

Eldric seemed agreeable. "It's worth a try."

Valmar flashed a confident smile. "I know exactly where they grow. With your permission, Captain, it will be faster to dimension travel."

"We don't know if Shadow Warriors are just in the Delta or have managed to infiltrate other provinces."

"With the Highlands so far north, I don't think so." Receiving a nod from Kell, Valmar vanished in the white light of dimension travel.

"What should we do?" Mona asked Kell.

"Return to your provinces and watch for any signs of Shadow Warriors. Especially you, Gresham. Dagar seems to have a liking for Midessex." He said to Eldric. "Make Jedrek comfortable until Valmar returns.

Armus remained while the rest departed and Eldric went to the bedroom. Once alone, he commented to Kell, "*Dire* is an understatement if we lose Jedrek."

"We won't!" Kell snapped with frustration.

"Kell, you can't be certain. Even Eldric doesn't know."

The captain stared at his lieutenant. There was no rebuke in his eyes rather intense entreaty. "We must stand united no matter what."

"Of course. However, you can't deny or diminish the situation. We all sense the gravity of what is happening."

"Jor'el will not abandon his faithful."

"No," said Armus with certainty. "Only it doesn't mean those of us remaining are not expendable to keep that promise."

All Kell's combativeness drained. This time he stared at Armus with dreaded resolution. After a brief moment, he crossed to a front window to look outside. "Let it not be so," he prayed under his breath. Light appearing in the room made Kell turn from the window.

Valmar stumbled from the fade of dimension travel. "With snow falling, I gathered what I could. Let's hope these are enough," he spoke with weariness.

Kell and Armus watched Valmar enter the bedroom. A moment later, he reappeared carrying a cup. He plopped into a chair and drank.

"Strengthening tonics taste better in wine than water," he complained.

Armus chuckled. "He probably put it in water as revenge for showing him up with your *medical* suggestion."

"Ay," Valmar grumbled into the cup. He finished the tonic.

"And he says warriors are prideful," Kell groused.

Valmar and Armus laughed at the unintended humor. Kell first appeared curious at their reaction then realized why, and chuckled. "I suppose that did sound funny coming me." His humor was short-lived. "When you feel strong enough, return to the Highlands. Set up a perimeter to secure the cottage until Jedrek is recovered," he spoke to Valmar and Armus respectively.

Chapter 13

CONSIDERING THE DRAMATIC TURN OF EVENTS, NILES STAYED with Berk after the King retired from the banquet. Despite some initial resistance, Berk yielded to Niles' reasoning.

During the night, Niles didn't sleep. His mind was too active and disturbed in recalling the extraordinary events. When Berk named Zared as Grand Master, suddenly all the baron's machinations made sense. Wilbur's pronouncement regarding the exclusion of Berk from the royal line of Tristan made Niles quiver with dread. The entire kingdom stood perched the brink of destruction, and little he could do to stop it!

Many nobles voiced protest, namely those on Council. It surprised Niles that Berk didn't order their arrest rather allowed them to retire for the night. Or more rightly, Berk yielded to Zared when the baron suggested the Council members leave Waldron at first light. Clever. Once separated, they would be less likely to unite against the decision. It pleased Niles that Abner and Gordon showed restraint by not reacting to Zared's intervention.

"Sir Niles," the voice of Alvin interrupted his thoughts. "The King is awake and says you are relieved."

"What time is it?"

"Nine o'clock in the morning."

His thoughts and prayers made the night pass quickly. Niles cocked a grin and said, "Past the time I should have seen to the morning watch." He left the King's chamber.

Abner paused in crossing the courtyard upon spying Zared and Patrin. Both wore cloaks, gloves, spurs and hats, as they headed for the stables. Abner diverted his course to intercept them.

"Good day, my lords," he made a cordial greeting. Neither of them looked pleased. "Are you setting an example for us to follow in departing, my lord?"

"No! I am called home on urgent business. But leaving is something *you* should be doing," Zared replied, emphatic.

The harsh tone did not deter Abner. He remained calm in speech and posture. "I shall leave once my valet is finished packing. Does the King know of *your* departure?"

"Of course!" Zared made move to leave when Abner again spoke. "With Patrin?"

Zared huffed in anger, which prompted Patrin to intervene. "The situation requires aid and I volunteered."

"Be about your business!" Zared roughly pushed passed Abner.

The contact was so physical it knocked Abner backwards into someone. This collision made Abner fall to the ground while the man stumbled in an attempt to keep his balance.

"Clumsy oaf!" the man scolded. He wore Zared's livery under a hooded cloak. The hood became partially knocked off the man's head and face.

Abner's eyes widened with recognition. Seeing the reaction, the man quickly pulled the hood and hurried after Zared and Patrin. Abner scrambled to his feet in hopes of catching sight of the man. His effort proved unsuccessful. Zared and his party left with the hooded man among them.

Abner didn't turn from his observation until they rode out the main gate. He hastened to the armory. He paused in the threshold looking for someone. Niles stood on the far side of the room speaking to several Jor'ellians. They greeted him with the Jor'ellian salute. He returned it.

"A moment with the Champion." The others obliged. Despite their departure, Abner drew Niles to a private corner to speak. "Zared and Patrin have left Waldron."

The statement surprised Niles. "When?"

"Just now. I questioned them, but got little more than an excuse of urgent business." He leaned very close. "Then I saw *him* … *the disgraced one* joined Zared."

Niles' brows rose with alarm. "Are you certain?"

"Ay, a brief revealing caused by a rather nasty collision. When I saw him, he pulled the hood back over his face and bolted." When Niles' eyes narrowed with consideration, Abner said, "After what happened, why would he join with Zared?"

Niles' answer came slow, as he pondered the news. "Only for evil purposes."

"The King or Akilles, perhaps?"

Niles looked sharply at Abner. "Not if I can help it!" He again inquired, "Are you certain it was *him?*" Abner stiffened at the question, so Niles said, "I do not doubt your word, however, we must be absolutely sure of who we are dealing with."

"Though I understand your hesitation, I *am* certain," chided Abner.

Niles made a conciliatory nod to the affirmation. "You said he left with Zared, so that should give us time to make preparation to deal with him also."

"Sir Niles!" Alvin hurried over. "The King sends for you, and he is not in a good mood."

"What caused this sudden change?"

"I don't know exactly. He received a note shortly after you left that made him fly into a rage."

Niles gave Abner friendly pat on the shoulder. "Until later." He left with Alvin. "Is he still in his chambers?"

"No, he quickly put on some clothes and went to his study."

Nearing the door, they heard Berk bellowing. Alvin took a deep breath before knocking.

155

"Come!" snapped Berk.

Alvin entered first to announce, "Sir Niles, Sire."

In brisk military step, Niles entered. "You sent for me, Sire?"

Berk marched up to Niles and demanded, "What have you done?"

With surprised uncertainty, Niles blinked at the question. "Nothing that I'm aware of, Sire."

"Don't play games! Answer the question. What have you done?"

"Sire, if there is something specific you refer to please enlighten me."

"Zared and Patrin have left Waldron. I'm certain it's because of you!" Berk's finger practically poked Niles in the face.

Niles straightened at the accusation. "I have not spoken to the Baron since last night."

"Don't lie! You could have done so after leaving me earlier this morning!"

Niles face flushed with anger at the insult. "Before Jor'el, I do not lie."

"Gibberish! A hollow oath." With narrow eyes of malice, Berk continued his assertion. "Zared told me you accosted him."

Niles didn't recoil rather challenged Berk. "When does he claim this happened? For Your Majesty knows where I've been since last evening."

Berk' upper lip quivered into a sneer at the rebuff. "Attend me this day, and we shall see whose truth bares out."

"I will attend you because it is my duty. Only how will that establish the truth between me and the Baron seeing as he has left?"

Berk snorted a mocking laugh only did not answer the question.

Alvin opened the door after a knock. "Sire, Her Majesty."

Myla entered. Again, Wilma accompanied her. Myla smiled at Niles.

"Why have you come, Madam?" asked Berk with severity.

"To beg Akilles be excused from his lessons today. He suffered a minor injury yesterday when learning a new wrestling technique from Baron Zared."

Berk's suspicious gaze passed between Myla and Niles. "Is this a conspiracy?"

To diffuse the situation, Niles asked Myla, "How bad is His Highness' injury?"

She smiled with relief at the diversion. "Nothing serious, yet enough to warrant being excused. At least for today," she added at Berk's displeasure.

Berk glared at Myla. "What do you know of Zared's departure?"

She grew curious. "I beg your pardon? The Baron has left Waldron?"

"Bah! You both claim ignorance that I find highly suspicious."

"Perhaps he left because of injuring Akilles."

"Why? If done during a wrestling lesson the injury was unintentional."

Myla clenched her hands to steady her agitation. "I'm merely offering a possible explanation, since I am ignorant of the real reason for his departure."

"He said there was a crisis at home that needed tending."

Niles drew alongside Myla in defense. "Sire, if you knew the reason for departure then why accost us when we were unaware of it?"

"To test your veracity. Of which, I still doubt!"

Niles stirred with anger, "Sire—" Myla took hold of his arm stop him. Instead, she spoke.

"You cannot have it both ways. To test Sir Niles, and then accuse him of causing the Baron's departure."

"Jealousy! Ay, he is jealous of Zared. Same as you are! Well, he is Grand Master now!" He waved a hand when she began to speak again. "Enough! Leave us."

Myla maintained her stance. "What about Akilles?"

"I'll find someone else to tutor him until Zared returns. Now, go! Both of you!" He waved at Myla and Niles.

Myla left. Wilma offered Berk a curtsey before following the Queen.

Niles gripped the hilt of his sword, made a curt bow and withdrew. He seethed with anger. Berk's erratic behavior, an unjust scolding and Abner's discovery of the Jor'ellian traitor at Waldron, already made this a very bad day. Not that such days were uncommon, quite the contrary. Daily life grew more contentious the past few months. Perhaps Zared will be gone long enough for voices of reason to bring Berk back to his senses. *May it be so, Jor'el,* he offered a silent prayer.

Instead of returning to the armory, Niles retired to his room. Cleaning up might help soothe him. He removed his sword and outer tunic to begin his toiletry. Before he poured the water from the pitcher into the basin, he noticed it. Next to the basin sat a piece of paper carefully folded to resemble a bird. He snatched it up to read. He dressed quickly and placed the note in pocket of his tunic.

Despite the buzz of daily activity, Niles moved casually toward the armory so as not to draw attention. He went to his office to retrieve a lantern then made his way to the old door in the back. Satisfied at seeing no one nearby, he unlocked the door, entered and locked it from the other side. Even during daylight, the room remained dark. The lantern provided light in moving from the threshold down the steeps stairs to the cellar. Nearing the bottom, he noticed another light. He held the hilt of his sword ready. Archimedes, Colin, Gordon and Abner waited. Their grave expressions alerted him to trouble.

Niles put the lantern on the table. This doubled the amount of light. "Has something more happened?" he asked Abner.

"According to Archimedes it is a disturbing discovery. He found me after we had spoken but not much else as we waited for you."

Archimedes began by speaking the Ancient. "Disturbing is an understatement. This will change *everything.*"

The ominous tone made Niles switch languages. "How?"

Archimedes motioned to Colin, who took up the explanation.

"During a heated bout at practice, Akilles uncovered an amulet Zared wears just under his collar." Colin held the neck of his tunic. "I didn't recognize the description so I sought Lord Archimedes' aid to learn what it could be."

Archimedes stepped close to Niles. "If you recall, we said only one *darkness* can hold such sway ..." He didn't finish. He didn't have to, not according Niles' sneering reaction.

"The Dark Way."

"In full force, for it is *Dagar's* talisman Zared possesses."

"*Jor'el, cuidich sinn!*" Niles spoke an earnest plea for aid. "Do you know Danior is with Zared?" he asked Archimedes. It was the First Jor'ellian's turn to sneer in glowering response.

"Who is Danior?" asked Gordon.

"A murderous traitor to his Oath!" Archimedes passionately replied.

"Easy. Gordon doesn't know the full history," Abner warned.

"He's right. Remember those involved," Niles said to Archimedes. He made a slight motion of his head toward Gordon.

"Judging by the visceral reaction, do I really want to know?" said Gordon with hesitation.

Niles' expression softened with compassion toward the young lord. "There are facts you may not be aware of concerning Danior. He was the commander of the Jor'ellian Guards. As such, he was often given the task of protecting dignitaries or those on special assignments regarding affairs of state."

"I heard he resigned after the Tulundian incident," said Gordon.

"That was the last in a string of problematic events. More troubling was his alleged involvement with certain unexplained … deaths." Niles' pointed glance made Gordon wary.

"What do you mean?"

"There is no gentle way of saying it," Archimedes said with sobriety.

"No," agreed Niles solemnly. He faced Gordon directly. "It is believed that several men under Danior's protection, did not die of natural causes, including—your father."

With astonished disturbance, Gordon stared at Niles. "You think Danior *murdered* him?"

Niles held Gordon's shoulder. "There was some evidence to suggest that possibility. In fact, when Wilbur confronted Danior, he offered his resignation thus avoided a full inquiry."

Gordon struggled to comprehend. "If he is believed guilty of murder, why allow him to resign and not suffer punishment?"

"The evidence was all circumstantial, not direct. The Jor'ellian Code is very specific about charges against a brother Knight. The evidence must be clear and convincing."

Gordon shook his head, obviously grappling with the news. "All of you believe it," he motioned to them. "Archimedes called him a murderous traitor!"

Archimedes tempered his words for Gordon's sake. "Belief isn't always based upon direct evidence. Behavior and actions of an individual can signal a guilty conscience while personal gut instinct also plays a part."

Niles stopped Gordon's objection to Archimedes statement. "None of which are admissible at an inquiry. Strong suspicion cannot condemn a man according to the Jor'ellian Code—and divine law," he added with emphasis.

Abner held Gordon's shoulder to get his attention. "If suspicion alone were the chief factor, the five of us would be condemned for treason based solely upon meeting like this. But is treason our real motive?"

After a moment, Gordon sighed with resignation. "I see your point. Our behavior, brought on by caution and great concern, could be viewed by others as something else." He blinked back a rising wave of emotion to speak to Niles. "Answer me truly, do you believe in your heart, Danior killed my father?"

"I do."

"So does the Vicar," said Archimedes. "Only it is left for Jor'el to level justice how and when the Almighty sees fit."

Abner comforted Gordon when Gordon lowered his head to compose his emotions. In response, Gordon spoke. "I always had difficulty accepting his death as an accident. Something about the explanation sounded wrong." He raised his head, showing sorrow replaced by determination. "That's why I completed the secret passage, along with all the other precautionary plans my father began." He then looked directly at Niles. "What are we going to do about Danior?"

"I don't know—*yet*. Until we discover Zared's reason for leaving Waldron, Danior is just one factor to consider in this wretched scenario."

Solemn warning came from Archimedes. "Having the talisman means Zared *is* the wielder of the Dark Way power. That's how he has been able to sway the king. With newfound *spiritual* and governmental authority, Zared won't stop there. He could employ Danior as an assassin."

"He would need to plan a complete coup, not just an assassination. Akilles would succeed Berk," said Colin.

"Unless he strikes the Prince first."

"I told you I placed Blake and Safford on guard before leaving. They will die before allowing harm to come to Akilles," insisted Colin.

Archimedes nodded agreement. "Ay, for tonight."

"With Zared away, I can continue watching over him."

"Unless Berk interferes," said Abner to Colin.

"We'll deal with that *if* it happens." Colin then asked Niles, "Are you attending Berk tomorrow as well?"

Nile shrugged. "I will present myself in the morning like usual, and see how he receives me."

"We can't cover all fronts or account for every possibility," groused Abner.

"We can ask for guidance." Archimedes reached down beside him to pick up a satchel. The others watched him withdraw a bottle of wine, cup and a loaf of bread. Understanding that Archimedes intended to conduct the Jor'ellian Refreshing Ceremony, Colin, Abner, Gordon and Niles prayerfully bowed their heads.

After placing all the elements beside the lanterns, Archimedes began speaking. "Great Jor'el, creator of the universe, we come before you with bread and wine to pay homage while beseeching you for strength and wisdom." He waved his hand over the lanterns. "May this, your light, give us insight into the enemy who threatens your appointed king."

"*Tangiel,*" said Abner, Niles, Gordon and Colin in agreement.

Archimedes poured wine into the cup. He held it up. "May this wine strengthen our hearts and spirits to faithfully fulfill our duties to you and your appointed king." He drank then handed the cup to Niles, who stood to his left. Niles repeated what Archimedes said, took a drink then passed it to Abner. Abner, Gordon and Colin did likewise, with Colin handing the cup back to Archimedes.

Archimedes took the bread. "May this bread strengthen our bodies for acts of righteousness in defense of your holy name and honor." He tore off a piece and ate. The others repeated the phrase and ate, ending with Colin giving the bread back to Archimedes.

"To your will we commend our prayers, our lives and our mission. Grant us—" Suddenly the lanterns flared into blinding light that knocked them all to the floor. The light faded back to normal.

Colin recovered first. He assisted Gordon to stand. Abner grabbed the table to pull himself up. Niles moved to Archimedes, who appeared unconscious.

"Archimedes?" Niles attempted to rouse the First Jor'ellian. With a defensive start, Archimedes bolted up into a sitting position. He reached for his sword. "Steady, old friend." Niles flashed a friendly smile.

Archimedes didn't calm down. Instead, he seized Niles arm. "We must make haste to the Temple! Wilbur is in danger."

"How do you know?" asked Abner.

"The light was Jor'el with a warning!" Archimedes rose. "You three, keep a sharp eye on things here."

"Wait!" began Colin in mild protest. "Berk will wonder where he is, and might accuse him of dereliction of duty," he spoke of his father.

"Tell him we were summoned by the Vicar!" Archimedes hastily said.

Chapter 14

ALTHOUGH TOLD TO RETURN TO HER PROVINCE WHEN LEAVING the Meadowlands cottage, Zinna didn't make her way directly back to the South Plains. A strong, compelling sense led her further northwest into Midessex. She wasn't able to discern the source, just that she had to follow it. She wondered if the sense would take her to Arundine. No. She bypassed the secret trail to continue on a northwesterly course to the crossroads leading to Waldron Castle. Could the source be there? No. The sensation turned in a more westerly trek away from Waldron.

Zinna continued on the new course for several miles. An overwhelming chill of evil caused her to duck into a thick grove of trees. She armed her bow before stretching out her senses to determine the origin of the disturbance. Her effort became interrupted at hearing the neighing of a horse. She crouched down to observe the approaching mortals. Even at half-strength, Guardian eyesight remained keen. Patrin rode with Baron Zared and another individual. Two valets and four soldiers followed them. Zinna recalled how Jedrek believed Zared possessed Dagar's talisman. If true, that could account for the evil.

By the directions they rode, Zared wasn't heading home to the Delta. More than likely he was accompanying Patrin to the South Plains. Zinna waited until they travelled a good distance past her concealment before she followed. With sunset coming early, they wouldn't reach the Lower Pass until the following day. They would have to find lodging in a couple of hours. When the group stopped at an inn, Zinna found a nearby vantage point to wait through the night.

Prior to full sunrise, the mortals left the inn to continue on their journey. Nearing the Lower Pass, Zinna paused to watch. They didn't make the turn to the South Plains! Instead they kept heading west. This meant Burleigh wasn't their destination. If they planned to visit Baron Fenton in the North Plains, the Upper Pass would be the best road. That required another few hours of travel.

Once again they continued without taking the Upper Pass into the North Plains. This meant they passed all roads to other provinces! It didn't make sense. There were no major towns in this part of Midessex, thus no safe accommodations for travelers. Few mortals chose to brave the hazards of night travel since society had so deteriorated that bandits ruled the highways. Before the Great Battle, the Guardian administration kept such thievery in check. Now what would they do?

Just after nightfall, they veered off the main road onto an old overgrown path. Suddenly, Zinna feared she knew their destination—the ruins of Ravendale, the once formidable castle of the Dark Way! This convinced her that Jedrek was correct and Zared did possess the talisman.

She needed to be careful and not come within a mile of the cursed meadow. She continually muttered the Ancient to endure the tremendous emanation of evil coming from the ruins. She made a parallel trek to keep them in sight. Even in the dark, she saw them a little over a mile away.

Finally, she stopped at a good vantage point in trees. A sharp immense pain caused Zinna to double over. She pulled herself up to her knees by use of a log. Firelight came from the ruins. The men dismounted beside some overgrown stones. She quickly covered her mouth to stop an unintended gasp at seeing Witter and Altari move from behind the stones. Altari carried a wrought iron tripod basin. After setting down the basin, the Warriors and mortals began conversing.

To eavesdrop on the conversation meant Zinna had to stretch out her sense of hearing. Not something she wanted to under the circumstances. A single use of power would alert the Shadow Warriors to her presence. She chose to watch.

Zared approached the basin. By his movements, he was speaking. Mist rose from the basin. An image appeared within the mist. It grew clearer to reveal a noble and awesome figure of perfection. He wore a scarlet doublet and breeches trimmed in gold. The white undershirt showed through slits in the doublet. His boots and belt were of finely crafted black leather. A jewel encrusted dagger hung from the belt. His sun-yellow hair, matching small beard and flawless complexion stood in marked contrast to the suit.

"Dagar!" Zinna covered her mouth with both hands and ducked behind the log. Granted, her voice was a low, but the unintended gasp not welcomed. She dared a glance. Witter motioned in her direction. She ducked down to crawl further into the trees. Another glance showed Witter headed toward her hiding spot. She bolted into the forest, running as fast as she could to put distance between she and the Warriors.

"Witter!" Dagar shouted.

The Warrior returned. "I'm sorry, my lord. I thought I heard something."

"The woods are crawling with bandits," said Zared.

"Can you be certain you weren't followed?" Witter rebuffed.

"Commander Altari reported the perimeter is secure," said Patrin.

Despite being displeased, Witter accepted the answer.

"Zared, how go the preparations?" asked Dagar.

"Well, my lord. Berk named me Grand Master of Enlightenment and Patrin as Regent. However, a slight problem requires the acceleration of our plans."

Dagar's bright mahogany eyes narrowed upon Zared. "What problem?"

"The Prince discovered the talisman." He tapped at his doublet, and proceeded to explain the incident. Dagar's lowly throaty growl of disapproval made Zared recoil a few steps.

"My lord, the troops are assembled at Deltoria," said Altari. His statement diverted Dagar's attention from the mortal.

"And Burleigh?"

"Nari and her team are in the South Plains."

"We came to inform you of the change before heading to Burleigh," said Zared. He recovered from his momentary discomposure to rejoin the conversation. Dagar remained unconvinced, so he continued. "My lord, this is Danior." He introduced a man with him. "He will complete the first phase of our plan."

Dagar eyed Danior, a wiry individual with small brown eyes and clean-shaven rugged features. "You hardly appear the assassin type."

Danior resisted the impulse to smile. "That is the idea, my lord. Once I change into suitable clothes, the Vicar will not suspect an innocent beggar. "

Dagar's inquired of Zared. "Has Wilbur named his successor?"

"No, my lord, and without a formal announcement, the man who replaces him will be appointed by the king. So you see, a few days won't really matter."

"Will Berk appoint our man to the Vicary?"

Zared smiled with triumphant pleasure. "Berk believes everything I tell him. He is totally swayed against the Queen, and anyone who attempts to interfere. He will agree to the suggestion."

"Of course, if for some reason, he balks, the appointment can be made after we succeed," Patrin added.

"True. However, he won't resist me."

Dagar turned his attention to the Warriors. "Any sign of Guardians?"

"No," replied Witter.

Dagar frowned and scratched at his beard. "Strange, *he* hasn't made an appearance. Futile though it would be. However, death of the Vicar should produce interest. Be on the alert for *any* indication of *his* presence."

"Who, my lord?" asked Zared.

Altari grunted a negative and waved Zared silent.

Dagar noticed the exchange yet made no comment. "I'll send Tor to the South Plains. Proceed as planned." Dagar's image vanished.

"Why stop my inquiry?" Zared asked Altari.

"Because it would upset Dagar, and you don't want to do that."

"Who did he mean?" asked Patrin.

"Kell. Captain of the Guardians." Altari snarled when he answered.

"Is this Kell powerful enough to thwart Dagar?"

When Altari's grey eyes flashed with insult, Witter stepped between him and Patrin. "Easy," he said to Altari. "His ignorance isn't worth your time." Witter continued his mediation by speaking to the mortals. "Take food and rest by the fire tonight. Danior will leave with us at first light."

Zared's upper lip quivered. "You are bold to speak to me in such a manner. When I gain my full authority as Grand Master—"

"Then I will be subject to you. For now, Commander Altari and I are in charge of this mission. In the morning, make your way to the South Plains border and wait a few days before returning to Waldron. You must make your excuse plausible before beginning phase two."

Patrin intervened to calm Zared. "We have important business. Dealing with him can wait until later." He nudged Zared away from the Warriors.

Altari spoke once they left. "Dagar is right. It is odd that *he* hasn't showed up."

Skeptical, Witter regarded Altari. "You want to face Kell?"

"Aligning with the Dark Way has increased our strength."

Witter shook his head. "Not under punishment. We too suffer the effects of half-strength. Though I also want to take revenge upon the Captain, we must wait until the right time."

Altari's glare turned merciless. "Not just Kell, but also Armus … and Avatar!"

Witter became curious. "You witnessed Avatar's destruction by Mahon."

"*Witnessed*, not convinced. He disappeared in white light, not grey. The bloody sword and Mahon's contrition might have swayed Dagar into believing the wound was lethal, but not me. It was all too easy."

"Well, whoever shows up, it will be too late. We'll make sure of that."

Zinna ran for several miles before stopping in a shaded ravine to assess the situation. This time she carefully stretched out her senses. She flinched at touching an essence close by. The brief contact caused alarm at possibly being followed. She armed her bow.

"You don't want to shoot me," a voice spoke from behind.

Zinna whirled about with her bow aimed. In annoyed relief, she lowered her weapon. "Gresham! Why didn't you identify yourself?"

"I did. I stopped you from shooting me." He flashed a toothy smile.

Annoyed by his humor, she moved passed him to continue south. "We can't stay here and argue. Witter and Altari are in the province."

Gresham drew his dagger to follow. "Jedrek reported they were in the Delta."

"Well, they're here now! I need to tell Kell what else I discovered. Back to the cottage."

"You're assuming Kell stayed there."

"With so few of us, I don't think he would leave until Jedrek is recovered. Or at the very least, out of danger." She stopped. "This should be far enough for safe travel." She put up her bow and held out her hands.

Gresham sheathed his dagger to take her hands. Speaking the Ancient, they disappeared in dimension travel. Upon reappearing at the cottage, her statement proved correct. Kell and Armus remained. They came off guard when the light faded.

"Is something wrong in the South Plains that you risk dimension travel?" Kell sheathed his sword.

"Not the South Plains." Zinna gave her report.

Kell's golden eyes narrowed with malice when she mentioned Dagar. Armus folded his arms across his chest, his expression grim.

"Summoning Dagar means Zared *does* have the talisman like Jedrek suspected," concluded Zinna.

"That's obvious!" groused Armus.

Kell walked to a front window. He stared outside. His expression perplexed, as he spoke under his breath. "Why haven't I sensed them?"

The others overheard him.

"Perhaps Dagar and the Dark Way have grown powerful enough to shield them from sensing," suggested Armus.

Kell tossed a none-too-pleased glance at Armus.

"It would explain a lot of recent activity going undetected," said Gresham. He now became the focus of Kell's displeasure.

"No matter how distasteful, you can't discount the possibility," said Armus.

Kell looked at the floor, took a deep breath and slowly exhaled. "No," he admitted. He said to Zinna, "Your report is appreciated."

"What about Jedrek? Is he any better?" she asked.

Kell smiled. "Ay. The Highland berries proved helpful. He will recover."

She also smiled at the news.

"Now, return *directly* to the South Plains. I'll go with Gresham to Midessex."

"Dimension travel is the most direct way."

Kell titled his head in consideration. "You already took a risk coming here. If what Armus suggests is actually the case, their senses may also be stronger."

"With things happening so fast, what choice do we have? We can't let them get the upper-hand."

He didn't argue her counterpoint. "Be careful when reappearing."

Zinna made the Guardian salute then disappeared in white light.

Zinna reappeared on the fringe of a thicket-ringed field halfway between the town of Burleigh and the South Plain's provincial castle. A startling sight greeted her. Shadow Warriors! Hundreds of them! Along with Shadow Archers and spirit stallions. Her astonishment turned to alarm upon hearing the *twang* of a bow. She barely stepped aside when a black and silver arrow lodged in the thicket beside her.

Twang! Twang! Bows fired in rapid succession. Zinna successfully dodged the second arrow but not the third. It ripped open a deep gash under the ribcage on her left side. She heard shouts of pursuit. Dimension travel was the only option of escape. However, with a wound, she couldn't travel very far. The foothills.

From the fading light of a difficult travel, she collapsed to all fours. The use of power aggravated her wound and sent searing pain through her body. She had to reach safety before any signs of pursuit. She ventured higher into the foothills.

Since being assigned the South Plains, she found a secure place to retreat for solace. The label of legend and disdain towards Jor'el and Guardians sometimes proved too much. Often, she needed to soothe her spirit. She managed to reach her safe haven without any signs of pursuit.

"Thank you, Jor'el," she prayed in relief. Using power and a serious wound combined to drain her energy. Before she realized it, she fell asleep.

***

Back in the field, Tor arrived at the line of Shadow Archer. "What are they shooting at?" he demanded of Nari.

"We sensed enemy presence," she replied.

"Who?"

Nari shrugged. "I couldn't clearly identify the essence."

A Shadow Archer raced over to give report. "I hit someone. Looks like a deep wound by the amount of blood." He showed them the arrow.

"Not a kill?" demanded Tor.

"I—" Before the Shadow Archer could react; Tor drew his sword and destroyed him. The Archer vanished in grey light. The arrow fell to the ground.

Tor addressed the disturbed onlookers. "Let that be a lesson! Destroy the enemy or be destroyed!" He picked up the arrow and shoved it at Nari. "Finish the job."

She snatched the arrow from her face. "It will delay our ultimate purpose."

The brazen rebuff made Tor accost her. "Are you defying my orders?"

"No, reminding *you* of *Dagar's* orders. Is a fleeting essence worth jeopardizing the plan?"

"That fleeting essence could alert Kell! You don't want that."

She held up the arrow. "If you can get Dagar's approval, I'll find the individual whose blood stains the arrow. If not, we continue."

Tor fiercely snarled. "Mark me well! If we experience any hint of Kell, I will do to you as I did the Archer."

At the threat, Nari righted her posture to remain steadfast under his punishing gaze. "So be it, Commander."

"Now get ready to march on Waldron!"

Chapter 15

ITH SUCH URGENCY, ARCHIMEDES AND NILES PRESSED their horses almost beyond endurance. Before leaving Waldron they took time to grab cloaks, gloves and flasks. They also placed an extra sword in their saddle sheaths.

Niles' horse began to stumble. He drew the animal to a stop and called to Archimedes, "We can't kill beasts or we'll never make it!"

Archimedes checked his mount. "We can't rest too long."

"Three to four hours at most. The horses need to recover, and it wouldn't hurt us to eat something either." Niles dismounted to lead his horse off the road. Archimedes mimicked Niles in walking his horse into the trees.

A half-mile off the road, they found a secluded ravine with a small stream. Niles took the reins of both horses and led the anxious mounts to the stream. The horses eagerly drank.

"That's enough for now." Niles brought the horses back to where Archimedes built a small fire. He tethered the animals with enough slack to feed on fall foliage and scrub grass. He then joined Archimedes.

"Doesn't look hot enough to cook anything," he said.

Archimedes ignored the comment to stoke the fire.

Niles continued with sarcasm, "I'll trap us something small."

Sure enough, Niles managed to snare a couple of rabbits. He prepared and cut them into pieces to fit on their swords. By that time, Archimedes had the fire hot enough to cook.

"What exactly did Jor'el tell you?" Niles asked.

Archimedes shrugged as he focused on cooking the rabbit. "Not much. Only that Wilbur is in grave danger and for us to ride to the Temple."

"Well, after what Wilbur said at high banquet—"

Archimedes sat up to confront Niles. "Every word was justified!"

"Easy! I agree." Niles grew serious in his verbal contemplation. "If Zared plans on employing Danior, it might not work. Wilbur put a fiat out on him. He goes anywhere near the Temple, he'll run afoul of all Jor'ellians and Temple Guards."

"Ay, but that doesn't explain why Jor'el appeared to me as he did."

"We may not know the reason until we get to Temple. All we can do is speculate and try to prepare for what we could encounter."

A brooding settled in. Archimedes tested the rabbit for cooking doneness.

Niles noticed the change to a sullen demeanor. "What's wrong? Other than us riding into unknown danger." He tried to add some levity.

Archimedes shied at answering which made Niles curious since shyness was not one of Archimedes' character traits.

"Truly, what is the matter?"

Archimedes scowled with frustration. "We rushed from Waldron without thought to anything or anyone else." His tone turned earnest, his expression entreating of Niles. "If something happens to me, I need you to help Wilma."

"Of course. Helping her and Myla is part of the plan."

"No, no, man, you don't understand! It's more than the plan." Archimedes sat perched on the log as if ready to pounce. His posture and tone suggesting deep seeded anxiety.

"I won't understand unless you clarify." Niles watched Archimedes wrestle with speaking. He took hold of Archimedes' arm. "We are brother Jor'ellians, and I think friends. You can trust me."

"I know," said Archimedes with a hint of a smile that quickly faded. "It's just, at this moment, I realize how much I love her. I mean I always did, but now, it's deeper than even I anticipated."

"Then marry her."

Archimedes looked directly at Niles. "I did."

Niles' initial surprise at the revelation turned into hearty laughter.

"*You* may think it's funny, but we wed in secret. With Berk's unpredictable behavior, there is no telling how he would respond to one of the Queen's lady marrying a mere knight." Archimedes grew reflective. "In truth, I've often wondered what she sees in me to make such a match. A commoner."

"My laughter is in rejoicing, not ridicule." Niles cocked a grin in regards of Archimedes. "As for what Wilma sees in you: a stouthearted man of courage, fortitude and a loyal heart toward to Jor'el."

Archimedes grew suspicious. "How would you know that?"

"Because, my friend, that is who you are. Your bearing of command, loyalty and courage are without question, even to the most cynical nobles at Court." Niles snickered. "Granted some don't like you due to those characteristics, but they are undeniable."

Archimedes appeared to blush and scowl at the same time. "Maybe, but it doesn't make me feel any better leaving her so suddenly. And in her condition! If something happens, I might not see my own child!"

"Ah, now I understand." Niles clapped Archimedes on the shoulder. "Put your mind at ease, my friend. If the worse should happen, I shall do as you ask."

Archimedes smiled in relief. "Thank you."

They consumed the rabbits in silence. Niles yawned, stretched and rubbed his neck in a weary gesture.

"I didn't realize you were so tired," teased Archimedes.

"I've been awake since yesterday morning. After the banquet, Berk allowed me to accompany him to his chambers. All the commotion prevented me from sleeping, so I stood guard all night. Then Abner's news about Danior, our urgent meeting and now we ride to the Temple."

"Sleep for a few hours. I'll keep watch."

"Wake me so you can sleep."

Archimedes simply nodded.

Niles wrapped his cloak about him and quickly fell asleep. The sleep went deeper than expected. He resisted the urging to wake, that was until he felt something cold and wet hit his face. He bolted up to a sitting position.

"That's better," said Archimedes. He held a flask.

Niles touched his face to discover what he felt was water. "Why did you do that?"

"You weren't waking up."

Being as the temperature was very cool, Niles used the corner of his cloak to wipe his face dry. He noticed the darkness and the fire out. "What time is it?"

"Around three in the morning. I let you sleep four hours."

"Don't you want to sleep?"

"No." Archimedes went to his horse, replaced the flask on saddlebow and mounted. He waited for Niles to mount before he spoke again. "A burrowing wombat appeared in camp. I snared it and cooked it for breakfast. You slept so soundly nothing woke you. Hence the water," he said with a teasing smile. "You'll find some of the wombat wrapped in a cloth in your saddlebag to eat as we ride."

For several hours they paced the horses between hard gallops and walking for recovery. They ate shortly after sunrise during a time of walking. When they made to continue the gallop, Archimedes' horse stumbled. This time Niles rode in the lead and didn't notice Archimedes pull up his mount.

"Niles!" Archimedes shouted. He jumped from the saddle to examine his horse's right foreleg.

Niles rode back. "What happened?"

"Not sure, but the leg feels lame."

"Good morning, gentlemen," they heard a female say.

On the road in front of them, she appeared. A forester by her clothing, complete with a crossbow and quiver. Auburn hair shone in the morning sunlight. In height, she was taller than most women, though

175

shorter than Archimedes, who had four inches on Niles. This made her in between the men in height.

"Good morning, miss," said Niles with perplexity. "Are you lost?"

She lightly chuckled. "No. But it appears you are in some trouble." She motioned to the horse.

"Lame. Hopefully nothing some rest won't cure," said Archimedes.

"May I?" she asked while approaching the horse.

"I don't know what help you can offer."

She widely smiled, her green eyes bright. "I have a way with animals." She reached into her pouch. "Along with some liniment that I'm certain will help her."

Archimedes stepped aside to allow her access to the horse's right foreleg. Once kneeling beside the horse, she applied the liniment. All the while she whispered in a breathy tone with indistinct syllables

"Sounds like a song," said Niles.

She glanced at him with a soft smile. "I find it soothes them." She took a cloth from her pouch to wrap it around the horse's leg. She stood up to stroke the animal's cheek. "There. That should help you."

The mare neighed and tossed her head in affirmative response.

Archimedes' eyes showed steady on the woman. "You do have a way with animals. Not to mention appearing from almost nowhere."

Her smile grew wide. "Take it as a gesture of divine good will."

"*Finn-seul!*" said Archimedes in amazement.

"Servant, same as both of you."

"Legends have names," Niles kindly insisted.

"Faith is all that matters in times like these." Wren's serious yet encouraging gaze shifted between them. "Gird your hearts and steel your courage, for you shall need both." She motioned to the horses. "Ride well and steady, faithful Jor'ellians."

Wren watched Niles and Archimedes follow her instructions. She thought to wait until they vanished from sight. She suddenly shivered with an overwhelming sensation of evil. She raced back under the cover of the forest where she immediately lost her shift and reverted to her

Guardian form. Disconcerted, Wren stared off in the distance across the road. Hearing something from behind, she whipped out her crossbow to face whatever approached.

Barnum stepped out with his arms raise. "No cause for alarm."

"What are you doing here?"

"I could ask you the same since we're both in Midessex rather than our own provinces," he said with rakish smile. It faded at her annoyance. "I've been staying close to the border in case of trouble. The unsettling sense is growing. I came to investigate. That's when I saw you. Why are you here?"

Wren put up her crossbow. "Like you, I've been staying close to the border. Each time I get a prompting by Jor'el; I respond. Lately my task is to shadow mortals on a journey. Archimedes and Niles are heading to the Temple in a hurry." She grew disturbed. "Just now a forceful evil drove me to take cover since I couldn't maintain my shift."

Contemplating the news, Barnum surveyed the road seen through the trees. "Did you ask them why they are going to the Temple?"

"No. I just helped one of the horses that had gone lame. Whatever the reason, I sense they *must* reach the Temple. Now, I shouldn't let them get too far ahead."

Chapter 16

K ELL APPEARED IN THE ANTECHAMBER TO WILBUR'S QUARTERS. He dimmed the light from his dimension travel. Being so late at night, he didn't expect anyone to notice. In fact, only a few mortals accepted the reality of Guardians. Still, it was better to be cautious than cause undue surprise since this visit required stealth and not direct contact like before.

Each time Kell visited the Temple, he immediately felt a surge of power, as if renewing his full strength. While a blessing to feel whole again, it was also a sad reminder of the present. This time he didn't relish the sensation, as the urging to visit the Vicar felt ominous.

Kell moved silently into Wilbur's bedroom. To his surprise, the Vicar lay sleeping, peaceful from the look of it. Kell leaned down to determine if Wilbur actually slept, or something worse. He heard the rhythmic breathing of sleep. Placing his hand gently on Wilbur's forehead, he sensed no distress. Strange. Why so urgent? He closed his eyes, bowed his head and folded his hands under his chin. "Jor'el, why did you send me here if he sleeps in peace?" he whispered a prayerful inquiry.

After a moment, Kell's eyes opened. He knelt beside the bed to once more place a hand on Wilbur's forehead. He leaned his mouth close to the Vicar's ear to speak the Ancient. "Hear me, Wilbur, Vicar of Jor'el, your task is not complete. Do not wait until morning. Rise and finish what you started, only keep it secret until the time of revealing. His name means *to think of Jor'el first.*"

When Wilbur stirred, Kell stepped into a dark corner. Though a clandestine visit, he remained to ensure the task was done. He watched Wilbur sit up on the opposite side of the bed. He lit a candle on the nightstand. Kell concealed himself partially behind a curtain. Wilbur didn't seem to notice any movement when he made his way across the room to a desk.

Kell continued to observe. The scratching of a quill on paper began. Ten minutes later, Wilbur sprinkled the paper with dusting power, gently blew it off. He picked up a bell on his desk and rang it. Several moments passed before a blurry-eyed man arrived.

"You rang, Vicar?"

"Summon Kincaid and Delbert immediately."

"Vicar, it's three o'clock in the morning."

"I don't care what time it is!" He roughly waved the man away.

Another ten minutes passed before the summoned men appeared. Delbert wore a dressing gown while Kincaid a hastily donned Jor'ellian uniform. Delbert yawned.

"You sent for us, Vicar?" asked Kincaid.

"The Writ of Succession." Wilbur indicated the document in front of him on the desk.

Kincaid straightened with surprised dignity.

Delbert's fatigue vanished at the statement. "Vicar, the duty of witness—" he began in dispute.

Wilbur's hand on Delbert's arm and kind smile stopped the objection. "It falls to you on this occasion."

Delbert's impulsive smile quickly faded. "May I inquire if the Headmaster's name—" he motioned to the document unable to finish.

Wilbur again smiled and shook his head. "One of whom Jor'el is more pleased." He held up the quill for them. "Now, gentlemen, propriety must be observed."

Delbert and Kincaid obliged by signing the document. Both grinned at reading the name. When they finished, Wilbur sprinkled more dusting powder on the document and gently blew it off. He offered up a prayer as he folded it, applied sealing wax then took his holy ring of office to stamp it closed.

Wilbur placed both hands on the document. "Your will is done, Jor'el. May my successor be worthy of so honored a position." He bowed his head with hands folded. "Tangiel."

"Tangiel," Delbert and Kincaid agreed.

"Now, gentlemen, your word of silence about this Writ. Not until absolutely necessary is the existence to be revealed."

Kincaid came to attention. "My oath as a Jor'ellian, I will keep silent."

"My word before Jor'el, not a word shall pass my lips," said Delbert.

Wilbur graciously said, "I bid you both, goodnight."

After Kincaid and Delbert left, Wilbur rose. It took effort for the aged Vicar to move the heavy, bulking desk. In the rear of the desk, he opened a compartment and placed the document inside. Using his weight helped to slide the desk back into place.

Wilbur took several breaths of recovery before he shuffled back to bed. With a yawn of great fatigue, he blew out the candle and nestled under the covers. His head no sooner hit the pillow then Kell appeared.

"Sleep. You have done well, faithful Vicar," said Kell. Almost immediately, Wilbur's body relaxed with the rhythmic sound of peaceful breath.

Kell returned to the antechamber, only he couldn't shut the door. Instead, he stared at Wilbur with concern. "Why do I still sense trouble?" He glanced upwards "Jor'el?" He didn't receive an answer. Kell vacillated about staying in hopes of determining the source of the continuing disturbance.

"Leave," said a soft, yet audible voice.

"Jor'el?"

"Leave," the voice said again.

Kell hesitated with befuddlement. "Are you certain?"

"You question me, Captain?"

"No, but—"

"Leave!" this time the voice spoke with command. "Return to the Meadowlands, and wait."

Although vexed by the command, Kell shut the door and disappeared in dimension travel.

Kell reappeared at the cottage in the Meadowlands. To his pleasant surprise, Jedrek sat at the table in the front room with Armus across from him. Eldric stood scowling at them. Not an unusual expression for the prime physician.

Kell smiled at Jedrek. "Ah, good to see you up."

"I couldn't resist the smell of Armus' cooking." Jedrek indicated the array of empty plates in front of him.

"He ate an entire boar, along with a dozen potatoes, five loaves of bread and four bottles of wine," said Armus.

Jedrek's grin grew mischievous. "I needed all of it to offset the taste of the tonics."

Eldric huffed at the jab and protested to Kell. "Don't let him fool you. He's out of bed sooner than he should be. That's why he put away more food than a *healthy* Guardian needs, which would be nothing, *if* he finished the treatment."

"Not too much food for one who must replenish his energy from healing," countered Armus.

Kell stopped Eldric's protest. "There is enough tension with the current situation. We don't need to add any more by squabbling." With Eldric subdued, Kell asked him, "Now, is Jedrek fully healed?"

Eldric placed a hand on Jedrek's forehead. The warrior went to resist, only thought better of it at Kell's interest. Eldric closed his eyes for a brief moment then spoke, "Ay, he's healed."

Jedrek smiled, wide and satisfied. "I told you."

"Good, because each of you must return to your provinces. Something is about to happen, which I believe involves the Vicar." Kell's expression turned worried.

"What makes you think that?" asked Armus.

"I couldn't determine why I sensed trouble when Jor'el sent me to Wilbur."

"Then why have you returned?" asked Jedrek.

Kell's brows furrowed deeper with consideration. "While Wilbur slept, Jor'el had me speak to his mind that it was time to name his successor. Yet when I inquired about the unsettling feeling, the response didn't sound like Jor'el."

"You mean in vocal quality?" asked Armus with some confusion.

"No, I mean in a way unthinkable." Kell looked directly at Armus. "Even with the Dark Way confirmed, and the trouble I felt in my spirit, Jor'el *ordered me* to leave Wilbur and wait in the Meadowlands!"

Stunned by the implication, Armus, Jedrek and Eldric started at Kell. After heavy moment of silence, Eldric asked, "Why would he leave the Vicar vulnerable?"

"Ay, there has always been a Guardian Overseer protecting the Vicar of Jor'el," said Jedrek.

"I don't know. And *that* has me greatly worried. There are times I sense things clearly and other times not!" Kell complained with vexation.

"A sad part of our punishment," groused Armus.

"I thought it was Wren's job to state the obvious," Jedrek said with flippancy.

Kell ignored the humor to ask Jedrek, "Are you capable of dimension travel?"

"Ay." Jedrek sent a sideways glare of warning to Eldric, even though the physician voiced no objection.

"Return immediately. *I* must wait." Angst crept into Kell's voice.

Jedrek made the Guardian salute. He disappeared in white light. Eldric gave Kell a nod before he too disappeared.

"You don't have to wait alone. This is my province. I don't need to go anywhere." Armus flashed a smile of encouragement.

Kell replied with a half-hearted nod. He glanced to the ceiling. "Please tell me the reason I'm to wait is for good and not ill." When his plea was met with silence, frustration spilled forth. He picked up a plate and threw it across the room where it smashed against a wall. "Why can I not act?"

Armus warily watched the unusual explosion of temper. "What do you mean?"

"Exactly what I said … act! Just like my senses are limited, I feel a restraint in acting upon what I *do* perceive. Oh, I've made visits to key mortals, but taking direct part is almost … forbidden!"

"Then don't fight the prohibition."

Kell glared crossly at Armus. "I am *captain!* It's hard to stand by and watch others suffer due to dangers I should be active in repelling."

Armus remained calm in the face of such a forceful argument. "When helping Tristan, you tried to prevent Avatar from fulfilling his assignment, only Jor'el made it clear his plans would not be thwarted. Perhaps, the Almighty is defining *your* role in this present situation."

Kell's great displeasure at the reasoning made Armus continue by quoting,

"Back then you said; *The moment my full strength returns, I will appear, and Dagar will curse the day he chose to rebel. For on that day, every Guardian and mortal who has suffered will be avenged!*" His voice filled with sympathetic certainty when concluding, "Kell, it's not your time yet."

The battle between realization and frustration showed on Kell's face. Even when taking a deep breath to regain his temper, a grunt of vexation escaped. He picked up another plate and threw it, only this time in a final release of emotion.

"There is an easier way to clean off a table," said a voice, though flat in tone.

Kell rolled his eyes before turning around. "Gresham, I'm in no mood for humor."

"Humor isn't what brings me here." Gresham's gaze direct on the captain. "Shadow Warriors have crossed into Midessex by way of the Upper Pass."

The news surprised Kell. "From the North Plains?" He inquired of Armus, "Did Mona send word of trouble while I was gone?"

"No. They could have crossed the Talmadge from the South Plains to make it appear that way."

"The bridge isn't finished," countered Kell.

"Maybe it is," said Gresham.

Kell cocked a dubious eyebrow. "Two years ahead of schedule? Mortals in the Plains are not that helpful toward one another."

"If the Shadow Warrior's powers are enhanced by the Dark Way, forging a river shouldn't be too difficult," said Armus.

"If that were the case, we should sense a large disturbance in the transverse!" chided Kell in dispute.

"Well, however they got to the North Plains, they are in Midessex *now*," said Gresham with emphasis.

Kell didn't argue further rather asked, "Are they heading toward Waldron?"

Gresham shrugged. "I don't know. I learned from overhearing some mortals that they made camp shortly after arriving in the province. Perhaps they are waiting for orders."

"We need to be certain!" snapped Kell. "Find them and learn what you can."

"On foot or dimension travel? One would be safer while the other faster."

Kell thought for a brief moment. "Dimension travel to Arundine and then proceed on foot."

Chapter 17

AFTER REAPPEARING AT ARUNDINE, GRESHAM TOOK A MOMENT to rest on the portico. Just like at the Temple, a sense of power came from being at Arundine. The short-lived surge of strength helped Gresham recover from his second dimension travel of the day. He used the added energy to stretch out his senses in careful search for any spiritual essence in the province.

He cried out in pain and staggered backwards into the massive ornate wooden doors. The repelling force that plagued them of late felt more powerful. Of course, the large presence of Shadow Warriors could enhance the force. He waited for the pain to subside before deciding on how to proceed.

Since Zinna reported activity at Ravendale that would be the most likely place for Shadow Warriors to gather. The ruins lay northwest. With speedy stealth, Gresham raced from Arundine. By dawn, he reached the confluence of waters where the smaller and gentle Samhach River met the mighty Bendix.

A division in sense made him halt. The spiritual sense of danger led west toward Ravendale while the uneasiness came from the east, in the direction of Waldron. For several moments, Gresham wondered about which sense to follow. The recent difficulty at Waldron dealt with Zared's influence over Berk. Zared left Waldron for Ravendale; meaning whatever happens at the ruins will impact Waldron. If he could discover Zared's plan, perhaps the Guardians could prevent anything from adversely affecting the royal family. He headed west along the banks of the Samhach.

At the narrowest and shallowest part of the river, he crossed to the other side. Going on foot was less risky than dimension travel. The depth of water reached shoulder high. The coolness didn't trouble him. Temperature variations were inconsequential to Guardians. Once across, he again ran. He slowed his pace when drawing closer to the ruins. He needed to conserve his strength in case he ran afoul of Shadow Warriors.

Upon reaching a knoll two miles from Ravendale, a cold dread gripped him so hard that it wrenched the breath from his lungs. He stumbled to take cover in a cleft on the knoll. The difficulty breathing lasted for several moments. Finally, he could breathe easy. Gresham touched his face to find he perspired, something unusual for a Guardian.

"What manner of evil have you concocted now, Dagar?" he muttered. He looked from his hand to the sky. "Jor'el, give me strength."

Recovered from the strangling dread, Gresham used the knoll as a screen to approach the ruins. The awareness of evil increased with each step. He gripped the hilt of his dagger for a quick draw. Under his breath, Gresham spoke the Ancient to shield him from discovery. He dashed behind an abandoned pile of overgrown bricks mixed with quarried stone. The ruins of Ravendale lay a mile away. He stopped at maxing sensing distance; at least the old maximum distance. What if the Dark Way enhancement extended that distance? It may also veil any nearby essence. He spoke in the Ancient before peeking out from the pile.

"Sight be great and ears be sharp, help to discern what lies in the dark."

With great concentration, Gresham's violet eyes glowed while making a scan of the ruins. He exhaled with exhaustion from the effort. He sat back against the pile confused at sensing nothing! Zinna reported the presence of Shadow Warriors. He confirmed they had been there, but now gone.

He rubbed his aching eyes before once again staring at the ruins. This time he attempted to gauge where they went. "North!" That could mean only one thing. The Shadow Warriors headed to the Pass of Peace! To The Temple!

Not bothering to hide his presence, Gresham ran north. He covered five miles in less than five minutes, expending a great deal of energy to locate them. He staggered to a halt on a rise where he could see the main road. The urgency of his travel made him out of breath, another unusual side effect of punishment.

Three miles ahead moved a very large contingent of Shadow Warriors with spirit stallions and Shadow Archers.

"Merciful heaven," he murmured.

Kell ordered him to learn what he could. He drew his dagger. It would be risky but … he disappeared in dimension travel.

Gresham reappeared on a foothill overlooking where the main road entered the Pass of Peace. The pass was a narrow valley of a half-mile wide between the foothills of the Tulairde Mountain Range. The foothills served as the border between Midessex and the Region of Sanctuary. The enemy's force now lay a couple of miles behind him.

Movement caught Gresham's attention. Two mounted mortals appeared riding up from the south. They pushed their horses at a frantic pace to enter the Pass. He recognized them. The speed of the Shadow Warrior army seemed to accelerate in nearing the pass. If they catch the mortals … Gresham had to act fast.

He raced back along the hillside using the evergreen trees and brush for cover. Of course, moving toward the Shadow Warriors meant possible discovery by sight not just sense. Spying the perfect combinations of rocks at an outcropping, Gresham got an idea. If he blocked the path, it could gain the mortals time to hopefully avoid detection.

"*Tuit a caill!*" he spoke the Ancient command and struck the overhanging boulder with his dagger.

A loud crack echoed. The boulder separated from the outcropping. Unfortunately, this loosened other parts of the ground, namely everything under Gresham. The breaking away of a large section swept him down the hillside along with the rocks. He desperately tried to control his descent.

The landside covered the road about a hundred yards in front of the Shadow Warriors. Gresham ended up sprawled on top of the back portion of the slide.

"A Guardian!"

Gresham pushed himself up to see four Shadow Warriors advancing towards him. Witter rode in the lead. Not good! He quickly looked for his dagger. It lay a few feet to his right. He had no choice but to call upon his power and reverse discovery. He snatched the dagger and placed it in front of his face.

"Time and space hear my sound, make the near past appear as now!"

The plain dagger transformed into one with sparkling jewels. From the jewels, a rainbow of colors swirled toward the Shadow Warriors. Everything became distorted in a spiral of colors. With a brilliant burst of blinding color, the scene reset to Gresham on top of the hill ready to strike the boulder. The Shadow Warriors were on the road, unaware of anything.

Again Gresham spoke *"Tuit a caill!"* However, this time when he struck the boulder, he disappeared in dimension travel.

Gresham reappeared on the portico of Arundine where he collapsed into unconsciousness. The dagger fell from his hand. Even the appearance of multiple flashes of white light didn't rouse him.

Chase and Priscilla rushed to Gresham

"How is he?" she asked.

Chase felt Gresham's face. "He's cool, too cool. Get the door. We'll take him inside." He tucked Gresham's dagger in his belt before lifting him.

Priscilla placed both hands on the massive ornate door. *"Fosgail!"* The doors opened upon command. The hinges creaked from lack of use. She let Chase enter first.

Chase laid Gresham on the floor in front of the Midessex chair. He examined Gresham. "He's barely breathing, and his lips are turning blue. Whatever happened, it drained his life-force to almost nothing."

"Eldric may still be at the cottage." She tried to sound hopeful.

Chase shook his head. "I don't believe Gresham could survive the travel. I'm hoping being in here will slow the lifeforce drain to give him a fighting chance."

"I'll fetch Eldric." Priscilla took a few steps away and vanished.

Chase gently stroked Gresham hair. "I'm not sure what you did, my friend, but I pray it's worth such a sacrifice." He sat back on his heels to look up. "Jor'el, how many more will we lose before you fulfill your promise of our restoration?" His voice cracked with emotion. He turned his attention to Gresham. "I'd gladly give you some of my strength if I knew it would help you recover."

"Then two would be sacrificed instead of one." Kell knelt opposite Chase.

Chase glanced around. "Where is Eldric?"

"He returned to the Lowlands now that Jedrek is well."

"And Priscilla? Where is she?"

"Taking a much needed rest after two quick travels. I told Armus to summon Eldric." Kell's brows furrowed with distress at Gresham's haggard state. "He must have encountered Shadow Warriors. He reported that they moved into Midessex from the North Plains."

"It forced him to use his power." Chase removed the dagger to show Kell. It remained in its original jeweled form.

Kell took the dagger to focus on the blade. "*Nochag mi.*"

At the captain's command, images appeared on the blade. Chase moved to Kell's shoulder to view the replay of events. The scene began with Gresham's first command and striking the boulder. They watched him fall with the rocks, his discovery and invoking his power to alter a short period of time. When Gresham hit the boulder a second time, he disappeared and arrived at Arundine. The blade gleamed with white light before reverting back to a plain looking dagger.

"It showed us what happened, but the question remains *why?*" said Chase.

"Obviously, he used the time reversion to wipe away any memory of his presence. Dagar can't learn we are around."

"I understood that from the images. But *why* create the landslide?"

Armus entered Arundine with Eldric. The physician appeared weary. No surprise since he already expended a lot of energy.

"I assumed you dimension traveled," said Kell.

"Ay," replied Armus.

Eldric's weariness became replaced by dreadful concern. He knelt to examine Gresham. "He's almost gone. Strengthening tonics won't work." He stared earnestly at Kell. "You realize that if I use my power, one or both of us, may not survive."

Kell held up Gresham's dagger. "He used *his* power to prevent our presence from being discovered by Shadow Warriors."

The sobriety of the news struck Eldric hard. "May Jor'el have mercy on us."

Armus took hold of Eldric's shoulder. "Take heart. We are at Arundine."

Eldric took a deep breath then placed one hand on Gresham's forehead and the other over Gresham's heart. "Eternal spirit, immortal strength, wrapped in fragile frame awake. Heed the Creator's call to serve and return to this mortal world." Underneath his hands, an amber glow appeared.

Eldric repeated the phrased several times. With each reciting, the amber glow spread out until the aura enveloped Gresham from head to toe. After the fifth recitation, Gresham gasped for air though his eyes remained close. Exhausted, Eldric collapsed back on his rump. Armus supported the prime physician.

Kell seized Gresham's shoulders. "Gresham? Can you hear me?"

Eldric spoke, low and weary. "He won't respond just yet. I healed him, but only to the point of not dying. If I expended any more effort, *neither of us* would be here," he spoke the last sentence with great emphasis.

"How long till he wakes?"

The physician heaved a shrug, still recovering. "Difficult to say. Minutes. Hours. I don't know." Eldric closed his eyes and held his head.

"You need to rest also," said Armus.

"Huh! What gave you that idea?"

Chase grinned. "Well, fatigue hasn't affected your surly bedside manner."

Eldric lied down on the floor to rest.

"Need a strengthening tonic?" Armus received no reply, as Eldric fell asleep.

Kell said to Chase, "Return to the West Coast." The light no sooner faded from Chase's departure than Kell's eyes widened with alarm. He hastily spoke to Armus. "Go to the Temple . . . as Finn."

"Why?"

"Just go!"

Chapter 18

ALTHOUGH FULLY DRESSED AND WEARING A CLOAK TO CONCEAL his identity, Odell moved with jerky anxiousness. Clandestine activity was unfamiliar to him, but he made an agreement. Despite the dwindling numbers of Jor'ellians, Kincaid still posted guards; thus navigating the Temple compound to the rear buildings required precaution.

Several anxious moments passed, as Odell waited in the shadows across from the postern gate. The nightwatch inspected the gate before proceeding. Once they disappeared from sight, Odell rushed to the gate. He continued to glance about for signs of anyone. A noise made him flinch. It took a moment to recognize the signal. He unlocked the gate and opened it just enough to allow a cloaked, hooded man to enter. With the man inside, Odell closed but didn't lock the gate.

"Danior?" he asked.

"No names, you fool! You knew the sign so why else open the gate?"

"I needed to be sure. I'm taking a great risk."

"They are waiting for you by the trees to take you to safety."

"Some may ask questions when I'm not found."

"Are you turning coward?" Danior challenged.

"No! Just cautious."

"All will be remedied when this done. Now, go!" Danior opened the gate and shoved Odell through.

Dawn broke over the horizon. Niles and Archimedes pushed their struggling horses to complete the last mile to the Temple.

Reaching the front gate, Archimedes called, "By order of the First Jor'ellian, open the gate!" He felt the horse beneath him tremble and snort, near the point of collapse. "Quickly!" he impatiently shouted upon hearing movement behind the gate.

A priest complied. Archimedes kicked the horse to move. The animal loudly protested. Struck by the reins, it lurched through the gate before stumbling. He managed to dismount before the animal collapsed.

Niles' horse barely stayed on its feet. Its head nearly touched the ground when Niles dismounted. "Where are the guards?" he asked.

"Doesn't matter!" snapped Archimedes.

Niles rushed after Archimedes in heading for the main entrance of the Temple. "Of course it matters! It's dereliction of duty not to protect the Temple."

"Morning prayers!" Archimedes said over this shoulder.

Niles understood. Despite being very early, the Vicar oversaw morning prayers before breakfast. They rushed inside the Temple.

Archimedes' jowls tightened at the disturbing sight. "No one?"

"Could they have already concluded morning prayers and be at breakfast?"

Shouting and high pitched calling came from outside. They emerged to find priests and guards rushing about the compound.

Disguised as Commander Finn, Armus ran from the barracks area. Surprised at seeing Niles and Archimedes, he asked, "What are you two doing here?"

"Never mind us, what is happening?" rebuffed Archimedes.

"A thousand talents to the one who finds the perpetrator!" shouted Kincaid.

"Here now, what's going on?" demanded Archimedes.

Kincaid made defense when someone grabbed his arm. It took a moment to recognize the First Jor'ellian. "The Vicar's been struck down!"

"Where is he?"

"His chamber."

Archimedes shoved Kincaid aside and raced to the building housing the Vicar's private quarters. Niles and Armus were close at his heels.

"Make way!" Archimedes pushed past grieving priests.

Lieutenant Markes lay in the threshold, bloodied from a very serious wound. He still held his sword. While Archimedes and Niles rushed into the chamber, Armus knelt. The lieutenant's eyes were shrouded but he showed signs of life.

With urgent sympathy, Armus held Markes' shoulder. "Lieutenant? It's Commander Finn. Can you hear me?"

Markes managed to open his eyes. He licked his lips to speak. "Commander ... I'm sorry ... I tried to stop him ..." His voice faded.

"I'm sure you did." Armus noticed the gravity of the wound. "You two!" He beckoned the priests. "Take him to the infirmary and see he gets the best of care."

Upon entering the room, Armus watched Niles and Archimedes lift Wilbur from the floor to place him on the bed. A grieving priest muttered prayers. Armus joined them at the foot of the bed. Blood stained the entire front of the Vicar's dressing gown.

"How is he?" asked Armus with a quiver of dread.

"Still alive," said Niles.

Archimedes examined the wound just above the heart. "Doubtful he'll survive much longer. Blood loss suggests it nicked the heart. The blow just missed being instantly fatal."

Niles stood on the opposite side of the bed from Archimedes. He accosted the priest. "Alfie, what happened?"

Alfie sniffled back a sob to reply. "I don't know. I came to help him prepare for morning prayers when I found him like this with Lieutenant Markes at the door, also wounded." He pointed to the threshold.

"I had them take Markes to the infirmary," said Armus.

"Where is Odell? Why isn't the he here?" chided Archimedes.

Alfie struggled with emotions and could only shrug ignorance.

"Find him!"

Alfie left to comply.

Wilbur stirred in an attempt to speak, only his words unintelligible.

Archimedes returned his attention to the Vicar. "My lord?"

With great agitation, Wilbur continued to mumble. Archimedes placed a comforting hand on Wilbur's forehead. "Easy, Wilbur."

The Vicar's eyes slowly opened. Unable to focus, he weakly asked, "Who?"

"Archimedes." He smiled kindly, his eyes compassionate upon Wilbur.

Wilbur's eyes opened wider with surprise, which quickly turned to concern. "Archimedes!" He grabbed hold of Archimedes' belt for he couldn't raise his arm any further. "Hear me." He tugged to bring Archimedes closer. The First Jor'ellian obliged by sitting on the bed.

"Are we alone?" asked Wilbur.

"No. Niles, Commander Finn and some other priests are here."

"Make everyone leave! Except Niles and Finn."

Armus heard and ushered the others out of the room. When he shut the door, he returned to stand by the head of the bed. "It is done as you requested, Vicar."

Looking into Armus' bright chestnut eyes, Wilbur managed a small smile. "Around my neck is a chain with an amulet. Give it to Niles."

When Armus complied, Niles examined the oddly shaped amulet. "What is it?"

Wilbur made a feeble shake of his head. "I don't know its purpose, only that it came from the heavenlies, and told I would know the person to whom it is to be given." His words came staggered due to difficulty breathing.

Hearing the origin, Niles asked in confusion, "Why me?"

"That is for you to learn. I was just to keep it safe." Wilbur gasped in great pain. His body relaxed. His eyes closed.

"Wilbur?" Archimedes seized the Vicar's shoulder.

The Vicar's eyes barely opened. His time nearly over, as told by the distant gaze in his eyes. With a feeble hand, he beckoned Archimedes closer. "It is in the secret compartment of my desk. Get it!" he whispered with urgency.

Archimedes moved to the desk. Uncertain of where to look, he said, "Help me find this compartment."

"Stay with him," Armus said to Niles in regards to Wilbur. He aided Archimedes to search every drawer and cubbyhole on the elaborate desk. Rather, Archimedes searched while Armus narrowed his eyes to focus on the desk in secret search. He reached behind the desk. *Click! Thud.*

Archimedes straightened at the sound. "What is that? Have you found something?"

"I'll have to move the desk to see clearly." Armus waited for Archimedes to step back. With little effort, he moved the desk from against the wall to view the backside. A door stood slightly ajar due to the wall preventing it from completely opening. Once away from any obstruction, it easily opened. Armus reached inside and pulled out a sealed document. He and Archimedes returned to the bed.

"Is this what you meant, Vicar? I found it in a back compartment," said Armus.

In a voice barely above a whisper, Wilbur said, "Give to Archimedes." A small shaky smile appeared when he said to Archimedes, "Read it, and do your position proud, as you have made me." He breathed his last.

Niles placed a hand on Wilbur's neck. By his forlorn expression, the Vicar was dead. For a moment no one spoke, each absorbing the grief of what just happened.

Tears filled Archimedes' eyes in regard of Wilbur. "Before Jor'el, I swear, we will find the person responsible."

"Before then you might want to read what he felt was so important," said Armus.

Archimedes broke the seal and unfolded the document to read.

Since Archimedes' expression remained unchanged, Niles couldn't tell the contents. "Well?"

Instead of answering, Archimedes gave it to Niles. Armus looked over Niles' shoulder. When finished, Niles inquired of Archimedes, "Will you accept?"

Armus watched with guarded anticipation of the answer.

Archimedes straightened to square his shoulders. "My heart and conscience compel me to do so."

Niles cocked a smile. "Odell may fight you."

Archimedes wryly replied, "Let him try." He took back the document.

Niles' smile faded. "Berk and Zared won't be pleased."

"They don't have a choice when the successor has been legally declared." He indicated the document.

Armus pointedly asked, "Are you ready to take on Zared? To face the Dark Way as Vicar?"

Switching to the Ancient, Archimedes replied with a voice inflection and facial expression suggesting comprehension. "I think you know the answer, *Commander Finn-seul.*"

Armus arched a brow of surprise at Archimedes' acknowledgement of his identity.

Niles flinched in wonder then grinned. "Two in one day."

"Two?" inquired Armus.

"A female we met on the road when my horse became lame," said Archimedes with grin. "After her *divine* aid, the animal wasn't lame anymore."

Niles glanced to the bed. "Alas, even with such help we didn't make it time."

"The Vicar lived long enough to impart what was needed," said Armus. His glance shifted between Niles and Archimedes. "Now, it's time for others to take up the cause. Be assured, Jor'el will not abandon his faithful no matter how bleak it may get."

The implication made Niles grip the hilt of his sword in readiness. Archimedes simply stared at Armus to inquire, "Will you remain to pay homage to him and witness my ordination?"

A poignant smile appeared, as Armus glanced to Wilbur while replying. "Alas, no. At present, duty takes me elsewhere." He then spoke directly to Archimedes. "We do grieve deeply with you on his behalf." After a brief, thoughtful glance back to Wilbur, he added, "Keep his wake and your ordination as secret as possible."

"Why? Surely Zared has knowledge of this!" Archimedes motioned to the bed.

"If not in some way responsible," chided Niles.

Armus shook his head. "Don't tip your hand too soon. If Zared believes he has the advantage, he may make a mistake that can be seized upon." He moved around the bed to Archimedes. He took hold of the mortal's shoulders to meet the steady gaze. "Like Wilbur, you will be tried and tested. During those times, remember, *you* are Jor'el's chosen for this task."

"I shall remember," affirmed Archimedes.

After taking a few steps from Archimedes, Armus spoke to Niles. "Remain to pay your respects and act as witness."

"I shall." Niles held up the necklace. "Can you tell me what this is?"

"No, I can't tell you anymore than Wilbur. Though forged in the heavenlies, we don't always know the reason, we simply obey the same as you." Armus came to attention and made the Jor'ellian salute. "For Jor'el, For Allon, be strong, Champion."

Niles returned the salute. Armus left.

Outside, Armus wandered the compound using his heavenly senses along with keen eyes to determine how such a thing could happen. To breach Temple security needed planning and stealth.

During his hour-long exploration of the compound, grief among the mortals was palpable. He had to ignore the mournful mood to concentrate on his task. The passing of the Vicar of Jor'el always caused deep sorrow in the Guardian ranks. Yet there was something profoundly disturbing about Wilbur's death. Being murder made Armus consider it directly linked to the rising tide of darkness.

Spying Alfie, Armus stopped to make inquiry. "Did you inform Headmaster Odell of the tragedy?"

"I can't find him, and no one knows where he is."

Not the answer Armus expected. "Did he give any indication of leaving on some errand prior to this?"

"I don't know. Some speculate … but I shouldn't repeat gossip," Alfie balked.

Gossip or not, he needed to know, so Armus pressed, "Speculate what?" When the priest hesitated, Armus insisted. "It could be of vital importance. The Headmaster may also be danger."

"That's not what they speculate," Alfie groused. "Some wonder if he left the order because Wilbur didn't name him as successor."

"Alfie!" another priest beckoned to him.

"I need to go." Alfie left.

Following up on what Alfie said, Armus made a few more inquiries about Odell. He discovered confirmation of what Alfie said regarding speculation of Odell's sudden absence but nothing to aid his investigation.

Unsuccessful at finding clues in the compound, Armus thought to investigate outside. He made his way to the postern gate. Unlocked! Well, it was now daylight, so the gate could be unlocked for various reasons. No, not with the current unrest, that would be foolhardy. Armus exited the gate. Two hundred yards of open plain lay between the compound and surrounding forest.

The moment Armus stepped outside, it hit him, and hard. The Dark Way! He hastened back inside the compound and waited a moment. No sensation of the Dark Way, so he again stepped outside. The Dark Way! Somehow the enemy managed to reach the postern gate, but not enter the Temple compound. Not good for them to come this close.

Armus carefully followed the sense of the Dark Way into the forest. He also used his tracking skills to search for visible signs. After a half-mile in the forest, he came to a small grove. He knelt when finding some disturbance on the ground. He focused on the spot and stretched out his senses. A mortal. Odell perhaps? Then others . . . the enemy! He gasped when a repelling force knocked him back onto his rump.

In bracing the fall, his right hand hit something sharp and hard. A brooch. The type used to hold a cloak closed, and fashioned with the Temple symbol in the center. The clasp was broken.

Armus stood. He stared back in the direction of the Temple. There was no way to tell exactly who or how the perpetrator accomplished his task, but he needed to return and make a sorrowful report.

Chapter 19

A T ARUNDINE, GRESHAM SAT IN THE MIDESSEX CHAIR. Although he appeared weary, some color returned to his face. Eldric sat in the chair beside Gresham, also recovering. Kell knelt and rummaged through Eldric's medical bag.

"You need to resupply ingredients for strengthening tonics," said Kell.

Bright light filled the hall, signaling the arrival of more than one Guardian. Kell rose in anticipation of the fading light. Barnum, Valmar, Jedrek, Wren, Priscilla, Chase and Mona arrived.

"What are all of you doing here?" Kell asked.

"We sensed a summoning in our spirits to come to Arundine immediately," said Jedrek.

"Has something happened at the Temple you haven't told us about?" asked Wren.

"I won't know until Armus returns," replied Kell.

"Well, there must be something because I aided Niles and Archimedes. They were in a tremendous rush."

"When was this?"

"Yesterday. They rode so hard it lamed a horse. I helped to heal her and refresh her strength to continue."

Not pleased by the answer, Kell pressed Wren. "Were you permitted to interact with them?"

"Ay! Jor'el has been prompting me to act as a clandestine escort between Waldron and the Region's border. But," Wren paused with frustration, "this last time an overwhelming evil caused me to lose my shift. Just like Armus reported."

"Only you didn't pass out," teased Barnum.

"Did you make any attempt to uncover the cause?" Jedrek asked Wren.

"No, I needed to make certain Niles and Archimedes arrived safely. One they neared the Pass of Peace, I withdrew."

"Since you were around, some help would have been nice," groused Gresham.

"I didn't see you or sense any trouble. If I had, I certainly wouldn't have left," she assured him.

A single flare of light interrupted the conversation. Armus appeared from the fading glow. Everyone noticed his somber expression.

Impatient, Kell asked, "What news?"

Armus didn't immediately reply rather took a deep sober breath before giving his report. "Wilbur was assassinated before I arrived."

Impulsive gasps of horror escaped from Mona and Priscilla while the others reeled at the shocking news. Even Kell recoiled.

"I tried to slow them down!" Gresham's passion came forth in pounding his fists on the arms of his chair.

"And my help proved futile," murmured Wren in distress.

"Take no blame," said Kell in a voice heavy with lament.

Dismayed, Armus shook his head. A downcast tone laced his words. "Kell's right. I don't know if much could have been done to prevent it. During my investigation, I discovered a very disturbing development: *they reached the postern gate*," he said with dreaded emphasis.

Shaken by the implication, fear filled Priscilla's voice. "Shadow Warriors at the Temple? I didn't think that possible."

Armus quickly spoke to reassure her. "Not inside, outside only."

"The postern gate is too close for my liking," complained Barnum.

"Agreed, which is why I made a thorough investigation. Whoever entered the compound was *not* from their ranks, which means a mortal. And more than likely, the assassin."

"With the enemy acting as handlers," groused Barnum.

"Ay, that's my assumption due to proximity and timing."

"Any witnesses?" Valmar asked Armus.

"None that I found. However, Odell went missing. Many speculate that he left because Wilbur didn't name him as successor. I'm don't think that's the reason." Armus took out the brooch he stuffed in his belt. "I found this in a grove where I tracked a large group of Shadow Warriors." He handed it to Kell. "The order's brooch."

"Broken," said Kell upon inspection. "Could mean they took him by force."

"Or he joined them. Either way explains why I found the postern gate unlocked. He either did so voluntarily or they made him."

Kell considered the brooch. "Do you think Odell killed Wilbur?"

Armus shrugged. "It's a possibility, but I can't say for certain."

"Maybe he left before it all happened, the brooch broke so he just discarded it where you tracked them," said Chase.

"That is also a possibility," agreed Armus. "We won't learn the reason until Odell is found."

"Do you know who Wilbur named as successor?" asked Jedrek.

Armus smiled with irony. "Archimedes."

It took a moment for the others to grasp the choice.

Kell spoke. "That is what I told Wilbur when permitted to visit him: to name Archimedes as the next Vicar of Jor'el. Being First Jor'ellian, he is not in the habit of backing down. He will be a force to be reckoned with." Kell's earlier lament returned. "Only I never expected it to happen this way."

Armus held Kell's shoulder. "Wilbur was a faithful servant, and though stout in faith, old in body. I witnessed his harrowing confrontation with Zared at the high banquet. I rushed him away before the Dark Way physically destroyed him. He earned his reward of eternal rest with Jor'el in the heavenlies."

"Ay," said Kell with small poignant smile. "I just mourn the violence of it rather than a peaceful passing."

"We all mourn him," said Mona gently.

Kell met her sympathetic gaze. "And like in times past, our mourning turns to embracing a new Vicar."

"Will you return to the Region now?" asked Wren.

Kell shook his head. "Not yet. With Waldron being the epicenter, I'll remain in Midessex. Armus will return to the Temple, discretely, until Commander Finn is again required."

"With me as secret escort." Wren flashed a wry grin at Armus.

Kell chuckled. He then glanced at the others ready to give orders when, "Wait. I just realized Zinna isn't here."

"I am now," a weary voice came from the threshold. Zinna leaned against the doorpost holding her wounded side.

Valmar and Jedrek rushed to help her to the South Plains chair. Still weak, Eldric stumbled in getting up to retrieve his bag. The others gathered around Zinna.

"What happened?" asked Kell.

"Shadow Archers in the South Plains. Also Warriors." Zinna hissed at Eldric's examination. "Once spotted, I managed to elude them."

"Not totally successful in that effort," huffed Eldric.

"I meant in covering my identity." She squirmed to get comfortable. "I hid in the foothills for a time to make certain they didn't sense me. Then I felt a prompting to come to Arundine. Only took me longer to get here on foot."

"How bad is the wound?" asked Priscilla.

"Minor. Only the delay in treatment caused a slight infection. Salve, bandage, tonics and a day of rest here with Gresham and me should suffice." Eldric took items out of his bag.

Kell's brows leveled in contemplating the latest development. "Shadow Warriors in the North Plains, Delta and South Plains leave the Lowlands as the next likely place to complete an arc."

Eldric paused in treatment of Zinna. "I haven't noticed any activity in the province. Then again, I haven't been able to stay in the Lowlands long enough to determine anything. Everybody keeps getting injured."

The physician's cynicism met with Kell's disapproval. Yet rather than argue, Kell asked Valmar, "Any activity in the Highlands?"

"No. So far north, Dagar seems to ignore the province."

Kell confronted Eldric. "Since your skills are presently needed elsewhere, Valmar will take temporary charge of the Lowlands."

Instead of replying to the rebuke, Eldric focused on Zinna.

Satisfied, Kell said, "The rest of you return, and keep a sharp eye."

"Also be on the lookout for Odell," Armus added to Kell's order.

Armus lingered while most of the others left. He drew Kell away from Eldric, Zinna and Gresham to speak privately. "Archimedes and Niles know who I am, or rather that Commander Finn is a *legend*."

"How?"

"Divine insight is my guess. Caught me a bit off guard when Archimedes' asked me what a legend would say to Wilbur's choice."

"Rather bold to speak so openly about legends."

"The three of us were alone in Wilbur's chamber when he addressed me in the Ancient. Although using the names Commander *Finn* and Captain *Seul* may go unnoticed by most mortals, those well studied in Verse and Prophecy can make a connection. Archimedes is the First Jor'ellian turned Vicar while Niles the King's Champion. He's the highest Jor'ellian next to Archimedes. Their faith and devotion runs deep. I may not have to be too clandestine with them."

"Any mention of Captain Seul?"

"Ay. Although they could mistake it as a code name for Jor'el since you only appeared to Wilbur in disguise. Unless there are times you spoke to Archimedes or Niles as Captain Seul and haven't told me?"

"No, just Wilbur." Kell considered the news. "Still be cautious with appearances around the compound. If the Shadow Warriors can get that close, they may sense your presence."

"Better me than you - before it's your time, that is." He wryly smiled.

Kell didn't accept the humor and nudged Armus to leave.

Chapter 20

RIDING SPIRIT STALLIONS, THE SHADOW ARMY CROSSED FROM the Region of Sanctuary into Midessex four hours after leaving the Temple Compound. Witter ordered the campaign to pull off the road for a halt. He dismounted and made a curt motion to Odell.

"Off your horse!"

Odell fretfully chewed on his lower lip, as he delayed in complying.

"I said, off the horse!" Witter seized the bridle, startling the animal.

Odell quickly dismounted. "What more do you want? I did as you asked," he said in anxious protest.

Witter didn't answer. Instead he waved to Danior. The assassin dismounted and took rough hold of Odell. "Fitch!" Witter shouted.

A vassal Guardian responded to the summons, though leery when doing so.

"You know what to do."

Fitch frowned with reluctance, which prompted Witter to seize him by the throat. Witter drew frightening close, nose-to-nose with Fitch.

"You don't want to lose more than your vocal chords, now do you?"

Terrified, Fitch managed to shake his head. Witter shoved him toward Odell. In a sudden move, Fitch grabbed Odell by the arm and placed a hand over the mortal's face. Instantly, Fitch transformed into Odell. The priest fainted. Danior caught him.

"Keep him alive until this is over," Fitch sternly told Danior.

"Why? And how can you speak?"

"By taking on mortal form, I inherit the ability to speak. Now do as you agreed, and keep the priest alive!"

"I still don't understand why? A dead witness is a silent one."

Witter intervened, "The *why* doesn't matter! Take him to the hideout and keep him alive! Unless you want to join him in silence?"

"No." Danior tied a gag around Odell's mouth then bound his hands. He carried the unconscious Odell to a small wagon. Even with supplies, there was enough room for Odell to sit. Danior used more rope to secure Odell to the wagon and prevent escape when he woke. Once finished, Danior sat in the driver's seat. He began to light a lantern attached to the wagon for night travel.

"No!" snapped Witter. "The horse will get you there without light."

Witter spoke to the animal in the Ancient. The horse neighed and tossed its head. Danior snatched the side seat rail to keep from falling off when horse lurched forward.

Witter, Fitch/Odell, Altari and the others waited until Danior was out of sight.

"Take the priest's horse and continue to Waldron. Meet with Zared and proceed to phase two," Altari instructed Fitch.

"Will he know who I really am?"

Altari cocked a sly grin. "No. While he might have plans to usurp the Vicar's position with one of his choosing, Dagar wants to destroy it!"

The answer concerned Fitch/Odell. "How long must I stay like this?"

"Until phase two is complete."

Fitch/Odell considered the situation. "Better hope Danior can keep the priest alive for the duration. I'll lose my shift if he dies."

Witter made a whistling sound followed by a wave toward the troops. A Shadow Archer separated from the group and ran in the direction taken by Danior. "Cleavon will make certain Danior doesn't fail."

"You mean kill him if anything goes wrong," groused Fitch/Odell.

"Now, go, only at a normal gallop. You don't want to arrive too soon and cause suspicion. We'll be waiting the signal to attack," said Altari.

Fitch/Odell mounted a smaller looking horse, yet in reality a spirit stallion disguised to pass as a mortal animal.

With Fitch/Odell away, Altari asked Witter, "Dimension travel or basin?"

"Basin. Less risky for us."

At a snap of Witter's fingers, two Warriors set up the basin for communication. Once ready, Witter cleared his throat before summoning Dagar. Steam appeared. Altari moved beside Witter to greet Dagar.

"Zared," began Dagar before his image was clearly visible. "Oh, Witter. Altari. Where is Zared?"

"On route to the South Plains, my lord," replied Witter.

"Before or after?"

"Before. We thought it best to conceal your alteration to phase two."

"Then I take it all went as planned?"

"Indeed. Wilbur is dead. Danior is taking the real Odell to the hideout while Fitch makes his way to Waldron."

A warped smile of satisfaction appeared on Dagar's face. "Excellent."

"My lord," began Altari with consideration. "I do not wish to belabor the point, but are you sure Fitch will be able to gain access to the Temple even disguised as a mortal? We have been forbidden entry since the Great Battle."

Surprisingly, Dagar took no offense to the question. "You know that only the most astute Guardian can detect a shapeshifter. Mortals are completely unaware of any difference."

Altari continued in his reserved manner. "However, Jor'el will know."

Dagar's agreeability vanished. "Altari, you have a bad habit of questioning me!"

"Only to better serve you, my lord!"

Dagar rebuffed, "Whether Fitch reaches the compound or not is immaterial. Once Zared publically uses his power to destroy the Vicar of Jor'el, the Dark Way will reign supreme! *That* is the objective, not the compound."

Altari and Witter exchanged astonished glances, which prompted Altari to say, "We didn't know."

Dagar heartily laughed. "That is because I give out information on a need to know basis. Until now, you didn't need to know."

"Sounds like Kell," Altari muttered a complaint to Witter.

"What did you say?" demanded Dagar. His mahogany eyes grew narrow with suspicion.

"Sounds reasonable," Altari dared to lie.

For a long moment, Dagar scrutinized Altari. "Set up a watch on the border between the Region and Midessex. I don't want *anything* to interfere. You'll find a few wolf *pets* in a nearby hollow. Use them at your discretion."

Understanding the reference for wolf *pets,* Altari and Witter flinched. Fortunately, Dagar didn't seem to notice, as he continued speaking.

"Contact me when Fitch has met with Zared." Dagar's image vanished.

Witter scolded Altari. "You're lucky he didn't hear you mention *Kell* by name!"

Altari lowly growled at the rebuke. He then called, "Carvel!"

The Commander of the Shadow Archer promptly arrived. "Ay?"

"Dagar wants to prevent any enemy interference. Since you are familiar with the road between the Temple and Waldron, assign two Archers and a Warrior to stop anyone suspicious."

"I'll see to it myself." He turned while shouted, "Ashby! Martel. Pathas."

At first the Warrior Martel seemed resistant to the Archer Commander.

"You heard him, Martel," Altari added his incentive for cooperation. "Oh, and employ a few *pets* you'll find in a nearby hollow."

To hide discomposure of the instruction, Martel grabbed the hilt of his sword. "How can I control them?"

"Tell them in the Ancient, *the master commands their aid.* They will listen until the task is complete."

Martel slapped his sheath in acceptance of the order.

"When were you going to tell me about these *pets?*" demanded Carvel.

Altari's stern expression showed his displeasure of the question. "I just did!"

Dagar angrily paced the audience chamber of the nether dimension. Such confinement proved infuriating when success depended upon the actions of others. He stopped in anticipation of the arrival a mere second before seeing light. Tor. It took a moment for Tor to recover from bridging the dimensional gap.

"Is there a problem?" asked Dagar in severe tone.

"No. I don't have a basin to utilize like Witter and Altari. I divided my forces as you requested, cutting off any support from the Lowlands or Meadowlands."

Dagar appeared slightly confused. "You said Zared reported Hagan agreed to cooperate so why blockade the Lowlands?"

"Hagan remains at Waldron, and has yet to prove his agreement is genuine."

"Mortal duplicity is insufferable!" Dagar complained.

"It's a trait we often exploit. Though I haven't completely blocked the main road, just placed it under heavy surveillance." Tor joined Dagar in front of a large map of the kingdom hanging on a cavern wall. "The only major road not monitored is to the Southern Forest."

Dagar's eyes brightened in regard of the map, as if stretching out his senses. "And there have been no reported encounters with Guardians?"

"Not in mass," said Tor.

The answer made Dagar's focus change to Tor. "Meaning?"

"There was a single essence in the South Plains, only brief and unable to determine identity."

"Did you send anyone to investigate?"

Tor shrugged. "Being indiscernible to exact identification, there was no trail to follow."

Dagar returned his attention to the map. "It is strange that Jor'el would not send at least one from the High Trio to investigate."

"Altari reported Mahon destroyed Avatar over two centuries ago."

Dagar scowled and folded his arm across his chest. "All the more reason for *him* to appear and avenge his intolerable protégé." He paced while thinking out loud. "The Vicar is dead, and there are nearly two thousand Shadow Warriors and three hundred Archers present in the kingdom. Those facts should generate interest!" He paused to confront Tor. "This is almost too easy!"

"And you're complaining?" said Tor with a wry huffing laugh. When Dagar resumed pacing, Tor said, "Since before the Great Battle you planned a coup. It partially succeeded in placing Ram on the throne and introducing the Dark Way. Now, we have an opportunity to publically destroy the Vicar of Jor'el, thus robbing the kingdom of spiritual guidance. This is no time for second-guessing."

Insulted by the statement, Dagar pulled to a halt. "I am *not* second-guessing. Rather considering *why* the enemy hasn't shown his face!"

"You mean *his* lack of appearance has baffled your superior intellect by not acting as anticipated."

Dagar's eyes grew deadly upon Tor. The latter began choking without Dagar touching him. Only when Tor reached the brink of fainting, did Dagar release his hold. Tor fell to the floor gasping for air. Tor looked up, still in some distress when Dagar stood before him.

"After you have recovered, return to your troops! Phase two will begin shortly." Dagar turned on his heels and left the main audience chamber.

Chapter 21

SUNRISE. THIS WAS NILES' FAVORITE TIME OF THE DAY. He stood on the eastern wall of the Fortress staring at the horizon. He enjoyed watching the growing light of day push back the darkest part of night. Perhaps symbolic of how he felt being at the Temple. Despite Wilbur's death, a new spiritual light was dawning with the appointment of Archimedes as Vicar. At least that is what he hoped. The discovery of Dagar's talisman meant the return of the Dark Way. Just like sunrise and twilight, the battle between light and dark took place every day.

"What challenges await us when they learn of your new Vicar? Will your light help us fight this rising darkness?" he asked with some dread.

"Jor'el will give the answer when it is needed."

Niles didn't turn toward the speaker since he recognized Archimedes' voice. He grinned. "That is why you make a better priest than me. I ask too many questions, while you take life as it comes."

Archimedes gave Niles a hearty pat on the shoulder. "You are mistaken in that assumption." He leaned on the battlement to gaze out at the sunrise. "I've spent many hours these past few days asking *Why me?* Although a priest, as First Jor'ellian I've done more fighting then preaching."

Niles turned to lean back on the wall to face Archimedes. "Exactly what is needed now, fighting and not preaching. Oh, don't misunderstand," he added at Archimedes' sour frown. "Wilbur made an excellent Vicar, stout in faith and upstanding in moral fortitude with Jor'el's law and Verse. However," he paused now that he had Archimedes' undivided attention, "he had not the mettle and discipline of

212

a Jor'ellian Knight to stand up to the Dark Way." He gripped Archimedes' arm. "*You* are a unique individual, for when you take on the mantle and staff of Vicar, you will be only one of three in our country's history who has been both knight and priest. The answer to *why* is because Allon needs *you*."

A bashful smile appeared. "Not many can make me blush. You've done that, while Jor'el has blessed in ways I never considered. Yet," Archimedes grew somber, "to ask Wilma to share such a burden ..."

"She would gladly do so!" Niles insisted.

"If word reaches Waldron before I can secure her ..." he began another objection.

"Which is why you agreed to send Abner a message about Wilbur, so they will be prepared for when we arrive. Don't let the enemy use your concern for her to weaken your resolve."

"Don't take your counsel too far, knight."

Niles heartily laughed. "Now that's the Archimedes I know, confident and bold. The one who will put Zared in his place by a surprise appearance."

Alfie arrived huffing and puffing, out of breath from running. "My lord! The ceremony is to begin within the hour. You must get ready!"

Niles grinned at Archimedes. "Go. I'll see the escort is ready before making my way to the Temple."

Even though everyone from the Fortress and Temple assembled for the ordination of a new Vicar, the atmosphere proved somber. Normally a service to install a new Vicar was met with hopeful enthusiasm. Not this time. They still grieved a dastardly, unthinkable deed. Three days earlier they held a quiet entombing ceremony for Wilbur inside the Fortress crypt rather than the Temple. This installing of a new Vicar required sobriety and alertness.

Sadly, inhabitants of the Region paid little attention to anything that happened at the Temple. Thus, with only four hundred people in a place capable of holding three thousand, Niles easily made his way to the front.

Orders were issued not to use trumpets or tower bells during the ceremony. Instead, a priest walked the aisle from the rear to high altar. He rang a handbell before making an announcement.

"Give heed! Give heed! By divine decree and right of succession, we, assemble for the purpose of ordaining to the honored position of Vicar of Jor'el, Archimedes." He motioned toward the back of the Temple then stepped aside.

Leading the procession came the captain of the Fortress Guard and Commander Kincaid of the Jor'ellian Knights. Behind them walked Archimedes, who was followed by four priests. Two priests carried the heavy blue and silver robe while the others carried the staff of Jor'el. Lastly came Delbert, Assistant Headmaster of the Fortress. He carried the Temple's sacred book of Verse.

The captain and Kincaid moved to opposite sides of the altar steps. Archimedes proceeded to mount the steps to the high altar. Upon a blue cushion, he knelt before the altar with his head bowed. The priests bearing the symbols of the office mounted the platform and each pair flanked Archimedes. Delbert made his way to stand in front of Archimedes, which was between him and the high altar.

"In the absence of Headmaster Odell, I, Assistant Headmaster Delbert, preside over this ordination." He opened the book of Verse.

> *"From among the faithful shall one come to bear*
> *The most sacred responsibility in service to Jor'el.*
> *To lead the priests and people in the ways of*
> *The Almighty by taking the title Vicar of Jor'el."*

Delbert closed the book and put it back in its place on the high altar. When he faced the crowd again, he withdrew the document from a pocket of his robe. He held it up for viewing. "By his own hand, and in accordance with divine law and authority, Vicar Wilbur named as his successor, Archimedes, First Jor'ellian Knight of the Realm. Once accepted, this appointment is irrevocable and binding."

Delbert lowered his arm. Looking soberly at Archimedes, he asked, "In Jor'el's name, I ask you, Archimedes, First Jor'ellian Knight of the Realm, do you accept this charge?"

Archimedes looked up to Delbert. "I so accept."

"Rise and place your hands upon the sacred book."

Archimedes did as instructed.

Delbert walked behind the high altar to continue the ordination. "Do you accept the sacred responsibility of guarding Jor'el's holy honor?"

"I so accept."

"Do you accept to be Allon's spiritual example of Jor'el's ordinances for righteous living?"

"I so accept."

"Do you accept that this position may require the ultimate sacrifice in the face of evil opposition?"

"I so accept."

"In Jor'el's name, do you accept all that is required of this oath?"

"I so accept the oath in Jor'el's name."

Delbert moved around to the front of the altar and took Archimedes' elbow to turn him to face the crowd. "Receive the robe of the office as a covering and daily reminder of your vow. Embroidered in silver thread are the Ancient words of your oath."

The two priests carrying the robe helped Archimedes put it on. When they resumed their places, Delbert continued.

"Receive the staff of Jor'el to act with righteousness."

The two priests bearing the large staff gave it to Archimedes. When they returned to their places, Delbert concluded.

"By the authority of divine writ and sworn oath, you are now Archimedes, Vicar of Jor'el."

At the pronouncement, everyone knelt on one knee while saying, "Long live Jor'el. Long live the Vicar."

"Rise, my brothers," said Archimedes. Once they were on their feet, he continued. "Our duty is sober and pressing, as the kingdom stands on the brink of darkness. The power that struck down our beloved Wilbur is at this moment corrupting the mind of our King. I speak of none other than the Dark Way!"

The stunned murmurs were measureable, so Archimedes put up a hand and loudly spoke. "Hear me! I know this for a fact. Dagar's talisman, long thought destroyed, has returned! Though it may require the ultimate sacrifice of me sooner than anyone of us would like, I must return to Waldron and confront this darkness. Pray for me, and the brave souls who will accompany me. But," he stressed when the murmurings again grew loud. "I do not leave you defenseless. Commander Kincaid!"

Kincaid turned to Archimedes from his position on the floor. "My lord!" He mounted the steps when beckoned by Archimedes.

From his doublet pocket, Archimedes produced the First Jor'ellian medallion. "From this day forward you are First Jor'ellian of the Realm." He placed it around Kincaid's neck. "To your duty of justice be true, and to Jor'el be faithful."

Kincaid made the Jor'ellian salute and bowed his head. "To this pledge I give my word. May my life be forfeited if I forsake my charge."

"Now lend me your arm. I must grow accustomed to the weight of this mantle when moving."

Archimedes leaned upon Kincaid in descending the platform. Once on the level floor, he slowly proceeded down the aisle. Kincaid and Delbert came behind him. Niles fell in step for departing the Temple. The rest followed them outside to awaiting escort. To their surprise Commander Finn stood next to a small second wagon.

"Commander," began Archimedes. "This is a surprise. I didn't expect to see you for quite some time."

Armus smiled. "I completed my task, hence my quicker return." He gazed directly at Archimedes. "As I escorted Wilbur, I will escort you."

"Your service is appreciated." Archimedes indicated Kincaid. "My second-in-command has accepted the charge of First Jor'ellian."

Armus focused on Kincaid. "A challenging time to take on such responsibility."

"I will not shrink from the challenge."

"Then will you accept my taking command of the escort?"

Kincaid returned Armus' smile. "Your reputation is well known, Commander Finn. I welcome your aid in escorting the Vicar."

"Indeed," began Niles in agreement. "However, two wagons were not in my original plan." He noticed the second wagon.

"Precaution for the Vicar's *personal items*." Armus replied to Niles, though he still looked at Archimedes. "No need to tip our hand."

Archimedes grinned. He gave the staff to Armus, who placed it in the wagon under a tarp. Archimedes struggled to remove the heavy robe, so Armus helped him. He then concealed it in the wagon alongside the staff.

"He should at least have a cloak. It is cold," chided Niles.

Armus reached into the wagon to pull out a cloak and hat for Archimedes. "Assistant Headmaster, I think you too should conceal your robes for the journey."

Delbert shed his priest robes and trapping for Armus to place in the wagon. "I don't suppose you have a cloak and hat for me also?"

Armus grinned and produced the items from the wagon. "When you are ready, Vicar, we shall be off."

"Ah, call me Archimedes! Don't want to tip our hand, Commander," he said in light retort.

Armus chuckled. "Your horse is waiting, *Archimedes*." He conducted Archimedes to the horse while Kincaid helped Delbert. Afterward, Armus mounted his horse.

In leading the escort from the compound, Armus made careful note of the surroundings. He didn't sense the enemy, though an essence felt close. With a small amount of energy, he explored the sensation. Wren. He fought a smile. *Mustn't get too close.* Even though the *huff* was in his mind, he could hear Wren's sarcastic tone attached to the reply.

217

Chapter 22

LATE AFTERNOON OF THE THIRD DAY, FITCH/ODELL REACHED THE plain surrounding Waldron. He moved off the road and into the forest. Twilight made the trees cast long shadows. He stopped to consider how to approach the castle. He needed to maintain his appearance of the mortal Headmaster. However, priests were not welcomed at Waldron, or so he learned from assuming Odell's identity. He discovered Odell to be a weasely man who played both sides to his advantage. This could work well in his clandestine role.

Fitch searched Odell's memory for any clue of how the Headmaster interacted with those at Waldron. Naturally, he had contact with Zared, so Fitch pursued that avenue of recollection. He reached into the pocket of the priestly robe-doublet and pulled out a small brooch with a raven on it. He smiled and quickly pocketed the brooch.

Fitch/Odell dismounted and tethered the horse to a nearby tree. He sat against the tree to watch and wait. From this vantage point, he could see the main gate and the road leading to the rear of Waldron. After dark is when he would attempt to gain entry at the postern gate.

Riders nearing the castle caught his attention. With clear visibility, a Guardian's eyesight was keen and precise up to two miles. They were noblemen with soldiers and servants. Being in the neither dimension for hundreds of years, he didn't recognize them. When he focused on one, he became struck with a sense of power. No mistaking the Dark Way. He rubbed the pain from his eyes.

"That must be Zared."

The mortal would be at Waldron. Now to wait until dark for contact.

In the courtyard, grooms scrambled to greet the arriving nobles. Once dismounted, Zared spied Akilles across the way. The Prince bolted inside.

Patrin noticed. "What are going to do about him?"

Zared drew Patrin away from the grooms to head for the main entrance. "Nothing. After our little trip, he and the others don't have much time left." He fought back a smile.

"He could still cause trouble," Patrin warned.

"Berk won't listen," said Zared with confidence. They entered the Grand Foyer.

"Speaking of, do we present ourselves to the King or just retire to our quarters?"

"Retire. We must make ourselves presentable." Zared headed down the corridor intent on reaching the guest quarters unhindered. That was not to be the case.

"Zared?" Berk's voice called from behind.

"A little alteration of plan, I think," said Patrin to Zared before both men turned. They bowed to Berk.

"When did you get back?"

"Just now, Sire," said Zared.

"I thought there was a crisis?"

Zared sighed with feigned anger. "Apparently the definition of crisis is something my steward doesn't understand. A rider met me part way with a notice that all is well. Rather than continue and give him the thrashing he deserves, I hastened back to Your Majesty. It was hardly the way I wanted to leave with our work here unfinished."

Berk widely smiled. He placed an arm around Zared's shoulder. "You're a good man. I was right to appoint you Grand Master. Come. There is work to do."

"Sire, I beg your pardon for this evening. After seven days of riding, I wish to retire so my mind can be fresh in the morning to begin our undertaking."

Berk laughed. "Enthusiasm of having you back clouded my mind." He leaned closer to speak with rough sarcasm. "You don't know what it's been like since you left! I have been inundated with aggravating audiences, all clamoring about your appointment." Berk patted Zared on the shoulder. "But enough. We'll take care of all that beginning tomorrow. Goodnight, gentlemen."

"Goodnight, Sire." They bowed to the departing Berk.

An hour after dusk, Fitch/Odell invoked the power of stealth to reach the postern gate unnoticed by the nightwatch. He couldn't keep up the stealth to gain entry. He dismounted to pound on the gate while shouting for admittance.

"What do you want?" demanded a guard from the battlement.

"It's a matter of urgency! Open the gate."

The guard disappeared for a moment. Shortly, the sight-hole in the postern gate opened. "Who are you?"

"I come with a message."

"From where?"

"I can't say."

The guard snarled. "You look like a priest."

Fitch/Odell reached into his pocket to produce the bird brooch. "Tell Rankin I'm here." He held up the brooch for the guard to see.

Frowning, the guard said, "Hand it through and I'll talk to him." Once he had the brooch, he slammed the sight-hole shut.

Fitch/Odell waited, and waited. He grew impatient at the time it took. Perhaps he gave away his only safe means to enter Waldron. He considered other ways to gain entry should the brooch fail. He jumped slightly when he heard metallic creaking. The postern gate opened.

"Hurry up." The guard waved Fitch/Odell inside.

Fitch/Odell led his horse into Waldron.

"Here" The guard gave the brooch back to Fitch/Odell. "Rankin says to meet him in the alcove off the kitchen."

"Thanks." He handed the reins to the guards.

"Put the nag over there!" The guard pointed to a place near the gatehouse.

Once he tethered the horse, Fitch/Odell used the mortal's memory to make his way to the alcove. He saw no one, and again forced to wait. Soon a middle-aged, husky man in servant's clothes and apron arrived. Upon sight of him, Fitch/Odell recognized Rankin, a cook at Waldron. Not who Fitch originally thought when asking for Rankin.

"You're bold to come here like this. He couldn't have summoned you. Unless you knew he just returned," complained Rankin.

"The news I bring is something he will want to hear immediately."

Displeased, Rankin surveyed Fitch/Odell. "I'm surprised you didn't come in disguise like other times. The sight of a priest around here isn't a good idea."

"I couldn't risk any delay. The matter is too pressing."

Rankin scratched his chin in thought. "I'll fetch you an old cloak."

He left before Fitch/Odell could speak either a question or objection. This wait took ten minutes, which made Fitch/Odell stay in the shadows to allow a patrol to pass. Finally, Rankin returned.

"This should do." He handed an old cloak to Fitch/Odell. It had a particularly strong odor.

"What is that smell?" Fitch/Odell asked while putting it on.

"Onions and garlic. It hangs in the storeroom for anyone to use for going outside." He turned Fitch/Odell around. "Fortunately for you, he takes the back guest room. The one nearest the stairwell." He looked down the back alley. "When the night patrol passes, you'll have ten minutes to reach the outer stairs to the guest wing."

"They just went by before you returned."

"Then go now!" Rankin shoved Fitch/Odell on his way.

Pulling the hood up, Fitch/Odell again tapped into the priest's memory for navigating the castle. Odell had obviously been to Waldron numerous times to develop a signal, use a disguise and move through the back portions of the castle.

Once up the back outer stairs, he carefully moved to the exterior door leading to the guest wing. Apparently, the latch on the brooch served as a key. It didn't take much effort to unlock the door, enter and lock it from the inside.

Rankin said Zared stays in the room closest to the stairwell, but there were two doors, one on each side of the hall. Ever so carefully, Fitch/Odell used his senses to search for the Dark Way. Again, he felt pain. However, with the pain came the location—the door across the hall.

Peeking out the stairwell, he spied two royal guards. Once more he invoked his powers to move unseen from the stairwell to the door. To his surprise, the door was unlocked. He swiftly entered yet carefully closed the door.

"Who are you and what are you doing here?"

Fitch/Odell came face-to-face with Zared holding a sword. He put up his hands. "I mean no harm, my lord."

"Your voice is familiar." He tried to look under the hood.

"May I?" Fitch/Odell placed his hand on the hood to remove it.

"Slowly," warned Zared. "Odell?" He lowered the sword, despite being irate. "I didn't send for you!"

"Where else would you expect me to go with *such horrible* news?" he spoke with a knowing inflection.

Zared fought a warped smile. "You mean Danior succeeded?"

"Indeed, my lord. The Vicar is dead."

"Tell me, did he name his successor?"

"Not that I am aware of."

"But you don't know for certain?"

"I pressed him upon the matter the evening before his death, and received the same answer of *not yet.*"

"Could he do so without your knowledge?"

"My lord, for the Divine Writ of Succession to be official, there must be witnesses in agreement to the choice and present when the holy seal is applied. That duty falls to the Fortress Headmaster and Commander of the Jor'ellians. I witnessed no such sealing. If only Commander Kincaid bore witness, the document is not binding."

This time Zared didn't fight the pleased smile. He guided Fitch/Odell further into the room. "Your faithfulness will be handsomely rewarded." He motioned to the sitting area. "For tonight, make yourself comfortable on the sofa. In the morning, we'll tell the King of this unfortunate incident."

"Why not now? I'm certain a messenger has been dispatched from the Temple."

"Surely that wouldn't have occurred until *after* you left. So we have a few hours, if not a day's head start, correct?"

"Ay, my lord."

Zared yawned and stretched. "Besides, I really do need some rest after a week of travel. You'll find pillows and blankets in that cupboard." He pointed to the named furniture behind the sofa.

Fitch/Odell fetched pillows and a blanket. Though rest was unnecessary for a Guardian, in his guise, he laid on the sofa in a pretense of sleep. He listened to Zared make ready to retire then finally fall asleep.

Turning on his back, Fitch/Odell stared at the ceiling. Agreeing to this charade was an act of self-preservation. After centuries of torture, anything seemed worth it to make the pain stop. This first assignment for Dagar showed him the reality of his choice. He knew that whoever denounced Jor'el forfeited their divine station. There would be no peaceful retirement from physical service to the heavenlies for eternity. Instead, he faced oblivion. He had no chance to receive the mercy he witnessed of mortals who embraced Jor'el.

Ironically, he had been a messenger of Jor'el to tell mortals about eternal peace. Now, he chose a different path. He could ill-afford regret or dwell on memories of the past. No, he must fully embrace his new identity as a servant of the Dark Way and enemy of Jor'el. Whatever Dagar or Zared commanded, he would fulfill.

At first light, Fitch/Odell put the pillows and blankets away. Zared must really be fatigued since he didn't stir when Fitch/Odell purposely made noise cleaning up his makeshift bed. This meant he had to again wait. Fitch recalled that a master of Dark Way had to be part Guardian to wield its power. Somehow it involved Dagar. Then he remembered that Ram and Razi were sons of Dagar by a mortal female. Would Zared also be a son? A half-breed? Sad how centuries of abuse clouded his memory, when before the Great Battle he had immediate clarity in recall.

There came a knock at the door followed by a voice calling for Zared. Fitch/Odell answered the summons. He discovered the same nobleman who rode with Zared along with a valet. According to Odell's memory, he was Lord Patrin.

The valet passed Fitch/Odell to tend to duty.

"My lord, the baron is still asleep," said Fitch/Odell.

Patrin didn't appear pleased and slammed the door to confront Fitch/Odell. "What are you doing here?"

"Danior succeeded," said Zared. He sat up in bed and stretched.

Patrin crossed to the bed. "The Vicar?" he asked in anticipation.

Zared simply smiled.

"Still doesn't answer why *he* is here rather than a messenger." Patrin jerked his thumb at Fitch/Odell.

Zared rose to begin his morning toilet. "Easier to convince Berk of *our* new appointee to Vicar since Wilbur failed to name his successor."

"I suppose." Patrin sat on the sofa while Zared used the privy. When Zared reappeared he continued. "When do you plan on approaching Berk?"

"This morning. Such news can't wait, nor should it. Our plan is in motion." Zared stood while the valet began to dress him for the day.

Servants arrived with breakfast.

"I took the liberty of ordering enough for two, my lord. I was unaware of anyone else," said the valet as he prepared the table.

"I can wait," said Fitch/Odell.

"No, there is plenty." Zared motioned for Fitch/Odell to join them.

In his role-playing, Fitch/Odell assumed the position to say a blessing for the meal. He balked at the harsh clearing of a throat from Zared. "I'm sorry. It is habit, my lord. Though shouldn't I keep up appearances?"

"In public," said Zared with some begrudging.

To maintain the façade, Fitch/Odell ate enough food to be convincing. Once finished, they left the quarters to head for the King's study.

"Let us do the talking," Zared said to Fitch/Odell in reference to he and Patrin.

"Of course, my lord."

Turning the corner of the Upper Galleyway, they spied a group of nobleman outside the King's study. This included Abner, Gordon, Jarrett, Mathis and Slater. By reactions, all were surprised to see them.

Zared widely smiled. "Good morning, gentlemen. Count," he said to Slater.

Slater replied in an unfriendly voice. "Baron."

Zared ignored the tone. "Is the King not in audience yet?"

"He is. We're awaiting his pleasure."

Zared's self-assured smile returned. He knocked on the door and identified himself. To the great annoyance of those waiting, he received immediate admittance, along with Patrin and Fitch/Odell.

Berk warmly greeted Zared. "At last! I've been waiting for you so we can deal with *them*." He impatiently waved at the door. Scrutinizing eyes fell upon Fitch/Odell. "What is *that priest* doing here?"

"I'm afraid he brings tragic news," began Zared in a feigned tone of upset. "Vicar Wilbur is dead."

At first Berk balked at hearing the report then began to laugh, almost uncontrollable. Zared, Patrin and Fitch/Odell waited for Berk to regain his composure.

On his part, Berk noticed their unaffected reactions. "Oh surely, you find more pleasure in this than to look so somber," he spoke to Zared. "Our nemesis is gone!"

Zared fought an impulsive smile. "There is decorum to maintain, Sire. At least temporarily before the Court."

Berk's expression grew sly. "You are a cunning devil, baron—I mean—Grand Master." He laughed again.

"This presents us with an opportunity to make those more resistant to change see things our way."

"How so?" Berk sat at his desk to give Zared due attention.

"It appears Wilbur made a horrible oversight in not naming his successor before his unfortunate passing. Without a Divine Writ, the position of Vicar can be filled by order of the *King.*"

Berk's smile widened with immense pleasure. "Do you have a candidate in mind, dear baron? A Grand Master perhaps?"

"Oh, Sire," began Zared with a hearty chuckle. "You are a wit."

Berk's smile faded. "I am serious, Zared, not being witty."

Zared's expression matched Berk's. "So am I."

"If I may be so bold as to make a suggestion," began Patrin. When he received attention, he continued. "So quick an appointment after the announcement of Zared's new position and Wilbur's untimely death, might be met with resistance. Please, Sire," he raised a quick hand when Berk started to object, "hear me out on this."

Berk made an impatient wave for continuance.

"An interim step would help to facility the ultimate plan." Patrin stood beside Fitch/Odell. "A man of your choosing, who can defer to Grand Master Zared's wisdom of enlightenment and subtlety guide the transition for a *brief* period."

Berk's eyes narrowed upon Fitch/Odell. "This priest is such a man?"

"This is Headmaster Odell of the Fortress of Jor'el, assistant to Wilbur, yet not fully of the same mind as the late Vicar. If you understand my meaning, Sire."

Berk's scrutinized of Fitch/Odell then asked Zared, "How familiar are you with the Headmaster?"

"We have corresponded frequently since you appointed me overseer of the Fortresses."

"So you can vouch for his differing views?"

"I vouch for his aligning with *our* views," Zared spoke with certainty.

Berk's thoughtful gaze shifted to Fitch/Odell. His eyes remained for a long moment on Fitch/Odell before inquiring, "How long should this transition be?"

Patrin replied. "A year. This gives enough time to establish places of enlightenment in each province to replace the local Fortresses."

"And fill the gap left by the dissolving of the Council," added Zared.

"So you agree with Patrin's proposal?" Berk asked Zared.

"It would help to facilitate our plan without facing too much opposition."

"A bloodless coup," murmured Berk.

Unseen by Berk, Zared and Patrin exchanged satisfied glances.

Berk smiled with approval. "Well thought out, my dear Patrin."

"Then you agree?"

"Ay." Berk came out from behind his desk. "How soon shall we convene a royal forum to make the announcement?"

Patrin took a moment to consider the answer. "With most of those *previously* on the Council still at Waldron, I would say tomorrow before word spreads of Wilbur's demise."

"Zared?"

"I agree, Sire. The more swiftly we move the better."

"Alvin!" Berk bellowed. He went to the hearth where a rope hung on one side of the mantel. He pulled it several times while again calling, "Alvin!"

In hasty response, Alvin entered the study. "You summoned me, Sire?"

"Cancel all my audiences and issue a summons for a royal forum at four o'clock tomorrow!"

Momentarily stunned, Alvin asked, "Tomorrow?"

"Is there a problem, lord chamberlain?"

"No problem, Sire. Merely surprised by the quickness. It shall be as you say." Alvin bowed and departed.

Soon raised voices of protest came from the hall.

Berk laughed. "The vultures' feathers are already ruffled!" He bid Zared, Patrin and Fitch/Odell good day. "Until this afternoon, gentleman. Headmaster."

By the time Zared, Patrin and Fitch/Odell left the study, guards had cleared the Upper Galleyway. Walking toward the guest wing, Zared spoke.

"You played your part exceedingly well, Patrin. Introducing our idea at precisely the right moment."

Patrin replied with antagonism. "I will continue to play my part as long as you remember the bargain."

Zared stopped to face Patrin. "I assure you, both of us will achieve what we desire." He then changed his heavy focus to Fitch/Odell. "The plan is only as strong as its weakest link. Do you understand, priest?"

It took a moment for Fitch to comprehend, as Odell's memories came quicker. "I understand completely, my lord. All will go as planned."

Zared held the neck of his collar in staring at Fitch/Odell. "Indeed," he said in happy agreement. His hand fell away. "For now, let us review *your* part." He continued their trek toward the guest wing.

Colin watched Akilles' agitation. Since seeing Zared return to Waldron, the Prince could barely concentrate on anything else. No matter how many times Colin made Akilles recite the Jor'ellian Creed, he quickly reverted to being upset.

Myla and Wilma arrived shortly after breakfast. Akilles practically knocked over Myla in his anxiety to speak with her.

"Marmi, what can I do now that he's back?" Akilles asked in desperation.

"We'll think of something." She led Akilles to the sofa to sit. "For now, try to relax. Sir Colin is with you."

"I have reminded him of the Jor'ellian Creed and Verse about courage instead of fear," said Colin.

Myla made a motherly frown. "Why haven't you listened to Sir Colin?"

Akilles heaved a sigh. "I don't know! He just makes me so uncomfortable."

"I beg your pardon, Highness?" asked Colin with curiosity.

"I mean Zared not you!" Akilles flung his hands in frustration.

Without a knock, the chamber door opened. Berk entered. Colin and Wilma paid their respects to the King. He ignored them to speak to Myla.

"I was told you were here, Madam," he spoke formal and harsh.

"Merely visiting our son. Is there a problem with that?"

"A *problem* has arisen that will be addressed at a royal forum tomorrow afternoon."

Surprise brought Myla to her feet. "Royal forum? Why?"

"You will learn the reason along with rest of Court. I expect you to attend. It begins promptly at four." Berk turned on his heels to depart.

"Marmi," began Akilles, although mindful of his mother's concern. "What is a royal forum?"

"Something that is rarely done," she said in disturbed reply.

"And only in times of great upheaval," added Colin with sobriety.

After a firm, determined look to Colin, Myla sat on the sofa. She took hold of Akilles' hands and spoke with grave urgency. "You *must* stay close to Sir Colin. Go nowhere by yourself."

Fear leapt into Akilles' eyes. "Marmi, I …"

She touched his face to stop his protest. "Trust me and do as I say."

He leaned closer to ask in a low voice, "What about going to the Fortress with him instead of Sir Niles?"

She took his head in both her hands so that her forehead touched his forehead. "Soon, which is why you must remain close, as the time to leave can come at any moment."

"I will."

She kissed his forehead. "I love you."

"I love you, too, Marmi."

Myla sent a last confident glance to Colin before leaving with Wilma.

"Your mother is a very brave woman," said Colin. Akilles' focus remained on the door. "She can face whatever comes due to her trust in Jor'el. You must do the same to harness such bravery."

Still staring at the door, Akilles recited the Jor'ellian Creed with more resolution in his voice than he had all morning.

Myla made her way to the family salon with Wilma still in attendance. Blaine, Calder and Delwin went about their day with blissful ignorance under the care of two nurses. Myla watched ten-year-old Blaine merrily interact with his younger brothers. Only two years younger than Akilles, Blaine's lighthearted personality stood in marked contrast to the more serious-minded Akilles. Some of that was to be expected with Akilles being the Heir Apparent.

Although the brothers clashed and exhibited sibling rivalry, she sensed no jealousy from Blaine toward Akilles. On his part, Akilles took being the eldest very seriously in looking out for their welfare. Perhaps, he acted too serious at times, but not under the current situation. Care needed to be taken to protect all her sons.

In playing tag, the boys ran circles around Myla and Wilma. The women laughed at the jubilant nature of children at play. Delwin pulled up when the door opened since he nearly ran into Gordon, who arrived with Abner.

"Little prince. I hope I didn't scare you," said Gordon.

"No. I just didn't expect the door to open."

Calder slapped Delwin on the back. "Tag! You're it."

Delwin pouted, unhappy at being caught.

Gordon knelt. "I'm afraid it was my fault. So, how about tagging me?" He held his hand out. Delwin slapped Gordon's hand.

"That's not how it's played! You have to run," protested Calder.

Gordon winked at Delwin then touched Calder on the shoulder. "Tag! Now, you're it. Run," he shooed Delwin away. With a merry laugh, Delwin ran off.

"Hey!" Calder huffed.

"Can't catch me!" Delwin teased, which made Calder pursue him.

Myla laughed. "Very clever for a bachelor."

Gordon chuckled. "I have four younger siblings. I do remember playing games."

"However, Majesty, we came on important business," said Abner.

"I suspected as much, my lord." Myla turned to the nurses. "Lianne, Emma, take the boys back to nursery."

"But, Marmi!" Calder sulked.

"You can continue playing in the nursery. It is larger, and with more places to hide. Now, off with you."

"Oh! Hide and seek," said a gleeful Delwin.

Myla motioned Blaine to the younger boys. He understood and helped the nurses usher Calder and Delwin from the salon.

"Please, Madam, sit. You too, my lady." Abner indicated a sofa across the room near the hearth. After they did as bade, he continued in a low voice. "It is best done without words. Guard your reaction." He handed an opened letter to Myla.

Upon reading, an impulsive gasp escaped, making Myla cover her mouth with a hand. She passed it to Wilma when motioned by Abner to do so. Wilma bit her lip to keep from making any sound. Abner snatched the letter and tossed it into the fire. He waited until the letter burned to ashes before speaking again.

"All must be ready when they return."

"I wonder if that is why Berk is calling a royal forum, because he knows about … this tragedy." Myla stopped short of saying a name.

"That is more than likely the case since Headmaster Odell accompanied Zared and Patrin to see him this morning."

"Without Divine Writ, Berk can name the successor," said Gordon with dread.

"Pray it is not … that … wretched man!" Wilma came close to swearing.

Myla took hold of Wilma's hand. "I'm sure a *certain someone* will have a say in who the next one shall be." She softly smiled.

"If his voice isn't shouted down by malcontents."

"Those of us loyal to the Council will add our voices," Abner assured Wilma.

Myla asked, "How long do you think before they return?"

"Well," began Abner in consideration. "It is a four day ride. Perhaps as early as tonight."

Myla stood, a glimmer of hope in her eyes. "Before the royal forum tomorrow afternoon?"

"I don't know. I suppose it's possible."

"Is that enough time for all to be ready?" asked Gordon.

"I'm not sure." Myla began to pace. "Getting Berk's permission will be difficult, to say the least."

Abner asked a probing, hard question. "Are you prepared for it to be done *without* permission should it become necessary?"

Myla stoutly squared her shoulders. "I'm prepared to do what is needed to protect my sons."

Abner softly smiled with admiration. "We shall leave to do our part." He bowed. Gordon followed his example and the men departed.

Chapter 23

EANWHILE, THE VICAR'S RETINUE ENCOUNTERED NO PROBLEM travelling the Region of Sanctuary. Once in Midessex, Armus' senses became heightened. He knew Wren shadowed them, yet every reported encounter with the Dark Way occurred in Midessex. He hoped Wren wasn't alone in covert surveillance.

With the late afternoon sun fading, they needed to find a place to camp for the night. By tomorrow evening, they should reach Waldron. In truth, they moved further into Midessex than Armus thought possible without a hint of trouble. He wasn't certain whether to be glad or wary of what they would discover at Waldron. He considered pushing his senses past his current surroundings to search for Kell's essence. If anything were wrong at Waldron, he would know by Kell's reaction to transverse contact. It could come in the form of a mental scolding, warning or call for help.

Armus began to stretch out his sensory perception when … "The Dark Way!" he said in alarm. He drew his sword and turned his horse around to shout a warning when the attack happened. A hail of arrows came from the western side of the road.

"For Jor'el, for Allon!" he raised the Jor'ellian battle cry.

Kincaid and Niles echoed the maxim.

The arrows inflicted damage by killing two Jor'ellians. Armus noticed Archimedes bent over his saddlebow. He hastened to the Vicar.

"Archimedes?"

Gritting his teeth against the pain, Archimedes grunted. "A passing arrow ripped open my abdomen. Not fatal, just inconvenient!"

Armus glanced around, but so far no enemy in sight. Eerie deafening howls came from the eastern side of the road. The mortals doubled over in agony at the noise. Those armed with swords tried to cover their ears. Armus snarled in painful anger at recognition of the sound.

Six *madah-dunes* rushed from the trees. The wolf-man creatures stood nine feet tall on two legs with the body of a man, face of a wolf and covered in fur. Their hands had razor sharp claws while drool dripped from the long fangs. Each wielded a spike club.

"By Jor'el's will I fight his enemies!" Armus spoke the Ancient in a breathy manner to call upon his special power.

He raised his sword and kicked his horse to meet them. He didn't yield when his sword made impact with a club. His face showed the effort needed to hold the club at bay. *"Aaagggrrh!"* Armus shoved the club aside and slashed the beast deep across its chest.

The *madah-dune* stumbled backwards from the impact. Before it could attack Armus again, an arrow pierced its throat. A horrid gurgling sound followed as it collapsed, dead. Whether the arrow came from the attackers or Wren's intervention, Armus couldn't take the time to determine.

When he turned to view the battle, his eyes momentarily averted from nearby trouble. Another beast's claws ripped into the horse's neck. It then struck the horse in the head with the spiked club. Armus fell with the horse yet managed to avoid getting caught beneath the dead animal.

He dodged the club now aimed at him. He regained his balance to make a stand. He avoided a second strike only unable to miss being grabbed by the arm. In jerking away, claws ripped his uniform, gouging flesh. Armus used his sword to knock aside another attempt at being seized. He unsheathed his dagger and thrust it hilt deep in middle of the beast's body.

With a snarling *oofff* the beast reacted. The raising of its club stopped in mid-swing at the *thud, thud* of impact. Armus sidestepped when the beast fell forward revealing two arrows, one between its shoulder blades and the other lodged in the base of the neck.

Knocked from his horse in a battle with a beast, Niles desperately fought the *madah-dune*. A backward swing from the beast's arm sent Niles hard to the ground. In defense of Niles, a mounted Jor'ellian plunged his dagger into the back of the beast's shoulders. Unable to pull out the dagger, he let go as the beast collapsed to its knees. Niles scrambled to his feet. He thrust his sword through the beast's chest to finish it. Niles swayed slightly and stumbled in backing away.

"Champion? Are you injured?" asked the Jor'ellian.

"Let's just say it hurts to breathe or move. Fetch my horse."

When the Jor'ellian moved off, Niles noticed Archimedes beside the small wagon holding his stomach. Delbert knelt inside the wagon, pale with fear. Taking a pain-ridden breath, Niles made his way to the wagon.

"Are you hurt?" he asked Archimedes.

"Arrow gouge. Not mortal, but I can't make defense."

Nile examined the wound. "Deep," he said with frustration. "What about you? Are you injured?" he asked Delbert.

Terrified, Delbert shook his head. "No! What are those things?"

"Nothing natural," chided Niles.

Armus arrived on foot. He sustained a gouging wound across his left shoulder. His face glistened with perspiration. "My lord, can you continue?" he asked Archimedes.

"Not without treatment."

Armus noticed all six beasts were dead or incapacitated. "Kincaid!"

Still mounted, Kincaid arrived. "Commander." He noticed Archimedes. "My lord, how badly are you hurt?"

"I'll live," he groused. "What of the others?

"Two dead, two badly wounded, and their horses killed."

"My horse is also dead," said Armus.

"What do we do now, Commander?" asked Delbert, still very shaken.

"Seek shelter and tend to the dead and wounded."

"There is a safe place not far from here," a female voice spoke.

Niles turned to discover the same forester woman who aided him and Archimedes. "You have a knack for showing up during times of trouble."

"You have a knack for attracting trouble," Wren retorted.

Archimedes began to laugh at her comeback, but quickly stopped due to pain.

Wren took hold of the reins to Archimedes' horse. "Come. The sooner we are off the road, the sooner your wound can be tended." She led the horse.

"Kincaid, tell the men to place the dead and wounded in the wagons. We'll give Cleary and Emmett a proper burial once we reach safety." Armus proceeded on foot after Wren and Archimedes.

For fifteen minutes, Wren led them through the forest to a sheltered cove with a creek. She helped Archimedes to dismount then sit on a fallen log beside the creek. She gave instructions to those arriving.

"I'll need one of you to build a fire. Also, a bowl, cup and cloth for bandages. Are those available among your supplies?" she asked Armus.

"There are cups and bowls are among the cooking supplies. Kincaid, see what can be found for bandages." While Wren went to fetch what she needed, Armus knelt beside Archimedes. "Let's see how bad it is."

A significant amount of blood stained the front of Archimedes' tunic. He tried to sit up straight for Armus to examine the wound. He hissed and flinched.

"It's pretty deep, but doesn't appear to have cut muscle, just flesh."

"Then why does it hurt so fiercely and makes me feel incapacitated?"

Armus looked directly at Archimedes. "Those were *not* normal arrows."

Archimedes' huffed. "Goes along with unnatural creatures." He nodded toward Armus' shoulder. "They clipped you too."

"Hard to completely avoid those claws. But, not too debilitating."

Wren arrived with a bowl, cup and cloth. She had filled the bowl and cup with water. She shooed Armus aside to kneel in front of Archimedes. He sat beside Archimedes. She then removed her pouch and proceeded to mix some herbs in the water of both cup and bowl. She handed the cup to Armus.

"Here, drink this while I tend to his wound then I'll take care of your shoulder."

One sniff, and Armus recognized a strengthening tonic, but for the sake of the mortals he asked, "What is it?"

"Something to stave off infection from whatever gouged you." She touched his face to wipe off some sweat and show him. "A hard fought battle."

"Those beasts didn't go down easily." Armus took a long drink and fought frowning at the taste. "I hope I need only one." He gave her back the cup.

Wren wryly grinned. "Being you are so strong, I doubled the dose just to make sure."

"She helped us before. You should be fine," said Archimedes.

"As should you. I'm going to check on the others." Armus joined Niles, who aided the two seriously wounded Knights. "How bad are they?"

In painful halting steps, Niles drew Armus away. "I don't think they'll be able to continue with us."

Armus noticed Niles discomfort. "What about you?"

Niles gingerly touched his chest while trying to breath. "I think it broke a couple of ribs, but I'm still standing."

Hearing the crackling of flames, Armus left Niles to approach the fire. Kincaid stoked the flames.

"How long do you think we'll need to stay here?" asked Kincaid.

"Depends upon the results of treatment. Archimedes' wound is not too severe, though very painful. Niles may have some broken ribs, while Osborn and Travis are more serious."

"And your gouged shoulder."

Armus let the comment slide. "In the meantime, we bury Cleary and Emmett. Then a good hot meal is in order."

Kincaid frowned to the contrary. "Osborn is our cook."

"No worries. I'll take care of the meal."

Wren heard, and spoke to Armus. "You'll find a young boar hanging on the side of that large oak tree. It's already prepared. I downed it this morning."

Armus grinned at Kincaid. "We'll eat well. But duty first."

⚜

Two miles west of where the attack happened, Carvel, Ashby, Martel and Pathas gathered in a grove of trees.

"That didn't go as planned," Martel chided.

"They are Jor'ellians," countered Carvel.

"And those were creatures of infrinn," insisted Martel.

"Which you were supposed to control! All we were to do is inflict damage without being discovered," Carvel boldly rebuffed.

Martel's chest heaved with insult but he didn't reply.

Irate, Carvel moved to edge of the trees. With great concentration, he stared at the horizon. "There is a familiar sense though nothing clear to explain how they survived!"

"What do you plan on telling Witter and Altari?" Ashby inquired.

Carvel shook his head, still considering the situation. "I'm not sure yet. However, Niles is the King's Champion while Archimedes, First Jor'ellian. Both are highly trained to deal with the unusual."

"I don't think that explanation will suffice," said Martel.

Carvel confronted Martel. "What do you suggest? You saw what happened! Did you sense anything out of the ordinary? Guardian presence that you're not telling me?"

"We didn't sense anything," insisted Ashby in reference to him and Pathas.

"Ay. Between the four of us, we should have sensed something," said Pathas.

"Well, Warrior?" Carvel pressed.

"I sensed nothing," Martel begrudgingly admitted.

"Then we must stand united *when* we report what happened."

Martel cocked a brow of suspicion. "When?"

Carvel grew sly in his reply. "They haven't reach Waldron yet, have they?"

Martel grinned with approval.

"But!" Carvel stressed. "Since the *madah-dune* failed, this calls for Archer stealth." He addressed Ashby. "Learn who accompanies Niles and Archimedes. I want to determine why something felt familiar but not a Guardian."

Ashby readied his bow and ran off.

Chapter 24

THE KNIGHTS SAT AROUND THE WARM FIRE EATING A HEARTY meal of roasted boar and a savory dish of onions, cabbage and potatoes. Two Knights fed their injured comrades a specially fixed boar broth with herbs for pain. They needed food for strength, but in measured portions for ease of digestion.

Armus made his rounds of the wounded. "Not too much," he instructed the Jor'ellian caring for Osborn. "Small amounts. Don't worry if he doesn't finish. It will keep until later."

"Ay, Commander."

"Commander, this is one of the best meals I've had in a while. You need to give Osborn the recipe," said another Jor'ellian.

Armus chuckled. "When he is well enough."

Osborn grunted what sounded like an agreement before accepting another spoonful of broth.

Kincaid paused in eating to address Wren. "In all this rush, we still don't know your name or where you come from."

She kindly grinned. "Call me Collie. I live in the forest."

Seeing Kincaid's marked interest of Wren, Niles spoke. "Well, Mistress Collie, thank you for your kindness."

"No thanks are needed. Our service and cause is the same."

Niles widely smiled. "I thank Jor'el for allowing our paths to cross."

"Here, here!" Archimedes raised his cup in salute.

The Jor'ellians did the same in salute to Wren. She slightly blushed.

Armus spoke to the group. "Once everyone has finished eating and cleaned up, get some sleep. We need to recover our strength to continue in the morning."

"What about the wounded? I don't think Osborn and Travis can be moved far," said Kincaid.

"If you can spare the smaller wagon, I will take them to a cottage for safety," said Wren.

"We could have brought them there rather than camp here."

She shook her head. "No, their wounds needed immediate attention to stabilize their condition. By the morning they can endure a couple of hours in the wagon."

Armus added his comments, "Going there would take us too far off course."

This piqued Kincaid's interest. "How do you know where this cottage is?"

Archimedes intervened. "You wrongly make interrogation when hospitality and aid is offered."

"My lord, I'm merely concerned for the safety of my men."

"There is no need ..." Archimedes began.

Realizing he needed to cover for his unguarded remark, Armus interrupted Archimedes. "My lord, I understand his concern. Perhaps disclosure is needed."

Archimedes stared at Armus, surprised by the statement. Niles also appeared taken aback while Wren wary when Armus approached her. He placed an arm around her shoulder and began to address Kincaid.

"These are perilous times. So, for reasons of security that you should appreciate, it is a closely guarded secret that Collie is in reality, *my sister.*" Armus stared emphatically at Kincaid.

Wren slightly relaxed in relief, though she responded with a thinly disguised rebuke of sarcasm. "I think you speak too freely, *brother.*"

Kincaid came to attention at the stunning revelation to recant. "Commander, I didn't mean for you to betray such a confidence. And surely not to everyone here."

"We are Jor'ellians, sworn to protect each other. Upon that oath I call for you to keep our secret," Armus firmly replied.

Kincaid made the Jor'ellian salute. "I so swear."

The other Knights capable of standing mimicked Kincaid's pledge.

"I may not be a Jor'ellian Knight, but by my priestly pledge, I will maintain your secret," said Delbert.

"I assumed as much, Headmaster," said Armus with a kind smile. Satisfied, he sent Wren a private wink. He then told the men, "Now clean up from dinner and get some sleep. I'll take the first watch."

"We both will keep watch." Wren tapped her crossbow.

It took an hour to clean the dishes, erect two lean-tos and prepare bedding for the night. Archimedes and Delbert slept in one lean-to with Niles and Kincaid taking pallets outside to act as guards. The other was erected around Osborn and Travis in an effort to protect them from the elements. Two Knights remained with them.

Armus stored the leftover boar for use in breakfast. Wren tended the fire to keep the mortals warm during the cool late autumn night. She once again spoke the Ancient in a breathy tone with no distinct syllables for the mortals to discern. With the fire sufficiently stoked, she joined Armus at the larger wagon where he stowed the boar.

"The nightwatch is set," she said with discretion in the Ancient. "*Brother*," she added with a snicker.

He leaned closer to ask in a teasing tone, "Would you prefer Avatar?"

She covered her mouth to prevent a laugh. She then replied in the same tone. "At least our rivalry would give credence to being siblings."

He cocked a grin. "We look more alike."

She lightly chuckled. "There is that."

He grew serious. "Between us, they should rest deeply and undisturbed."

She turned her back to where the mortals slept. "If there aren't any more creatures of infrinn around."

"Did you sense something when setting the watch?"

Wren's brows drew level with consideration. "A faint essence. Familiar somehow, but nothing identifiable."

"Friend, perhaps?"

Wren frowned with further thought. "Gresham isn't well enough yet. A certain *captain*, maybe. After I tend your shoulder, I'll make a search of the perimeter."

"No reason for delay."

"I won't accept another excuse. It *must* be tended."

Armus didn't argue further rather sat on the back of the wagon. Wren withdrew the jar of salve from her pouch. He gritted his teeth against the discomfort when she applied the salve. He relaxed when she finished.

She flashed irate eyes at him. "If you had let me treat it earlier, there wouldn't be any inflammation."

"Others had more pressing needs."

Wren replaced the jar in the pouch, which she left on the wagon. She readied her crossbow.

Armus caught her shoulder when she started to move away. "Be careful."

Wren flashed a confident smile then disappeared into the darkness.

Moving a quarter mile from the campsite, Wren made a wide arc around the area. Occasionally she caught glimpses of the campfire, yet more interested in the growing sense of familiarity. Of course, if she sensed whoever it was, they may be able to sense her. She hoped her mortal persona helped to shield her Guardian essence from clear identification.

A sudden chill stopped her. Not due to the cold since weather and temperature didn't affect Guardians. The night had grown unusually still and silent. Wren held her bow ready. She carefully stretched out her senses to communicate with the animals on the nightwatch.

Someone seized her from behind, one arm wrapped around her chest to pin her arms, while the other hand pressed a dagger to her throat. Held against his body, she reckoned him to be about a foot taller than her mortal disguise of five feet ten inches. She dare not cry out.

"Who are you? And don't lie. I can sense you are more than you appear," demanded a male voice in her left ear.

She heard his voice before, though not immediately recognizable. She attempted to disguise her voice with a higher tenor than normal, hoping he'd mistaken it for fright. "I live here."

"I said don't lie!" He pressed the dagger closer.

She winced when the blade nicked her throat. The warmth of blood trickled down her neck. Any use of power to summon Armus, would give away her true identity. She continued the pretense while deciding how to break free. "I'm not. I'm an orphan and live here to survive."

She still held the crossbow, so she slowly lowered her hands. When she felt him slightly shift his weight from one foot to another, she acted. She shifted the opposite way he moved and used all her might to jam the butt of her crossbow into his abdomen. The strength of the blow made him gasp for air. Another blow from the crossbow into his body allowed her to duck under his arm and break free. Turning to face him with bow ready, she froze in shock.

"Ashby!" the name leapt from her lips.

He glared at her with brief confusion then his eyes widened in recognition. "Wren!"

At her momentary indecision, Ashby attacked. He knocked aside the crossbow to alter her aim. He thrust out with his dagger. Wren barely avoided being impaled. As it was, the dagger ripped her doublet, but missed flesh. She dodged another attack by diving under his arm. She rolled, came up to her knees and fired. The arrow hit Ashby squarely in the chest and knocked him back into a tree. The smashing impact brought him to the ground where he vanished in grey light.

Tears swelled, as Wren stared at the tree. Not since the Great Battle had she been forced to destroy someone she once knew well. Even in their brief battle, she saw he wore the uniform of a Shadow Archer. Why else attack after recognizing her? She lowered her head and wept, biting her lower lip to keep silent.

Wren felt the concern of an essence reaching toward her. Armus. She needed to relax or he would leave the others to come looking for her. She sat back on her heels to wipe her eyes and compose her emotions before returning to camp. When she reached the perimeter of camp, Armus rose from beside the fire to meet her.

He noticed her pale features and the blood. He touched her neck to ascertain the extent of injury. "I sensed something wrong. What happened?"

Wren fought new tears. "The essence … Ashby turned … I had to—"

Armus understood her broken words, and held her when she sobbed.

"Commander?" asked Kincaid with soft-spoken curiosity.

"I thought you were asleep."

"A disturbance in my mind woke me." Kincaid's concern turned to Wren. "Has something happened?"

Armus still held Wren. "She killed to keep us from being discovered. Thank Jor'el she only sustained a minor cut."

Kincaid gazed with sympathy at Wren's wound. "You're very brave, and we are in your debt." He took her hand. "Jor'el comfort and strengthen you, mistress."

She simply nodded and wiped her eyes.

"Thank you," Armus said to Kincaid. "Check on Osborn and Travis. They seemed to be sleeping soundly, but make sure before returning to sleep yourself."

With a compassionate smile at Wren, Kincaid left.

Armus drew Wren to the larger wagon. "Sit, while I make you a tonic." He took the pouch to the front of the wagon. By the time he returned with the pouch and cup, she appeared calmer.

She accepted the cup without comment. Surprise registered in her gaze when drinking. "Wine."

He softly smiled. "You needed something more soothing than just water."

Choked words stopped further speech. She finished the tonic.

Armus used a wet cloth to gently wipe the dried blood from Wren's neck. Once the area was clean, he saw the nature of the wound. "A blade nick. Not too serious. Still, a dab of salve will keep it from turning into something unexpected."

Early the next morning, Armus and Wren examined Osborn and Travis. After having slept well, color returned to their faces.

"I feel better than I expected," said Osborn.

"You're still too weak to do anything more than recover," said Wren.

"I didn't mean that. I just thought I'd feel a lot worse with such wounds."

"I'm afraid that assessment won't last once we move you to the wagon."

Osborn's questioning glance shifted to Armus. "Must I go, Commander?"

"Ay, you and Travis need treatment. We are enough to see them safely to Waldron." Armus signaled to the waiting Jor'ellians. "As gently as you can."

Alas, Wren's assessment proved correct, though Osborn tried not to show too much discomfort. The evidence appeared in his newly paled features. Travis held his breath to resist the pain.

Wren placed a hand on Osborn's shoulder. "We gave as much cushion as possible for the journey. I'll try to take it slow and easy, however, the drive will take a couple of hours through the wilderness.

Osborn took a breath before replying. "We understand and are ready."

Archimedes appeared beside the wagon to speak to Osborn and Travis. "Before we separate, and to renew all our spirits, we shall partake of the *Mismich*."

Everyone gathered around the wagon. Delbert held a candle, Kincaid a loaf of bread and Niles an open bottle of wine.

Archimedes presided over the refreshing ceremony. He spoke the Ancient. "Great Jor'el, creator of the universe, we come before you with bread and wine to pay homage, beseeching you for strength and wisdom." He stuck a match and lit the candle Delbert held. "May this, your eternal light, give us insight into the enemy that threatens your kingdom."

246

"*Tangiel,*" everyone said.

Archimedes took the bottle from Niles. "May this wine refresh our hearts and strengthen our spirits to complete the great task you have set before us."

"*Tangiel,*" they spoke in agreement.

Archimedes drank and handed the bottle to Armus, who helped Osborn and Travis to drink. Armus took a drink and passed the bottle to Wren. The bottle passed to each in the group to take a drink.

Kincaid handed Archimedes the loaf of bread. The Vicar continued. "May this bread strengthen our bodies to endure what is to come."

"*Tangiel*", the group said in unison.

Archimedes broke off a piece and ate. Armus did the same then again aided Osborn and Travis. The bread passed around the group with each tearing off a piece to eat. When finished, Archimedes spoke the concluding statement. "To your will we commend our prayers, our lives and this mission. *Tangiel.*"

"*Tangiel*", they repeated for the last time.

Archimedes raised his hands and eyes to heaven. "Jor'el, we ask you to grant safe passage to Mistress Collie and our companions. May you allow their recovery to be speedy and complete. *Tangiel.*"

Wren hopped onto the driver's seat. "Jor'el watch over you, my lord," she said to Archimedes. She glanced to Armus with a small smile. "Brother."

Armus simply grinned and winked in response.

When the wagon was out of sight, Kincaid spoke to Archimedes. "My lord, it is obvious someone knows we are coming."

Archimedes flashed a grin. "That shouldn't surprise you."

"It doesn't. However, it does concern me on how to proceed after this attack."

"In disguise. Or at the very least attempt to look non-threatening," said Armus. He went to a trunk on the wagon. "Common clothes to appear like travelers."

Niles scowled with annoyance. "Something else I missed when I should have been considering security."

Armus spoke with compassion. "Champion, your mind was understandably divided between duty and grief. I merely filled in where necessary."

"Your kindness and forethought is greatly appreciated, Commander."

Kincaid distributed the clothes. "This will take care of our appearance. What about gaining entry to Waldron?" he asked Armus.

"We'll use the Chapel undercroft."

Puzzled, Kincaid paused in changing. "Chapel undercroft?"

"A secret passage into the castle that very few remember, or even know about," said Archimedes. He tossed a careful glance to Armus.

The answer didn't clarify much for Kincaid, so Armus explained while they changed clothes. "Tristan ordered it built during the original construction. He won the throne, but the kingdom remained in turmoil. He wanted a means of escape for his family should the worse happen before he achieved total unity. It will serve our purpose. Once we reach the safe zone, we'll change back into our uniforms, but with cloaks as concealment then enter via the Chapel undercroft. "

"If very few *remember* or know the secret, how is it that you know?"

Armus grinned at Kincaid. "Captain Seul told me."

With frustration, Kincaid straightened his common tunic. "Maybe someday I'll meet this Captain Seul I've heard so much about."

Archimedes laughed and slapped Kincaid's arm. "I'll introduce you next time he calls upon me. Now, let's finish changing and continue."

Chapter 25

AT POINTS DURING THE LONG, SLOW DRIVE, WREN SPOKE THE Ancient under her breath seeking protection and comfort for Osborn and Travis. She also wondered about how to get them into the cottage without revealing her true nature. A mortal female would not be able to single-handedly carry them.

No roads led to the cottage, only a few old narrow paths wound through the woods. When a path ended, the journey became rough in navigating the forest. Wren stopped several times to help Osborn and Travis when their pain became too great. She added some poppy juice to the water in hopes of inducing sleep. Unfortunately, stopping or taking detours to avoid hazards lengthened the journey from her original estimate of two hours to three hours.

When they finally reaching the cottage, Osborn's eyes were closed with his face screwed in pain. Travis had fainted after the last jostling. As hard as Wren tried to keep the wagon steady, it proved totally impossible to miss every rut or divot.

To her surprised, two individuals waited outside the cottage: Eldric and Kell. Although both were disguised as mortals, she recognized them. Eldric appeared in his usually mortal physician disguise while Kell assumed the role of a commoner. He retained his black hair with mortal golden hazel eyes.

"Greetings, Collie," began Eldric in address.

Hearing a male voice made Osborn open his eyes. "Who's that?" he spoke with anxiety.

"Have no fear," soothed Wren, still on the driver's seat. "It is Master Godwin."

"And my assistant, Conrad." Eldric motioned to Kell.

The answer confused Osborn. "Assistant of what?"

Wren climbed down from the wagon to reassure Osborn. "Godwin is a physician to the poor and unfortunate."

Eldric joined Wren at the wagon. "Indeed. We never come to this part of the province without visiting Collie. Judging by the wounds of you and your friend, it is good we did."

Wren spoke to Kell. "Stay with them while Godwin and I prepare beds and medicine."

Kell simply nodded. When Osborn warily eyed him, Kell kindly smiled. "Be at peace, sir. Your secret is safe with us."

"What secret?" Osborn demanded.

Kell lightly chuckled. "I do recognize the Jor'ellian uniform."

Osborn started at Kell. The gold of the hazel eyes seemed to intensify and Osborn relaxed. "Oh, ay." He then winced in pain. He exhaled in relief when the discomfort subsided.

Travis loudly groaned, so Kell moved to ascertain his injuries. "Your comrade is in great pain," he said to Osborn.

"His wounds are more serious than mine."

"Don't minimize your injuries."

"I don't. Only the severity is obvious. Mine are numerous and inhibiting, his are life-threatening."

Wren and Eldric returned with Eldric speaking to Kell. "We need to gently carrying them inside. Collie, take care of the wagon."

After Eldric and Kell took Travis and Osborn from the wagon, Wren drove the wagon behind the cottage. She placed the horse in a secluded pen. She then used a spoken word of power to create a canopy of overgrowth and tree branches to hide the wagon. She lowered her head with a sigh at the expenditure of energy of what used to be so normal and easy.

Inside the two-room cottage, Travis and Osborn were taken to the bedroom. Two cots had been well prepared. Wren entered the bedroom to help. She tended Travis while Kell aided Osborn. Eldric divided his time between them, though more concerned for Travis. Treatment ended with Eldric administering two extra strong sleeping tonics. They left so the Knights could rest undisturbed.

Eldric shut the bedroom door. "They should sleep until tomorrow."

"What of their wounds?" asked Wren.

"Osborn will make a full recovery. Travis, well, the deep wound severed muscles and tendons in his arm. You did well in stopping the bleeding. It helped me to surgically repair the damaged areas. Still, I fear there could be some paralysis."

Kell switched to the Ancient and asked Wren, "What attacked them?" only Eldric answered.

"*Madah-dune.* I can tell by the wounds."

Kell grew wary at the reply, but Wren confirmed the answer.

"Ay. Along with Shadow Archers." Her voice quivered when speaking of Archers. She shied away.

"Wren?" Kell held her shoulder, concerned by her change in mood.

With discomposure she said, "Ashby. We fought. I shot ..."

"That accounts for the nick on your neck," said Eldric in mild assessment.

"And the tear in your jerkin?" asked Kell.

"Same reason," she weakly said. She gathered her emotions to complete the report. "Archimedes suffered an abdominal wound from an arrow. Niles has a few cracked ribs and Armus gouged by claws," she motioned to her left shoulder. "All manageable. Two Knights were killed along with three horses. We spent the night in the wilderness before I brought Osborn and Travis here for safety and treatment."

With level brows, Kell listened. After a moment he asked Eldric, "How long for Osborn and Travis to recover?"

"At least ten days for Osborn. Two weeks would be better. Travis longer. His left arm is the major concern. It will take months to recover movement or sensation, *if* allowed."

Kell shook his head. "They can't stay here for weeks."

"I wasn't suggesting that," disputed Eldric. "I meant Jor'el granting full restoration of the arm."

"How long until they can travel back to the main Fortress?"

"Ten days, at least."

"No, three."

"Kell, recovery time is not negotiable," chided Eldric.

"A week maybe all the time we have left!" Kell hotly rebuffed.

"Quiet!" Wren scolded in a low harsh voice. She waved toward the bedroom.

Kell and Eldric took a moment to calm down.

"I can have them ready to leave in a week," said Eldric.

"No! *Three* days," Kell said with emphasis, though he kept his voice low. "It will take Wren three days to drive them to the Fortress thus six days before she can rejoin us."

"We can shorten that time *if* we take them back using our way," said Wren.

Eldric pursed his lips in consideration. "I don't know what dimension travel would do to them. Healthy mortals don't tolerate it well. It could set them back in recovery, *or* they might not survive the trip."

Despite the dismal prognosis, Kell spoke with sobriety. "We can only act within the parameters of our orders." He placed both hands on Eldric's shoulders to look directly at the physician. "We are only twelve against thousands of the enemy! We must all assemble to be ready to face whatever is to happen. As Jor'ellians, they too know the risks. Service to Jor'el is paramount over the cost."

"Sacrifice some to save the whole. As a physician, I never like that," grumbled Eldric.

"You think I do?" probed Kell.

Eldric gazed steadily at Kell. The answer obvious, for despite Kell's stalwart façade as captain, his eyes showed a depth of emotional pain that came with the position. Eldric's combativeness faded. "I know you don't. I'll have them ready for dimension travel in three days."

Kell patted Eldric's shoulder in gratitude.

"Where we will take them? Legends can't just appear in the Fortress infirmary." Eldric usual sarcasm returned.

After a brief moment of thought, Kell replied. "The Temple's abandoned guesthouse a mile south of the Fortress." He spoke to Wren. "Once there, go to the Temple and ask for Alfie. Say Captain Seul sent you with word about Osborn and Travis."

"Who will shadow Armus and the others?"

"I will. If they ask, tell them you sent *Conrad* on ahead to your next patient." After a nod from Eldric, Kell drew Wren outside. "I am sorry about Ashby. It's not easy to face an old friend as an enemy."

Conflicting emotions kept her mute.

Kell continued, a bit awkward in his sympathy. Such situations were always hard. "I realize that might not help much, but it's all I can say."

"Go, take care of Armus and the others." Wren went back inside.

Even though he understood sorrow made Wren reply gruffly, Kell stared at the cottage. Centuries of conflict didn't make it easy to deal with former comrades turned to the Dark Way. Alas, it became a necessary part of their duty.

"Peace to you, Wren," Kell spoke an Ancient blessing under his breath before vanishing in dimension travel.

Chapter 26

MYLA DIVIDED HER TIME BETWEEN THE YOUNGER BOYS AND visiting Akilles. Since Zared's return, she made excuses to Berk that Akilles was ill and needed to remain in his chambers under care. Berk acted unusually agreeable, even kind. He used to be kind when they were first married, and sometimes romantic. Zared's influence changed all that. The past six years Berk grew more hostile towards her, but turning on Akilles? That was too much!

Myla realized she and Niles took a great risk in formulating the plan. However, with the safety her sons and the future of the kingdom at stake, it was a necessary risk. Jor'el willing, Niles and Archimedes will arrive before the royal forum. If not, she might have to rely on Colin to execute the plan.

After lunch, Myla made her way to Akilles' chambers. The Jor'ellian standing guard admitted her without knocking. Colin remained with Akilles, as did Wilma. While Wilma did needlepoint, Colin and Akilles sat at a table near the hearth where Colin conducted lessons.

"Marmi!" Her arrival gave Akilles an excuse to leave the table.

She accepted his hug and kiss of greeting. "I see you are wisely spending your time in study." She winked at Colin.

"Since he must not appear too active, study is the best alternative," said Colin with a smile.

Akilles rolled his eyes. "I could use some fresh air."

"Then open the window," said Wilma with a large teasing smile.

This further frustrated the Prince.

Myla sat on sofa. "We discuss this each time I visit."

Akilles joined her. "I know, and I'm trying," he said with exasperation.

Myla tenderly touched his cheek. "I understand your need for activity." She then lowered her voice. "*You* must understand the need for discretion."

"I do, and I can't wait for him to leave!"

"*Shhh!*" she scolded.

Akilles slumped back into the sofa.

Colin huffed a wry chuckle. "For being so intuitive, you must stop allowing your emotion to get the better of you. In a couple of months, you will be thirteen, an adult. It's time to start putting into practice the skills needed to navigate the adult world."

Akilles sat up, straight and formal. "I have been succeeding more times than not."

"To succeed at all times, you must temper your frustration during situations out of your control. This is where patience and trust in Jor'el must guide you. Hence, the lessons." Colin motioned to the books on the table.

Akilles' brows leveled in thought. "I never realized Jor'ellians were as knowledgeable in Verse and Prophecy as they are in arms and military tactics."

"We must be grounded in Jor'el's law in order to be effective in service to the Almighty. It is upon that foundation all other aspects of our training depend."

Akilles regarded Colin while considering the statement. "Niles often said the same." With a heavy sigh of lament, he lowered his head. "I wish my father and I were as much alike as you and Niles."

In a gesture of silent sympathy, Myla took hold of Akilles' hands.

There was a ruffle of skirts as Wilma knelt beside Akilles. "Jor'el knows your heart. If all goes as planned, there may be hope in winning him back to faith."

"Do you really believe that?"

"While there is life, there is always hope. Don't give up on that."

Myla wiped away a tear. "My dear Wilma, thank you."

Wilma gently smiled.

Myla squeezed Akilles' hand to get his attention. "Continue your studies with Sir Colin, yet be ready at a moment's notice."

The statement made Colin ask, "Has there been progress?"

"Some. I will know for certain after the royal forum this afternoon." She then spoke to Akilles. "Wilma must leave with me to prepare for the forum. Listen closely to Sir Colin." She kissed Akilles on the forehead.

"To your studies. I'll be there in a moment," said Colin to Akilles. He accompanied Myla and Wilma to the door. He detained Myla to speak privately. "Madam, be wary of Zared at the forum."

"Oh, I shall," she replied with certainly. She then smiled fondly at Colin. "Akilles is right. You and Niles are very much alike. For that, I thank Jor'el."

Colin made a reverent bow as she and Wilma left.

Fitch/Odell paced Zared's chamber. He spent nearly two days holed up in the room. For security, Zared told him. Although agreeing to assume the Headmaster's identity, he didn't realize it meant so much inaction. Of course when trying to save one's life, the ramifications of rash agreements didn't factor into the decision. Once broken by reconditioning, Dagar commanded, and he obeyed.

Odell's memories and personal machinations informed Fitch somewhat of the plan. Or at least what the Headmaster believed; Wilbur would be killed and Odell assume the role of Vicar by royal appointment. Fitch tried to find any clue to something other than what he discovered from Odell's mind by questioning Zared. Unfortunately, the cagey mortal evaded any direct answers.

Fitch/Odell picked up a piece of cold roast beef from the tray of food brought him. Although he ate to keep up appearances, the taste was appealing.

Zared arrived with his valet. "Time to get ready for our most awaited performance!"

"My lord? I have no clothes but these," said Fitch/Odell.

Zared laughed. "Don't worry. They will soon be replaced by those more fitting your new station."

Fitch/Odell flashed a cool, calculating smile.

"Now to make ready for my first royal act." While the valet tended to the duty of preparing Zared, the baron spoke to Fitch/Odell. "When we leave for the forum, you must hide beneath the hooded cloak of discretion. Hiller," he spoke of his valet, "will take you to an alcove off the Great Hall to wait. At the appointed time, he will escort you into the Hall where *I* will reveal the chosen candidate for Vicar." Zared's eyes narrowed in warning upon Fitch/Odell. "Pay close attention to the words I'm about to tell you and remember to speak them only when appropriate."

"Ay, my lord."

In his guest chambers, Abner stood before a full-length mirror finishing his preparation for the royal forum. Gordon arrived. The younger lord was suitably dressed for the formal occasion though somber in expression. Abner dismissed his valet. When the door closed upon the man's departure, Abner made inquiry.

"This may be gloomy business but we must play our parts."

It took a moment for Gordon to understand. In fact, it wasn't until Abner smiled and Gordon saw the reflection in the mirror. "Oh, sorry. My mind is rather preoccupied."

"Understandable."

Gordon plopped in a chair. "I don't mean about this evening."

His curiosity piqued, Abner moved from the mirror. "What about?"

Gordon sat forward to confront Abner. His voice low yet harsh. "My father! And what was said about ... the disgraced one."

Abner pulled up another chair. "I'm sure it was a difficult way for you to learn the truth."

Gordon's expression hardened. "How long have you known?"

Abner didn't take offense at the harsh tone. "Niles reluctantly told me shortly after *his* resignation when I pressed for answers."

"Six months." Gordon sat back, face fixed with anger.

"For five years *he* evaded suspicion until it finally caught up with him. Clues from Hoyt's death lead to Wilbur finally confronting him. Apparently, Hoyt was last in the string of questionable circumstances involving him."

Gordon looked askew. "What was different about my father's death?"

Abner shrugged. "I don't know. All Niles said is that Hoyt's death brought to light other issues. Don't be angry at Niles for telling me. I knew something wasn't right, and wouldn't let him get away with evading questions. For your sake, I wanted to learn the truth."

"How for *my sake* if you withheld such information?"

Abner sighed with regret and frustration. He replied with honest discretion. "Back then, you were a vulnerable lad of nineteen and needed to believe Zared so you could assume your rightful place on the Council. If, at any time before being installed, Zared suspected you knew the truth, doubtful you would be sitting here now. Remember, until six months ago, *he* was still in our ranks. We swore to protect you until a time came to reveal the truth."

Gordon stared at the floor, his face rapt in consideration.

"All I can I do is apologize, and assure you we had your best interest at heart." Abner touched Gordon's knee to get attention. Abner softly smiled. "You've grown into a fine man. Hoyt would be proud, as I am proud to call friend. Better yet, my Jor'ellian brother. No harm was intended."

A small quick smile appeared that quickly faded. "But *he* still inflicts harm!" Gordon chided.

"We seek to prevent it. To do so, let us partake of *mismich* to refocus and strengthen our hearts and mind for this evening."

Gordon joined Abner at small table where Abner already placed what was needed for the refreshing. He asked in a whisper, "Have you heard anything about certain plans?"

"She believes it all hinges on his mood after the forum. Now, let's begin."

Nobles assembled in the Great Hall. Unlike at high banquet, only the royal thrones were prepared, everyone else remained standing. Although Berk dissolved the Council, eight wore the chain and crest of their province, a sign of their station as overlord and position on the Council. Three dissenters were Zared, Patrin and Hagan.

They approached a group that included Abner, Gordon, Slater and Mather. Zared wore a disapproving sneer. "Gentlemen, you are bold in your attire."

"Why?" began Slater. "This is a royal forum, and requires protocol."

"The *King* may not see it that way. Rather as willful defiance," scolded Patrin.

"If the King issues a formal writ of disestablishment then we shall remove our chains as required. Until then, the Council exists in form, though not function."

Zared stopped Patrin from protest. "Your point is taken, Count Slater." He, Patrin and Hagan left.

"That was telling," grumbled Mather.

Slater's narrow glance followed Zared in departure. "It tells me that for all his cleverness, Zared overlooked a point of order."

Abner coughed to cover a chuckle.

Slater's grin at Abner's reaction quickly faded into warning. "You can laugh now at his miscue, but it won't be easy for us when he has Berk issue the writ."

"Then perhaps you shouldn't have reminded him," said Mather.

Slater touched his crest. "It is our only defense for being so bold. Actual defiance would incur worse than a writ."

"What will we do when it happens?" asked Gordon.

Slater patted the younger lord on the shoulder. "We will make that decision when the time comes. At present, the forum requires our full attention." He looked again to find Zared. He and Patrin chatted cordially with other nobles near the main platform. "Being made *Grand Master* is just the first step in his plan. The forum will tell us more."

The herald pounded the staff and called for order. When Berk and Myla made their way from the back of the Hall to the platform, everyone paid their respects. No one followed the royal couple. Wilma, and several of the Queen's ladies, waited near the platform. Myla sat first. Berk looked with smug satisfaction at those assembled before taking a seat.

"Rise," he said at length.

When the Hall grew quiet from the activity of movement, Berk continued.

"News has reached us that required the summoning of a royal forum. News that will shake the very foundation of Allon." He paused for dramatic effect. "It is my solemn duty to inform the Court of Vicar Wilbur's death ..."

Stunned gasps, murmurs and exclamations of grief came from those gathered. A few women appeared on the verge of fainting. Despite prior knowledge, witnessing the reactions made Myla misty eyed. She bowed her head to contain her emotions.

Slater eyes grew wide with shock while Mather mumbled a somber prayer. Abner and Gordon remained stone-faced at the announcement. The only visible sign of their disturbance came in clenched fists and narrow eyes.

Slater stepped forward. His voice troubled yet loud enough to be heard over the reactions. "Sire, do you know how the Vicar died?"

Berk feigned sympathy. Even to the casual observer, the King seemed too aloof to be sincere. "He was old. Who is to say which of his many aliments made him succumb?"

"He was not in ill-health!" Gordon protested.

Abner seized Gordon to stop further words. Abner's expression of warning made Gordon regret his hasty actions.

Seeing Berk stirred with insult, Zared spoke. "Everyone witnessed Wilbur's weakened condition at the high banquet. So while you may want to see things through the eyes of youth, Sir Gordon, those of us older and wiser know the truth."

Berk took advantage of Zared's speech to calm down. "Well said, Grand Master."

"Thank you, Sire."

Berk addressed Gordon. "Considering the shock of this news, we shall overlook your outburst, Sir Gordon."

Gordon bowed in acknowledgement.

Berk's gaze once again swept over the assembly. Many regained their composure while some women shed silent tears. "Alas, Wilbur neglected to provide a Divine Writ of Succession. This leaves us in the position of appointing a new Vicar. One who will work with Grand Master Zared and help guide the kingdom to enlightenment."

"Does Your Majesty have a candidate in mind?" asked Patrin.

Berk motioned to Zared, who stepped in front of the platform to address the assembly. "The man is known to all, and well qualified." He waved to the left side of the hall.

A slender hooded and cloaked individual entered from an alcove. He kept his head slightly bent in his approach of the Grand Master. Zared removed the hood and cloak as Fitch/Odell stood to his full height.

"Headmaster Odell," announced Zared.

The reaction was measureable, some in favor, some not and others wary.

"Please, please!" Zared tried to get attention with little success.

Berk stood and shouted, "Silence!" Once he received everyone's attention, he sat. "This appointment is not up for debate or question." After a brief moment of haughtily glaring at the crowd, he nodded to Zared. "Proceed."

Zared spoke to Fitch/Odell. "Headmaster, you may explain."

Fitch/Odell assumed a formal posture and cleared his throat to begin. "For five years I have served as Vicar Wilbur's personal assistant and Headmaster of the Fortress of Jor'el. According to canon law, if Divine Writ is not formally declared, the next in line is the Headmaster of the Fortress. This must meet with royal approval. If not, the King is authorized to appoint a new Vicar."

Berk took up the formal address. "I have interviewed Headmaster Odell and find him to be of like mind. He is willing to work closely with Grand Master Zared and myself in bringing Allon into a new age of illumination and progress. We will no longer stagnate in the ways of our forefathers—"

"Heresy!" shouted Slater, Abner, Gordon and several others.

"There is no heresy where royal will and law is concerned!" Berk shouted. He waved at the guards. Quickly five guards surrounded Slater, Abner, Gordon and Mather. "Now, curb your tongue. And remove those chains of office! I have dissolved the Council."

Slater stopped a guard from reaching for his chain. "Where is the Writ of Disestablishment, Sire? When I see it, I will retire."

"As will I," said Abner. Gordon and Mather echoed their agreement.

Berk fought his fury at the counterpoint. He set an irate sneer to Zared, which prompted the Grand Master to calmly nod. Berk then spoke with reluctance. "It will be posted later this evening!" He waved the guards from the group.

Berk took a deep breath before concluding. "Tomorrow morning at ten o'clock, Headmaster Odell shall conduct a chapel service for us. He will then journey to The Temple and be properly installed as Vicar. I expect full attendance at Chapel." He spoke the last sentence to the group of dissenters. He abruptly stood to leave.

Myla cast worried eyes to Wilma before she hurried to follow Berk. Wilma fell in step behind her mistress. Wilma sent a fretful glance to Abner on her way out.

Gordon leaned close to Abner. "I think departure will be delayed."

"Or expedite it. I'll find out," replied Abner.

Not until midnight did Abner manage to contact Wilma. He needed to be discrete rather than approach the Queen directly. Although inside, she wore a cloak with the hood partially raised for protection against clear identification. She lowered it enough for Abner to recognize her.

They met in a dark rear corner of the hallway connecting the royal wing to the guest wing.

"Well?" he asked.

Wilma whispered in the Ancient. "He wants all his sons present at Chapel."

Abner scowled with annoyance at the news. "It needs to be soon."

"Ay, maybe taking advantage of activity during Odell's departure."

Abner grinned. "An interesting option. You have learned to speak the Ancient very well. No doubt thanks to a certain *Jor'ellian*."

She quelled an embarrassed smile. "Be ready for the signal. Now, I must go." Taking a caution look around, she hurried back toward the royal wing.

Chapter 27

THE FOLLOWING MORNING, COLIN ACCOMPANIED MYLA, WILMA and the young princes to the Chapel. Despite the gathering crowd, guards held open a path for the royal family. Colin took up position on the wall side of the row where Myla sat with her sons. Wilma sat on the aisle, thus she and Colin flanked the Queen and Princes. Berk stood at the base of the high altar with Zared, Patrin and Fitch/Odell.

Colin observed all, from the assembly of people to the clean and bright state of the Chapel. Servants must have worked all night to make the Chapel look this good. Even the Chapel priest appeared reinvigorated. Colin wasn't quite sure what to make of this sudden transformation. He had never seen the Chapel immaculate, but something in his spirit sensed a foreboding.

Last evening when Myla informed Akilles about the Chapel service, Colin grieved for Wilbur. What a blow it must be to his father and Archimedes. In truth, it was devastating news to all those true and loyal to Jor'el. But why haven't they returned? Surely they know about Odell. Or do they?

Colin's considering gaze focused on the Headmaster. During his time at the Fortress training to become a Jor'ellian, Colin saw Odell frequently. As if sensing interest, Odell met Colin's stare. A shiver racked Colin's body accompanied by a momentary discomposure he found disturbing. He broke eye contact with Odell to assume a formal stance. In actuality, he needed to consider the uneasiness.

Promptly at ten o'clock the Chapel bells tolled. Again, this was not a regular occurrence. Colin's spirit grew more troubled when Fitch/Odell mounted the steps to high altar. Everything within Colin wanted to cry out to stop whatever unsettled him. Since he didn't know *what*, he had to remain silent.

Fitch/Odell faced the altar and raised his hands. "Almighty Jor'el, we come beseeching you to grace us this day with your presence—"

"Stop!" a loud echoing shout came from the Chapel entrance.

Four soldiers barred a group of cloaked and hooded men from entering further.

"Who dares interrupt the service?" demanded Fitch/Odell.

"I—" began a tall man, when a hand on his shoulder made him pause.

The man who made the gesture shed his cloak. Niles! Upon seeing The King's Champion and his angry sneer, the soldiers stepped aside to let him pass but prevented the others from following. Niles advanced down the aisle until Zared bolted to his feet then Niles stopped.

"You?" Zared thundered. "Why have your returned? To disgrace the King further?"

"No, to stop an affront to Jor'el!" Niles pointed to Fitch/Odell. "That man is not fit to be Vicar. Nor is he the appointed one."

Zared moved from the pew to confront Niles. "With no writ of succession King Berk has the right to appoint whom he will."

"There is a writ!" Niles withdrew the copy from his belt. "Duly witnessed and official. Canon law prevails over royal choice."

This brought Berk to his feet. "A forgery! I received no such document."

"We discovered it after Wilbur's *murder!*" Niles loudly declared.

The revelation brought horrified gasps and mutters from those gathered.

"Silence!" Berk shouted.

A pounding from the group of men caught attention. The agitated crowd grew silent, at least for moment.

Curious about the pounding yet determined for answer, Berk accosted Niles. "First you claim, that I, *The King,* cannot appoint

Headmaster Odell to be Vicar, now you say Wilbur was murdered. You are filled with outrageous boldness, Knight."

Zared joined Berk's rebuff. "What proof do you bring besides a forgery?"

"Witnesses to the Writ and the *real* Vicar." Niles returned to the group. "Stand down!" he ordered the soldiers. Though reluctant, they moved aside. "Behold, Jor'el's appointed Vicar!"

Everyone in the group shed their cloaks. Astonishment reigned at seeing Archimedes in the robes of high office and the holding the Staff of Jor'el.

Zared grabbed the neck of his collar, momentarily discomposed. He quickly righted himself with a snarl of fury.

Wilma covered her mouth to stop calling out Archimedes' name. Her eyes swelled with tears of proud admiration. She caught Archimedes' eye when he moved forward with Niles. He didn't react, he couldn't.

Kincaid, Delbert, Armus and the Jor'ellians followed Archimedes and Niles. Rather than focus on the mortals, Armus' attention stayed on Fitch/Odell. The Headmaster grew uneasy in watching the group walk the center aisle.

Archimedes and Niles stopped at the fourth row. Archimedes' stalwart gaze shifted between Zared and Berk, ending on Berk. "You want proof. Myself, Niles and Commander Finn found Wilbur moments before he died of his wound. A single thrust nicked the heart. He gave me this." He took the paper from Niles and handed it to Berk. "As required by canon law, Headmaster Delbert and First Jor'ellian Kincaid witnessed Wilbur's choice and authenticated the document."

"I am Headmaster not Delbert," objected Fitch/Odell.

"You forfeited your position when you abandoned the brethren in a time of crisis," rebuffed Archimedes. "Now we find you here continuing your disgraceful behavior by making a false claim."

Zared stood beside Berk to inspect the Writ of Succession.

"This is a forgery!" Berk said again, only in weak protest.

"Then show me the Writ for Odell," challenged Archimedes.

"I don't need a writ!" began Fitch/Odell. He too sounded a bit shaky, yet masked it with determination. "I was Wilbur's assistant and Fortress Headmaster, next in line. You!" he pointed to Archimedes, "are not legitimate."

Armus stepped out from behind Archimedes to confront Fitch/Odell. "You are not who you claim."

Fitch/Odell stared into Armus' eyes. A gasp of alarm escaped, as he stepped back into the altar.

At the reaction, Archimedes demanded of Fitch/Odell, "Who are you?"

Fitch/Odell righted himself with renewed vigor. "You shall see power this day." He raised his eyes and arms toward the ceiling. "Mighty one, lord of d—"

Archimedes pounded his staff on the floor. "Jor'el is the only mighty one, creature of darkness!"

A sudden aura of light surrounded Archimedes. A focused bright beam radiated from the head of the staff to blind Fitch/Odell. With an outcry of pain, Fitch/Odell fell. His face briefly transformed back to Fitch then returned to Odell. Unmasked! He scrambled to his feet, ran off the side of the platform and down the hall leading to the back of the Chapel.

"Stay with them!" Armus ordered Kincaid before pursuing Fitch/Odell.

At the display of power, people screamed. In a panic, most rushed from the Chapel. Abner, Gordon, Slater and Mather remained in rapt anticipation. Myla and Wilma comforted the frightened younger princes. Akilles watched in mesmerized awe. Colin made his way to Akilles, his sword ready for defense. The corners of Colin's mouth twitched with a smile of relief, yet wary of the scene.

Zared trembled with rage. He gripped the collar so tight his knuckles turned white. Stunned, Berk's legs gave way, which forced him to sit. The paper slipped from his hand.

Niles retrieved the Writ. "Any more questions, Sire?"

Berk couldn't answer.

With lethal tone and expression, Zared spoke so only those close to Niles could hear. "You will regret this." He then addressed Archimedes in a raised voice. "It would be wise for you to leave before the King takes action for this effrontery!"

Archimedes grinned in triumph. "I have discharged my duty in confronting an imposter. However, I will not leave before I claim what is mine."

"You already proved you are the Vicar. What more do you want?" demanded Berk.

"My wife." With a tender smile, Archimedes held out his hand to Wilma.

When she rose to take his hand, there were no murmurs of surprise. By now all who remained in the Chapel were Archimedes's group, the royal family, Colin, Zared, Patrin and four Council members.

Wilma held onto Archimedes' arm as they left the Chapel. Outside she asked, "Where are we going?"

"The Temple, of course. Our new home." He smiled at her.

"I don't get say to good-bye to Myla?" she asked with dismay.

He touched her cheek to wipe away a tear. "You know that's not possible."

She clung to him even harder when walking across the Grand Courtyard. Warily she watched, waiting to be accosted.

He patted her hand. "After Jor'el made his presence known, they won't prevent us from leaving."

Kincaid sent a Knight running to the open gate. There the Knight whistled several times and used both arms in a waving signal.

When the wagon arrived, Archimedes took hold of Wilma's hand. "It's not a carriage because we needed to be discrete. All your needs will be provided for when we reach The Temple." He helped her climb into the wagon then joined her.

Meanwhile, Armus raced to find Fitch. The fleeting glimpse provided enough clarity for identification. Armus sensed something odd about the

Headmaster, even suspected a Guardian somehow. Seeing the shapeshifter, he immediately understood what was happening.

Armus followed Fitch out the rear door where he lost sight of the wily shapeshifter. He closed his eyes in an attempt to discern if Fitch was nearby. Though briefly unmasked, Fitch could hide his essence completely beneath Odell's semblance. No good. He slipped away.

For a moment, Armus vacillated between pursuing Fitch, and returning to Archimedes. The latter won out since protecting the new Vicar was his primary task. With Archimedes' identity revealed, the return journey would be more hazardous.

Armus arrived at the gate just after Archimedes sat beside Wilma in the wagon.

"Commander Finn. Did you find him?" Archimedes asked.

"No. I will resume my search after I see you safely returned to the Temple." Armus kindly grinned at Wilma. "My lady, I'm sorry the mode of transport is not as comfortable as it should be in your delicate condition."

Wilma marveled. "What do you know of my condition?"

Archimedes chuckled. "My dear, you will find Commander Finn is gifted with heavenly insight."

"Archimedes." Niles began with a conflicted expression. "I'm staying. My duty is here. Finn and Kincaid will see you safely back."

"You risk a great deal by remaining."

"I can't leave them again! No matter what it may cost me." Niles' grim determination became obvious the more he spoke.

Archimedes held Niles' arm, staring intensely at him. "Whether we meet again in this life or the next, Jor'el keep you safe, Niles of Pollux."

The sentiment touched Niles, who spoke in earnest reply. "May he bless you, my lord Vicar." He made the Jor'ellian salute.

Armus watched the exchange with great interest. His observance became interrupted when Kincaid, said, "Your horse, Commander," and gave him the reins.

Armus made a sharp glance around the castle entrance. "Let's move quickly. They won't stay inactive for long." When Kincaid went to his horse, Armus clapped Niles on the shoulder. For a moment, he held the Champion's gaze then spoke in Ancient. "Trust Jor'el, and act as you feel necessary." He mounted and the group left Waldron.

In agitated strides, Berk led Zared and Patrin to his study. He slammed the door. He furiously muttered under his breath. Occasionally, he knocked over an object as he paced the room. Zared and Patrin said nothing. Their faces showed the same fuming anger spouted by the King.

Berk halted in front of Zared. "Odell was your idea! How could you not know about the Writ naming Archimedes as Vicar?"

Zared swallowed back his temper to reply, still irritation laced his words. "I took Odell's word that no Writ existed. He deceived us both!"

Berk swore. "If I get my hands on that duplicitous priest, I'll hang him!"

"I don't think you'll find him."

"What makes you say that?"

"If he is resourceful enough to deceive us, then he had a back-up plan should the situation go awry."

"I fear Zared may be correct, Sire," groused Patrin.

Berk once again paced. "What can be done about Archimedes?"

Zared forced an ill-tempered reply. "Other than keeping him in check, nothing."

"Nothing? You told me that as *Grand Master* you have the power to persuade the Vicar to our plans."

Confident, Zared squared his shoulders. "Oh, I have power. However, Archimedes is not as willing as Odell." He heaved a shrug of indifference. "We merely amend our strategy by swaying others to our side rather than influencing Archimedes."

Berk considered the suggestion. "How much longer will it take?"

Zared flashed a small smile of intent. "*If* you allow me to be aggressive in my position to execute our plans, the timetable shouldn't change."

The answer satisfied Berk. "Do so! I want total control."

Zared's smile widened. "It shall be total when complete." He bowed to Berk and left.

Chapter 28

FTER LEAVING ARCHIMEDES, NILES QUICKLY MADE HIS WAY TO the rear of the main building. He entered a back door and travelled the servants' corridor to the staircase they used to reach the royal wing. He wanted to speak with Colin and Myla before Berk learned he remained at Waldron. Hard to miss how upset the younger princes became, so Niles chose to visit the nursery. He assumed correctly. Myla and the nurses diligently tried to calm the boys. Upon sight of him, Myla met him at the door.

"Don't come in any further," she said in a hurried whisper. She pushed him back and away from the nurses. "Hide behind the chair while I dismiss them. We must talk in private." She indicated a large chair near the door.

Niles did so. He listened as Myla spoke. One woman seemed reluctant, citing concern for Delwin, but Myla's insisted. He shrunk as low as possible behind the chair at hearing footsteps. Myla escorted the women to the door.

"You can come out now," she said.

Niles emerged. "Is there a problem with boys? I noticed their upset earlier." He glanced to where Delwin and Calder slept in bed together. Blaine sat dozing in a chair beside the bed.

"Delwin cried so hard with fear that he fell asleep from exhaustion. Calder fought to stay awake because he feared nightmares. It always happens when he gets upset. I pretended to give him his favorite drink only secretly mixed with a sleeping tonic. Blaine is strangely silent though helpful with his brothers."

"What about Akilles?"

"I don't know yet. Colin remains with him." She kindly grinned. "Your son has been of great help to Akilles, and to me."

"You realize now is the time?" he asked.

"Ay. We hoped to use Odell's departure as cover to take all of them from here." Using her eyes, she motioned back to the boys. "Under the circumstances, I fear for them if Akilles is found missing."

Niles took several moments to consider the new wrinkle.

Myla misunderstood his silence. "Please, cousin. Save them for me." Her eyes filled with imploring tears.

Her plea could not be ignored. "By taking them all, I will need more than Akilles' medallion," he spoke in earnest.

"I thought of that." She reached into the pocket of her skirt to produce a signet ring. "This is Delwin's. He is too young to wear it, so it won't be missed."

Niles placed the ring in his tunic pocket. "When you bring them to Akilles' room, they must understand this not a game. They must move silently, and do exactly as they are told."

"They will. Since you sent word about the tragedy, Wilma and I have been diligent with instruction. To Delwin, it is a *silent* escape game. Blaine is more serious while Calder fights fear. He has improved with each practice," she assured him.

"Then let us pray for success." A small smile appeared in regard of her. "Until later. Dear cousin." He quietly left the room.

Spying guards, Niles ducked into a darkened alcove to wait. Once clear, he dashed from his concealment to Akilles' room. To his surprised annoyance, he found the door locked.

He harshly whispered in the Ancient. "*Colin, fosgial rib uh athair!*"

Click! The door opened just wide enough to admit Niles.

"Thank Jor'el," said Colin with relief. "I didn't know if you would remain after all the commotion and Zared's threat."

"Niles!" exclaimed Akilles with delight.

Niles accepted Akilles' hug of greeting. He held Akilles by the shoulders to ask directly; "Are you ready to move on my command?"

"Ay! What happened at the Chapel when—"

Niles put up his hand to stay the anticipated question. "There is no time to explain."

"I meant that it made me realize my father has truly turned his back on Jor'el." When Akilles couldn't stop a sob, Niles held him. After several moments, he escorted Akilles to the sofa where he made the Prince sit. "I must speak with Colin then go make arrangements for tonight. You must steady your nerves and steel your resolve."

"I *will* be ready," Akilles stoutly said.

Niles took note of Akilles' determination with an approving nod. He then drew Colin aside. "Myla wants us to take them all."

"All?" Colin tried to digest the news. "It'll be hard enough with one."

"We can hardly refuse."

"Based upon family relations or her status as Queen?"

Niles rebuffed Colin for his surly question with an elbow jab to the side. "You should know better than to ask. She fears for their safety should Akilles be found missing. I don't blame her."

"Sorry," he droned. "It's just getting dangerous and complex."

"It will become more so until this business is done." Niles glanced to Akilles. The Prince remained on the sofa with expectant eyes on the duo. "Keep his spirits up. I'm going to make contact with Gordon and Abner and come up with an altered plan." He returned to the sofa and said to Akilles, "*Easba Jor'el, agus easba sinn.*"

"Trust goes with faith, so you have always told me."

A fond smile crossed Niles' lips. He ruffled Akilles' hair. He glanced to Colin before disappearing into the privy.

"Where is he going?" asked Akilles, a bit confused.

Before Colin replied, Niles reappeared and looked very satisfied.

"It hasn't been discovered," he said to Colin.

"What?" Akilles asked.

"Something we will make use of."

"Shouldn't you test it?" suggested Colin.

"Exactly my intention. If for some reason anything goes awry, take charge."

"Ay," said Colin with dread.

Niles told Akilles, "This time when I go into the privy, I won't be coming back immediately. Have no fear, it's part of the test."

Akilles scowled at the cryptic remark.

Moving back to the privy, Niles spied something on the table where Colin and Akilles spent time studying. He picked up a chunk of dark grey material. "Molding clay?" he asked Colin.

"During a lesson, I showed Akilles how to make impressions."

"Impressions," Niles muttered in thought. He slyly grinned. "An excellent idea. I need to borrow this."

Niles shut the door to the privy, more for safety than privacy. Behind the water closet he found the secret passage. In the holder was a half-used candle. He took another candle and shoved it in under his belt. He lit the candle in the holder before he entered the passage. He closed the panel from the other side then held the candle to light his way.

After the defeat of a King's Champion, it was customary to hand down all the secrets of Waldron in protection of the royal family. For a couple of weeks the old King's Champion showed Niles every nook, cranny, secret passageway and compartment. Over the years since, Niles took occasional night tours of the passageways to commit everything to memory. Someday such knowledge could be invaluable. *Now*, became that someday.

The passageway descended from the second floor for quite some distance. At the bottom, it divided into two directions. Niles headed right. Hearing voices near the end, he paused to listen. The voices moved away, and faded as they went. He waited a moment before he carefully peeked out of the kitchen pantry. Between midnight and four in the morning, no one worked in the kitchen. However, leaving meant quietly crossing the rear compound to the postern gate. Not a good option with four boys.

Closing the passageway entrance, Niles doubled back to the divide and went down the left passage. This one descended a bit further where it ended at a locked door. Being charged with Waldron's secrets, Niles produced a key from inside his tunic. He unlocked the door, walked through and locked it on the other side.

This part was an earthen tunnel. For about two hundred yards, Niles travelled before ascending a flight of stone steps. Seeing light up ahead, he blew out the candle. He heard no voices so he slowly opened a peephole. No one appeared to be around. Niles left the candle on the floor of the tunnel and emerged into a tack room at the end of the stable. The building joined the postern gatehouse. The tack room would serve better than the kitchen with two hundred feet to the postern gate instead of the entire rear courtyard.

He pulled up the hood of his cloak to move to the gatehouse. With no one inside, he locked and barred the exterior door. On a tabletop, he flattened the molding clay to one inch in depth. He took a gate key off the hook next to the door and pressed it into the molding clay. When satisfied with the impression, he wiped any clay residue off the key then placed it back on the hook.

He grabbed the impression and left the gatehouse. He casually entered the tack room. After one last look to ensure no prying eyes, he entered the tunnel. He removed his hood for better visibility. He picked up the candle but didn't light it until far enough away from the door as not to be seen.

Niles retraced his steps to the kitchen. The half-candle was nearly gone so he replaced it with the second one he stuffed in his belt. He left both inside the passageway when he emerged into the kitchen pantry. The kitchen staff busily went about their chores. Seeing a break in flow, Niles stepped out. If he could cross to the exterior door without being seen ...

"Hey, you!"

Niles turned in such a way as to hold one hand behind his back to hide the impression.

"Sir Niles?"

"Rankin," he gruffly greeted the cook.

"What are you doing in the kitchen?"

"You know I always inspect the King's food."

"I just haven't seen you in a few days. Then I heard about some ruckus in the Chapel."

"Which is why I'm being extra cautious about the King's food!" Niles sternly rebuffed.

"Everything is in order," said Rankin with offense.

Niles continued in his harsh manner. "If I found otherwise, you wouldn't be standing there rather thrown in guardhouse!" He made an impatient wave. "Now, go about your business." He again turned in such a way as to hide the impression and leave by the back door.

Niles hurried across to the armory. Not trusting the task to anyone else, he went to a locker where old keys and broken pieces of metal were stored for smelting and re-forging at a later date. At the moment, no one was in the locker, however he still used caution in making a selection. He matched several older keys to the impression. Three appeared to be closest. He shoved them inside his belt and grabbed a metal file. He ducked into his office and locked the door.

Moving to the farthest corner, Niles used the file to alter the older keys to fit the impression. Once satisfied, he destroyed the impression by stomping on the molding clay. Such force would obliterate any hint of being used. He tossed it into the brazier. It made the coal hiss. With fire needed to heat the room, the clay would disintegrate. He put the three keys in his tunic's hidden pocket. Now he needed to make contact with Abner and Gordon.

Niles heard rain. A good cover since most would seek shelter. He pulled up the hood of his cloak. Instead of rushing from the armory to the main building, he made his way at a steady pace. Once more, he utilized the back entrance. This time he headed for the guest wing. Even inside, he kept the hood up. The last thing he needed to do was run into Zared or Patrin. As he neared the staircase ...

Praise Jor'el. Niles noticed Gordon ready to climb the steps. *"Psst!* Sir Gordon!" he called in low, urgent voice.

Gordon paused, though uncertain.

"Gordon, Jor'ellian brathair!" Niles spoke the Ancient Jor'ellian greeting. He stepped out from the shadow of the stairwell to carefully push back to hood for recognition. When Niles beckoned, Gordon carefully made his way to join him under the stairwell.

"Why did you stay behind?" Gordon hurriedly asked in the Ancient.

"Because it's tonight."

Gordon understood. "We thought so too. We separated after the Chapel, for caution and to initiate our parts."

"Well, there is a slight change. *All* are going. For safety."

Gordon's brows leveled in surprise.

Niles drew Gordon further into the shadows. He turned their backs to shield the exchange. He handed Gordon two copies of the key. "Postern," he said to Gordon's curious gaze. "One for each." He gave Gordon the signet ring. "The little prince." He firmly held Gordon's arm. "Keep them safe."

"Upon my life."

"Until tonight." Niles made the Jor'ellian salute before nudging Gordon to leave. Niles listened to Gordon ascend the stairs. He waited a couple of moments before exiting the rear door.

Chapter 29

FITCH BARELY REACHED THE FOREST SURROUNDING WALDRON before losing his shift. The brief unveiling by Jor'el compromised his power. He had to flee! He stumbled into some thick underbrush to rest. Despite not being his fault, his unmasking would not go over well with Witter and Altari. If he didn't make a report, they could come looking for him, which would make matters worse. It did last time. The thought made him shiver. He never again wanted to experience reconditioning.

After several moments to regain his composure, Fitch headed for the rendezvous. He thought about dimension travel, only he felt too weak to make the attempt. He walked the first two miles then ran. Within a mile of the rendezvous, Fitch slowed to a walking pace. Any moment he expected to be accosted by sentries.

"What are you doing here, vassal?" demanded a Shadow Warrior.

Unable to speak in Guardian form, Fitch glared intently at the Warrior.

"Ah!" the Warrior cried out in pain, blinked and rubbed his eyes. "Why did you do mind speech?" He impatiently waved. "Never mind. I'll take you to Witter." He seized Fitch, who didn't resist the manhandling.

Witter and Altari stood in front of the basin. Dagar's image appeared in the steam as they conversed. Fitch swallowed back nervousness. He hoped to give his report to the Commanders before facing Dagar.

"Commander Witter," the Warrior said.

Witter snarled at the interruption until he saw Fitch. "What are you doing back so soon?"

"Who are you talking to?" demanded Dagar.

"Fitch."

"Bring him here!"

Witter waved Fitch over to stand before Dagar. Fitch fought against appearing unsettled. He bowed to Dagar.

"Is your task complete that you return in your natural state?"

Fitch shook his head at Dagar. He clasped his hand together in a pleading gesture.

"I take it there is an explanation," said Altari.

Fitch eagerly nodded.

"My lord," Altari began to Dagar, "is there any way to assist him with speech?"

"Is there no mortal in the camp?"

"No. Danior is watching Odell at a secure location."

Dagar inquired of Fitch, "Did you lose your shift voluntarily?"

Fitch vigorously shook his head.

"Can you take Odell's persona a second time after what happened?"

At first Fitch appeared uncertain then nodded.

Frustrated Dagar snapped. "This could take all day. Fetch the priest."

Altari ordered the Warrior who brought Fitch to get Danior and Odell. "By dimension travel. We can't waste time."

"Did this adversely affect Zared?" Dagar asked with impatience.

Fitch shook his head. He shared Dagar's impatience. Mind speech was only used for short bursts of communication. What he had to tell was best done verbally. Of course, if Dagar hadn't damaged his vocal cords during reconditioning this wouldn't be a problem. No need to bring up that unpleasantness or face worse.

The Warrior reappeared with both mortals. Danior and Odell fainted. A common occurrence since mortal bodies aren't fit for dimension travel. Danior came around first. When Odell regained his senses, Fitch acted quickly in seizing the priest. Once again, Odell fainted when Fitch became him.

"Keep him from regaining consciousness," Fitch/Odell told Danior.

"Now, I want a full report," said Dagar sternly.

Fitch swallowed back his nervousness to begin his report. "All was going according to plan when … Jor'el showed up!"

Dagar's loud throaty growl and narrow mahogany eyes made Fitch/Odell take a step back.

"Please, hear me, my lord!" he urged. "After I made contact with Baron Zared, he informed me of my—Odell's—part in the plan to become Vicar by appointment at a royal forum."

"And?" pressed Dagar.

"All went well until the Chapel service."

"Chapel service? That wasn't in the plan," chided Dagar.

"The King ordered it!" he said in hast to forestall Dagar's temper. "We obliged to facilitate the plan and help the people accept Odell as Vicar."

The answer worked, as Dagar seemed appeased. "Continue."

"That's when *he* arrived," Fitch/Odell said with emphasis.

"Jor'el," sniggered Dagar.

Fitch/Odell hesitated. Whereas he succeeded just a moment ago, what he had to say now would anger everyone. "No, the *real* Vicar."

Altari jerked on Fitch/Odell's arm. "Wilbur is dead!"

"Archimedes!" Fitch/Odell blurted out the name, then proceeded with the full hurried explanation. "Apparently, Wilbur *made* a Divine Writ of Succession naming Archimedes as Vicar. During the confrontation regarding the legality of canon, a large Jor'ellian accused me of not being whom I claimed. Naturally, I rebuffed him. That's when Archimedes acted and … Jor'el showed up!" He swallowed back rising discomposure to continue. "Heavenly light surrounded Archimedes, like when Jor'el appeared at the Palace. It created a panic among the mortals. Then a sudden beam of bright light came from the staff towards me. For a brief moment I became unmasked, my real face exposed. Only by using every ounce of power could I replace Odell's face! Fearing total loss of my shift, I fled!"

With arms folded, Dagar intensely regarded Fitch/Odell.

"I swear, my lord! Fleeing was my only option," he pleaded with desperation.

After a moment of uncomfortable silence, Witter spoke. "My lord, you contacted us because of a disturbance in the transverse. This could explain it."

Dagar's eyes briefly went to Witter before returning to Fitch/Odell. "What happened after you left?"

"I don't know. Once I lost my shift, I came to give my report rather than return to Waldron. Being unmasked could cause trouble with the mortals."

Dagar scratched at his beard in thought. "Describe the large Jor'ellian."

Fitch/Odell's brows drew level in recollection. "Tall, brown hair, muscular." He shrugged. "Nothing unusual, if that is what you mean?"

"You sensed no heavenly essence?"

Fitch/Odell shook his head, still remembering the situation. "No, although I didn't think to search for any as it all happened so fast."

Dagar pressed his interrogation with incredulity. "He accused you of not being who you claimed. That didn't give you pause to wonder how?"

"Not past the fact he is a Jor'ellian commander."

"My lord," began Altari, "Jor'ellians are spiritually astute mortals."

"Perhaps, only this particular Jor'ellian seems *more* unusual. The description sounds very much like the individual Carvel experienced—twice!" Dagar argued.

"Jor'ellians are capable of killing creatures of infrinn," insisted Altari.

"Archimedes was First Jor'ellian," Witter added his voice to the argument.

Dagar snarled at the counterpoints. "I still find it difficult to believe that Jor'el showed up, yet has not sent his *captain* or others to interfere."

"With two thousand Warriors and three hundred Archers, they would be no match for us," said Altari with certainty.

Dagar glanced askew to Altari. "Contact Zared. No new Vicar will stop us. Waldron falls tonight!" The image and steam disappeared.

A heavy moment of silence passed before Altari instructed Fitch/Odell, "Return to Waldron."

"It would be too dangerous." Fitch made the brief protest before a cunning smile appeared. "Why not send our mortal assassin with a message?"

Danior's ears perk-up. He watched over an unconscious Odell.

"To do so means getting rid of Odell, and any chance of you assuming his identity again," said Witter.

Fitch/Odell answered with deadly earnest. "Once a shapeshifter has assumed a mortal's identity, that individual becomes sensitive to a Guardian's essence. He's too much of risk to leave alive."

Witter tossed a considering glance to Altari, which prompting Altari to nod agreement. "Very well." Witter turned to Danior, who remained silent during the discussion. "You know what to do, only take him out camp. Then you will proceed to Waldron. Let Zared know, it is tonight."

"How can I make it to Waldron before tonight? It's a two day ride."

Witter cocked a lopsided smile. "Leave that to us."

Danior's countenance fell. "Not that dimension stuff again?"

Witter showed his patience exhausted. "Take care of the priest!"

Before Danior took hold of Odell, Fitch reached into his pocket.

"Take this to gain entry into the castle. Ask for Rankin." He went to hand Danior the cloak brooch.

The assassin smiled. "I don't need it. I have my own ways of getting in." He lifted Odell over his shoulder and left camp.

"I best revert to normal before the deed is done," said Fitch.

"Why?" Witter asked.

"Because in his persona, I feel everything short of actually dying." Fitch brought his hand together and lowered his head. In a moment, he transformed into his Guardian form.

Altari smiled and made a side comment to Witter. "At least he is silent again."

Danior returned. He sheathed his dagger.

"That was quick. We didn't hear a sound," said Altari with skepticism.

"Of course not, he was unconscious. It only takes a single cut." Danior made a motion across his throat.

Fitch momentarily closed his eyes. He opened his eyes and nodded to Witter, who said to Altari, "It is done."

"Of course it is. I'm not foolish enough to cross you," chided Danior.

"We needed to be certain." Altari whistled. A whinny came in response then a black spirit stallion appeared. "You should reach Waldron in two hours."

"Only don't fall off," snickered Witter with warped amusement when Danior mounted.

With Danior out of sight, Altari said, "We need to get word to Tor."

"Send him." Witter jerked his thumb at Fitch.

"With what? A written note?"

Witter continued in his sardonic humor. "No, let him mind speak to Tor."

Altari laughed at the comment. He calmed down enough to say to Fitch, "Go."

Fitch made a nasal huff before he disappeared in dimension travel.

Chapter 30

K ELL'S GOLDEN EYES GLOWED BRIGHT WITH GREAT INTENSITY, as he focused on Waldron. He and Gresham stood on a knoll two miles from the castle.

"Kell!" came Jedrek's shout a moment before the warrior arrived. He became the object of Kell's attention. He slightly balked since the severity of the captain's gaze did not diminish. "They are on the move!"

Zinna arrived in a rush from the southwest. "More troops!"

Kell looked back at Waldron. His black brows deeply furrowed, as he announced, "The time has come."

"Will Jor'el send help?" asked Zinna with desperation.

"I don't know," said Kell almost under his breath.

Gresham seized Kell's arm. "Then what are we going to do with just twelve of us against more than two thousand?"

"We will do whatever is needed." Kell's resolve clearly visible. "Quickly, fetch the others," he ordered them.

When alone, Kell again regarded Waldron. He prayed with earnest importunity. "Jor'el, this cannot be the last stand, for your promise has yet to be fulfilled. What is the reason for this?" He lifted his eyes to the sky. "Will you send help as Zinna asked?" After a moment of silence, "Maybe just Avatar," he pleaded in speaking of his second lieutenant. At the continued silence, he lowered his head in a wince of dismay.

"Don't let the others see your discouragement," said a familiar voice from behind, not like Jor'el's voice that usually surrounded him.

"Avatar!" Kell cheered. He greeted his aide and second lieutenant with hearty embrace. He held Avatar by the arms, his voice filled with confident exuberance. "The High Trio together again. A good sign."

285

Avatar flashed a plaintive smile at Kell's enthusiasm. His silver eyes held disappointment. "I'm sorry, Kell, but I'm not here to help. Only to bring a message."

Kell's demoralization was immediate. "A ... message?"

"What is to happen, *must* happen, for from destruction will come hope."

Fighting vexation, Kell moved away from Avatar. "More waiting."

Avatar stepped in front of Kell, his tone demanding of compassionate attention. "Those of us who are not here are also waiting! Along with our comrades trapped in the nether dimension."

Kell's jowl flexed with grit and determination. "I *will* free them!"

Despite distress, Avatar said, "You are *only* allowed to help the few mortals affected, but prohibited from interfering or making any attempt to stop the enemy."

Thunderstruck, Kell's golden eyes flared with angry brightness. "My orders are to stand aside?"

"It is Jor'el's command! He sent *me* so you could see the tangible reason attached to this order. Kell," Avatar added with pleading urgency, "*our* future restoration depends upon complete obedience."

Kell saw the depth of entreaty and truth in Avatar's steady silver gaze. Pricked to the core, Kell closed his eyes to steady his temper. After a moment, he bowed his head to confess, "I live to serve and obey."

Kell felt Avatar take hold of his shoulder. He raised his head to see Avatar's regard turn sympathetic.

"This was the most difficult message I ever delivered." Avatar glanced to Waldron. "Too bad Tristan's descendants didn't remain faithful."

"Ay," Kell dolefully agreed. "Return in peace knowing it will be as Jor'el commands." He embraced Avatar.

"You know I'd rather stay, only I don't have a choice." Avatar took a few steps from Kell and immediately disappeared. No white light, he simply vanished.

Armus arrived with the rest of the Guardians, and in his natural form. He appeared puzzled. "Who were you talking to just now?"

Kell flashed a poignant smile. "Avatar. He came with a message."

"What did he say? And why did he leave? We could use his help." Armus sounded as enthusiastic as Kell earlier.

Kell placed an arm about Armus' shoulders. "Obedience is needed now, not questions."

"So you won't tell me what he said?" asked Armus, a bit puzzled.

Kell looked along his shoulder at Armus. "I just did." Before Armus could inquire further, Kell questioned Wren and Eldric. "How are Osborn and Travis?"

"Well enough to survive the journey back to the Region," replied Eldric with his normal ill-humor.

"I just finished contacting Alfie when Jedrek found me," said Wren.

Kell nodded. "Good."

"What's the plan, Captain?" asked Barnum.

Kell's thoughtful gaze shifted among the others, ending on Armus. "The plan is to follow Jor'el's orders, as relayed by Avatar." He paused to consider his words. They would be as difficult for him to speak as for Avatar. "No matter what happens at Waldron, we can only help a few mortals, and must leave the enemy alone."

Jedrek couldn't believe his ears. "You mean let Dagar's forces take the castle?"

"Fulfillment of prophecy depends upon it."

The statement rendered them speechless. Jedrek gaped at Kell in an effort to comprehend. Armus stared mercilessly at the ground. He clenched the hilt of his sword so tight that his knuckles turned white. Barnum and Valmar also gripped their swords. Priscilla covered her mouth in disbelief. Chase and Gresham shook their heads bewilderment. Neither Wren nor Eldric moved, frozen in astonishment.

Mona appeared to be the first to recover from the devastating blow, or at least able to proceed with the conversation. "How do we help those we can?"

Kell pursed his lips in consideration of his words. "Difficult to say exactly. It will more than likely require Captain Seul and Commander

Finn for direct contact, with the rest in support." He nudged Armus, who appeared to be recovered from the initial reaction.

"You'll need this." Eldric pulled out two paper packets from his pouch. "Double dose of strengthening tonic. Mix it all in one flask." He handed them to Armus. "With all the energy you've expended lately, drink it before and after. Kell might need a sip or two, but you drink most of it."

"Thanks," Armus said then spoke to Kell. "Who exactly can we help? Aside from Niles, Colin and Myla."

"Abner is Niles' good friend, and a Jor'ellian," said Wren.

"Gordon is also a friend and Jor'ellian. He and Abner act in support of Niles," added Gresham.

Kell briefly considered the names then made an assenting nod. "Those five for now. Others if you sense a directing in your spirit. Only avoid Zared, Patrin and Berk. They will be left to their fates."

"When do you think they will arrive?" asked Valmar.

"Jedrek and Zinna reported they are on the move." Kell directed his attention to Waldron during his analysis. "I would say tonight. At least move into position. It will startle the mortals to find the castle surrounded when they wake."

"I don't think they need to wait until dark," groused Armus.

"With Zared, it could be a bloodless coup," said Kell.

Armus continued his counterpoint with renewed irritation. "They tried it with Fitch posing as Odell. May be if we—"

Kell's frustration came out in rebuke. "Our orders are not to interfere!"

Armus backpedaled. "I wasn't meaning ..." His voice trailed off. Again, he clenched the hilt of his sword to contain his vexation.

"At least Avatar got to leave and not see this," Wren complained.

Kell flashed a sardonic smile. "He would have stayed if not for *Jor'el's orders* to return." He made a point to emphasize the situation. With Wren subdued, he gave out the assignments. "To facilitate our task of aiding those allowed, we will take up surveillance around Waldron. Valmar, you and Mona take the north watch. Wren and Barnum to the east. Jedrek, Priscilla and Zinna go to the south while Chase and Eldric go west. Gresham will remain with Armus and me until we find a way to help those permitted. Remember!" he stressed with stern warning, "*no* interference with the enemy's forces. Not even the slightest use of power. We must remain undetected. The future of the mortals, our restoration and the lives of imprisoned comrades depend upon *complete* obedience."

The gravity of the final statement had the desired effect. Armus, Barnum, Valmar and Jedrek came to attention with the Guardian salute and motto, "We live to serve and obey."

Chase, Wren, Priscilla, Mona, Zinna, Gresham and Eldric mimicked the warriors. Kell returned the salute. He watched them disperse to their assignments. Gresham resumed his surveillance on the high point of the knoll, leaving Kell and Armus alone for the moment.

"I was going to suggest being proactive in helping the mortals we can—not disobedience," said Armus.

Kell nodded. "How?"

"You mentioned Captain Seul and Commander Finn. Niles chose to remain after Archimedes confronted Fitch. We could contact him."

"Interesting thought, only we can't get caught at Waldron."

"If your assessment about it being tonight holds, we have a few hours."

"I can send a prearranged signal should they be sighted," Gresham began over his shoulder before he turned to face them. "Or give you thirty seconds to escape." He patted his dagger.

"The last option is too risky for your lifeforce, and in disobedience to our orders," Kell stoutly said.

"Less risky than you two masquerading as mortals inside Waldron?"

"I've done it twice," said Armus with grin.

Kell heaved a sigh of disappointment. "No, Gresham's right, it's too risky." He cast a side-glance to Armus. "We'll have to wait for our opportunity rather than initiate action."

Disgruntled, Armus chided, "Wren is right, at least Avatar is spared this restriction."

Kell cocked a contrary brow at the comment. "He wouldn't see it that way, and I'm surprised you do."

This time Armus didn't back down. "Tell me, Kell, what was your reaction to this news of allowing Dagar to succeed?"

Kell stiffened to his full height. His jowls flexed with insult. The offense didn't last long; it couldn't, as he was forced to admit, "Not very well, I'm afraid."

"Then why expect me to react differently?"

"I expect you to be supportive, especially in front of others."

Armus scowled at the rebuff. "Granted, I should not have disputed your assessment publicly. Being ordered to stand down in the face of the enemy is not an easy thing to accept."

Kell huffed an ironic chuckle. "I must be compelled to obey, you can't accept it and Avatar called it the most difficult message he ever delivered."

"Well, you are the High Trio. You're supposed to think and act alike," said Gresham. Becoming the focus of their displeasure, he returned to his surveillance.

"And *obey* orders from the Almighty as one," Kell said privately to Armus.

"We will, regardless of feelings," Armus said with unwavering certainty.

Chapter 31

DANIOR EXPERIENCED THE MOST HARROWING RIDE OF HIS LIFE. He couldn't really control the horse rather let the stallion run its course through the woods, meadows and farmlands. Jumping obstacles proved the most frightening. He closed his eyes and held on with all his might. He did manage to pull the stallion to a halt at the tree line north of Waldron. He sat for a moment to catch his breath and calm his racing heart after such a hair-raising ride. Maybe he should have agreed to another dimension thing.

Rain clouds made it hard to tell the exact time. By what shadows he could see, he reckoned the hour around one o'clock in the afternoon. Feeling rested, he raised the hood of his cloak.

"Now, let's take it at a more reasonable speed," he said.

The stallion snorted and pawed the ground.

"I hope that's an agreement. We don't need to cause suspicion. At a walk." He kicked the sides of the stallion. It lurched forward before starting to a walk.

The sloshing grass and mud told the earlier rain had been heavy. It slacked off to a light, steady shower. Instead of heading for the main gate, he drew rein a few yards from the closed postern gate.

"Hello, the castle!" he shouted.

A soldier appeared on the battlement. "Who calls?"

"One whom the Grand Master has summoned."

"I think you'd use the front gate."

Danior smiled at the counter phrase. "Front or rear matters not when the Master calls."

The soldier touched his helmet in acknowledgement and disappeared from the battlement.

Danior didn't wait long for the gate to open. He steered the horse to a tethering post just past the gatehouse. Once dismounted, he headed for the main building's rear exterior stairway. Being a rainy day meant fewer people outside. Still, he kept his head lowered to conceal his face within the shadows of the hood.

Inside, he encountered a couple of lower ranking servants. They scurried aside at his gruff command and wave. He paused at the top of the stairs to the guest quarters to assess the hallway. No guards or soldiers in sight. *Interesting.*

Knowing the location of Zared's quarters, Danior swiftly approached the room. He discovered the door locked. He pulled a metal pick from up his sleeve and used it to unlock the door. He locked it after entering.

"My lord?" He stepped further into the room. "Baron Zared?"

Danior made a quick search of the room to find it empty. He removed his cloak, shook off the rain and tossed it over the back of chair. Spying a decanter of brandy, he poured himself a liberal glass to help ward off a chill from the rain. He sat on the sofa with his feet up. Nothing to do but wait and enjoy a drink.

Mona stood on the spot previously occupied by Danior. She watched Valmar kneel to examine the ground. "Well?" she asked.

"A spirit stallion though the rider is mortal." He rose and brushed the mud off his hands.

"That surprises you?"

Valmar shook his head, and wary in his regard of Waldron. "Surprised, no. Curious, ay. I suppose he could be an advance scout. Less attention than the appearance of a Shadow Warrior." He instructed her, "Report this to Kell. I'll keep watch here in case he leaves the same way."

Mona took off in a run heading east to make a wide circuit around Waldron. Nearing the main road from the castle north toward the Region of Sanctuary, a dreadful chill gripped her. She raced to find a spot to hide. She hoped a mile would be enough distance from where she experienced the chill. She waited for either the sense of danger to pass or catch sight of the enemy. Several anxious moments passed with no change.

Although a breach of orders, she dare not proceed without knowing if the way was clear. At first sense of anything, she would break off the effort. Taking a deep breath, Mona focused on the road. As slowly as possible, she stretched out her sense to search for enemy presence. *Nothing!* She could press further, but no. Kell's emphasis of Jor'el's command prohibited even what she did.

Mona did a semi-crawl, low quickstep further into the woods. After a hundred yards, she experienced a sense of relief. She took off running again. From behind several trees she saw Armus, Kell and Gresham become alert.

"It's me, Mona!" she called.

"What are you doing here?" asked Kell.

"Valmar sent me to tell you that a mortal riding a spirit stallion arrived at Waldron not too long ago. They are *very* close," she said with certainty. "Perhaps no more than four miles."

"How do you know that?"

"An overwhelming sense of danger as I made my way here. I saw and sensed nothing nearby—"

"Sensed? You used your power?" Kell demanded, irate.

"I mean I *felt* the danger," she stammered in defense of her miscue. "I waited five minutes. I didn't dare move or risk giving myself away. I saw no evidence of the danger I *felt*. Yet something that powerful must be close, just not within sighting distance."

Kell didn't appear convinced.

Armus came to Mona's defense. "She's right about such a large force creating a massive disturbance."

"Kell," she began with contrition. "I would do nothing to risk our lives here or those in the Cave. However, you must admit, it will take everything within us not to act, to resist the very reason for our existence." Her statement softened his mood until ...

Armus and Kell drew their swords. Gresham pulled his dagger. She too became alert.

"I told you!" she insisted.

"Shhh!" Kell made an impatient wave for silence. He carefully moved to the edge of the knoll with Armus at his shoulder. Gresham and Mona stayed back in the shadows.

With tremendous concentration, Kell slowly scanned the horizon. The others neither spoke nor moved while he scrutinized the surrounding area. Kell barely breathed during his sweeping gaze. He finally let out a long exhale from effort and blinked several times. He and Armus rejoined Gresham and Mona.

"Did you use your power?" asked Mona.

Kell shook his head since he rubbed his eyes. "Stopped just short of employing it. Though it might have been easier."

Armus uncorked the flask containing the strengthening tonic. He handed it to Kell. "A sip won't hurt."

"See anything?" asked Gresham.

Kell swallowed before replying. He gave the flask back to Armus. "No, but Armus is right. The large number is what we *felt* not exact proximity." He smiled at Mona. "Your quadrupling of the normal range is close enough."

"Should we warn the others?" asked Gresham.

"No. It's too dangerous to be moving about unnecessarily." Kell said to Mona, "Remain with us instead of risking a return encounter."

Mona grinned with relief. "I hoped you would say that. Though I don't want to abandon Valmar."

Kell cocked a grin. "Valmar can take care of himself."

"What about my earlier suggestion of Captain Seul and Commander Finn contacting Niles to learn about this mortal?" Armus asked.

Kell turned back to the vista, thoughtful. "Maybe after dark we can slip in. For now, we'll keep watch and try to discern the approaching sense more clearly."

An empty decanter and glass sat on the floor beside the sofa where Danior slept. He felt a hard shove on this shoulder. A loud voice shouted, "Wake up, you fool!" Startled, he opened his eyes. He blinked to focus on the person responsible for the rude awakening. "My lord!"

Zared's displeasure showed in holding up the empty decanter.

Danior swung his legs off the sofa to sit up. "I can explain! They sent me on one of those unnatural beasts, the speed of which I was lucky to stay in the saddle. Pelted by cold rain and eyes whipped by the wind, I needed a drink to get warm."

"The whole decanter?" asked Zared with skepticism.

"Have you ever ridden one of those beasts?" he challenged. "No man should ride that fast. Travelling sixty miles in under two hours! It didn't break a sweat."

Zared set the decanter on a side table. "Are you admitting fear?"

"You would too if you experienced what I did."

Zared folded his arms in observance of Danior. "Why are you here?"

Danior glanced around the room to notice the light fading. "What time is it?"

"What does that matter?"

Danior stood to insist, "What time is it?"

"Four o'clock. I came to prepare for dinner with the king only to find you passed out on the sofa!"

Danior sighed with relief. "There is still time."

"Time for what?"

Danior stepped closer to Zared to speak confidentially. "It is *tonight.*"

Zared smiled with pleasure. "I thought as much."

"I suppose you will need my services again." Danior flashed a swaggering smile.

"We shall see after dinner."

"Speaking of," began Danior a bit cocky. "I could use some food."

Zared snorted a wry chuckle. "To counteract the effects of alcohol no doubt." He crossed to the wall and pulled a bell rope. Hiller came from the antechamber. "Fetch some food and wine then help me prepare for dinner with the king."

Hiller appeared perplexed. "My lord, if you are dining with the king—?"

"Just do as you're told!" He shoved the man toward the door. "Oh, and, Hiller, not a word about any visitor to my quarters."

"Ay, my lord."

When the door shut upon Hiller's departure, Zared spoke to Danior. "Remain here until I decide exactly how to dispose of our *former* king." He went to the privy.

Chapter 32

O N AND OFF RAIN JOINED WITH THE GLOOMINESS OF THE DAY
kept most people indoors. This worked to Niles' advantage, as
he continued to explore the secret avenues of the castle. True,
he determined a course of escape, but it never hurt to have alternate
plans should something go wrong.

He wore his cloak and hood against the rain, and to avoid being
clearly identified. Near the postern gatehouse, he spied an unusually large
black horse. Curious, he moved closer to examine the stallion. It
appeared nervous to his approach then touch.

"Steady," he said, only the animal kept snorting in anger. It tossed it
head to tug against the tether, all the while eying him.

Something wasn't right, not only the animal's size but also its
reaction. Niles tried speaking the Ancient. "*Fursada. Mi spiocaire no beud.*"
The stallion began to grow quiet, so Niles repeated the phrase. "Easy. I
mean no harm." He again touched the animal. This time the stallion just
chomped on the bit.

Niles stroked the stallion's neck, as he continued in the Ancient.
"See. I won't hurt you." He worked his way to the horse's head to take
the bridle. He gazed up into its eyes. "I don't think you are a normal
horse, are you?"

The stallion's mouth moved in what appeared to be an attempt at
words. The grunts seemed like syllables. Niles managed to hear Ancient
for what sounded like *spirit* and *dark*. He repeated to make sure he heard
correctly.

"*Spiorad? Dorcha?*"

The stallion tossed its head like a nod.

Niles suddenly understood. A beast of the Dark Way was at Waldron! In alarm, he looked to the second floor of the main building. Whoever came on the beast could mean harm to Akilles. At least he could stop the individual from escaping. He quickly undid the tether and led the beast to the postern gate.

"Open!" he ordered the gatekeeper.

"By whose authority?"

Niles removed his hood. "The King's Champion!"

Reluctantly, the gatekeeper complied.

Niles took the horse just outside. "*Siuthad!*" He commanded in the Ancient and struck the stallions' flank as hard as he could. With a great whinny and buck of protest, it ran off. Niles waited until it was out of sight to return inside.

"Close it!" he ordered the gatekeeper. "Did you see the rider?"

"Not clearly. He wore a cloak and hood. I did hear him say something to a guard about the Grand Master."

Niles' jowls clenched and eyes narrowed. "If you see him again, call the guards to detain him!" He raced to the main building.

Inside, Niles grabbed a lit candle from a stand and made his way to the servant's stairway leading to the royal wing. Certain of no one around, he ducked under the stairwell and unlocked a secret door hidden in the paneling. He mounted uneven steps, long neglected. He continued past the landing for the first floor up another set of stairs to the bedchamber level. Once on the second floor, he navigated his way to Akilles' room. He entered the privy through the same way as the other passage. Seeing light from the main chamber, he extinguished the candle. He heard raised voices so he listened.

"You will do as you are told!" Berk yelled.

"Sir, I can't," Akilles argued with a voice that sounded resolute.

"You can and you will! I don't give a fig what nonsense he and Niles have told you! Zared is your tutor and you will join us for dinner or risk my wrath for disobedience!"

Niles heard what sounded like stomping followed by slamming. He waited to determine if Berk left. Akilles spoke.

"What should I do? I can't go and jeopardize the plan."

"We'll think of something," Colin replied.

Knowing Berk left, Niles emerged from the privy. "Sounded like the conversation didn't go well."

"Niles!" Akilles accosted him. "When can we leave?"

"*Shhh!*" he scolded. In a gesture of caution, he motioned to the room door. He lowered his voice when he switched to the Ancient. "When your brothers are ready, and not before. Patience is a manly virtue. You must act like a man and not a child any longer."

Akilles squared his shoulders in offense to reply in the Ancient, though he stumbled on some words. "That is what I've been doing since the Chapel."

"Indeed. He's been reading and praying during your reconnaissance. Also most of our conversations have been in the Ancient," said Colin.

"Good, because he will need all the courage he can muster," said Niles.

"Do you mean I must go to dinner?" asked Akilles with guardedness.

"No. Like Colin said, we will find a way to keep you here." Niles laid a heavy hand on Akilles' shoulder. "Normally I would keep such information from you, but not under these circumstances. I discovered the *enemy* of the light has gained access to Waldron."

Akilles' eye widened with the horror of understanding. He could barely utter the Ancient term for, "The Dark Way!"

"You mean other than Zared?" Colin asked.

"Ay. Someone brought here on an unnatural horse commanded by the Dark Way. I found it tethered in the rear courtyard and sent it fleeing," said Niles.

A whimper of distress escaped so Akilles bit his lip.

"Courage, my prince."

"You're asking a lot of him in the face of great evil," objected Colin.

"Lives depend upon him like never before!"

Akilles spoke with a clear, strong voice. "My *concern* is for my mother and brothers, not myself. I will do what is necessary to keep them safe from Zared, my father and the Dark Way." Despite the bravado, misty tears filled his eyes.

Niles hugged Akilles about the shoulders and felt a few shivers. "Now," he held Akilles by the arms. "Continue seeking Jor'el, and be ready." He nudged Akilles to the table and waited for the Prince to sit and pick up a book.

Colin moved closer to Niles. "Why do I think you know who is here?"

Niles' expression turned lethal. "According to the gatekeeper, he said the Grand Master summoned him."

Colin made a careful motion with his head toward the table. "Him or Berk?"

"Both." Seeing the answer concerned Colin, Niles continued. "Why else want Akilles at dinner?" Niles scratched his beard in thought. "What time did Berk say?"

"Seven. It's now six. We have an hour to figure out some excuse."

Niles grinned. "I have just the counter that will work perfectly to our advantage." He approached the table, still smiling. This time he spoke in Allonian. "I'll be back shortly." He hastened to the privy.

"Why does he keep going to the privy every time? Is there some in there I don't know about?" Akilles demanded of Colin.

"Hush!" Colin quickly sat at the table.

Akilles realized he was correct. "So there is," he said in a low voice.

Colin firmly tapped on the book for Akilles to continue reading.

In a private formal dining room, Berk sat at a lavish table with Zared and Patrin. Finely crafted silverware, gold plates and glassware graced the table. Food lined the buffet located at the far end of the room. Servants dressed in handsome uniforms, awaited their cue to tend the King and his guests.

Berk scowled with impatience. "He's late!" He threw the napkin on the table. "I told him not to incur my wrath for disobedience. His head is so full of Jor'ellian nonsense as to be openly defiant." He leaned on the table and pointed his finger at Zared. "Come the morning, I want all Jor'ellians banished from Waldron!"

Zared fought a smile. "What of the Chapel?"

"Tear it apart! I don't want a single relic of that old gibberish anywhere in sight."

Alvin arrived. With a hesitant expression, and avoiding direct eye contact, he spoke. "Sire. Her Majesty insists His Royal Highness be excused for dinner."

"Oh, she does?" he scoffed. "Do you hear that, gentlemen? *She* dares to interfere. Come! We shall remedy her meddling once and for all."

Berk led Zared, Patrin and Alvin to Akilles' chamber. Upon nearing the door, they heard laughter and boyish squeals. Without knocking, Berk briskly entered. All four of his sons were roughhousing around on the floor.

"What is going on here?" he shouted in demand.

The boys immediately stopped playing. Fearful, Delwin ran to Akilles, who picked him up for comfort. Myla, Colin and two nurses turned their attention to the speaker.

"Sire," Myla cordially said in greeting.

"What is meaning of this, Madam? Akilles is supposed to be dining with me and my ministers not rolling around on the floor!"

She made a gentle motion to the other side of the room. "May we speak privately?"

"We will not. I want an answer."

"The boys were very frightened and upset after Chapel. Delwin in particular. We gave him a calming tonic, and he slept for a few hours. When he woke this afternoon, he cried because he wanted Akilles. He feels safe with his eldest brother. So, I brought him here for supper and play. As you can hear, it has helped."

Delwin clung to Akilles' neck. He leaned against Akilles to hide his face from Berk. Akilles closely watched the exchange between his parents.

Berk scowled at the boys. "Delwin is as skittish as a rabbit."

Myla stepped into Berk's line of sight. "He's a five-year-old boy terrified by power beyond his comprehension. You should show concern for your youngest. For all your sons! What is a dinner compared to their state of mind?"

Berk's anger rose. "You lecture me, Madam?"

"No, Sire. I care for your sons by nurturing their relationship instead of causing rivalry. This protects *your* throne." Her eyes briefly flashed to Zared and Patrin before she continued her argument. "You can teach what *enlightenment* you want, but without unity of your sons, the future of your reign and heritage is in jeopardy."

With a wry smile, Zared said, "Well played, Madam."

Myla confronted him. "Sir, I do not play games with the welfare of my sons."

Zared casually touched the neck of his doublet and bowed his head in acknowledgement. He didn't close his hand, merely rested it on the collar. He caught Colin's studious glare. "Sire, I believe Her Majesty has made her point."

"Very well. However," stressed Berk, "do not interfere again, Madam."

"As you say, Sire." Myla graciously inclined her head in agreement.

When the door slammed shut, Myla carefully locked it. She sighed in relief.

Niles moved from hiding in the privy to Myla. "Well done."

"For now."

"All we can do is deal with what is presented until the time."

Delwin frowned when he asked Akilles, "Why was Father so angry that I wanted to see you?"

"I don't know. He's been angry a lot lately." Akilles kindly smiled. "Don't let that ruin our fun."

"Indeed," agreed Niles. "There will be time enough later for seriousness." He tickled Delwin, who giggled.

Instead of returning to the dining room, Berk went to his study. Zared, Patrin and Alvin respectfully followed.

"Sire, will you require dinner sent here?" asked Alvin.

"No, I do not require dinner sent here!" he mimicked the Chamberlain. "I've lost my appetite. You gentlemen may enjoy the meal. I want to be left alone. Attend me in morning." He turned his back to them.

"Have dinner sent to my apartment," Zared told Alvin. After the Chamberlain left, Zared addressed Berk. "Until the morning, Sire."

When they reached Zared quarters, Danior was there, only this time dressed in a royal servant's uniform.

"My lord, I waited in the rear hall like you said. Only when you left with the King, I thought it best to return," said Danior.

Zared snapped with ire. "The Queen interfered!"

"Could she have gotten wind of our guest?" Patrin said of Danior.

"No one saw me arrive," insisted Danior

Zared added his support to Danior's refute. "You know he can come and go unseen. Part of his deadly nature."

"Then how do you account for her intervention?" pressed Patrin.

Zared took a few steps, thoughtful. "It could well be as she said. The younger princes were frightened by events."

"Along with most of Court," snickered Patrin. "So what now?"

Zared grinned with confidence. "We wait."

"Wait?" asked Patrin with skepticism.

Zared heaved a nonchalant shrug. "This part failed, but later tonight, we *will* totally succeed."

Chapter 33

THE BOYS REMAINED IN AKILLES' APARTMENT UNDER THE watchful eyes of Myla, Niles and Colin. Delwin and Calder fell asleep around nine o'clock after hours of playing. Myla dismissed the nurses when the younger boys fell asleep. Blaine stayed awake a bit longer, but by ten o'clock he too succumbed to fatigue. Whenever Akilles started to doze, he woke himself.

Niles checked the clock. It read fifteen minutes until midnight. "We should wake them, so we can reach the postern by midnight and take advantage of the change in shift."

He, Colin and Myla began the task of rousing the young boys. Niles started with Akilles, who once again dozed. He woke to Niles' grip on his shoulder.

"It's time," said Niles.

Akilles practically jumped to his feet to put on his cloak. He already wore his sword and dagger, taking time to prepare while waiting.

Myla gently urged Delwin from sleep. "Delwin, dear, it's time to wake up." He groaned in opening his eyes. "Time to play the escape game." Delwin rubbed his eyes. Myla continued. "Here's your cloak." She put it on him and closed it.

"What about Guffy?" he sleepily asked.

She smiled. "I didn't forget Guffy." She took a stuffed ragged dog off a side table for him.

Akilles came to fetch Delwin. "Remember, Marmi said you have to keep Guffy quiet. This means, no talking to him until we reach our safe place. Can you do that?"

Delwin nodded since he yawned. He held Guffy in one hand against his body while taking hold of Akilles' hand with his other hand.

Colin helped Calder put on his cloak. Blaine fastened a dagger onto his belt before donning his cloak. He would not be armed with a sword.

Myla fought to contain her emotions in regard of her sons. "Now, promise me to listen to everything Sir Niles and Sir Colin tell you."

"We promise. Don't we, Delwin?" said Akilles.

Delwin again nodded, fighting to stay awake.

Akilles sent a prompting glance to Calder and Blaine.

"We promise," they said in near unison.

Myla kissed each, starting with Delwin and ending with Akilles. Her eyes grew misty upon her eldest. "I will meet you at the Temple ..."

The sound of bells broke the late night silence. In sudden fear, Myla asked Niles and Colin, "The alarm bell?"

"They're here," said Niles with dread.

"Go! Quickly," she urged.

Niles grabbed Myla's arm. "You're coming with us."

"No! This will embolden Zared. I will create a distraction. No time to argue. Take my sons to safety!"

The bells kept tolling.

"Marmi?" asked Akilles.

"Go!" She nudged Akilles toward the privy.

Niles and Colin herded the boys into the privy. Niles lit two lanterns. He gave one to Colin then opened the secret passage. "I'll lead. Akilles follows with Delwin. Calder then Blaine with you in the rear. Make sure to secure the passage. Boys, hold hands! We must hurry!"

In order the specified, they proceeded. Dark gloom of the passage made Delwin whimper.

"Easy. Remember the silent rule of the game," Akilles tried to encourage Delwin.

"He's not the only one finding it hard," complained Calder.

"Do as Marmi said, and be quiet!" Akilles lowly chided.

Even in the passage, they heard the muted sounds of bells. Soon they heard screams, shouts and sounds of fighting. Niles and Colin urged the boys to continue despite their increasing fear of the noises.

Delwin sniffled and tugged on Akilles' hand. "This game isn't fun!"

"Hold on tight to Guffy. He's probably scared."

Delwin did so, to the point of the ragged dog covering his face to just below his eyes.

At the tunnel door, Niles gave Akilles the lantern then produced the key. "Go through and wait for everyone else," he instructed Akilles.

When Colin was the last to step through, Niles locked the door. He retrieved the lantern from Akilles. He spoke a gentle reminder to Delwin.

"This is the important part, so you must keep Guffy very quiet." Niles placed a finger to his lips.

Delwin nodded. He shied behind the stuffed dog.

Niles said to Calder and Blaine, "The same goes for you two."

Calder flinched in fear at the louder sounds of battle. Blaine placed a comforting hand on Calder's shoulder then nodded to Niles.

Near the end of the earthen tunnel, light came from just beyond. Niles extinguished the lantern. He drew his sword. Colin followed his father's lead with lantern and sword.

Niles whispered to Akilles. "Keep your sword sheathed to help your brothers."

"All right, but where are we?"

"The tack room of the rear stables. It's a short distance to the postern gate. We must move quickly regardless of what we encounter in the courtyard. Are you ready?"

Akilles' jowls tightened with determination. "Ay."

After a cautious, conferring glance to Colin, Niles opened the secret door. He and Colin ushered the boy inside then Niles closed the passage.

Loud, fierce battle sounds came from the courtyard. Niles carefully peeked out the window. Frightened servants and nobles attempted to flee the invaders while royal soldiers engaged tall men clad in black.

Colin came to peer over Niles shoulder. "Those must be Shadow Warriors," Niles lowly said to Colin.

"Jor'el help us," murmured Colin.

"What is it?" asked Akilles.

"Worse than we thought." Niles made Delwin look up at him. "You and Guffy must run as fast as you can to the postern gate."

"He has four legs, I only have two."

Niles grinned with encouragement at the reply. "You're bigger."

Delwin flinched in fear when a woman screamed. He clenched Guffy over his face as a shield.

"Marmi?" cried Calder in terror.

Blaine covered Calder's mouth. He whispered in Calder's ear. "She is inside not outside."

Niles motioned Colin to the door. "On the count of three."

Delwin held up three fingers. Niles used them to count by placing one down at a time when he spoke. "One ... two ... three!"

Colin jerked open the door and stepped out first, armed and ready. Akilles pulled Delwin from the tack room. Calder and Blaine followed with Niles in the rear. Chaos filled the courtyard with dead and wounded scattered about.

"Don't let them look!" Nile shouted to Colin.

Colin tried to block any view but with little success. "The gate door is open, but the gate broken and partially blocking the entrance!"

"Keep them moving to the door!"

The boys stopped in fright at seeing the devastation. Colin urged Calder and Blaine to keep moving ahead of the others. Delwin froze in terror.

"Run!" Niles nudged the youngest prince.

Delwin lost his balance and fell to the ground. He started crying. Akilles lifted Delwin to his feet to start running. This made Delwin lose hold of the ragged dog.

"Guffy!" Delwin pulled away from Akilles.

"Delwin, no!" Akilles tried to pursue when Niles stopped him.

"Go! I'll get him." When Akilles hesitated with indecision, Niles insisted. "*You must* leave!"

With a painful grunt, Akilles continued after Colin, Calder and Blaine.

By the time Niles moved from Akilles, he couldn't see Delwin. He headed back toward the tack room.

"Going somewhere?"

"Danior!" Niles snarled in rage. "I don't have time to deal with you!"

Danior blocked the path and leveled a sword at Niles' face. "I think you do."

Niles ducked under the first swing then met the second attack. This did not need to happen right now! Niles tried to find a way to disengage from Danior. The wily turncoat thwarted his attempts.

A stunning blow from the flat of Danior's blade knocked Niles sideways into a building wall. A blocking blade stopped Danior from attacking Niles when he was down. Niles recognized his rescuer. "Finn."

A swing from Armus' sword relieved Danior of his weapon. A clout from Armus sent Danior backwards off his feet. Danior struck his head against a wagon and lay unconscious.

"Quickly!" Armus helped Niles to his feet.

"I need to find Delwin."

"No time. Captain Seul is waiting with the others outside. We must hurry."

Niles retrieved his sword to go with Armus. They encountered some of Zared's men thus forced to fight their way to the postern door. Once outside Waldron, Niles pulled up to look for the others.

"Where are they?"

"The trees." Armus led the way. Two Shadow Warriors rode toward them on spirit stallions. Not good! "Sight unseen, move swift and true," Armus muttered the Ancient under his breath.

Niles didn't hear Armus, instead, he made ready for battle. The Warriors rode past them without stopping or giving any hint of recognition. Niles' befuddlement was momentary when Armus pulled on his arm to continue.

Under the cover of trees, Armus made a whistling signal. There came a reply. Armus led Niles to where Kell waited with Colin and the Princes in a sheltered cove. Kell appeared like a mortal with black hair and golden hazel eyes wearing the uniform of a high-ranking Jor'ellian.

"Where is Delwin?" demanded Akilles.

Niles expression showed he loathed answering the question. "I don't know. I couldn't find him."

"You left him?"

Armus detained Akilles when he moved to leave. "I saved Sir Niles from being killed."

Akilles stared into a pair of compassionate yet commanding chestnut eyes. "What about my brother?"

"I didn't see him anywhere nearby. Trust Jor'el to keep him safe."

Calder fought crying out loud. Blaine wiped away a silent tear.

Niles spoke softly to Akilles. "You have two others who need you to be strong in faith and resolve. Besides, as small as Delwin is, you know he can hide very well."

Calder couldn't contain his sobs any longer. Akilles hugged him. His expression shifted between anger, sorrow and determination.

"We can't stay here. We need to get you to safety," said Kell.

"We're supposed to meet Marmi at the Temple," said Blaine.

"That is the first place they will look. We'll take you somewhere safer, for the time being." Kell flashed a compassionate smile at Blaine.

"Can she join us there?" asked Calder between sniffles.

"Ay," said Kell. He then spoke to Colin and Niles. "We'll head east." He took the lead with Armus guarding the rear.

Niles glanced over his shoulder as they travelled. "I'm surprised they didn't double back when we ran past them to get here."

"Who?" Kell asked with guarded curiosity.

"Shadow Warriors, I think. At least that's what I guess from the descriptions I've read of large men in black uniforms."

"They didn't see us," said Armus.

"How? They rode right past us," insisted Niles.

"Obviously, they were more intent on where they headed and ignored us." Armus looked over Niles' head to Kell as he continued to speak. "If they perceived us, they would be after us. Since they aren't in pursuit, we can safely assume they saw nothing."

"And that's a good thing," said Kell.

Chapter 34

I N THE REAR COURTYARD, GORDON AND ABNER'S SOILED APPEARANCE and bloody swords told of battle. Although the fighting shifted to the front, they couldn't take any chances and hid behind a damaged wagon.

"Any sign of Niles and the Princes?" asked Abner.

"No," said Gordon with distress. "Look!" He seized Abner and pointed up to the second floor of the main building. Flames shot out from the windows of four different rooms. "Merciful heaven!"

"We can't give up hope. Go that way. I'll return to the barracks and Chapel. We'll try to meet up …"

When Abner hesitated with resignation, Gordon encouraged his friend. "You said don't give up. Now where shall we meet?"

"The same place we met Niles outside Waldron. Jor'el go with you, my brother." Abner held his arm out for the Jor'ellian parting gesture.

Gordon clasped Abner's arm to speak the response. "And may the Almighty be with you, Brother Jor'ellian."

Gordon ran in the direction indicated. He didn't envy Abner taking the more dangerous path. He couldn't think about that. He had to find Niles and the Princes. Smoke poured out when he tried to enter a rear door. He backed away, coughing from brief smoke inhalation.

He made his way to the far corner of the main building. On this side of the castle, a small alleyway ran between the main building and the western wall. From what he could see, nothing appeared disturbed. Perhaps this would serve as a place to hide until all was quiet.

Gordon slowly walked down the alley, keeping his eyes and ears open for any signs of a presence. He stopped when he heard shouting. He realized he stood under a window and the voice came from inside. Before moving further along the alley, there came a tiny squeal followed by sniffles and a feeble cough. Gordon listened more closely. Another cough. It came from just up ahead.

"Hello? Who's there?" asked Gordon.

Hearing a gasp of fright, Gordon knelt beside plank of old wood leaned against the wall. "I can hear you."

Movement, as a small body crawled out ready to bolt.

"Delwin?"

The boy stopped. He clenched Guffy in frightened defense when he turned to face Gordon. Tears stained his face and he trembled. "Who—who are you?"

"It's me. Sir Gordon. We played tag, remember?" He held out his hand and gently tapped his own palm.

Delwin cocked his head, as if inspecting Gordon. "Oh, ay."

"Why were you hiding here? I thought you went with Sir Niles?"

Delwin held out the dog doll. "I dropped Guffy. I couldn't leave without him. I got lost!" He wept.

Gordon held Delwin to comfort him. "I'm sure Akilles and Niles are looking for you, just like I have been looking for them."

"I tried to find Marmi, but there's too much smoke."

Gordon heard more shouting. He covered Delwin's mouth. When the voices stopped, he spoke hurried and low. "To find Akilles and your mother means taking you from Waldron. To do that, you must trust me and be quiet."

"The escape game again?" Delwin asked with a pout.

Gordon kindly stroked Delwin's face to wipe away the tears. "I'm afraid so. I tell you what, we can play tag when reach safety, all right?"

"Promise?"

"Ay." Gordon widely smiled. He pulled Delwin's hood up and closed the cloak. "Make sure the hood stay ups and hold Guffy so tight that he doesn't fall out from under your cloak." Gordon picked up Delwin. He rushed back to the rear courtyard.

The courtyard appeared empty while the noise of battle significantly decreased. Fire now engulfed the first floor of the royal wing. No reason for the invading force to contain the flames. Debris fell from the building, so Gordon kept close to the rear wall away from the fire. He shielded Delwin. At the postern gate, he peeked outside in search of any enemy. The way appeared cleared. He whispered to Delwin.

"I'm going to run as fast as I can for trees, so hold on tight."

Delwin gripped Gordon as hard as he could.

Gordon prayed, "Jor'el, protect us!" Taking a deep breath, he ran for the trees. The two hundred yards felt like an eternity. They managed to reach the woods without any hindrance. Gordon hid behind a large old oak tree to catch his breath.

"Thank you, Jor'el." He gulped for air. "I need to put you down for a moment to rest."

"Are Marmi and Akilles out here?"

Gordon shook his head, still recovering his breath. "I don't know where they are exactly. But," he said when Delwin began to protest. "When we get to my home, I'll send word to them that you are safe."

"Why not send word now?"

Gordon knelt to turn Delwin to view Waldron. "With the fire, word won't reach them right now. They have to put it out first. By the time we get to my home, the fire will be out and word can reach them."

"Where is your home?"

"In the Meadowlands. A castle called Milton. It has plenty of places to play tag." Gordon smiled. When Delwin frowned with consideration, Gordon added, "I think Guffy would like Milton. Lots of open spaces to run around." He turned the ragged dog to look at it. "What do you think, Guffy? Does Milton sound fun?" He made a pretend voice for Guffy to reply. "I think so."

"He doesn't talk out loud," protested Delwin. He asked Guffy. "What do you think?" He held the ragged dog up to his right ear.

"Well? I didn't hear an answer."

"He says he likes you and Milton sound likes fun."

Gordon laughed. "Then let's go to Milton."

Delwin nodded since he yawned.

"Are you tired?"

"And cold." Delwin sniffled and held Guffy close.

Gordon again picked up Delwin. "We need to find a warm place to get some sleep. We'll continue to Milton in the morning."

Meanwhile, Myla left Akilles' chamber intent on reaching the King's Study. At the end of the corridor to the royal wing, she heard sounds of fighting. She also recognized Zared's voice shouting a command.

"Fetch those rotten brats and bring them to the King's study!"

If they found the boys missing … she had to think fast! She raced back toward Akilles room. A pungent smell of smoke stopped her. Something nearby was burning.

"Fire!" she muttered with concern. Yet, this gave her an idea.

She rushed into Akilles' room. The evening fire had not totally extinguished. She stoked the coal to produce flames.

"Hurry!" she scolded during her efforts to revive the fire.

When sparks caught fresh wood, she used her skirt to wrap her hands and remove a burning log from the hearth. First she set the curtains on fire, then the bed, and anything else she could. Finally she threw several burning logs into the privy. After lighting various objects on fire, the smoke grew thicker. She choked from the smoke. Her eyes burned and she was forced from the room into the hallway. She coughed uncontrollably and fell to her knees in desperation to breath.

"Majesty?" One of the nurses hurried to Myla.

Zared arrived with several of his men and two large black clad individuals.

"Seize them!" he ordered his men in regards of the women.

Myla forced herself to stop coughing so she could confront him. "What are you doing?"

He didn't immediately answer. "Fetch the brats," he told the black clad men.

"The room is on fire!" Myla's shout stopped them. "I couldn't reach them!" she spoke with rising tears.

Zared glared with skepticism. "They were *all* in there?"

"You saw them last night. The younger ones fell asleep." Myla wept.

"My lord, the entire room is engulfed. The fire will move out in corridor soon," said one the Warriors standing at room's threshold.

Zared seized Myla's arm. "Take her to join the other servants," he said concerning the nurse.

Myla didn't fight her captors, as they moved from the family wing to the King's Study. Although the smell of smoke hung heavy, the fire hadn't reached this part of the castle yet. Berk sat at his desk surrounded by two more large black clad men. One had a nasty scar on his face, the other cold grey eyes. Patrin stood beside Berk.

"Berk, what is this about?" she asked, almost pleading.

Dumbfounded, Berk shook his head. "I don't know."

"Oh, come now," began Zared with bitter sarcasm. "Neither of you are that naïve. A coup, of course."

Berk spoke with intense anger. "You betray me?"

"No, you betrayed yourself. But we haven't time for discussion. The fire is moving quickly. Fortunately, it saved me the trouble of dealing with your brats."

The statement baffled Berk. "What?"

Myla fought tears. "The fire."

Astonished, Berk stared at her. "All of them?"

"All of them," confirmed Zared with dispassion. "Shortly, the unfortunate royal couple, as well. First, you will sign this paper naming your successor." He snapped his fingers. Witter pulled a document out from his belt and gave it to Zared.

"Who? You?" Berk challenged Zared when the baron placed the paper on the desk in front of him.

"No, me." Patrin made a satisfied smile. "Remember, you named me Regent."

Zared picked up a quill from the ink well. "Sign it!"

315

Berk didn't move, totally overwhelmed by the scope of what was happening. Zared forced the quill into Berk's hand. With pitiful eyes of regret, Berk looked to Myla.

She maintained her composure enough to reply. "What difference does it make? Your weakness brought us to this end."

A beaten man, Berk signed the document. Altari tied Berk to his desk chair and gagged him. Witter secured Myla to another chair. Zared, Patrin and the Warriors ran from the study to the Grand Courtyard and awaiting horses. They rode from Waldron.

After a half-mile, they stopped to watch. Flames erupted from various parts of the castle.

Patrin marveled. "I've never seen a fire spread so fast."

"Come morning, every stone and timber will be totally consumed. Only charred earth will remain," said Witter.

"Such is the power the Dark Way, *Sire,*" said Zared to Patrin.

Patrin stared at Zared. He covered a slight shiver of fear, by turning his attention back to the fire. "I shall remember that, Grand Master."

A man in Zared's livery arrived on horseback. "My lord. A group of men have gathered about a mile from here. Should I send soldiers to apprehend them?"

"Any identification?"

"They appear to be noblemen."

"No arms or soldiers?" asked Patrin.

He shook his head. "No, my lord."

"They probably fled the fire," said Zared. The flames rose higher. "Unless they move to interfere, leave them be."

"Why?" Patrin asked.

"Because when they see nothing left of Waldron, word will spread of the tragedy robbing Allon of the royal family."

"My lord," began Witter with objection. "They witnessed our invasion."

Zared's ire rose. "We can't kill the entire royal family *and* the Council!"

316

"Dagar may not agree."

Zared was hot to dispute. "Dagar's objective was to topple the House of Tristan and replace the worship of Jor'el with the Dark Way." He waved at Waldron. "There goes the House of Tristan. Once Patrin is crowned, the Dark Way will have won the day."

"There is still the matter of the *Vicar of Jor'el.*"

"My power will render Archimedes ineffective!"

"So will the presence of over two thousand Shadow Warriors and Archers," said Altari.

Zared flashed a thin smile of impatience. "Then that should render any further argument moot!" This made Witter and Altari fall silent. "Now, let us begin phase three." Zared turned his horse. Patrin followed.

Chapter 35

WITH YOUNG BOYS, KELL AND ARMUS ONLY MANAGED to lead the group four miles northeast from Waldron. The emotional toll, lateness of the hour and travel wearied Calder and Blaine. Akilles appeared to bear up well, though he also showed signs of fatigue.

They stopped in a sheltered hollow. Armus built a fire while Kell scouted the perimeter. Niles and Colin arranged fallen leaves into pallets near the rock-rimmed fire for warmth. Akilles tended to Calder and Blaine. He spoke with encouraging tenderness not often heard between brothers. Calder needed the most bolstering. When Blaine became gruff, a stern word from Akilles curbed his attitude.

Kell returned with a couple of rabbits and handful of wild tubers. "These will serve for breakfast." He told Armus.

"Is everything secure, Captain?" Colin asked.

"Ay. I found no signs of pursuit. They can rest until dawn."

Akilles coaxed Calder and Blaine to lie down on the pallets.

"You too," said Niles to Akilles. He took gentle hold of Akilles' arm, but roughly shook off. Akilles stormed to edge of the firelight, facing the direction from whence they came.

"Leave him be for now," Kell quietly said to Niles. "He has much to consider."

"His silence concerns me. He's usually not one to keep to himself."

"This is not a usual time." Kell clapped Niles' shoulder. "You also must rest. And don't tell me about Jor'ellian training to stay awake. They need you to be clearheaded and alert for what lies ahead."

"We can take turns on watch."

"No. Finn and I will remain awake." Kell heard disturbed moaning. Calder stirred in what appeared to be a nightmare. "He needs you. Lay beside him for comfort."

Niles did so and wrapped his cloak around Calder. Holding the boy seemed to relax him.

The noise caught Akilles' attention. Kell prevented him from approaching Calder.

"Sir Niles has calmed him. And you *do* need to rest to keep up your strength."

"It's hard not knowing what has become of my parents and Delwin."

"You can't think of that to the point of distraction. All you can do is deal with what you know at present. A time will come to sort out the rest. For now, your responsibility is to help you brothers and find a place of safety." Kell motioned to Calder and Blaine.

For a moment, Akilles' gazed upon his brothers. "I'll try." He went to lie between Calder and Blaine.

"*Sleep in peace, most favored one,*" Kell spoke low in the Ancient.

"I wonder why we haven't been followed?" Armus asked Kell in the Ancient.

"Divine intervention, perhaps. Let's just be grateful."

"Where do you plan on taking them?"

Kell thought for a moment before answering. "A place most won't dare to venture."

Armus drew Kell away from where the mortals slept. "You don't mean Dorgirith, do you?"

"Ay."

Armus grew dubious of the destination. "That's over one hundred miles. Mortals take four days of constant riding from Garwood to Waldron. Dorgirith is five miles beyond that." He glanced back at the group. "There are too many for us to take them by way dimension travel. And we don't want to leave any of them vulnerable."

Kell cocked a smile. "I summoned your *sister* to help us."

"With her help we can manage dimension travel."

Kell shook his head, grim in this reply. "Waldron has more than likely fallen, which means Dagar will send out troops when he finds them missing. Though permitted to help, using your power to shield escape was risky," he said in mild rebuke. "Our current persona keeps our essence hidden, but any *further* use of power could help them track us."

"So why summon Wren?"

"Factor in small boys and walking could take two weeks. She can bring the wagon used for Osborn and Travis to transport the boys while the rest of us walk. This could lessen the journey to six or seven days."

"Weather and other hazards permitting," grumbled Armus.

Key grinned. "The weather will be favorable."

Armus looked suspiciously at Kell. "You dispatched Priscilla, didn't you?"

"I wasn't idle while waiting for you to fetch Niles."

Armus became sarcastically cross. "Is there anything else I should know about besides Wren and Priscilla?"

Kell shook his head. "The others are still monitoring the enemy. Now let's set stand watch."

<hr />

Niles and Colin woke to the smell of cooking. They noticed the warm grey light of pre-dawn. Armus roasted rabbits on a spit. The tubers lay on rocks rimming the fire for slower cooking.

Niles didn't see Kell. "Where is Captain Seul?"

"Scouting for the safest route. He should be back shortly," replied Armus.

Akilles yawned and stretched. He sniffed the air. "That smells good."

Armus smiled. He used his knife to cut portions of the cooked rabbit.

Blaine became the next to stir. Colin encouraged him to wake.

"Calder," said Niles gently. "It's time for breakfast."

"It's morning already?"

Niles chuckled. "Ay. How did you sleep?"

Calder thought for a moment then smile. "I slept well." He rubbed his arms. "It's cold."

"Sit next to fire to warm up and eat."

Armus held out a rabbit leg to Calder. "It's hot, so you might want to put it on a rock between bites." He handed another leg to Blaine then gave breast pieces to Akilles, Niles and Colin. "Try the tubers. They have a sweet carrot-like flavor."

"I love carrots," said Calder. He took a tuber and ate. He smiled. "It is good!"

Colin picked up the flask for a drink. He balked in surprise at the taste. "That's not water."

Armus laughed. "It is water. I just added some sweet clover honey and ginger to help lift the spirits."

"Where did you find ginger and honey around here?"

"I brought them." Wren stepped forward from her position beside a nearby tree.

Colin stirred with mild alarm, to which Niles took hold of his son. He smiled to explain, "Mistress Collie is Command Finn's sister. A huntress who is well versed in wilderness survival."

"A woman?" asked Akilles.

Wren wryly smiled at the elder prince. "Survival knows no gender. Whether male or female, the rules of living in the wild are the same; hunt, find food and shelter, and be familiar with your surroundings."

Akilles accepted the answer.

"Now, finish eating. When Captain Seul returns, we will leave," said Armus. He distributed the last bits of rabbit and tubers.

"Aren't you going to eat?" Akilles asked.

"Captain Seul, Collie and I ate earlier."

Hearing a horse neigh brought Niles and Colin to their feet ready for defense. Kell returned.

"Easy, gentlemen. The horse you hear belongs to Collie. I just finished hitching it to a small wagon," he said.

"So we don't have to walk where we're going?" asked Blaine.

"No, you and your brothers get to ride in the wagon. The rest of us will walk."

"Except me. I drive." Wren smiled and winked at Akilles.

Kell ignored the humor. "It will take about a week to reach our destination."

"What is our destination?" asked Akilles.

"That is best kept secret until we arrive. Be assured, it is the safest place in the kingdom." Kell softly smiled. "Now, if you are finished, help your brothers into the wagon. We'll break camp so it appears that no one was here."

When that was done, Kell took the lead. Wren drove. Niles and Colin walked beside the wagon when the forest trail was wide enough. Armus kept the rear guard.

After a couple of hours, Calder grew frustrated at the bumpy ride. "Aren't we going to use the road?" he complained.

"When we can, but staying off the road is safer," replied Wren.

"Not less bumpy," Blaine complained.

They emerged from the forest into a meadow. Wren spoke the Ancient under her breath for protection. Up ahead, Kell drew his sword. Niles, Colin and Armus also proceeded with weapons ready. Once through the meadow, they traveled a well-worn cart path for a smoother ride into more woods.

Three miles later, "Captain!" Wren called. Kell paused to give attention. "In two miles there is a turn onto a small road that heads due east to the river. It's less travelled, yet more direct."

Kell waved an acknowledgement and resumed the trek. The small road took them through another meadow. The boys squirmed to get comfortable. Not due to bumps rather for more legroom and long periods of inactivity.

"I think everyone needs to get out and stretch their legs," teased Wren. She halted the wagon short of the trees. She motioned for the boys to climb out. Colin and Niles helped them.

"My stomach hurts also," groused Calder.

Niles grew concerned. "Hurts as in a stomach ache?"

"No, hungry."

"Then I guess it's a good thing I brought provisions," said Wren with a large smile.

Kell had entered the trees and ran back to the wagon when he noticed Wren stopped. "Something wrong?"

"Leg cramps and hunger," she replied to his chagrin.

"You could have waited until we got under the cover of trees to stop," he chided her.

"That's where I'm heading so we can eat."

Wren snapped the reins and drove the wagon into the trees. She pulled slightly off the road. She hopped down from the driver's seat. Reaching under the seat, she pulled out a long covered basket. Inside were three large loafs of bread and some sausage. She passed out good chunks of bread to the others, including Kell and Armus. Using her knife, she cut off sausage for each person. She even set aside food for herself. When finished, she replaced the basket under the seat.

"This will serve for during the day. After we make camp, I'll set traps for dinner," she said.

They all sat beneath several large pine trees to eat. Everyone shared from the flask to wash down the quick meal.

Calder appeared sheepish bordering on pain.

"Is there a problem?" Colin asked the boy.

Calder flashed abashed eyes at Wren, and leaned close to ask Colin, "What does one do for a privy in the wilderness when you need to sit down?"

Colin couldn't help a chuckle at the question. He stifled his reaction to appease the blushing young prince. "Come with me." He took Calder by the hand and shortly disappeared behind a cluster of trees.

Armus widely smiled at Wren. "I think you embarrass him."

Niles grinned at the exchange. He approached Kell to speak privately. "Heading for the river, means crossing into the Southern Forest. You aren't taking us to Garwood, are you? I don't know what has become of Abner. Nor would I want to place him danger."

"No, not Garwood."

For a moment, Niles studied Kell's steely expression. Hit with sudden understanding, Niles turned his back to Akilles and Blaine and spoke in a low guarded voice. "I believe I know our destination. A place even the Dark Way no longer goes."

Kell didn't reply. He didn't have to. His confirming gaze enough to satisfy Niles. At length, Kell said, "When they return, we best continue."

Each afternoon, the provisions Wren pulled out of the covered basket surprised Akilles. The bread tasted fresh and the sausage delicious. A few times she even gave them sweet, juicy apples. At night, she managed to trap or hunt a small boar, rabbits or quails.

Armus continued to impress with his cooking skills. With just a few meager ingredients scrounged in the forest and added to the meat, he prepared delicious food at night. Even the picky eater, Calder, enjoyed the meals. Armus then served the cooled leftovers for breakfast.

The most open and dangerous part of the journey came when crossing the bridge over the River Conn. Kell timed it so they made it during the early hours of the morning before sunrise. Once on the Southern Forest side, they proceeded for two more days.

The long hours of riding in the wagon or walking to stretch his legs, gave Akilles a lot of time to think. There were so many questions swirling in his mind that he didn't know where to begin. He wondered if he would ever learn the answers.

When not thinking, Akilles kept an eye on his brothers, especially walking. Blaine occasionally fell into his mood of complaining. However, those times grew short-lived. Mostly Blaine listened and followed instructions. Calder appeared thoughtful, more so than Akilles could remember for the eight-year-old. It pleased him that Calder slept without nightmares. Considering the harrowing escape, being on the road to an unknown destination and uncertain future, Calder sleeping soundly proved a blessing.

At times, Akilles wondered about Seul, Finn and Collie. Several nights he talked quietly with Niles. He learned Seul and Finn were well respected Jor'ellians. Niles just recently met Collie, yet trusted her due to her relation to Finn. Still, Akilles sensed something highly unusual about them, not concerning or frightening. No, he felt safe, even liked them. There was just a difference he couldn't quite figure out.

By late afternoon of the seventh day, they stopped a hundred yards before a large, dense forest. Akilles watched Seul and Finn approach the trees. They bowed their heads.

"Collie, what are they doing?" Akilles asked Wren.

"Thanking Jor'el for our safe arrival."

He rose from sitting in the wagon to standing behind her seat. "They brought us to a forest?"

"It's not just any forest." She saw Kell wave. "Now, sit. You'll learn more soon enough." She snapped the reins.

Even in late autumn, numerous large, tall pine trees created a dense canopy in the forest. Shafts of twilight penetrated only through the bare branches of leaf shedding trees. It took two hours of navigating the woods before they finally stopped at a very large mound with hanging vines.

Niles drew alongside Kell. "What is this place?"

"Your new home."

"A mound?" asked Colin.

"A cave. Safely hidden because it's not easily recognized as such. Fetch the boys." Kell waited for them to follow instructions.

"Is this our safe place?" Akilles asked Kell.

"Ay."

Wren gave Kell a lantern. He led them inside. After a short tunnel entrance, they emerged into a large room with two smaller alcoves on the other side. Old pieces of wooden furniture, buckets and pots showed signs of occupants.

"Does someone live here?" asked Niles.

"Not anymore," replied Wren. "Long ago, thieves and malcontents took advantage of hiding here. Those who weren't afraid that is."

Annoyed by the answer, Kell jabbed an elbow in her side.

"Afraid?" asked a nervous Calder. "What did they have to fear?"

"Nothing," said Kell. "Rumors, myths and legends now. Which is why this place is safe to hide."

"Dorgirith!" Akilles said with sudden comprehension.

"You've heard of it?" asked Armus.

"In my studies. A cursed forest once used by a man named Magelen."

"Cursed?" echoed Calder with terror.

"We're to live in a cursed cave?" added Blaine.

"Not cursed any longer." Kell reassured them. "However, many people still believe the legends, so they stay away. No one will trouble you here."

"How will Marmi find us?" asked Calder fighting back upset.

"Ay, we're supposed to meet her at the Temple," said Blaine.

Kell became sorrowful in regard of the young Princes. "I'm afraid, she won't be able to meet you anywhere."

"Have you learned something?" demanded Niles.

Wren spoke up, sympathetic. "When I arrived, I told Captain Seul and my brother the news. We agreed to wait until we arrived here, and it was safe to speak."

Akilles practically accosted Wren with anxiety for information. "What news?"

Wren eyes grew misty. "Waldron was totally destroyed by fire. There were no survivors ..." her voice trailed off to ... "I'm so sorry."

"Marmi?" Blaine whimpered.

Calder sobbed.

Akilles stared with wide eyes of angry astonishment. When Wren reached to comfort him, he bolted.

"Akilles!" called Niles.

"No! Let me," insisted Kell. "There are things he needs to hear." Although Akilles recklessly ran from the cave, Kell overtook him. In passion and grief, Akilles tried to fight Kell.

"Leave off! I need to go back! To avenge my mother ..." He wept.

Kell held Akilles. It took almost five minutes for Akilles to spend his sorrow. Hearing a pause, Kell said, "Someday your family will be avenged, and the House of Tristan restored. *You* were brought here to make certain that happens.

Akilles stepped away from Kell. "How do you know the future?"

"Didn't Niles teach you prophecy?"

Upset, Akilles chided, "What does prophecy have to do with this?"

Kell seized the impassioned Akilles by the shoulders. "Everything!"

Akilles knocked away Kell's hold. "You're saying the destruction of my family is fulfillment of prophecy?"

"No, *your* survival is the fulfillment!" Kell's expression became kind and encouraging. "From you, will come the hope of Allon."

"Me? I'm still a boy! Now without parents or a home!"

"You are highly favored by Jor'el. You need not fear the future, Akilles, Son of Tristan."

"You call me *Son of Tristan* when my father was Berk," he chided.

"Son of Tristan is a prophetic title."

With bewildered frustration, Akilles rebuffed, "You speak of prophecy and my future, but how do you know any of this?"

Kell straightened. "To mortals I am Captain Seul." Before Akilles' eyes, he transformed back to his Guardian form. At seven and half feet, he towered over Akilles. Kell's golden eyes were bright and compassionate in their regard, as he continued. "In reality, I am Kell, Captain of Jor'el's Guardians."

In wonder, Akilles gaped up at Kell. He blinked several times at what he just saw. "Guardians! You're real?" He reached out to touch Kell.

Kell laughed. "We are very real." He held Akilles' hand on his arm.

Akilles' brows furrowed as he attempted to comprehend. "How long will this take? I'm ready to destroy Zared now!"

"I appreciate your willingness, only it is not now. Perhaps when you're older. May be your son or grandson. Just know that it is through *you* Jor'el will right this wrong and destroy the Dark Way." He gently made Akilles face him when the Prince turned away in anger. "I know that is not what you want to hear because of grief and passion. But Jor'el has spoken so it *will* happen. Your task is to survive, grow in grace and pass on your faith, knowledge and resolve."

Dejected, Akilles moved from Kell. "Seems of little use in the face of what has happened."

"It's not. Do you remember the story of your ancestor Tristan?"

Akilles looked along his shoulder at Kell. "Of course. It's told in Verse, stories and song."

"All seemed hopeless then yet Tristan's faith won the day. He learned about Jor'el and faith from his grandfather Lord Razi. Same as you learned from your mother." He clapped Akilles on the shoulder. "Faith is the essence of things hoped for, the evidence of things not seen. I have told you more than most mortals know of their future." Kell patted Akilles' left breast. "Hide it here with the confidence of knowing it *will* come to pass."

Akilles became downcast. "It still hurts losing Marmi and Delwin."

"Naturally. Grief takes time while faith is eternal. Now come, Niles is worried, and your brothers need you." Kell steered Akilles back inside the cave.

Upon sight of Akilles, Calder ran to embrace him, weeping.

"I gave him something to calm down, only he wanted to see you before trying to sleep," Wren said the Akilles. She helped Akilles take Calder and Blaine to a small alcove with two worn cots.

Niles approached Kell, who remained in Guardian form. "Why do I recognize you? And not as *Captain Seul.*"

Kell kindly grinned. "Because we spoke in the Chapel at Waldron."

Niles smiled in remembrance. "The legend named Kell."

"Guardian, I take it," said Colin.

"*Captain* of the Guardians," Niles stressed. "So are Finn and Collie. Otherwise, we wouldn't have made it safely."

Kell chuckled. He glanced to the alcove. "Akilles knows what is required of him according to Prophecy regarding the House of Tristan. Your task," he said to Niles and Colin, "is to continue being diligent to help him grow in his faith and knowledge until he feels the call to leave and seek a wife."

Niles spoke with sobriety. "Just one question. Did anyone escape before the flames consumed Waldron?"

"I heard no report to that effect."

Niles blinked back tears. "Then Abner and Gordon ..." He couldn't finish and felt Colin's supportive hand on his shoulder.

Seeing Wren emerge from the alcove, Kell again spoke. "We must leave. Jor'el is with you, King's Champion, and you, loyal Jor'ellian," he said to Niles and Colin respectively. He, Armus and Wren withdrew.

Chapter 36

T THE RUINS OF RAVENDALE, ONE HUNDRED NOBLEMEN GATHERED. Twice as many Shadow Warriors ringed the area around a makeshift platform. Upon the platform sat the tri-pod wrought iron basin and a chair. A single rough-hewn step led to the platform. By the mood of the noblemen, they assembled under compulsion and not voluntarily.

Abner, Slater and Mather stood together. They conversed in low, hushed voices. All were wary of the makeshift platform.

"Most of Council is here save Archimedes and Gordon," said Slater.

"You shouldn't expect Archimedes to set foot on this cursed ground," chided Abner, his face set with disgust.

"What about Gordon? Surely he received the same summons."

Abner shook his head, as he attitude turned somber. "I don't know if he managed to leave Waldron before the fire."

Slater placed a comforting arm about Abner's shoulders. "He, Niles and Colin did as they swore, died in service to Jor'el."

Abner stiffened with painful frustration. "That is not a certainty. Once this fiasco is over, I intend to find out."

"Give heed, gentlemen!" called the raised voice of Zared. He, Patrin, Witter and Altari stepped onto the platform. Witter carried a large ornate wooden box.

Zared wore a handsome embroidered black robe trimmed in rich scarlet velvet. From a heavy silver chain hung the raven crested talisman. Patrin was finely arrayed in a noble suit of cream with black and scarlet trim. Witter and Altari assumed their places on either side of the chair and basin.

Zared fingered the talisman while his self-satisfied gaze swept over the assembly. "I'm certain you are all wondering why I, Grand Master of Allon, summoned you to the ruins of Ravendale, of all places." He paused a moment for reaction. No one spoke. "I will tell you. Allon needs a new king, and shall have one." He motioned to Patrin, stood in front of the chair.

"Why him?" asked Slater.

"A legitimate question, Count Slater." Zared reached into his pocket to produce a document. "If you all recall, our late King Berk named Lord Patrin as Regent for Prince Akilles. Berk also, wrote this." He unfolded the paper. "A Writ of Royal Succession, naming Lord Patrin his heir should a most unfortunate and tragic occurrence befall the royal family."

"A forgery!" Abner could barely contain his anger.

"I would curb your tongue, Sir Abner," warned Zared.

Abner didn't heed the warning. "This was a planned coup, not a—"

Slater's restraint stopped Abner. "Be still!" he scolded.

Abner's expression showed ire at the intervention.

"Wisely done, Count. You may have just saved Sir Abner's life," said Zared, pointedly. "Now, gentlemen, if there are no other objections, we shall proceed with the coronation of our new king."

After Abner's outburst, no one moved or spoke.

Zared opened the box Witter held. He removed a finely crafted silver crown studded with rubies and onyx. He moved to where Patrin waited. "By the power vested in me by royal decree, and right of office, I crown you, Patrin, King of Allon."

Patrin bowed his head to receive the crown. Deep silence met the new king; no kneeling or acknowledgement only faces of disapproval. This prompted Patrin to rebuke them. "I expect fealty and will not tolerate any form of sedition. Do I make myself clear, gentlemen?"

The noblemen remained fixed in their unwillingness to bow.

Zared gripped the talisman in both hands and shouted, "*Nochdadh!*"

Instantly, the water in the basin boiled. In the rising steam, Dagar's full image appeared. He held an unsheathed sword. His mahogany eyes blazed with unquestioning authority and evil.

Zared spoke to the stunned crowd. "Behold, the mighty immortal Lord Dagar!"

Scared beyond words, many noblemen fell to their knees. Several balked when compelled by Shadow Warriors to kneel. Zared marked attention found Abner, Slater and Mather. Mather yielded to Zared's penetrating glare and became the first to submit. Slater's jowls flexed with indecision before he bent the knee. Only Abner remained standing in the face of oppression. The effort to withstand the evil before him, showed in the sweat on his brow and narrow eyes of determination.

"You risk exhausting my patience by your refusal, Sir Abner," said Patrin.

"I will respect the position of king, as is my sworn duty, but I will not bow to the Dark Lord!"

When Dagar brought his sword up in front of his face, Abner drew to his full height ready to meet whatever.

"*Sguir!*" a voice from behind the crowd bellowed the Ancient for *stop*.

Dagar's action came to an abrupt halt. "Who dares to speak?" he demanded.

Using a staff, Archimedes knocked aside a Shadow Warrior to step where he could be seen. He wore all the trappings of his office of Vicar.

"You?" Dagar hissed with outrage.

Archimedes moved to stand beside Abner. "Did you think you could appoint a king without my presence?"

Dagar flashed a thin impatient smile. "Your presence is unnecessary. Be gone before I destroy you and anyone else who objects."

Archimedes firmly planted the staff in sign of immobility. "As long as Jor'el is sovereign over all, and remnant of the faithful shall remain there is nothing you can do about it, creature of darkness."

Dagar snarled. "You make bold threats in the face of overwhelming odds. Ravendale will be rebuilt, Patrin king and Grand Master Zared free to employ Shadow Warriors." His sneering gaze shifted to Abner then back to Archimedes. "Take your lone ally and leave, while I allow it!"

Archimedes paused only a moment to survey the crowd. Ninety-nine remained in a position of submission. He took hold of Abner. "Come.

Abner made no objection when Archimedes led him from the area. Kincaid waited with three Jor'ellians where the nobles had tethered their horses. They fell in behind Archimedes and Abner as they rode away. For an hour they continued until Abner pulled up his horse.

Archimedes noticed. "Why did you stop?"

"I appreciate your intervention, my lord, but I must take my leave."

"You're not going to return to confront Dagar, are you?"

"No, I travel to Milton to learn what has become of Gordon. The last I saw him was at Waldron when we went our separate ways to find Niles and Princes."

Archimedes anxiously asked, "Did you find them?"

Abner shook his head. "No. Alas, it is reported there were no survivors of those who didn't escape in time."

Archimedes muttered a prayer. "I did not want to believe the report, so I rode to Waldron. There I viewed the destruction for myself. I also learned of the summons and made haste." He nodded with pride at Abner. "You are a credit to your oath and vow." He made the Jor'ellian salute. "Go with Jor'el. Report to me to what you learn."

Abner returned the salute. "I will, my lord Vicar." He turned his horse to head southeast.

***

A week later, Abner arrived at Milton. The grand sprawling manor house sat in the heart of the Meadowlands. From spring through early fall, sheep and horses grazed around the manor. By late fall, the livestock were penned in corrals for safety and ease of feeding and shearing.

Abner waited in the study. At least he knew Gordon was alive by the fact the housekeeper went to fetch him.

In a rush, Gordon arrived and warmly greeted Abner with a hearty embrace. "Thank Jor'el! I didn't know if you survived."

"Nor I you!" Abner widely smiled and hugged Gordon again. His joy turned to downcast. "Have you heard about—?"

"I know all about them," said Gordon in somber haste to forestall Abner.

"What of the summons? Why didn't you come?"

Gordon hesitated in answering. "I couldn't leave. Not yet anyway."

"Why? Did injury prevent you from traveling?" He surveyed Gordon for signs of injury.

"No. I am whole." Again Gordon acted reluctant.

"What's wrong? You seem out of sorts."

Gordon led Abner to sit in one of two chairs separated by a small table. He flashed an abashed smile. "Well, I've recently become a father."

The stunning news was not what Abner expected to hear. Flabbergasted he could barely bring himself to ask, "You fathered a child out of wedlock?"

"No!" Gordon insisted at the misunderstanding. "You remember my sister. The one who went astray?"

"Iona."

"Ay. Well, she unexpectedly died and left a five-year-old son. Despite father's shame and my disapproval of her behavior, I couldn't leave the boy alone. I adopted him."

Abner listened and observed his friend. Gordon spoke with a halting, uncertain attitude. "You regret your actions?"

"No, not at all. He is a bright and loving child." Gordon smiled with fondness that soon faded. "I regret the circumstances."

"You're not responsible for your sister's choices."

Gordon looked to Abner with remorse. "Not her choices. Those I must make to protect him from his past. At five years old, he mourns his mother, though he doesn't fully understand." He rose to pace. "The past couple of weeks, I've spoken to him on the level a child can understand. He grasps some concepts now. But in the future there will be days of trying to answer questions I can't. Do you understand?" he asked in an almost pleading tone.

"Somewhat, though I'm not yet a father," replied Abner with a quick grin. "However, you can't keep him isolated from reality."

"I realize that. Yet for now, I must stay close to him, and secluded from responsibilities. At least until he can come to terms with his new surroundings and me as his father."

"What is his name?"

"Holden. Named after my grandfather." Gordon took Abner by the arm to escort him from the study. "I do not wish to seem rude, my friend, but I can't offer you hospitality right now. Please try to understand."

"Of course," Abner spoke in gracious reply. "Perhaps you'll bring him to Garwood for our New Year's celebration."

Gordon grinned. "Hopefully, he will be settled in by then."

Abner stopped in the foyer threshold. "Is there anything I can do to help?"

With earnestness, Gordon said, "Pray for us."

"Always, my friend. Jor'el's peace be upon this house."

"And may he grant you safe passage home." Gordon's smile faded, as he watched Abner mount, wave and ride off. He heard a small voice squeal with delight.

"Gordon, look what I did!"

Gordon quickly shut the door. He scooped up Delwin. The boy held a badly folded piece of paper. "Call me Papi now, remember?"

"Papi," Delwin repeated. He held up the paper. "I did it like you."

Gordon chuckled. "Well, it's a good attempt."

Delwin made an angry pout.

"Holden," began Gordon in a mild scolding tone. "There is no need to pout. Just try again."

Delwin pouted again, only this time to speak. "Will this new name game end?"

Gordon gently lifted Delwin's chin to look at him. "This is no game, remember? Word came from Waldron that your mother and brothers are with Jor'el. We don't want the bad men to find you or Guffy."

Delwin nodded and sniffled.

Gordon kissed the boy's forehead. "I know it is hard to understand. But before Jor'el, I promise you, this all for best." He held Delwin close. "Now, let's have supper."

Chapter 37

FROM A KNOLL OVERLOOKING WHERE WALDRON ONCE STOOD, Kell stared at the charred earth. Destruction by the Dark Way was complete in less than a day.

"I knew I'd find you here."

Kell didn't reply. Even when Armus moved beside him, Kell remained focused on the rubble.

"Everyone is waiting at Arundine," said Armus.

Kell took hold of Armus' shoulder and nodded. They disappeared in dimension travel, and reappeared on the portico of Arundine. Each took several breaths of recovery before moving inside.

The others sat in the chair of their province. Kell paused at the beginning of the arch of chairs to observe each Guardian. Most wore pensive or brooding expressions. None spoke a greeting or acknowledgement when he caught their eye. Kell walked to the raised platform to take his place. Rather than sit in the high chair, he remained standing.

"Such times of bleakness are not easy to accept," he said.

"Don't you mean *failure?*" chided Jedrek, the warrior fiercely scowled.

"No!" Kell rebuffed. "We didn't *fail*, we obeyed our orders."

Jedrek's passion made him bolt up from the Delta chair. "To watch the Dark Way destroy any hope of our return?"

"It is not destroyed!"

"No? Waldron is utterly razed and the House of Tristan massacred."

"No, they live," said Wren loud enough to be heard over Jedrek's vehement objection.

"What?" Jedrek asked with befuddlement.

"Three sons survived. Including Akilles, the rightful heir."

"She's right," began Kell. "Armus, Wren and myself, escorted them to Dorgirith. Along with Niles and Colin, who are charged with keeping them safe."

"Why didn't you tell us?" Jedrek demanded of Wren.

"Because I arrived a moment before Kell."

"That is why I called this meeting," said Kell. "To inform you of the escape and survival of the heir. It is through Akilles that Jor'el will fulfill his promise."

Armus motioned for Jedrek to resume his seat. The warrior obeyed.

"What of Wilbur's murder?" asked Valmar.

"We already know it happened to reveal Archimedes as Vicar," said Armus.

"For now, all we can do is wait. I will return to the Temple to—" began Kell.

"No!" said a booming voice that echoed all around. A bright haze descended from the ceiling to the high chair.

Kell scrambled off the platform. "Jor'el!" He knelt. The rest followed his lead in paying homage to the Almighty.

Jor'el's hazy frame assumed a sitting position in the high chair. Kind opalescent eyes gazed at each, ending on Kell. "You will not return to aid Archimedes."

Kell appeared befuddled. "Holy One, I have always protected your Vicar, while the Region of Sanctuary is my responsibility."

"Dagar will be expecting *you*. It is not time for you to be seen. Armus will go, thus fulfill his duties as Guardian of Allon. He will appear as Commander Finn when needed."

"Your pardon, Holy One, with the Dark Way rising they may sense Armus. By his presence, they will know my appearance is not far behind," insisted Kell.

"They assumed the same about Kell when Avatar arrived and we helped Tristan," said Armus.

Jor'el addressed the First Lieutenant. "It didn't happen then, did it?"

"No, Holy One."

"It won't happen now. You will return to the Temple."

"As you command." Armus saluted and bowed his head.

"The rest of you will wait and be prepared for when the time comes."

"How long? It's been over four hundred years since the Great Battle," said Jedrek.

"Valiant Jedrek, you should know time is irrelevant," said Jor'el.

"I do, but—"

Kell held up a hand to stop Jedrek. "We all know that, Holy One. We just yearn to see things as they once were."

The haze moved when Jor'el shook his head. "Things will never be as they once were. The past is done. A new promise of everlasting hope is what I offer the mortals."

"Then," began Wren, timidly, "those of us who have remained faithful will not regain what was lost from the punishment?"

Jor'el's eyes grew tender. "Dear Wren, Kell has reassured you many times that the Guardians will be *fully* restored." Jor'el's gaze swept over them. His voice grew stern when he next spoke. "Yet mortals are stubborn. Thus is now the appointed time from which they will fear no escape. A time of great testing, and purging. Only when those who have incurred my displeasure are consumed will the way be cleared for the Son of Tristan and Daughter of Allon to appear. Until then, stay strong and true, my faithful ones."

Jor'el vanished in burst of light that knocked them to the floor.

For the continuation of the series, read ...

Allon

Book 1

It has been five hundred years since the Great Battle drove the Guardians from Allon and gave rise to the Dark Way.

As the mortals suffer under the tyranny and supernatural oppression of the Dark Way, ancient prophecies are being fulfilled, bringing hope of the Promised Prince, and the return of the Guardians.

Explore the Kingdom of Allon

www.allonbooks.com

Featuring:

- Read excerpts of Allon books
- News and Events
- Photos and Videos
- Links to:
  - Facebook - The Kingdom of Allon Page
  - Newsletter
  - Contact Shawn Lamb

www.ingramcontent.com/pod-product-compliance
Lightning Source LLC
Chambersburg PA
CBHW071049250626
47159CB00002B/412